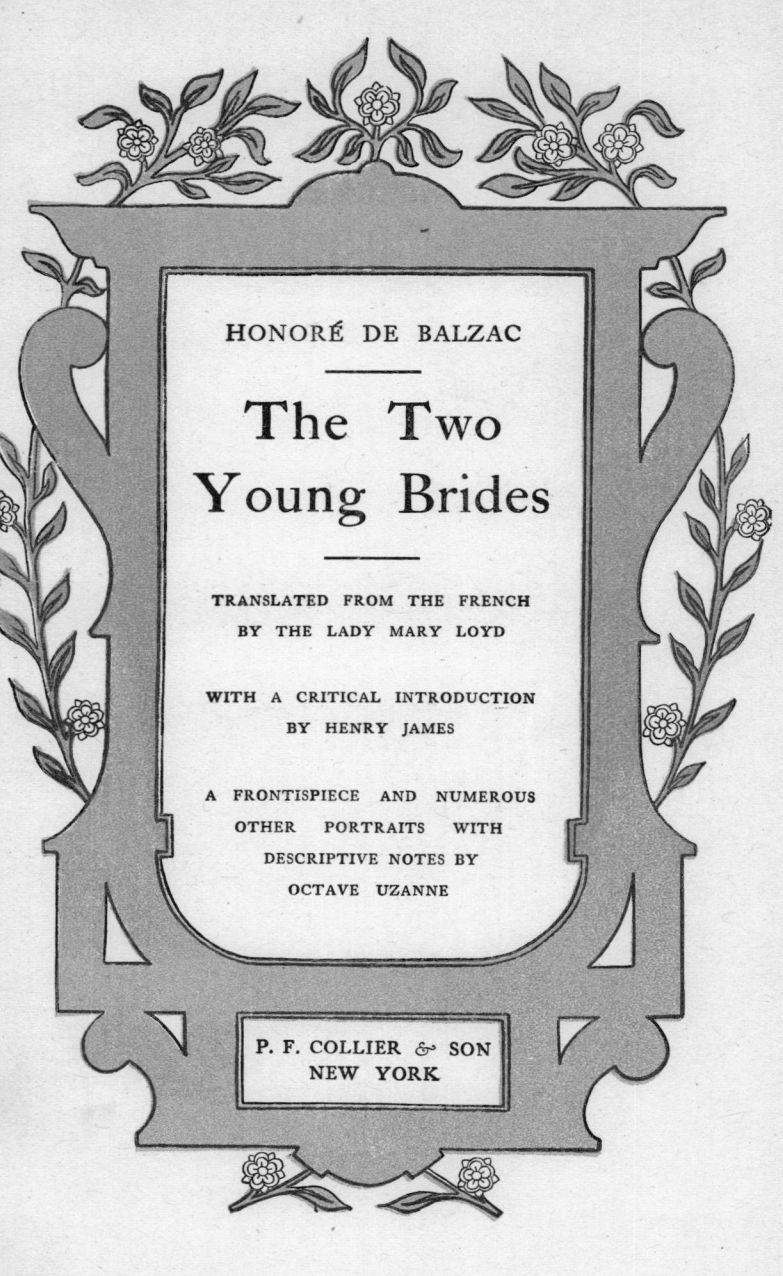

HONORÉ DE BALZAC

The Two Young Brides

TRANSLATED FROM THE FRENCH
BY THE LADY MARY LOYD

WITH A CRITICAL INTRODUCTION
BY HENRY JAMES

A FRONTISPIECE AND NUMEROUS
OTHER PORTRAITS WITH
DESCRIPTIVE NOTES BY
OCTAVE UZANNE

P. F. COLLIER & SON
NEW YORK

COPYRIGHT, 1902
BY D. APPLETON & COMPANY

HONORÉ DE BALZAC

I

STRONGER than ever, even than under the spell of first acquaintance and of the early time, is the sense—thanks to a renewal of intimacy and, I am tempted to say, of loyalty—that Balzac stands signally alone, that he is the first and foremost member of his craft, and that, above all, the Balzac-lover is in no position till he has cleared the ground by saying so. The Balzac-lover only, for that matter, is worthy to have his word, on so happy an occasion as this, about the author of *La Comédie Humaine,* and it is indeed not easy to see how the amount of attention so inevitably induced could, at the worst, have failed to find itself turning to an act of homage. I have been deeply affected, to be frank, by the mere refreshment of memory, which has brought in its train, moreover, consequences critical and sentimental too numerous to figure here in their completeness. The authors and the books that have, as the phrase is, done something for us, formed a solid part of the answer to our curiosity when our curiosity had the freshness of youth, these particular agents exist for us, with the lapse of time, as the substance itself of knowledge: they have been intellectually so swallowed, digested, and assimilated that we take their general use and suggestion for granted, cease to be aware of them because they have passed out of sight. But they have passed out of sight simply by having passed into our lives. They have become a part of our personal history, a part of ourselves, very often, so far as we may have succeeded in best expressing ourselves. Endless, however, are the uses of great persons and great things, and it may easily happen in these cases that the connection, even as an " excitement "—the form mainly of the connections of youth—is never really broken. We have largely been living on our benefactor—which is the highest acknowledgment one can make; only, thanks to a blessed law that operates in the long run to rekindle excitement, we are accessible to the sense of having neglected him. Even when we may not constantly have read him over the neglect is quite an illusion, but the illusion perhaps prepares us for the finest emotion we are to have owed to the acquaintance. Without having abandoned or denied our author, we yet come expressly back to him, and if not quite in tatters and in penitence like the Prodigal Son, with something at all events of the tenderness with which we revert to the parental threshold and hearthstone, if not, more fortunately, to the parental presence. The beauty of this adventure, that of seeing the dust blown off a relation that had been put away as on a shelf, almost out of reach, at the back

Honoré de Balzac

of one's mind, consists in finding the precious object not only fresh and intact, but with its firm lacquer still further figured, gilded, and enriched. It is all overscored with traces and impressions—vivid, definite, almost as valuable as itself—of the recognitions and agitations it originally produced in us. Our old —that is our young—feelings are, very nearly, what page after page most gives us. The case has become a case of authority *plus* association. If Balzac in himself is indubitably wanting in the sufficiently common felicity we know as charm, it is this association that may on occasion contribute the glamour.

The impression then, confirmed and brightened, is of the mass and weight of the figure, and of the extent of ground it occupies; a tract on which we really might all of us together pitch our little tents, open our little booths, deal in our little wares, and not materially either diminish the area or impede the circulation of the occupant. I seem to see him in such an image moving about as Gulliver among the pigmies, and not less good-natured than Gulliver for the exercise of any function, without exception, that can illustrate his larger life. The first and the last word about the author of *Les Contes Drolatiques* is that of all novelists he is the most serious—by which I am far from meaning that in the human comedy as he shows it the comic is an absent quantity. His sense of the comic was on the scale of his extraordinary senses in general, though his expression of it suffers perhaps exceptionally from that odd want of elbow-

Honoré de Balzac

room—the penalty somehow of his close-packed, pressed-down contents—which reminds us of some designedly beautiful thing but half-disengaged from the clay or the marble. It is the scheme and the scope that are supreme in him, applying it, moreover, not to mere great intention, but to the concrete form, the proved case, in which we possess them. We most of us aspire to achieve at the best but a patch here and there, to pluck a sprig or a single branch, to break ground in a corner of the great garden of life. Balzac's plan was simply to do all, to give the whole thing. He proposed to himself to turn over the great garden from north to south and from east to west; a task—immense, heroic, to this day immeasurable—that he bequeathed us the partial performance of, a huge imperfect block, in the twenty monstrous years, years of concentration and sacrifice the vision of which still makes us ache, representing his productive career. He had indeed a striking good fortune, the only one he was to enjoy as an harassed and exasperated worker: the great garden of life presented itself to him absolutely and exactly in the guise of the great garden of France, a subject vast and comprehensive enough, yet with definite edges and corners. This identity of his universal with, so to speak, his local, national vision is the particular thing we should doubtless call his greatest strength were we preparing agreeably to speak of it also as his visible weakness. Of Balzac's weaknesses, however, it takes some assurance to talk; there is always plenty of time for

Honoré de Balzac

them; they are the last signs we know him by; such things, truly, as in other painters of manners often pass for the exuberances of power. So little in short do they earn that name even when we feel them as defects.

What he did above all was to read the universe, as hard and as loud as he could, *into* the France of his time; his own eyes regarding his work as at once the drama of man and a mirror of the mass of social phenomena, the social state, the most rounded and registered, most organized and administered, and thereby most exposed to systematic observation and portrayal, that the world had seen. There are happily other interesting societies, but these are, for schemes of such an order, comparatively loose and incoherent, with more extent and perhaps more variety, but with less of the great inclosed and exhibited quality, less neatness and sharpness of arrangement, fewer categories, subdivisions, juxtapositions. Balzac's France was both inspiring enough for an immense prose epic and reducible enough for a report or a table. To allow his achievement all its dignity we should doubtless say also treatable enough for a history, since it was as a patient historian, a Benedictine of the actual, the living painter of his living time, that he regarded himself and handled his material. All painters of manners and fashions, if we will, are historians, even when they least put on the uniform: Fielding, Dickens, Thackeray, George Eliot, Hawthorne, among ourselves. But the great difference between the great

Honoré de Balzac

Frenchman and the eminent others is that, with an imagination of the highest power, an unequalled intensity of vision, he saw his subject in the light of science as well, in the light of the bearing of all its parts on each other, and under pressure of a passion for exactitude, an appetite, the appetite of an ogre, for *all* the kinds of facts. We find, I think, in the combination here suggested something like the truth about his genius, the nearest approach to a final account of him. Of imagination, on one side, all compact, he was on the other an insatiable reporter of the immediate, the material, the current combination, perpetually moved by the historian's impulse to fix them, preserve them, explain them. One asks one's self as one reads him what concern the poet has with so much arithmetic and so much criticism, so many statistics and documents, what concern the critic and the economist have with so many passions, characters, and adventures. The contradiction is always before us; it springs from the inordinate scale of the author's two faces; it explains more than anything else his eccentricities and difficulties. It accounts for his want of grace, his want of the lightness associated with an amusing literary form, his bristling surface, his closeness of texture, so suggestive, yet at the same time so akin to the crowded air we have in mind when we speak of not being able to see the wood for the trees.

A thorough-paced votary, for that matter, can easily afford to declare at once that this confounding

Honoré de Balzac

duality of character does more things still, or does at least the most important of all—introduces us without mercy (mercy for ourselves, I mean) to the oddest truth we could have dreamed of meeting in such a connection. It was certainly *a priori* not to be expected we should feel it of him, but our hero is, after all, not, in his magnificence, totally an artist: which would be the strangest thing possible, one must hasten to add, were not the smallness of the practical difference so made even stranger. His endowment and his effect are each so great that the anomaly makes at the most a difference only by adding to his interest for the critic. The critic worth his salt is indiscreetly curious and wants ever to know how and why—whereby Balzac is thus a still rarer case for him, suggesting that curiosity may have exceptional rewards. The question of what makes the artist, on a great scale, is interesting enough; but we feel it in Balzac's company to be nothing to the question of what, on an equal scale, frustrates him. The scattered pieces, the *disjecta membra,* of the character are here so numerous and so splendid that they prove misleading; we pile them together, and the heap, assuredly, is monumental; it forms an overtopping figure. The genius this figure stands for, none the less, is really such a lesson to the artist as perfection itself would be powerless to give; it carries him so much further into the special mystery. Where it carries him, however, I must not in this scant space attempt to say—which would be a loss of the fine thread of my argument. I stick to

Honoré de Balzac

our point in putting it, more concisely, that the artist of the *Comédie Humaine* is half smothered by the historian. Yet it belongs as well to the matter also to meet the question of whether the historian himself may not be an artist, in which case Balzac's catastrophe would seem to lose its excuse. The answer of course is that the reporter, however philosophic, has one law, and the creator, however substantially fed, has another; so that the two laws can with no sort of harmony or congruity make, for the finer sense, a common household. Balzac's catastrophe—so to name it once again—was in this perpetual conflict and final impossibility, an impossibility that explains his defeat on the classic side and extends so far at times as to make us think of his work as, from the point of view of beauty, a tragic waste of effort.

What it would come to, we judge, is that the irreconcilability of the two kinds of law is, more simply expressed, but the irreconcilability of two different ways of composing one's work. The principle of composition that his free imagination would have, or certainly might have, handsomely imposed on him is perpetually dislocated by the quite opposite principle of the earnest seeker, the inquirer to a useful end, in whom nothing is free but a born antipathy to his yoke-fellow. Such a production as *Le Curé de Village*, the wonderful story of Mme. Graslin, so nearly a masterpiece, yet so ultimately not one, would be, in this connection, could I take due space for it, a perfect illustration. If, as I say, Mme. Graslin's creator was

Honoré de Balzac

confined by his doom to patches and pieces, no piece is finer than the first half of the book in question, the half in which the picture is determined by his unequalled power of putting people on their feet, planting them before us in their habit as they lived—a faculty nourished by observation as much as one will, but with the inner vision all the while wide-awake, the vision for which ideas are as living as facts and assume an equal intensity. This intensity, greatest indeed in the facts, has in Balzac a force all its own, to which none other in any novelist I know can be likened. His touch communicates on the spot to the object, the creature evoked, the hardness and permanence that certain substances, some sorts of stone, acquire by exposure to the air. The hardening medium, for the image soaked in it, is the air of his mind. It would take but little more to make the peopled world of fiction as we know it elsewhere affect us by contrast as a world of rather gray pulp. This mixture of the solid and the vivid is Balzac at his best, and it prevails without a break, without a note not admirably true, in *Le Curé de Village*—since I have named that instance—up to the point at which Mme. Graslin moves out from Limoges to Montégnac in her ardent passion of penitence, her determination to expiate her strange and undiscovered association with a dark misdeed by living and working for others. Her drama is a particularly inward one, interesting, and in the highest degree, so long as she herself, her nature, her behaviour, her personal history, and the relations in

Honoré de Balzac

which they place her, control the picture and feed our illusion. The firmness with which the author makes them play this part, the whole constitution of the scene and of its developments from the moment we cross the threshold of her dusky, stuffy old-time birth-house, is a rare delight, producing in the reader that sense of local and material immersion which is one of Balzac's supreme secrets. What characteristically befalls, however, is that the spell accompanies us but part of the way—only until, at a given moment, his attention ruthlessly transfers itself from inside to outside, from the centre of his subject to its circumference.

This is Balzac caught in the very fact of his monstrous duality, caught in his most complete self-expression. He is clearly quite unwitting that in handing over his *data* to his twin-brother the impassioned economist and surveyor, the insatiate general inquirer and reporter, he is in any sort betraying our confidence, for his good conscience at such times, the spirit of edification in him, is a lesson even to the best of us, his rich, robust temperament nowhere more striking, no more marked anywhere the great push of the shoulder with which he makes his theme move, overcharged though it may be like a carrier's van. It is not therefore, assuredly, that he loses either sincerity or power in putting before us to the last detail such a matter as, in this case, his heroine's management of her property, her tenantry, her economic opportunities and visions, for these are cases in which

Honoré de Balzac

he never shrinks nor relents, in which, positively, he stiffens and terribly towers, reminds us again of M. Taine's simplifying sentence, his being a great painter doubled with a man of business. Balzac was indeed doubled, if ever a writer was, and to that extent that we almost as often, while we read, feel ourselves thinking of him as a man of business doubled with a great painter. Whichever way we turn it the oddity never fails, nor the wonder of the ease with which either character bears the burden of the other. I use the word burden because, as the fusion is never complete —witness in the book before us the fatal break of "tone," the one unpardonable sin for the novelist— we are beset by the conviction that, but for this strangest of dooms, one or other of the two partners might, to our relief and to his own, have been disembarrassed. The disembarrassment, for each, by a more insidious fusion, would probably have produced the master of the interest proceeding from form, or at all events the seeker for it, that Balzac fails to be. Perhaps the possibility of an artist constructed on such strong lines is one of those fine things that are not of this world, a mere dream of the fond critical spirit. Let these speculations and condonations at least pass as the amusement, as a result of the high spirits—if high spirits be the word—of the reader feeling himself again in touch. It was not of our author's difficulties—that is of his difficulty, the great one—that I proposed to speak, but of his immense positive effect. Even that, truly, is not an impression

Honoré de Balzac

of ease, and it is strange and striking that we are in fact so attached by his want of the unity that keeps surfaces smooth and dangers down as scarce to feel sure at any moment that we shall not come back to it with most curiosity. We are never so curious about successes as about interesting failures. The more reason therefore to speak promptly, and once for all, of the scale on which, in its own quarter of his genius, success worked itself out for him.

It is to that I *should* come back—to the infinite reach in him of the painter and the poet. We can never know what might have become of him with less importunity in his consciousness of the machinery of life, of its furniture and fittings, of all that, right and left, he causes to assail us, sometimes almost to suffocation, under the general rubric of *things*. Things, in this sense, with him, are at once our delight and our despair; we pass from being inordinately beguiled and convinced by them to feeling that his universe fairly smells too much of them, that the larger ether, the diviner air, is in peril of finding among them scarce room to circulate. His landscapes, his " local colour "—thick, in his pages, at a time when it was to be found in his pages almost alone—his towns, his streets, his houses, his Saumurs, Angoulêmes, Guérandes, his great prose Turner-views of the land of the Loire, his rooms, shops, interiors, details of domesticity and traffic, are a short list of the terms into which he saw the real as clamouring to be rendered and into which he rendered

Honoré de Balzac

it with unequalled authority. It would be doubtless more to the point to make our profit of this consummation than to try to reconstruct a Balzac planted more in the open. We hardly, as the case stands, know most whether to admire in such an example as the short tale of *La Grenadière* the exquisite feeling for " natural objects " with which it overflows like a brimming wine-cup, the energy of perception and description which so multiplies them for beauty's sake, and for the love of their beauty, or the general wealth of genius that can count so little and spend so joyously. The tale practically exists for the sake of the enchanting aspects involved—those of the embowered white house that nestles, on its terraced hill, above the great French river, and we can think, frankly, of no one else with an equal amount of business on his hands who would either have so put himself out for aspects or made them, almost by themselves, a living subject. A born son of Touraine, it must be said, he pictures his province, on every pretext and occasion, with filial passion and extraordinary breadth. The prime aspect in his scene, all the while, it must be added, is the money aspect. The general money question so loads him up and weighs him down that he moves through the human comedy, from beginning to end, very much in the fashion of a camel, the ship of the desert, surmounted with a cargo. " Things " for him are francs and centimes more than any others, and I give up as inscrutable, unfathomable, the nature, the peculiar avidity of his interest

Honoré de Balzac

in them. It makes us wonder again and again what then is the use, on Balzac's scale, of the divine faculty. The imagination, as we all know, may be employed up to a certain point, in inventing uses for money; but its office beyond that point is surely to make us forget that anything so odious exists. This is what Balzac never forgot; his universe goes on expressing itself for him, to its furthest reaches, on its finest sides, in the terms of the market. To say these things, however, is, after all, to come out where we want, to suggest his extraordinary scale and his terrible completeness. I am not sure that he does not see character too, see passion, motive, personality, as quite in the order of the " things " we have spoken of. He makes them no less concrete and palpable, handles them no less directly and freely. It is the whole business, in fine—that grand total to which he proposed to himself to do high justice—that gives him his place apart, makes him, among the novelists, the largest, weightiest presence. There are some of his obsessions—that of the material, that of the financial, that of the " social," that of the technical, political, civil—for which I feel myself unable to judge him, judgment losing itself, unexpectedly, in a particular shade of pity. The way to judge him is to try to walk all round him—on which we see how remarkably far we have to go. He is the only member of his order really monumental, the sturdiest-seated mass that rises in our path.

Honoré de Balzac

II

We recognise, none the less, that the finest consequence of these re-established relations is linked with just that appearance in him, that obsession of the actual under so many heads, that makes us look at him, as we would at some rare animal in captivity, between the bars of a cage. It amounts to a kind of doom, since to be solicited by the world from all quarters at once—what is that, for the spirit, but a denial of escape? We feel his doom to be his want of a private door, and that he felt it, though more obscurely, himself. When we speak of his want of charm, therefore, we perhaps so surrender the question as but to show our own poverty. If charm, to cut it short, is what he lacks, how comes it that he so touches and holds us that—above all, if we be actual or possible fellow-workers—we are uncomfortably conscious of the disloyalty of almost any shade of surrender? We are lodged perhaps by our excited sensibility in a dilemma of which one of the horns is a compassion that savours of patronage; but we must resign ourselves to that by reflecting that our tenderness at least takes nothing away from him. It leaves him solidly where he is and only brings us near, brings us to a view of *all* his formidable parts and properties. The conception of the *Comédie Humaine* represents them all, and represents them mostly in their felicity and their triumph—or at least the execution does: in spite of which we irresistibly find ourselves thinking of him,

Honoré de Balzac

in reperusals, as most essentially the victim of a cruel joke. The joke is one of the jokes of fate, the fate that rode him for twenty years at so terrible a pace and with the whip so constantly applied. To have wanted to do so much, to have thought it possible, to have faced and in a manner resisted the effort, to have felt life poisoned and consumed, in fine, by such a bravery of self-committal—these things form for us in him a face of trouble that, oddly enough, is not appreciably lighted by the fact of his success. It was the having wanted to do so much that was the trap, whatever possibilities of glory might accompany the good faith with which he fell into it. What accompanies *us*, as we frequent him, is a sense of the deepening ache of that good faith with the increase of his working consciousness, the merciless development of his huge subject and of the rigour of all the conditions. We see the whole thing quite as if Destiny had said to him: " You want to 'do' France, presumptuous, magnificent, miserable man—the France of revolutions, revivals, restorations, of Bonapartes, Bourbons, republics, of war and peace, of blood and romanticism, of violent change and intimate continuity, the France of the first half of your century? Very well; you most distinctly *shall*, and you shall particularly let me hear, even if the great groan of your labour do fill at moments the temple of letters, how you like the job." We must of course not appear to deny the existence of a robust joy in him, the joy of power and creation, the joy of the observer and the dreamer who finds a

Honoré de Balzac

use for his observations and his dreams as fast as they come. The *Contes Drolatiques* would by themselves sufficiently contradict us, and the savour of the *Contes Drolatiques* is not confined to these productions. His work at large tastes of the same kind of humour, and we feel him again and again, like any other great healthy producer of these matters, beguiled and carried along. He would have been, I dare say, the last not to insist that the artist has pleasures forever indescribable; he lived, in short, in his human comedy, with the largest life we can attribute to the largest capacity. There are particular parts of his subject from which, with our sense of his enjoyment of them, we have to check the impulse to call him away—frequently, as, I confess, in this connection, that impulse arises.

The connection is with the special element of his spectacle from which he never fully detaches himself, the element, to express it succinctly, of the "old families" and the great ladies. Balzac frankly revelled in his conception of an aristocracy—a conception that never succeeded in becoming his happiest; whether, objectively, thanks to the facts supplied him by the society he studied, or through one of the strangest deviations of taste that the literary critic is likely to encounter. Nothing would in fact be more interesting than to attempt a general measure of the part played, in the total comedy, to his imagination, by the old families; and one or two contributions to such an attempt I must not fail presently to make. I glance at them here, however, the delect-

Honoré de Balzac

able class, but as most representing on the author's part free and amused creation; by which, too, I am far from hinting that the amusement is at all at their expense. It is in their great ladies that the old families most shine out for him, images of strange colour and form, but "felt," as we say, to their finger-tips, and extraordinarily interesting as a mark of the high predominance—predominance of character, of cleverness, of will, of general "personality"—that almost every scene of the comedy attributes to women. It attributes to them in fact a recognised and uncontested supremacy; it is through them that the hierarchy of old families most expresses itself; and it is as surrounded by them, even as some magnificent, indulgent pasha by his overflowing seraglio, that Balzac sits most at his ease. All of which reaffirms—if it be needed—that his inspiration, and the sense of it, were even greater than his task. And yet such betrayals of spontaneity in him make, for an old friend, at the end of the chapter, no great difference in respect to the pathos—since it amounts to that—of his genius-ridden aspect. It comes to us as we go back to him that his spirit had fairly made of itself a cage, in which he was to turn round and round, always unwinding his reel, much in the manner of a criminal condemned to hard labour for life. The cage is simply the complicated but dreadfully definite French world that built itself so solidly in and roofed itself so impenetrably over him.

It is not that, caught there with him though we

Honoré de Balzac

be, we ourselves prematurely seek an issue: we throw ourselves back, on the contrary, for the particular sense of it, into his ancient, superseded, comparatively *rococo* and quite patriarchal France—patriarchal in spite of social and political convulsions; into his old-time, antediluvian Paris, all picturesque and all workable, full, to the fancy, of an amenity that has passed away; into his intensely differentiated sphere of *la province*, evoked in each sharpest or faintest note of its difference, described systematically as narrow and flat, and yet attaching us if only by the contagion of the author's overflowing sensibility. He feels, in his vast comedy, many things, but there is nothing he feels with the communicable shocks and vibrations, the sustained fury of perception—not always a fierceness of judgment, which is another matter—that *la province* excites in him. Half our interest in him springs still from our own sense that, for all the convulsions, the revolutions, and experiments that have come and gone, the order he describes is the old order that our sense of the past perversely recurs to as to something happy we have irretrievably missed. His pages bristle with the revelation of the lingering earlier world, the world in which places and people still had their queerness, their strong marks, their sharp type, and in which, as before the platitude that was to come, the observer with an appetite for the salient could, by way of precaution, fill his lungs. Balzac's appetite for the salient was voracious, yet he came, as it were, in time, in spite of his so often speaking as if what he sees about him is but the last desolation of the modern. His conservatism, the most entire, consistent, and convinced that ever was—yet even at that much inclined to whistling in the dark as if to the tune of " Oh, how mediæval I *am!*"— was doubtless the best point of view from which he could rake his field. But if what he sniffed from afar, in that position, was the extremity of change, we in turn feel both subject and painter drenched with the smell of the past. It is preserved in his work as nowhere else—not vague, nor faint, nor delicate, but as strong to-day as when first distilled.

It may seem odd to find the taste of sadness in the fact that a great worker succeeded in clasping his opportunity in such an embrace, that being exactly our usual measure of the felicity of great workers. I speak, I hasten to reassert, all in the name of sympathy—without which it would have been detestable to speak at all; and this sentiment puts its hand instinctively on the thing that makes it least futile. This particular thing then is not in the least Balzac's own hold of his terrible mass of matter; it is absolutely the convolutions of the serpent he had with a magnificent courage invited to wind itself round him. We must use the common image—he had created his Frankenstein monster. It is the fellow-craftsman who can most feel for him—it being apparently possible to read him from another point of view without getting really into his presence. We undergo with him from book to book, from picture to picture, the con-

Honoré de Balzac

volutions of the serpent, we especially whose refined performances are given, as we know, with but the small common or garden snake. I stick to this to justify my image, just above, of his having been " caged " by the intensity with which he saw his general subject as a whole. To see it always as a whole is our wise, our virtuous effort, the very condition, as we keep in mind, of superior art. Balzac was in this connection then wise and virtuous to the most exemplary degree; so that he ought logically, doubtless, but to prompt to complacent reflections. No painter ever saw his general subject half so much as a whole. Why is it then that we hover about him, if we are real Balzacians, not with cheerful chatter, but with a consideration deeper in its reach than any mere moralizing? The reason is largely that, if you wish with absolute immaculate virtue to look at your subject as a whole and yet remain a theme for cheerful chatter, you must be careful to take a subject that will not hug you to death. Balzac's active intention was, to vary our simile, a beast with a hundred claws, and the spectacle is in the hugging process of which, as energy against energy, the beast was capable. Its victim died of the process at fifty, and if what we see in the long gallery in which it is mirrored is not the defeat, but the admirable resistance, we none the less never lose the sense that the fighter is shut up with his fate. He has locked himself in—it is doubtless his own fault—and thrown the key away. Most of all perhaps the impression comes—the impression of

Honoré de Balzac

the adventurer committed and anxious, but with no retreat—from the so formidably concrete nature of his material. When we work in the open, as it were, our material is not classed and catalogued, so that we have at hand a hundred ways of being loose, superficial, disingenuous, and yet passing, to our no small profit, for remarkable. Balzac had no open; he held that the great central, normal, fruitful country of his birth and race, overarched with its infinite social complexity, yielded a sufficiency of earth and sea and sky. We seem to see as his catastrophe that the sky, all the same, came down on him. He couldn't keep it up—in more senses than one. These are perhaps fine fancies for a critic to weave about a literary figure of whom he has undertaken to give a plain account; but I leave them so on the plea that there are relations in which, for the Balzacian, criticism simply drops out. That is not a liberty, I admit, ever to be much encouraged; critics in fact are the only people who have a right occasionally to take it. There is no such plain account of the *Comédie Humaine* as that it makes us fold up our yard-measure and put away our note-book quite as we do with some extraordinary character, some mysterious and various stranger who brings with him his own standards and his own air. There is a kind of eminent presence that abashes even the interviewer, moves him to respect and wonder, makes him, for consideration itself, not insist. This takes of course a personage sole of his kind. But such a personage precisely is Balzac.

Honoré de Balzac

III

By all of which, none the less, I have felt it but too clear that I must not pretend here to take apart the pieces of his immense complicated work, to number them or group them or dispose them about. The most we can do is to pick one up here and there and wonder, as we weigh it in our hand, at its close, compact substance. That is all even M. Taine could do in the longest and most penetrating study of which our author has been the subject. Every piece we handle is so full of stuff, condensed like the edibles provided for campaigns and explorations, positively so charged, in a word, with life, that we find ourselves dropping it, in certain states of sensibility, as we drop an object, unguardedly touched, that startles us by being animate. We seem really scarce to want anything to be *so* animate. It would verily take Balzac to detail Balzac, and he has had in fact Balzacians nearly enough affiliated to affront the task with courage. The *Répertoire de la Comédie Humaine* of MM. Anatole Cerfberr and Jules Christophe is a closely-printed octavo of 550 pages, which constitutes, in relation to his characters great and small, an impeccable biographical dictionary. His votaries and expositors are so numerous that the Balzac library of comment and research must be, of its type, one of the most copious. M. de Lovenjoul has laboured all round the subject; his *Histoire des Œuvres* alone is another crowded octavo of 400 pages; in connection

Honoré de Balzac

with which I must mention Miss Wormeley, the devoted American translator, interpreter, worshipper, who in the course of her own studies has so often found occasion to differ from M. de Lovenjoul on matters of fact and questions of date and of appreciation. Miss Wormeley, M. Paul Bourget, and many others are examples of the passionate piety that our author can inspire. As I turn over the encyclopedia of his characters I note that whereas such works usually commemorate only the ostensibly eminent of a race and time, every creature so much as named in the fictive swarm is in this case preserved to fame: so close is the implication that to have *been* named by such a dispenser of life and privilege is to be, as we say it of baronets and peers, created. He infinitely divided moreover, as we know, he subdivided, altered, and multiplied his heads and categories—his *Vie Parisienne*, his *Vie de Province*, his *Vie Politique*, his *Parents Pauvres*, his *Études Philosophiques*, his *Splendeurs et Misères des Courtisanes*, his *Envers de l'Histoire Contemporaine*, and all the rest; so that nominal reference to them becomes the more difficult. Yet without prejudice either to the energy of conception with which he mapped out his theme as with chalk on a huge blackboard, or to the prodigious patience with which he executed his plan, practically filling in, with a wealth of illustration, from sources that to this day we fail to make out, every compartment of his table, M. de Lovenjoul draws up the list, year by year, from 1822 to 1848, of his mass of work, giving us thus the

Honoré de Balzac

measure of the tension represented for him by almost any twelve-month. It is wholly unequalled, considering the quality of Balzac's production, by any other eminent abundance.

I must be pardoned for coming back to it, for seeming unable to leave it; it enshrouds so interesting a mystery. How was so solidly systematic a literary attack on life to be conjoined with whatever workable minimum of needful intermission, of free observation, of personal experience? Some small possibility of personal experience, of disinterested life, must at the worst, from deep within or far without, feed and fortify the strained productive machine. These things were luxuries that Balzac appears really never to have tasted on any appreciable scale. His published letters—the driest and most starved of those of any man of equal distinction—are with the exception of those to Mme. de Hanska, whom he married shortly before his death, almost exclusively the audible wail of a galley-slave chained to the oar. M. Zola, in our time, among the novelists, has sacrificed to intensity of production in something of the same manner, yet with goodly modern differences that leave him a comparatively simple instance. His work, assuredly, has been more nearly dried up by the sacrifice than ever Balzac's was—so miraculously, given the conditions, was Balzac's to escape the anticlimax. Method and system, in the chronicle of the race of Rougon-Macquart, an economy in itself certainly of the rarest and most interesting, have spread so from centre to cir-

Honoré de Balzac

cumference that they have ended by being almost the only thing we feel. And then M. Zola has survived and triumphed in his lifetime, has continued and lasted, has piled up, and, if the remark be not frivolous, enjoyed in all its *agréments* the reward for which Balzac toiled and sweated in vain. On top of which he will have had also his literary great-grandfather's heroic example to start from and profit by, the positive heritage of a *fils de famille* to enjoy, spend, save, waste. Balzac, frankly, had no heritage at all but his stiff subject, and, by way of model, not even, in any direct or immediate manner, that of the inner light and kindly admonition of his genius. Nothing adds more to the strangeness of his general performance than his having failed so long to find his inner light, groped for it for nearly ten years, missed it again and again, moved straight away from it, turned his back on it, lived, in fine, round about it, in a darkness still scarce penetrable, a darkness into which we peep only half to make out the dreary little waste of his numerous *œuvres de jeunesse*. To M. Zola was vouchsafed the good fortune of settling down to the Rougon-Macquart with the happiest promptitude; it was as if time for one look about him—and I say it without disparagement to the reach of his look—had sufficiently served his purpose. Balzac, moreover, might have written five hundred novels without our feeling in him the faintest hint of the breath of doom, if he had only been comfortably capable of conceiving the short cut of the fashion practised by others under his eyes.

Honoré de Balzac

As Alexandre Dumas and Mme. George Sand, illustrious contemporaries, cultivated a personal life and a disinterested consciousness by the bushel, having, for their easier duration, not too consistently known, as the true painter knows it, the obsession of the thing to be done, so Balzac was condemned by his constitution itself, by his inveterately seeing this " thing to be done " as part and parcel, as of the very essence, of his subject. The latter existed for him, as the process worked and hallucination set in, in the form, and the form only, of the thing done, and not in any hocus-pocus about doing. There was no kindly convenient escape for him by the little swinging backdoor of the thing *not* done. He desired—no man more—to get out of his obsession, but only at the other end, that is by boring through it. " How then, thus deprived of the outer air almost as much as if he were gouging a passage for a railway through an Alp, *did* he live? " is the question that haunts us—with the consequence, for the most part, of promptly meeting its answer. He did *not* live—save in his imagination, or by other aid than he could find there; his imagination was, in fine, his experience—he had provably no time for the real thing. This brings us to the rich if simple truth that his imagination alone did the business, carried through both the conception and the execution—as large an effort and as proportionate a success, in all but the vulgar sense, as the faculty, equally handicapped, was ever concerned in. Handicapped I say because this interesting fact about him,

Honoré de Balzac

with the claim it makes, rests on the ground, the high distinction, that, more than all the rest of us put together, he went in, as we say, for detail, circumstance, and specification, proposed to himself *all* the connections of every part of his matter and the full total of the parts. The whole thing, it is impossible not to keep repeating, was what he deemed treatable. One really knows, in all imaginative literature, no enterprise to compare with it for courage, good faith, and sublimity. There, once more, was the necessity that rode him and that places him apart in our homage. It is no light thing to have been condemned to become provably sublime. And looking through, or trying to, at what is beneath, behind, we are left benevolently uncertain if the predominant quantity be audacity or innocence.

It is of course inevitable at this point to seem to hear the colder critic promptly take us up. He undertook the whole thing—oh, exactly—the ponderous person! But *did* he "do" the whole thing, if you please, any more than sundry others of fewer pretensions? The answer to this is one that it is a positive joy to give, so sharp a note instantly sounds as an effect of the inquiry. Nothing is more interesting and amusing than to find one's self recognising both that Balzac's pretensions were immense, portentous, and that yet, taking him—and taking *them*—altogether, they only minister, in the long run, to our fondness. They affect us not only as the endearing eccentricities of a person we greatly admire, but fairly as the very condition of

Honoré de Balzac

his having become such a person. We take them thus in the first place for the very terms of his plan, and in the second for a part of that high robustness and that general richness of nature which made him, in the face of such a plan, believe in himself. One would really scarce have liked to see such a job as *La Comédie Humaine* tackled without swagger. To think of the thing really as practicable *was* swagger, and of the very highest order. So to think assuredly implied pretensions, pretensions that risked showing as monstrous should the enterprise fail to succeed. It is for the colder critic to take the trouble to make out that of the two parties to it the body of pretension remains greater than the success. One may put it, moreover, at the worst for him, recognise that it is in the matter of opinion still more than in the matter of knowledge that Balzac offers himself as universally competent. He has flights of judgment—on subjects the most special as well as the most general—that are vertiginous, and on his alighting from which we greet him with a peculiar indulgence. We can easily imagine him to respond, confessing humorously—if he had only time—to such a benevolent, understanding smile as would fain hold our own eyes a moment. Then it is that he would most show us his scheme and his necessities, and how, in operation, they all hang together. *Naturally* everything about everything, though how he had time to learn it is the last thing he has time to tell us; which matters the less, moreover, as it is not over the question of his knowledge

Honoré de Balzac

that we sociably invite him, as it were (and remembering the two augurs behind the altar), to wink at us. His convictions it is that are his great, pardonable "swagger"; to them in particular I refer as his general operative condition, the constituted terms of his experiment, and, not less, as his consolation, his support, his amusement by the way. They embrace everything in the world—that is in his world of the high-coloured France of his time: religion, morals, politics, economics, physics, æsthetics, letters, art, science, sociology, every question of faith, every branch of research. They represent thus his equipment of ideas, those ideas of which it will never do for a man who aspires to constitute a state to be deprived. He must take them with him as an ambassador extraordinary takes with him secretaries, uniforms, stars and garters, a gilded coach and a high assurance. Balzac's opinions are his gilded coach, in which he is more amused than anything else to feel himself riding, but which is indispensably concerned in getting him over the ground. What more inevitable than that they should be intensely Catholic, intensely monarchical, intensely saturated with the real genius—as between 1830 and 1848 he believed it to be—of the French character and French institutions?

Nothing is happier for us than that he should have enjoyed his outlook before the first half of the century closed. He could then still treat his subject as comparatively homogeneous. Any country could have a Revolution—every country *had* had one. A

Honoré de Balzac

Restoration was merely what a revolution involved, and the Empire had been, with the French, but a revolutionary incident, in addition to being, by good luck, for the novelist, an immensely pictorial one. He was free, therefore, to arrange the background of the comedy in the manner that seemed to him best to suit anything so great; in the manner, at the same time, prescribed, according to his contention, by the noblest traditions. The church, the throne, the noblesse, the bourgeoisie, the people, the peasantry, all in their order, and each solidly kept in it, these were precious things, things his superabundant insistence on the price of which is what I refer to as his exuberance of opinion. It was a luxury for more reasons than one, though one, presently to be mentioned, handsomely predominates. The meaning of that exchange of intelligences in the rear of the oracle which I have figured for him with the perceptive friend bears simply on his pleading guilty to the purport of the friend's discrimination. The point the latter makes with him —a beautiful, cordial, critical point—is that he truly cares for nothing in the world, thank goodness, so much as for the passions and embroilments of men and women, the free play of character and the sharp revelation of type, all the real stuff of the drama and the native food of the novelist. Religion, morals, politics, economics, æsthetics, would be thus, as systematic matter, very well in their place, but quite secondary and subservient. Balzac's attitude is again and again that he cares for the adventures and emotions

Honoré de Balzac

because, as his last word, he cares for the good and the greatness of the state—which is where his swagger, with a whole society on his hands, comes in. What we on our side in a thousand places gratefully feel is that he cares for his monarchical and hierarchical and ecclesiastical society because it rounds itself, for his mind, into the most congruous and capacious theatre for the repertory of his innumerable comedians. It has, above all, for a painter abhorrent of the superficial, the inestimable benefit of the accumulated, of strong marks and fine shades, contrasts and complications. There had certainly been since 1789 dispersals and confusions enough, but the thick tradition, no more, at the most, than half smothered, lay under them all. So the whole of his faith and no small part of his working omniscience were neither more nor less than that historic sense which I have spoken of as the spur of his invention and which he possessed as no other novelist has done. We immediately feel that to name it in connection with him is to answer every question he suggests and to account for each of his idiosyncrasies in turn. The novel, the tale, however brief, the passage, the sentence by itself, the situation, the person, the place, the motive exposed, the speech reported—these things were, in his view, history, with the absoluteness and the dignity of history. This is the source both of his weight and of his wealth. What is the historic sense after all but animated, but impassioned knowledge seeking to enlarge itself? I have said that his imagination did the whole thing,

Honoré de Balzac

no other explanation—no reckoning of the possibilities of personal saturation—meeting the mysteries of the case. Therefore his imagination achieved the miracle of absolutely resolving itself into multifarious knowledge. Since history proceeds by documents, he constructed, as he needed them, the documents too—fictive sources that imitated the actual to the life. It was of course a terrible business, but at least, in the light of it, his pretensions to infinitude are justified—which is what was to be shown.

IV

It is very well, even in the sketchiest attempt at a portrait of his genius, to try to take particulars in their order: one peeps over the shoulder of another at the moment we get a feature into focus. The loud appeal not to be left out prevails among them all, and certainly with the excuse that each, as we fix it, seems to fall most into the picture. I have indulged myself so as to his general air that I find a whole list of vivid contributive marks almost left on my hands. Such a list, in any study of Balzac, is delightful for intimate edification as well as for the fine humour of the thing; we proceed from one of the items of his breathing physiognomy to the other with quite the same sense of life, the same active curiosity, with which we push our way through the thick undergrowth of one of the novels. The difficulty is really that the special point for which one at the moment observes him melts into all the other points, is swallowed up before one's eyes in the formidable mass. The French apply the best of terms to certain characters when they speak of them as *entiers,* and if the word had been invented for Balzac it could scarce better have expressed him. He is " entire " as was never a man of his craft; he moves always in his mass; wherever we find him we find him in force; whatever touch he applies he applies it with his whole apparatus. He is like an army gathered to besiege a cottage equally with a city, and living voraciously, in either case, on all the country about. It may well be, at any rate, that his infatuation with the idea of the social, the practical primacy of " the sex " is the article at the top of one's list; there could certainly be no better occasion than this of a rich reissue of the *Deux Jeunes Mariées* for placing it there at a venture. Here indeed, precisely, we get a sharp example of the way in which, as I have just said, a capital illustration of one of his sides becomes, just as we take it up, a capital illustration of another. The correspondence of Louise de Chaulieu and Renée de Maucombe is in fact one of those cases that light up with a great golden glow all his parts at once. We needn't mean by this that such parts are themselves absolutely all golden—given the amount of tinsel, for instance, in his view, supereminent, transcendent here, of the old families and the great ladies. What we do convey, however, is that his creative temperament finds in such *data* as these one of its best occasions for shining out. Again we fondly recognise his splendid, his attaching

Honoré de Balzac

swagger—that of a "bounder" of genius and of feeling; again we see how, with opportunity, its elements may vibrate into a perfect ecstasy of creation.

Why shouldn't a man swagger, he treats us to the diversion of asking ourselves, who has created, from top to toe, the most brilliant, the most historic, the most insolent, above all the most detailed and discriminated of aristocracies? Balzac carried the uppermost class of his comedy, from the princes, dukes, and unspeakable duchesses down to his poor barons *de province*, about in his pocket as he might have carried a tolerably befingered pack of cards, to deal them about with a flourish of the highest authority whenever there was a chance of a game. He knew them up and down and in and out, their arms, infallibly supplied, their quarterings, pedigrees, services, intermarriages, relationships, ramifications, and other delectable attributes. This indeed is comparatively simple learning; the real wonder is rather when we linger on the ground of the patrician consciousness itself, the innermost, the esoteric, the spirit, temper, tone—tone above all—of the titled and the proud. The questions multiply for every scene of the comedy; there is no one who makes us walk in such a cloud of them. The clouds elsewhere, in comparison, are at best of questions not worth asking. *Was* the patrician consciousness that figured as our author's model so splendidly fatuous as he—almost without irony, often in fact with a certain poetic sympathy—everywhere represents it? His imagination lives in it, breathes its scented air, swallows this element with the smack of the lips of the connoisseur; but I feel that we never know, even to the end, whether he be here directly historic or only, quite misguidedly, romantic. The romantic side of him has the extent of all the others; it represents, in the oddest manner, his escape from the walled and roofed structure into which he had built himself—his longing for the vaguely-felt outside, for the rest, so to speak, of the globe. But it is characteristic of him that the most he could do for this relief was to bring the fantastic into the circle and fit it somehow to his conditions. Was the tone of his duchesses and marquises but the imported fantastic, one of those smashes of the window-pane of the real that reactions sometimes produce even in the stubborn? or are we to take it as observed, as really reported, as, for all its difference from our notion of the natural—and, quite as much, of the artificial—in another and happier strain of manners, substantially true? The whole episode, in *Les Illusions Perdues*, of Mme. de Bargeton's " chucking " Lucien de Rubempré, on reaching Paris with him, under pressure of Mme. d'Espard's shockability as to his coat and trousers, and other such matters, is either a magnificent lurid document or the baseless fabric of a vision. The great wonder is that, as I rejoice to put it, we can never really discover which, and that we feel, as we read, that we can't, and that we suffer at the hands of no other author this particular helplessness of immersion. It is *done*—we are always thrown back on that; we can't get out of it; all we can do is to say that the true itself can't be more than done, and that if the false in this way equals it we must give up looking for the difference. Alone among novelists Balzac has the secret of an insistence that somehow makes the difference nought. He warms his facts into life—as witness the certainty that the episode I just cited has absolutely as much of that property as if perfect matching had been achieved. If the great ladies in question *didn't* behave, wouldn't, couldn't have behaved, like a pair of frightened snobs, why, so much the worse, we say to ourselves, for the great ladies in question. We *know* them so—they owe their being to our so seeing them; whereas we never can tell ourselves how we should otherwise have known them or what quantity of being they would, on a different footing, have been able to show us.

The case is the same with Louise de Chaulieu, who, besides coming out of her convent school, as a quite young thing, with an amount of sophistication that would have chilled the heart of a horse-dealer, exhales—and to her familiar friend, a young person of a supposedly equal breeding—an extravagance of complacency in her " social position " that makes us rub our eyes. Whereupon, after a little, the same phenomenon occurs; we swallow her bragging, against our better reason, or at any rate our startled sense, under coercion of the total intensity. We do more than this, we cease to care for the question, which loses itself in the hot fusion of the whole pic-

Honoré de Balzac

ture. He has "gone for" his subject, in the vulgar phrase, with an avidity that makes the attack of his most eminent rivals affect us as the intercourse between introduced indifferences at a dull evening party. He squeezes it till it cries out, we hardly know whether for pleasure or pain. In the case before us, for example—without wandering from book to book, impossible here, I make the most of the ground already broken—he has seen at once that the state of marriage itself, sounded to its depths, is, in the connection, his real theme. He sees it of course in the conditions that exist for him, but he weighs it to the last ounce, feels it in all its dimensions, as well as in all his own, and would scorn to take refuge in any engaging side-issue. He gets, for further intensity, into the very skin of his *jeunes mariées*—into each alternately, as they are different enough; so that, to repeat again, any other mode of representing women, or of representing anybody, becomes, in juxtaposition, a thing so void of the active contortions of truth as to be comparatively wooden. He bears children with Mme. de l'Estorade, knows intimately how she suffers for them, and not less intimately how her correspondent suffers, as well as enjoys, without them. Big as he is he makes himself small to be handled by her with young maternal passion and positively to handle her in turn with infantile innocence. These things are the very flourishes, the little technical amusements of his penetrating power. But it is doubtless in his hand for such a matter as the jealous passion of Louise de

Honoré de Balzac

Chaulieu, the free play of her intelligence, and the almost beautiful good faith of her egotism, that he is most individual. It is one of the neatest examples of his extraordinary leading gift, his art—which is really, moreover, not an art—of working the exhibition of a given character up to intensity. I say it is not an art because it acts for us rather as a hunger on the part of his nature to take on, in all freedom, another nature—take it by a direct process of the senses. Art is for the mass of us who have only the process of art, comparatively so stiff. The thing amounts with him to a kind of shameless personal, physical, not merely intellectual, duality—the very spirit and secret of transmigration.

HENRY JAMES.

LIFE OF BALZAC

HONORÉ DE BALZAC *was the eldest of the four children of an officer in the commissariat, settled in that service at Tours. Here, at No. 39 Rue Royale, the future novelist was born on the 16th of May, 1799. He was dull and dreamy as a child, sometimes so absorbed as to seem positively comatose. At school at Vendôme, and afterward in Tours, he seemed to make little intellectual progress. In 1814 the family moved to Paris, and from 1816 to 1819 Honoré studied the law. By his twentieth year, however, the vocation of letters had appealed to him so strongly, and he seemed to have so little aptitude for any other business, that his parents consented to leave him alone in Paris (for the family now retired to Villeparisis), in an attic near the Arsenal Library, where he devoted himself entirely to preparation for the literary life. Between 1822 and 1826 Balzac produced a great number of stories, extravagant and dull, under such pseudonyms as " Lord R'Hoone," " Villerglé," " Horace de St. Aubain," and " M. D." These valueless romances he sold for very small sums to eke out the slender allowance which he received from his father. Balzac was aware of the worthlessness of these productions, and he set himself,*

Life of Balzac

with heroic resolution, to begin his labours over again. His genuine works, therefore, start with the four volumes of "Le Dernier Chouan" (afterward "Les Chouans"), published in 1829, the earliest book to which Balzac attached his name. This magnificent romance attracted some notice, and the author was encouraged to bring out his pseudo-metaphysical essay, the "Physiologie du Mariage," and the collection of short stories, "Scènes de la Vie Privée," both in 1830. The next year saw the issue of "La Peau de Chagrin" and "La Maison du Chat-qui-Pelote," which enjoyed a decided success, and from this time forth, for nearly twenty years, Balzac was engaged, almost without intermission, in the furious composition of stories. It is impossible to name here a tenth part of so fertile an author's most important works; to deal with the bibliography of Balzac is to try to count the stars upon a frosty night. But it may be recorded that the "Contes Drolatiques" began to be issued in 1832; that the "Études de Moeurs" (which included "Eugenie Grandet," "Les Illusions Perdues," and "Le Colonel Chabert") appeared between 1834 and 1837; and the more fantastic "Études Philosophiques"—among which are "Louis Lambert," "Seraphita," and "Une Passion dans le Désert"—date from 1835 to 1840. But before the latter date, Balzac had settled down to more detailed studies of contemporary life, beginning in 1835 with "Le Père Goriot." Among the splendid novels which followed we can not omit to mention "Le Lys dans la Vallée" (1836), "César Birotteau" (1838), "Mémoires de Deux Jeunes Mariées" (1842), "Modeste

Life of Balzac

Mignon" (*1844*), "*La Cousine Bette*" (*1846*), *and* "*Le Cousin Pons*" (*1847*). *It was in 1842 that Balzac's books were first collected, in seventeen volumes, as* "*La Comédie Humaine,*" *although for many years the idea had occurred to him of bringing them together under a common heading. The greater part of the extremely laborious life of Balzac was spent in Paris, and finally in a pavillon of the Hôtel Beaujon, where he arranged around his writing-table a rich collection of paintings and bric-à-brac. His brief periods of repose were spent with his friends, and there were in particular certain women whose names will be always honoured in connection with his. During his early struggles he received the most charming kindness from Madame de Berny; for many years Madame Zulma Carraud was his sympathetic confidante; and from 1833 to the close of his life he found absolute happiness in his friendship with Madame de Hanska. Although the latter became a widow in 1843, difficulties stood in the way of her marriage with Balzac, until March, 1850, when they were united in Warsaw under very fortunate conditions. Unluckily, Balzac had worked too strenuously and had postponed happiness too long. As early as May it was seen that his health was failing, and the couple hurried to Paris for advice. Nothing, however, could stem the progress of heart-disease, and on the night of the 18th of August, 1850, Balzac died; his widow survived him until 1882.*

E. G.

TO
GEORGE SAND

THIS DEDICATION, my dear George, can add nothing to the glory of your name, which will cast its magic ray over my book. Yet it argues neither calculation nor modesty on my part. My desire is thereby to attest the true friendship which has endured between us two, through all our travels and our partings, in spite of our labours, in spite of the ill-nature of the world about us. This feeling will never weaken, I am sure. The procession of affectionately remembered names which will accompany my works mingles a pleasure with the pain their number has cost me—for they all cost me suffering, if it were only the vituperation my alarming prolificness calls down upon me—as though the world I picture were not even more fecund yet! Will it not be a grand thing, George, if the future antiquary, delving, some fine day, among dead literatures, discovers in this array none but great names, high hearts, friendships holy and pure, and all the most glorious reputations of this country? May I not claim greater pride in this assured good fortune than in successes which are always subject to dispute? To any one who knows you well, is it not a happiness to be able to call himself, as I do here,

Your friend,
DE BALZAC.

PARIS, June, 1840.

CONTENTS

	PAGES
Honoré de Balzac	v–xliii
Henry James	
Life of Balzac	xlv–xlvii
Edmund Gosse	
Dedication	xlix
The Memoirs of Two Young Brides .	1–354
Curious unpublished or unknown Portraits of Honoré de Balzac . . .	355–368
Octave Uzanne	

THE MEMOIRS
OF TWO YOUNG BRIDES

THE MEMOIRS OF TWO YOUNG BRIDES

PART FIRST

I

LOUISE DE CHAULIEU TO RENÉE DE MAUCOMBE

WELL, my dear! I, too, have reached the outer world, and if you haven't written to me from Blois, I am the first to keep our delightful epistolary rendezvous. Now lift up the beautiful black eyes you have fixed on this first sentence of mine, and keep your exclamations for the letter which shall tell you of my first love! People always talk about a *first* love; is there a second, then? "Hush!" you'll say. "Tell me rather," you'll add, "how you escaped from the convent in which you were to have taken your vows?" My dear, the miracle of my deliverance, though it did happen in the Carmelite convent, was the most natural thing in the world. The clamour of a terrified conscience finally prevailed over the fiat of an unwavering policy, and there's an end. My aunt, who did not choose to see me die of a consumption, got the better of my mother, who had always prescribed the novitiate as the one and only cure for

The Memoirs of Two Young Brides

my malady. The state of deep melancholy into which I fell when you departed hastened this happy solution. And I am in Paris, my dearest, and I am in all the delight of being there! My Renée, if you could have seen me, that day, when I found myself all alone, you would have been proud of having inspired so deep a feeling in so young a heart! We have dreamt so many dreams in company, we have spread our wings so often, and lived so much together, that I believe our souls are welded one to the other just like those two Hungarian girls, whose death-story was told us by M. Beauvisage, who certainly wasn't like his name —never was convent doctor better chosen! Were you not ill, too, when your darling fell sick? In my state of gloomy depression, I could only recognise, each in its turn, the bonds that make us one. I fancied separation had broken them. I loathed existence like some widowed turtle-dove. The thought of death was sweet to me, and I really was dying softly away. To be left alone at the Carmelite convent at Blois, tortured by the fear of having to take the veil, without Mlle. de la Vallière's previous experience, and without my Renée, that was illness, indeed—a mortal sickness! The monotonous round in which each hour brings a duty, a labour, or a prayer, all so precisely alike that at any hour of the day or night any one may know exactly what a Carmelite nun must be doing—that hateful life, in which it matters not whether the things about us exist or not—had grown full of variety to us. The flight of our imagination

The Memoirs of Two Young Brides

knew no limit. On us fancy had bestowed the key of all her realms. Each of us in turn was the other's winged steed. The liveliest stirred the dullest pulses of the other, and our fancy frolicked at will, in undisturbed possession of that outer world which was forbidden us.

Even the lives of the saints helped us to understand the things most carefully hidden from us. The day which robbed me of your sweet company saw me become that which we know a Carmelite to be—a modern Danaid, whose task does not, indeed, consist in filling a bottomless cask, but who daily draws, out of some hidden well, an empty bucket on the unceasing rope that she may find it full. My aunt knew of our inner life. To her, who had made herself a heaven of happiness within the two acres encircled by her convent walls, my loathing of existence was inexplicable. The girl who, at our age, embraces the religious life, must either possess an excessive simplicity (which we, my dear creature, cannot claim) or else that passion of devotion which makes my aunt so noble a figure. My aunt sacrificed herself to a brother whom she adored; but what girl can sacrifice herself to people she doesn't even know, or to an idea?

For almost a fortnight, now, I have been keeping back so many hasty remarks, and burying so many meditations deep in my heart, I have so many things to say, so many stories to tell, which I can confide to none but you, that but for this makeshift plan of writing you my confidences, and thus replacing our beloved talks, I really should choke! How indispensable is the life of the affections. This morning I begin this journal of mine, fancying that yours, too, is begun, and that in a few days I shall live in the depths of your beautiful valley at Gémenos, of which I know only what you have told me, just as you will live in Paris, of which you know nothing but what we used to dream together.

Well, my sweet child, on a morning which will always be written in rose-colour in the book of my life, a *demoiselle de compagnie* and my grandmother's last man-servant, Philippe, arrived from Paris to escort me back. When my aunt sent for me to her room and told me this piece of news, my joy quite struck me dumb and I stared stupidly at her.

"My child," said she in her guttural voice, "it is no grief to you to leave me, I can see that. But this farewell is not our last. We shall meet again. God has set the mark of the elect upon your forehead. You have the pride which either leads a woman up to heaven or down to hell. But you have too much nobility in you to sink. I know you better than you know yourself. Passion, in your case, will not be what it is to the common run of women."

She drew me gently towards her, and kissed me on the forehead, so that I could feel the fire that consumes her—that has blackened the azure of her eyes and weighted her eye-lids, lined her smooth temples, and sallowed her beautiful face. It made my flesh creep. Before I answered her, I kissed her hands.

The Memoirs of Two Young Brides

Then I said: "Dear aunt, since your adorable goodness has not made your Paraclete seem either healthy to my body or dear to my heart, I must shed so many tears before I came back, that you could hardly wish for my return. I never will come back, unless my Louis XIV betrays me. And if I once lay my hand on one, nothing but Death shall take him from me. No Montespan shall frighten me!"

"Hush, giddy child," she said, with a smile. "You must not leave those vain thoughts here behind you. Take them away with you, and know that there is more of the Montespan than of the La Vallière in your composition."

I kissed her. The poor soul could not resist coming with me to the carriage, and her eyes wandered backward and forward between the family coat of arms and me.

At Beaugency night overtook me, still lost in the moral stupor caused by this strange farewell. What is my destiny in this outer world for which I have so greatly longed? In the first place, I found nobody to meet me. The demonstrations of affection I had prepared were all wasted. My mother was at the Bois de Boulogne, my father was at the Council-board. My brother, the Duc de Rhétoré, never comes in, I am told, except to dress before dinner. Miss Griffiths (she has claws) and Philippe showed me to my rooms.

These rooms belonged to that beloved grandmother, the Princess de Vaurémont, to whom I owe a

The Memoirs of Two Young Brides

fortune of some kind, which nobody has mentioned to me. As you read these words, you will share the sadness that overwhelmed me when I entered the apartments hallowed to me by so many memories. They remained just as she had left them. I was to sleep in the very bed in which she died. I sat down on the edge of her sofa, and burst into tears, quite forgetting that I was not alone. How often, I thought, I had knelt here beside her—so as to catch her words more easily—and from this couch had watched her face, half hidden amid yellowish laces, and worn as much by age as by the sufferings of approaching death! The room still seemed full of the warmth she had always kept up in it. How comes it, thought I, that Mlle. Armande Louise Marie de Chaulieu is obliged, like any peasant, to sleep in her grandmother's bed almost on the day of her death? For to me it seemed that the Princess, who had really passed away in 1817, had died only on the previous night. There were things in this room which should not have been there, and which proved how careless people taken up with the affairs of the kingdom are apt to be about their own, and how little thought was given, once she was dead, to the noble-hearted woman who will always remain one of the great feminine figures of the eighteenth century. Philippe had an inkling of the cause of my tears. He told me the Princess had left me all her furniture, and also that my father had left the great reception rooms in the condition into which they had fallen during the Revolution.

The Memoirs of Two Young Brides

Then I rose to my feet, Philippe opened the door of the small drawing-room leading into the saloons, and I found them in the state of complete ruin I recollected. Above the doors the empty panels, once filled by valuable pictures, still gape; the marble figures are all smashed, the looking-glasses have been carried off. In the old days I used to dread going up the great stair-case and crossing the huge lonely, lofty rooms, and I used to pass to the Princess's apartment by a small stair-case which runs under the hollow of the great one, and leads to the wainscot door of her dressing-room.

The apartment, consisting of a sitting-room, a bed-room, and that pretty vermilion and gold dressing-room of which I have often spoken to you, is in the wing that lies towards the Invalides. The house is only separated from the boulevard by a creeper-covered wall, and by a splendid double row of trees, whose foliage mingles with that of the elms on the side of the boulevard. But for the gold and blue dome and the gray outlines of the Invalides one might fancy one's self in a forest. The style of these three rooms and their position marks them as having formed the old state apartments of the Duchess of Chaulieu. Those of the Duke must have been in the opposite wing. The two are decently parted by the principal building and by the front wing, which contains those great dark, resounding rooms, which, as Philippe had shown me, are still stripped of their splendour, and just as I used to see them in my childish days. When Philippe per-

The Memoirs of Two Young Brides

ceived the astonishment depicted on my countenance he took on a confidential air. "In this diplomatic household, my dear, every servant is mysterious and discreet." He informed me that the passing of a law which was to restore the value of their property to the *emigré* families was shortly expected. My father is putting off the decoration of his house till that restitution is made. The King's architect has calculated the expense at three hundred thousand francs. The result of this confidence was to send me back to my sofa in the drawing-room. What! Then my father, instead of using this sum of money for my dowry, would have let me die in a convent? This was the thought that struck me on the threshold of that door. Ah, Renée! how I did lean my head against your shoulder, and how my mind went back to the days when my grandmother's presence filled these two rooms with life! She, who lives nowhere now, save in my heart, and you, who are at Maucombe, two hundred leagues away from me, are the only two human beings who love, or ever have loved me! That dear old lady with the young eyes delighted to be roused in the mornings by my voice. How we understood each other! The memory of her brought a sudden change in the feelings I had first experienced. That which had seemed a profanation now appeared to me something almost holy! It was sweet to me, now, to breathe the vague odour of *Poudre à la Maréchale* that hung about the room. It would be sweet to sleep under the protecting yellow satin curtains with their white pattern, in which her eyes and her breath must surely have left something of herself. I told Philippe to restore their bright polish to the bits of old furniture and to impart a look of habitation to my rooms. I showed him myself how I wished things to be arranged, pointing out where each piece of furniture should stand. I looked over everything, and took formal possession, explaining how he was to freshen up the antique things which are so dear to me. The decoration of the room is all white, somewhat dimmed by time, and the gilding of the fanciful arabesques shows a touch of red here and there. But this is all in harmony with the faded tints of the *Savonnerie* carpet, given to my grandmother, with his own portrait, by Louis XV. The clock was a present from the Maréchal de Saxe, the china on the chimney-piece a gift from the Maréchal de Richelieu. My grandmother's picture, painted when she was five-and-twenty, hangs in an oval frame facing the King's portrait. There is no picture of the Prince. I like this frank omission, which, in a flash, without a touch of hypocrisy in it, depicts her fascinating personality. Once, when my aunt was very ill, her confessor pressed her to allow the Prince, who was waiting in the drawing-room, to enter the sick-room.

"With the doctor and his prescriptions," said my grandmother.

Over the bed there is a canopy, the bed-head is padded, and the curtains looped up in fine ample

The Memoirs of Two Young Brides

folds. The furniture is of gilt wood, covered with the same yellow damask, patterned with white flowers, of which the window hangings are made, and which is lined with a white silken material something like moire. I do not know who painted the panels over the doors, but they represent a sunrise and a moonlight effect. The chimney-piece is treated in a very peculiar style. It is clear that in those days people spent a great deal of their time at their own firesides. All sorts of important events took place there. The fire-place, all of gilt bronze, is a wonderful bit of work; the chimney-piece itself is exquisitely finished, the shovel and tongs are beautifully modelled, the bellows are quite lovely. The tapestry in the fire-screen comes from the Gobelins works, and it is exquisitely mounted. The merry figures that run along the outline, the feet, the cross-bar of the frame, are all enchanting; the whole is carried out as carefully as if it had been for a fan. Who gave her that pretty bit of furniture, of which she was so fond? I wish I knew. How often have I seen her, with her foot on that cross-bar, leaning back in her easy chair, her gown lifted half-way up to her knee by her posture, taking up her snuff-box, laying it down, and then taking it up again from its place on the shelf between her bonbonnière and her silk mittens. What a coquette she was! Till the day of her death she took as much care of her person as if it were still the morrow of the time when that beautiful picture had been painted, and as if she were still expecting the

The Memoirs of Two Young Brides

flower of the Court to gather round her. That easy chair made me think of the inimitable wave she would give her skirts as she dropped into it. The women of that period have carried away with them certain characteristic secrets peculiar to their times. The Princess had a way of moving her head and a way of dropping her words and her glances, and a particular fashion of speech, especially, which I never was able to discover in my own mother. It was both clever and good-natured; there was purpose in it, but there was no affectation. Her conversation was at once prolix and laconic; she could tell a story well, and she could sketch a thing in half a dozen words. Above all, she had that excessive breadth of judgment which has certainly influenced my own turn of mind. From my sixth year to my tenth I spent my life in her pocket—she was as fond of having me with her as I was of going to her. This fondness gave rise to more than one quarrel between her and my mother. Nothing fans a sentiment like the ice-cold wind of persecution. What a charm there was in the way she would say to me, " Here you are, little witch! " when, curious as any snake, I had slipped through doorway after doorway to reach her rooms. She felt I loved her, and she loved my artless love, which brought a ray of sunshine to her winter days. I don't know what went on in her rooms at night, but she had a great many visitors. In the mornings, when I crept tip-toe to see if her windows were open, I used to find the furniture in her drawing-room all pushed hither and thither, card-tables set, and snuff lying here and there in heaps. The drawing-room is in much the same style as the bed-room. The furniture is of curious shapes, with deeply moulded wood-work and claw feet. Wreaths of flowers, richly carved and finely modelled, twine across the mirrors and hang in festoons along their edges. On the marble tables there are beautiful Chinese vases. The prevailing shades in the furniture and hangings are poppy-colour and white. My grandmother was a stately and striking brunette. Her complexion accounts for her favourite colours. In the drawing-room I found a writing-table, the figures on which used to keep my eyes very busy in the old days. It is adorned with chiselled silver plaques, and was given her by one of the Genoese Lomellini. Each side of this table represents the occupations appropriate to one of the four seasons. The figures are all in relief, there are hundreds of them in each scene. I spent two hours quite alone, gathering up my memories, one by one, in the sacred precincts within which one of the most famous women, both for beauty and for wit, at the Court of Louis XV, breathed her last sigh. You know how suddenly I was parted from her in 1816.

"Go and say good-bye to your grandmother," said my mother to me.

I found the Princess not at all surprised, but apparently unmoved by my departure. "You are going to the convent, my treasure," she said. "You'll see your aunt there—a most excellent woman. I'll take

The Memoirs of Two Young Brides

care you are not sacrificed; you shall be independent, and able to marry whomsoever you may choose."

Six months later she was dead. She had given her will into the keeping of one of her most trusted friends, the Prince de Talleyrand, who contrived, when he came to see Mlle. de Chargebœuf, to let me know, through her, that my grandmother forbade me to take religious vows. I very much hope that sooner or later I may meet the Prince, and then, no doubt, he will tell me more.

So, my dear, though I found nobody waiting to greet me, I consoled myself with the shade of my dear Princess, and I set myself to fulfil one of our agreements, which—do you remember it?—was that we should mutually inform each other of the tiniest details concerning our dwellings and our lives. It is so sweet to know the where and how of the existence of the beloved being! So be sure you describe all the very smallest matters about you, every single thing, even to the effects of the sunset among the tall trees!

October 10th.

It was three o'clock in the afternoon when I arrived. Towards half past five Rose came to tell me my mother had returned, and I went downstairs to pay her my respects. My mother's rooms are on the ground floor; they are planned just like mine, and are in the same wing. I live just above her, and we have the same private stair-case. My father lives in the opposite wing. But as he has all the space on the court-yard side, which in our case is taken up by the grand stair-case, his rooms are much larger than ours. In spite of the social duties incumbent on the position to which the return of the Bourbons has restored my parents, they still continue living on the ground floor, and are able to entertain there, so roomy are the houses built by our forefathers. I found my mother in her own drawing-room, in which nothing has been altered. As I went down the stairs I kept asking myself how this woman, who has been so little of a mother to me that in eight years she has only written me two letters you wot of, would receive me. Thinking it unworthy of myself to simulate a tenderness I could not feel, I had composed my countenance after the fashion of a silly nun, and when I entered her room I felt, inwardly, exceedingly embarrassed. This shyness soon passed away. My mother was perfectly charming. She made no pretence of sham tenderness. She was not cold; she did not treat me as if I had been her best beloved daughter.

She welcomed me as though we had only parted the night before. She was the gentlest, the frankest of friends. She spoke to me as to a grown-up woman, and began by kissing me on the forehead.

"My dear child," she said. "If you are to die of your convent, you had much better come and live with us. You have upset your father's plans and mine, but the days of blind obedience to parents are gone by. M. de Chaulieu's intention, with which mine agrees, is that nothing shall be left undone which can make your life pleasant and enable you to see the world. At your age, I should have thought as you do. So I have no feeling against you on that score; you are not capable of understanding what we asked of you. You will not find any absurd severity in me. If you have doubted my affection you will soon find out you were mistaken. Though I intend to leave you in perfect freedom, I think you will do wisely to listen, at first, to the advice of a mother who will treat you as if you were her sister."

The Duchess spoke in a soft voice, and as she talked she straightened my school-girl's cape. She fascinated me. She is eight-and-thirty, and she is an angel of beauty. She has blue eyes that are almost black, eye-lashes like silk, not a line on her forehead, her skin so pink and white you would fancy she painted, wonderful shoulders and bust, a waist as slight and well curved as your own; an extraordinarily beautiful hand, as white as milk; finger-nails that hold the light, they are so polished; her little finger a little separate from the other four, her thumb as smooth as ivory. And then she has a foot to match her hand —the Spanish foot of Mlle. de Vandenesse. If she is like this at forty, she will be beautiful still, at sixty.

I answered her, my dear, as a submissive daughter should. I was all she had been to me, and I was better still. Her beauty had conquered me; I forgave her for forsaking me. I realized that such a woman had been swept off her feet by her queenly position. I said all this to her, simply, as though I had been talking to you. Perhaps she had not expected to hear words of affection from her daughter's lips. The tribute of my honest admiration touched her deeply, her manner changed and grew even more gracious; she dropped the second person plural.

"You are a good child," she said, "and I hope we shall continue friends."

The words struck me as being exquisitely artless. I would not have her see how I took them, for I realized at once that I must let her think she has much more wit and cleverness than her daughter. So I played the ninny, and she was delighted with me. I kissed her hands several times over, saying how happy I was at her treating me in this way, that I felt quite relieved, and I even confessed my terrors to her. She smiled, and put her arm round my neck with an affectionate gesture to draw me close to her, and kiss me on the forehead.

"Dear child," she said, "we have company to dinner to-day. I dare say you'll agree with me that you had better not make your appearance in society until the dressmaker has made you some clothes; so, after you have seen your father and your brother, you had better go back to your own rooms."

To this arrangement I agreed with all my heart. My mother's exquisite gown was my first revelation of the world of which we had glimpses in our dreams. But I did not feel the slightest touch of jealousy.

My father entered the room.

"Sir," said the Duchesse, "this is your daughter."

The Memoirs of Two Young Brides

My father suddenly became quite tender in his manner to me. So perfectly did he play the father's part, that I believed he felt it.

"So here you are, unruly daughter," he cried, taking my two hands in his and kissing them in a way that was more gallant than paternal. Then he drew me close, put his arm round my waist and clasped me to him, kissing my cheeks and forehead.

"You'll make up for the sorrow your change of vocation has caused us by the pleasure your success in society will bring us.

"Do you know, Madame, she is very pretty, and some day you may be proud of her. Here's your brother Rhétoré. . . . Alphonse," said he to a good-looking young man who had just come in, "here's your nun-sister who wants to cast off her habit."

My brother came forward in a very leisurely fashion, took my hand and shook it.

"Why don't you kiss her?" said the Duke. And he kissed me on each cheek.

"I am very glad to see you, sister," he said, "and I'm on your side against my father."

I thanked him, but I think he might have come to Blois, when he used to go to Orleans to see our brother, the Marquis, in his quarters there. Fearing strangers might appear, I beat a retreat. I settled a few things in my own room and laid out all I needed for writing to you on the red velvet top of my beautiful table, pondering, meanwhile, over my new surroundings.

The Memoirs of Two Young Brides

Thus, first and last, dearest love, has come to pass the return of the eighteen-year-old daughter of one of the greatest families in France to the bosom of her kindred, after an absence lasting some nine years. The journey had tired me, and so had the emotions of this family meeting. Wherefore I sought my bed, just as I should have sought it in the convent, as soon as I had eaten my supper. They have even kept the little Dresden knife and fork and spoon my dear old Princess used whenever she took it into her head to have a meal served to her apart, in her own rooms.

II

FROM THE SAME TO THE SAME

November 25th.

THE next morning I found my rooms had been set in order and prepared for me by old Philippe, who had put flowers into all the vases, so I settled down at last. But it had never occurred to anybody that a school-girl from the Carmelite convent was likely to feel hungry early in the morning, and Rose had the greatest difficulty in getting me some breakfast.

"Mademoiselle went to bed just when dinner was being served, and she got up just after her father had come home," she said.

I sat down to write. Towards one o'clock my father knocked at the door of my little sitting-room and asked if he might come in. I opened the door, he entered and found me writing to you.

"My dear," he said, "you have to buy your clothes and settle down here. In this purse you will find twelve thousand francs. That represents one year of the income I shall allow you for your personal expenses. You must settle with your mother about engaging a governess who will suit you, if you do not care about Miss Griffiths, for Madame de Chaulieu will not have time to go out with you in the mornings. You will have a carriage and a servant at your orders."

"Let me keep Philippe," I said.

"So be it," he answered. "But do not worry yourself, your own fortune is large enough to prevent your being a burden either to your mother or to me."

"Should I be taking a liberty if I asked you to tell me the amount of my fortune?"

"Not in the least, my child," he replied. "Your grandmother left you five hundred thousand francs. These were her savings, for she would not rob her family of a single foot of land. The money was invested in the *Grand Livre*; the interest has accumulated, and it now brings in about forty thousand francs a year. I had intended to apply this sum to settling a fortune on your second brother, and you have greatly upset my plans. But in time, perhaps, you will agree to them. I shall depend on you for everything. You seem to me far more sensible than I had thought. There is no need for me to tell you how a Demoiselle de Chaulieu should conduct herself. The pride stamped on your features gives me full security as to that. Among us, such precautions as are taken with regard to their daughters by smaller folk would be insulting. Any light word spoken about you might cost the life of the person who dared to utter it, or that of one of your own brothers, if Heaven should prove unjust. I will say no more to you on that head. Farewell, dear child!"

He kissed me on the forehead and departed. The

The Memoirs of Two Young Brides

thing I cannot explain to myself is that after having persevered in it for nine years he should have abandoned his plan. I like the straightforwardness with which my father spoke. There was nothing ambiguous in what he said. My fortune is intended for his son, the Marquis. Who has shown pity on me, then? Was it my mother? Was it my father? Can it have been my brother?

There I sat on my grandmother's sofa, staring at the purse my father had left on the mantel-piece, at once pleased, and yet displeased, with an attention which had attracted my mind to a question of money.

It's true, indeed, that I need not think about it any more. My doubts are cleared up, and there was something fine in the way he spared me all hurt to my pride in connection with the subject. Philippe has spent the day going about to the different shops and tradesmen who are to undertake my metamorphosis. A famous dressmaker of the name of Victorine has been with me, as well as a *lingère*. I am as impatient as a child to know what I shall be like when I have cast off the sack in which the regulation costume of our convent has hitherto enveloped us. But all these people expect to be allowed a great deal of time. The stay-maker says he must have a week if I don't want to spoil my figure. So I have a figure! This grows serious. Janssen, the shoemaker to the Opera, has positively assured me I have my mother's foot. I have spent my whole morning over these important matters. I have even seen a glovemaker, who came to take the measure of my hand. I have given my orders to the *lingère*. At my dinner-time, which was that of the family lunch, my mother told me we were to go together to the milliner's, so as to form my taste, and teach me how to order my own bonnets. This beginning of my independence makes me feel as giddy as a blind man who has just recovered his sight. I can judge now of what a Carmelite is like beside a society girl. The difference is so great that we could never have conceived it. During lunch my father was very absent, and we left him to his own thoughts; he is much mixed up with all the King's secrets. He had utterly forgotten me; he will only remember me when I happen to be necessary to him—that I saw clearly. In spite of his fifty years, my father is a most attractive man. His figure is young, he is well built, fair; his appearance and ways are charming. He has the face of a true diplomat, speaking and silent at once. His nose is slight and delicate; his eyes are dark. What a good-looking couple they are! How many strange thoughts crowded upon me then, when I clearly perceived that these two beings—each of them noble, rich, and cast in a superior mould—never live together, have nothing in common but their name, and yet keep up an appearance of union before the world. Yesterday the *élite* of the Court and diplomatic body were in the house. In a few days I am to go to a ball given by the Duchesse de Manfrigneuse, and shall be presented in that society I so greatly long to know. I am to have a dancing-master every morning.

The Memoirs of Two Young Brides

I must know how to dance within a month, on pain of not being allowed to go to the ball. Before dinner my mother came to see me about my governess. I have kept Miss Griffiths, who was recommended by the English ambassador. This lady is a clergyman's daughter. She is perfectly well-bred. Her mother was of noble birth. She is thirty-six years old, and she will teach me English. My Griffiths has some fairly well-grounded pretensions to good looks; she is a Scotchwoman, poor and proud; she will be my chaperone; she will sleep in Rose's room, and Rose will be under Miss Griffiths's orders. I saw in a flash that I was destined to govern my governess. During the six days we have spent together she has realized perfectly that I am the only person who can possibly do anything for her; and in spite of her marble countenance I have thoroughly realized that she will be very obliging to me. She seems to me a good-natured creature, but I have not been able to find out anything about what passed between her and my mother.

There is another piece of news, which does not strike me as being particularly important. This morning my father refused the Ministry which had been offered him. This accounts for his absence of mind yesterday. He prefers an embassy, he says, to the worry of public debates. He has a fancy for Spain. All this I heard at lunch, the only moment in the day when my father, my mother, and my brother see each other in a certain amount of intimacy. On these

The Memoirs of Two Young Brides

occasions the servants do not come into the room unless they are rung for. The rest of the time, my brother, as well as my father, is out of doors. My mother is always dressing, and is never to be seen between two o'clock and four. At four o'clock she goes out for an hour's drive, she receives her friends from six to seven, unless she is dining out, and the whole evening is spent in amusement—plays, balls, concerts or visits. Her life is so full, indeed, that I don't believe she ever has a quarter of an hour to herself. She must spend a good deal of time over her morning toilet, for she is perfectly beautiful when she appears at breakfast, which is served at half past eleven. I am beginning to understand the meaning of the noises I hear in her rooms. She first of all takes a bath of very nearly cold water; then she drinks a cup of coffee with cream, and cold; then she dresses. Except on extraordinary occasions, she is never awake before nine o'clock. In the summer she rides early in the morning. At two o'clock a young man, of whom I have not yet been able to catch a glimpse, comes to see her. This is our household life. We meet at breakfast and at dinner, but at this latter meal I am often alone with my mother, and I fancy that oftener still I shall dine with Miss Griffiths in my own rooms, just as my grandmother used to do, for my mother very often dines out. The scanty interest my family has taken in me no longer causes me any astonishment. In Paris, my dear, it is a mark of heroism to care for people who are really near us, for we are not very often in our own

The Memoirs of Two Young Brides

company. How all absent folk are forgotten in this town! Nevertheless, I have not as yet put my foot outside the door. I know nothing. I am waiting to sharpen my wits, waiting till my dress and my appearance shall be in harmony with this outer world, the stir of which astounds me, although I only hear its distant murmur. So far I have only been out in the garden. The Italian opera opens in a few days. My mother has a box. I am wild with longing to hear Italian music and to see a French opera. I am beginning to break my convent habits and take up those of the outer world. I am writing to you to-night until I go to bed—a moment which is now put off until ten o'clock, the hour at which my mother goes out, unless she is attending some theatrical performance.

There are a dozen theatres in Paris. My ignorance is gross, and I read a great deal, but my reading is confused. One book leads me on to another. I find the names of several fresh ones on the cover of the one I have in hand. But nobody can direct me, and consequently I come across some very dull ones. All the modern literature I have read treats of love, that subject which used to occupy our thoughts so greatly, since our whole fate hangs on man and is shaped for his pleasure. But how inferior are these authors to those two young girls whom we used to call the White Doe and the Pet Darling, Renée and Louise. Ah, my sweet! How paltry and fantastic are their incidents! How shabby their expression of the tender feeling! Two books, however, have strangely delighted me.

The Memoirs of Two Young Brides

One is called Corinne, the other Adolphe. Talking of this, I asked my father if I could get a sight of Mme. de Staël. My mother and he and Alphonse all began to laugh.

Alphonse said: "But where has she been?"

My father answered: "We are rare simpletons. She has been with the Carmelites."

"My child," said the Duchesse, gently, "Mme. de Staël is dead."

"How can a woman be deceived?" said I to Miss Griffiths, when I had read to the end of Adolphe.

"Why, when she is in love!" quoth Miss Griffiths.

Tell me, Renée, do you think any man could deceive us? . . . Miss Griffiths has ended by finding out that I'm only half a fool, that I possess a secret education—that we gave each other means in our endless discussions. She has realized that my ignorance is limited to external matters. The poor soul has opened her heart to me. That brief answer of hers, weighed in the balance against every imaginable misfortune, made me shiver a little. Griffiths told me, over again, that I am not to let myself be dazzled by anything on earth, and that I must be on my guard against everything, and chiefly against that which will delight me most. She knows no more, and can tell me nothing further. This style of discourse is too monotonous. She is like the bird that can only chirp one note.

III

THE SAME TO THE SAME

December.

DARLING: Here I am, ready to make my entrance into the gay world, and I have striven to reach the wildest height of frolic, before I compose my countenance to face society. This morning, after many attempts, I beheld myself well and truly laced, shod, my waist drawn in, my hair dressed—myself gowned and adorned. I did as the men who fight duels do before a hostile meeting. I practised within four walls. I wanted to see myself in my full armour. I noted very complacently that I had a sort of little conquering and triumphant look, to which folks will have to submit perforce. I have looked myself over, and passed judgment on myself. I have reviewed all my forces, and so carried out that fine maxim of the ancients, "Know thyself." I found immense delight in making my own acquaintance. Griffiths was the only person in the secret of this doll's play of mine, in which I was child and doll at once. You think you know me? Not a bit.

Here, Renée, I give you a portrait of this your sister disguised as a Carmelite, and now returned to

The Memoirs of Two Young Brides

life as a gay and worldly young lady. Provence always accepted, I am one of the most beautiful people in France. That seems to me a truthful summing up of this delightful chapter. Deficiencies I have, but if I were a man, I should love them. They are all points that are rich in future promise. When a girl has spent a fortnight admiring the exquisite roundness of her mother's arms, and that mother, my dear, the Duchesse de Chaulieu, she is naturally grieved when she observes her own arms to be thin. But she consoles herself when she perceives that her wrist is delicately formed, and that there is a certain tenderness of outline about the hollows which the soft flesh will soon round and fill up and make shapely. The somewhat spare outline of the arms repeats itself in the shoulders. In fact, I have no shoulders. I have only two hard shoulder-blades, which make two sharp lines, and there is nothing supple about my figure—my sides look stiff and rigid. Oh, now I've told it all! But all the lines are clear and refined, the warm pure colour of health shines in the sinewy curves, life and blue blood course freely under the transparent skin. Why, the fairest daughter ever born of the fair-haired Eve is a negress beside me! Why, I have a foot like a gazelle! All my joints are daintily modelled, and I have the correct features of a Greek drawing. The flesh-tints are not softly merged together, my dear—I know it—but they are lively enough. I am a very pretty unripe fruit, and I have all the unripe charm pertaining to my condition. To sum it up, I'm

The Memoirs of Two Young Brides

like the figure rising out of a purplish lily, in my aunt's old missal. My blue eyes don't look foolish—they are proud eyes, with rims of pearly flesh about them, prettily tinged with tiny thread-like veins; my long and close-set eye-lashes fall like a silken fringe. My brow shines, my hair grows enchantingly in little waves of pale gold, that looks darker in the shadows, with rebellious tendrils here and there, telling plainly enough that I am not one of your sickly fair-haired maidens given to fainting fits, but a full-blooded blonde from the South country—a blonde who strikes before any one has time to strike her. The hair-dresser, if you please, actually wanted to smooth my hair down into two bands and to hang a pearl on a gold chain upon my forehead, telling me I should make a " Middle Ages " effect. " Let me tell you," said I, " that I am not so near middle age as to need any adornment calculated to make me look younger! "

My nose is delicate, my nostrils are well-cut, and the membrane that parts them is of a dainty pink. It is an imperious and scornful nose, and in the composition of its tip muscle predominates over flesh to an extent which will prevent it ever growing thick or red.

My dear creature, if all this is not enough to make a man marry a portionless girl, I'm sorely mistaken. My ears are bewitchingly curled, a pearl in each lobe would look yellow beside them. My neck is long—it has that serpentine movement which imparts so great an appearance of majesty. In the shadow its white-

The Memoirs of Two Young Brides

ness takes on a golden tinge. Ah, my mouth is a thought too big, perhaps! But, then, it's so expressive! The colour of my lips is so brilliant, my teeth laugh so merrily behind them! And then, my dear, the whole thing is in harmony. I have a way of moving, and a voice. I remember how my grandmother managed her skirts without ever laying her hand upon them. I am pretty, then, and I am graceful. If it so pleases me, I can laugh as we used to laugh together often, and I shall still be respected. There will be something imposing always in the dimples light-fingered Mirth will make in my fair cheeks. I can drop my eyes, and look as though my snowy brow concealed an ice-cold heart. I can sit Madonna-like, with melancholy, drooping, swan-like neck, and all the virgins ever painted will be fathoms deep below me. I shall throne higher in Heaven than they will. The man who would speak with me will be fain to set his voice to music.

Thus I am armed at all points, and I can play the gamut of the coquette from its most solemn notes up to its sweetest trills. It is an immense advantage not to be uniform. My mother is neither wanton nor virginal. She is altogether dignified and imposing. The only possible change for her is when she becomes *leonine*. If she inflicts a wound she finds it difficult to heal it. I shall know how to wound and how to heal too. Thus there is no possibility of any rivalry between us, unless we fall out about the relative perfections of our feet and hands. I take after my father.

The Memoirs of Two Young Brides

He is subtle and clever. I have my grandmother's ways and her delightful tone of voice—a head voice, when I force it, a melodious chest-voice in ordinary *tête-à-tête* conversation. It seems to me it is only to-day I have come out of the convent. As yet I don't exist, as far as society is concerned, I am utterly unknown. What an exquisite moment! I am still mine own, like a newly opened flower on which no eye has lighted. Well, dearest, when I walked up and down my sitting-room and looked at myself, when I saw my simple convent garments lying cast aside, something, I know not what, rose up in my heart. There was regret for the past, dread of the future, fear of the great world, farewells to our pale daisies, so innocently culled, so carelessly pulled asunder. All these there were. But there were other things—those wayward fancies that I drive back into the depths of my soul, whither I dare not descend, and whence they rise up to me.

Renée, I have a trousseau like a bride's. Everything is carefully laid away with bags of perfume in the cedar-wood drawers faced with lacquer-work in my beautiful dressing-room. I have ribbons, shoes, gloves, quantities of them all. My father, in the kindliest way, has given me a young lady's necessary treasures—a dressing-case, a toilet service, a perfume box, a fan, a parasol, a prayer-book, a gold chain, a cashmere shawl. He has promised to have me taught to ride; and further, I have learnt to dance. To-morrow, yes, to-morrow night, I am to make my *début*. I have

The Memoirs of Two Young Brides

a white muslin dress. My hair is to be dressed *à la Greque*, with a wreath of white roses. I shall put on my Madonna expression. I mean to look very simple, and to have all the women on my side. My mother doesn't dream of anything of what I am writing to you. She believes me incapable of any serious thought. If she were to read my letter she would be stupefied with astonishment. My brother honours me with the most utter scorn and continues to treat me with the good-nature born of his indifference. He is a handsome young fellow, but pettish and low-spirited. I know his secret—neither the Duke nor the Duchesse have guessed it. Though he is a Duke and though he is young, he is jealous of his father. He has no State position, he has no office at Court. He can't say, " I'm going to the House of Parliament." I am the only person in this house who has sixteen free hours in which I can think. My father is absorbed in public business and his own pleasures. My mother, too, is busy. Not one of them ever turns back to their own thought, they seem always out of doors. There is not time enough for their life. I am excessively curious to know what invincible charm there can be about this society that keeps you out of doors from nine o'clock every night till two or three the next morning, that induces you to take so much trouble and endure so much fatigue. When I longed to reach it I never dreamt there could be such distances and such intoxications: but, in truth, I forget that this is Paris. So you see, the members of a family may all live together

The Memoirs of Two Young Brides

and not really know each other. Enter a sort of nun, and in a fortnight she discovers what a statesman can not perceive in his own house. But perhaps he does see it, and there is something paternal in his deliberate blindness. I must probe this dark matter.

IV

FROM THE SAME TO THE SAME

December 15th.

YESTERDAY at two o'clock, on just such an autumn day as those we used to enjoy so much by the banks of the Loire, I went for a drive in the Champs Elysées and the Bois de Boulogne. So I have seen Paris at last! The effect of the Place Louis XV is really fine, but its beauty is of the order that mankind creates. I was well dressed, pensive, though ready enough to laugh; my face looked calmly out under a bewitching hat; my arms were folded. I did not win a single smile. Not one poor young man stopped short in his astonishment; not a soul turned round to look at me; and yet the carriage progressed with a deliberation that was in harmony with my attitude. But I was mistaken. One fascinating Duke, who passed me by, turned his horse sharply back. This man, who saved my vanity in the public sight, was my own father, whose pride, he tells me, was agreeably tickled by my appearance. I met my mother, who wafted me a little greeting that looked like a kiss upon her finger tips. My Griffiths, who knows not what an *arrière pensée* means, glanced carelessly about her, this way and that. To my thinking, a young lady should always

The Memoirs of Two Young Brides

know exactly what she is looking at. I felt furious. One man scrutinized my carriage most attentively and took no notice of me whatever. This latter individual was probably a coach-builder. I have been mistaken in my estimate of my own power: beauty, that rare privilege that God alone bestows, is more common in Paris than I had fancied. Simpering beings reaped courteous salutations. Red-faced women came in view, and men said to themselves, " There she is!" My mother was enormously admired. There is an answer to this riddle, and I will seek it out. Speaking generally, the men, my dear, struck me as being very ugly. The good-looking ones are unpleasing likenesses of us women. I know not what evil genius invented their dress. Compared with that of the last two centuries its awkwardness is something surprising. It has no brilliancy, no colour, no poetry. It appeals neither to the senses, the intellect, nor the eye, and it must be inconvenient. It is scant and short in cut. The hats struck me particularly. They are like the segment of a pillar. They don't follow the shape of the head. But I am assured it is easier to bring about a revolution than to bring in becoming hats. In France a man's courage fails him at the idea of wearing a round-crowned felt head-piece, and for want of one day's bravery they suffer absurd hats all their lives. And then we are told Frenchmen are fickle! Anyhow, the men are perfectly frightful. All the faces I have seen are hard and worn, without the slightest look of peace or calm. The lines are harsh,

The Memoirs of Two Young Brides

and there are wrinkles that tell of disappointed ambitions and unsatisfied vanities. A fine forehead is a rare occurrence.

"So these are the Parisians!" said I to Miss Griffiths.

"Very charming and witty men," she answered.

I held my peace. An unmarried woman of thirty-six keeps a mine of indulgence for others in her heart.

That evening I went to a ball, and stood beside my mother, who took me on her arm and was well rewarded for her pains. All the honours of the evening were hers. I was a pretext for the most pleasing flatteries. She was clever enough to set me dancing with various idiots, who all descanted on the heat, as if I were freezing, and on the beauty of the entertainment, as if I were blind. Not one of them failed to fall into ecstasies over one strange, unheard of, extraordinary, singular, whimsical fact—that of beholding me for the first time. My dress, which I had thought so enchanting when I walked alone up and down my white-and-gold sitting-room, was barely noticeable among the wonderful adornments worn by most of the women present. Each lady had her faithful circle, and they all watched each other out of the corner of their eyes. Several, like my mother, blazed with triumphant beauty. A girl does not count at a ball at all, she is a mere dancing-machine. With a few rare exceptions, the men were no better than those I saw in the Champs Élysées. They look worn-out, there is no character about their faces, or rather they all have

The Memoirs of Two Young Brides

the same character. The proud and vigorous expressions we see in the pictures of our ancestors, who united physical strength with moral force, no longer exist. Yet at this gathering there was one highly gifted man, whose great beauty of face made him stand out from the general crowd. But he did not impress me as he should have done. I do not know his works, and he is not of noble blood. However great may be the genius and the qualities possessed by a *bourgeois*, or a man who has been ennobled, not one drop of blood flows in my veins for him. And besides, this individual seemed to me so self-occupied, so little concerned about others, that he made me feel we can only be things, not beings, in the eyes of such great seekers after thought. When a man of talent falls in love, he must give up writing. Otherwise he does not really love; for there is something in his brain that takes precedence of his mistress. All this I seemed to read in the demeanour of this gentleman, who is, I am told, an orator, a teacher, a writer, and whom his ambition turns into the humble servant of all greatness. I made up my mind at once. I concluded it was quite unworthy of me to bear society a grudge for my own lack of success, and I began to dance quite unconcernedly. Further, I found I enjoyed dancing very much. I heard various uninteresting pieces of gossip about people with whom I had no acquaintance. But perhaps one has to know a great many things of which I am still ignorant before one can understand these stories, for I saw that most men and women took a lively pleasure in saying or listening to certain sentences. Society is full of riddles, the answers to which seem difficult to find. There are manifold intrigues, too. I have fairly sharp eyes and keen ears, and as to my powers of comprehension, you know them, Mlle. de Maucombe!

I went home weary and delighted with my weariness. I very artlessly expressed my sensations to my mother, and she told me I was never to confide that sort of thing to any one but her.

"My dear child," she added, "good taste consists as much in knowing when to keep silence as when to speak."

This warning helped me to understand the nature of certain sensations concerning which one should be silent to every one, perhaps even to one's own mother. With a single glance I took in the whole field of feminine dissimulation. I can assure you, dear soul, that we two, with the boldness born of our innocence, would be two tolerably wide-awake little gossips. How much teaching lies in a finger laid on lip, a word, a glance! In one instant, I felt timid to a degree. What! must I not express the natural delight I found in dancing? "Then," said I to myself, "what about my inner feelings?" I went to bed feeling sad. I am still sharply conscious of the effect of this first collision between my frank and joyous nature and the hard laws of the social world. Already I have left some scraps of my white fleece hanging on the wayside brambles. Adieu, my angel!

V

FROM RENÉE DE MAUCOMBE TO LOUISE DE CHAULIEU

October.

How deeply your letter moved me, especially when I compared our two destinies! How brilliant is the society in which you are to live! How peaceful the retreat in which I shall end my obscure career! One fortnight after my arrival at the Château de Maucombe—of which I have talked to you so much that I need not speak of it again, and where I found my own room very much as I had left it—though now I can appreciate the splendid outlook upon the Gémenos Valley, on which, in my childish days, I used to gaze with unseeing eyes—my father and mother, accompanied by my two brothers, took me to dine with one of our neighbours, an old M. de l'Estorade, a nobleman who has grown very rich, as provincial people can grow rich, by dint of avarice. This old gentleman had not been able to protect his only son from the greedy hands of Bonaparte. After having saved him from conscription, he was obliged, in 1813, to send him to serve in the army in the *Garde d'Honneur.* After the battle of Leipsic, the old Baron heard no more tidings of his son. In 1814, he waited

The Memoirs of Two Young Brides

on M. de Montriveau, who told him he had seen his son taken prisoner by the Russians. Mme. de l'Estorade died of grief, while fruitless inquiries were still being made in Russia. The Baron, a very religious-minded old man, practised that noble theological virtue which we used to practise at Blois—Hope! Hope brought his son before his eyes in dreams, and for his son he laid aside his income, and looked after his boy's share in the inheritance due to him from Mme. de l'Estorade's family. Nobody ventured to make game of the old gentleman. I guessed, at last, that the unhoped for reappearance of this son had been the cause of my own recall. Who would ever have guessed that while our thoughts roved idly hither and thither, my future husband was slowly making his way on foot across Russia, Poland, and Germany. His evil fate never forsook him till he reached Berlin, whence the French minister assisted him to get back to France. The celebrity of the name of the elder M. de l'Estorade, a small provincial nobleman, with an income of some ten thousand francs a year, is not sufficiently European to have kindled any special interest in the Chevalier de l'Estorade—a title with a decided smack of the adventurer about it. The accumulations of an annual income of twelve thousand francs, Mme. de l'Estorade's own fortune, together with the father's savings, have provided the poor *Garde d'Honneur* with what in Provence is a considerable fortune—something like two hundred and fifty thousand francs, independent

The Memoirs of Two Young Brides

of real estate. Just before his son came back to him, old M. de l'Estorade bought a fine bit of property which had been badly managed, and proposes to plant it with ten thousand mulberry trees, which he had reared in his nursery garden with a special view to this very purchase. When the Baron recovered his son, his one idea was to find him a wife, and that wife a girl of noble birth. My father and mother fell in, as regards me, with their neighbour's plan, as soon as the old gentleman informed them of his willingness to accept Renée de Maucombe without any dowry, and to formally settle on the said Renée the amount she should legally have inherited from her parents. As soon as my second brother, Jean de Maucombe, came of age, he signed a deed acknowledging the receipt of an advance on the family inheritance amounting to one-third of the sum total. Thus do well-born Provençal families evade the Sieur de Bonaparte's vile *Code Civil*, which will send as many girls to the convent as it has already assisted to the altar. According to the little I have heard said on the matter, there is great difference of opinion among the French nobility as to these important subjects.

That dinner, my dear creature, was for an interview between your darling and the exile. Let me recount everything in its proper order. The Comte de Maucombe's servants put on their old embroidered liveries and laced hats, the coachman got into his big boots. We sat, five of us, in the old coach, and we arrived in

The Memoirs of Two Young Brides

all our majesty by two o'clock, for dinner at three, at the country-house which the Baron de l'Estorade makes his home. My father-in-law does not possess a château—it is a plain country-house, standing at the foot of one of our hills, at the mouth of our lovely valley, the pride of which certainly is our own old Castle of Maucombe. This country-house is just a plain country-house—four flint walls, faced with a yellowish cement, and roofed with curved tiles of a beautiful red colour. The rafters bend under the weight of these tiles. The windows, cut in the walls without any attempt at symmetrical arrangement, have huge yellow-painted shutters. The garden around the dwelling is a regular Provençal garden, shut in by low walls built of big round pebbles, arranged in layers, and in which the mason's skill is exemplified by the fashion in which he laid the said pebbles, one row flat and the next standing up on edge. The layer of mud that incases them is falling off in places. What raises this country-house to the dignity of a mansion is the ironwork entrance gates opening on to the high-road. Those gates cost many a sacrifice. They are so thin and poor they remind me of Sœur Angélique! The house has a flight of stone steps, the door is graced with a pent-house porch that no peasant of the Loire would endure on his neat white-stone house with its blue roof on which the sun laughs. The garden, like all the surrounding ground, is horribly dusty, the trees are all burnt up. It is easy to see that for many a long day the Baron's whole life has been

The Memoirs of Two Young Brides

spent in getting up and going to bed and getting up again, without giving a thought to anything save to laying by one copper coin after another. He eats the same kind of food as his two servants—a Provençal lad and his wife's old maid. There is very little furniture in the rooms. Yet the De l'Estorade household had done its best, ransacked its cupboards, taxed all its resources for this dinner, which was served to us on old, black, battered, silver plate. The exile, my dear, is like his gates, very thin and poor. He is pale, he has suffered, he is taciturn. He is seven-and-thirty, and he looks as if he were fifty. The ebony of his once splendid tresses is streaked with white like a lark's wing. His fine blue eyes are sunk in his head. He is a little deaf, which makes him like the Knight of the Sorrowful Countenance. Nevertheless, I have graciously consented to become Mme. de l'Estorade and to accept a dowry of two hundred and fifty thousand francs, but only on the express understanding that I am to be allowed to rearrange the country-house and lay out a park round it. I have extracted a formal promise from my father to make over to me a small water supply, which can be carried hither from Maucombe. Within a month I shall be Mme. de l'Estorade. For I am loved, my dear! A man who has dwelt in Siberian snows is very much disposed to admire those black eyes which, so you used to tell me, ripen the very fruit I look at. Louis de l'Estorade appears exceedingly happy to marry " the fair Renée de Maucombe," thus is your friend proudly described. While you are making yourself ready to reap all the joys of the fullest of lives—that of a daughter of the House of Chaulieu in Paris, where you will reign supreme—your poor love, your Renée, that child of the desert, has fallen from the Empyrean heights to which we both had soared, down to a fate as ordinary as that of a field daisy.

Yes, I have vowed to myself that I will be the consolation of this young man who has had no youth, who passed from his mother's lap to that of the war goddess, and from the delights of a country home to Siberian frosts and toils. The uniform tenor of my future existence will be varied by the humble pleasures of a rural life. I will extend the oasis of the Gémenos Valley all about my house, which shall stand in the majestic shade of splendid trees. Here, in Provence, I will have lawns that are always green. I will spread my park up on to the hill, and on its highest point I will set some dainty summer-house, whence, perhaps, I may get a glimpse of the shining Mediterranean. Orange and lemon trees, all the richest products of botany, shall embellish my retreat, and here I shall be the mother of children; a natural, imperishable poetry will environ us. If I am faithful to my duty, I need fear no ill-fortune. My father-in-law and M. de l'Estorade share my feelings about religion. Ah, dearest! Life looks to me just like one of our great French high-roads, smooth and quiet and shaded by everlasting trees. There will hardly be two Bonapartes in this one century! I shall be able to

The Memoirs of Two Young Brides

keep my children, if I have any, to rear them and bring them up to man's estate. I shall enjoy my life in theirs. If you do not fail to reach your appointed destiny—you who will be the most powerful woman upon earth—your Renée's children will have an active protectress. Then farewell, for me at least, to the romantic tales and fantastic situations of which we used to fancy ourselves the heroines. I know the story of my life already and beforehand. It will be marked by such great events as the teething of the young De l'Estorades, their meals, the havoc they will wreak on my shrubberies and my person. To embroider their caps, to be loved and admired by a poor ailing man, here at the mouth of the Gémenos Valley —these will be my pleasures. Some day, perhaps, this country lady will go and spend her winters at Marseilles. But even then she will only appear on the tiny provincial stage, where but little danger lurks behind the scenes. There will be nothing for me to fear, not even one of those admirations which may give just cause for a legitimate pride. We shall take a deep interest in silkworms, because we shall have mulberry leaves to sell. We shall learn to know all the strange vicissitudes of Provençal life, and the storms of a household in which there can not be any possible quarrel. M. de l'Estorade has formally announced his intention to be ruled by his wife. Now, as I shall do nothing to keep him up to this wise resolution, he will most probably persist in it. You, dear Louise, will constitute the romantic side of my existence. So, mind you tell me all about your balls and parties. Let me know how you are dressed, what flowers you wreathe in your beautiful fair hair, what the men say and how they behave. I shall be with you, listening, dancing, feeling the tips of your fingers gently squeezed. How I should like to amuse myself in Paris, while you played house-mother at La Crampade —that is the name of our country-house! Poor dear man who thinks he's only marrying one woman! Will he find out we are two? I am beginning to talk foolishness, and as I must cease doing it, except by proxy, I'll stop short. A kiss, then, on each of your cheeks. My lips are still maiden lips. He has not dared to do more than hold my hand. Oh, there's something rather alarming about his respectfulness and propriety! Well there, I am beginning again! Farewell, my dear one!

P. S.—I have just opened your third letter. My dear, I have about a thousand francs at my command. Please spend them for me on pretty things that could not be had in this neighbourhood, nor even at Marseilles. Remember that none of the old folk on either side know any one with good taste, to do their Paris commissions for them. I will answer the letter later.

VI

FROM DON FELIPE HENAREZ TO DON FERNANDO

PARIS, *September.*

THE heading of this letter, my dear brother, will show you that the chief of your family is in no danger. If the massacre of our ancestors in the Court of Lions did turn us, despite ourselves, into Spaniards and Christians, it left us a legacy of Arab caution—and I owe my safety, perhaps, to the blood of the Abencerages that flows in my veins. Fright turned Ferdinand into so good an actor that Valdez believed his protestations. But for me the poor admiral would have been lost. None of the Liberals will ever learn to know the nature of a King. But I had long been familiar with the character of that particular member of the Bourbon House. The more his Majesty averred he would protect us, the more deep were my suspicions. A true Spaniard does not need to reiterate his promises. The man who talks too much seeks to deceive. Valdez got on board an English ship. As for me, when the fate of my beloved Spain was lost in Andalusia, I wrote to my steward in Sardinia to provide for my safety. Some skilful coral fishers waited for me in a boat at a certain place on the

The Memoirs of Two Young Brides

sea-coast. While Ferdinand was begging the French authorities to seize my person, I was safe in my Barony of Macumer, surrounded by bandits, who set every law and every vengeance at defiance. The head of the last Hispano-Moorish house in Granada found an African desert, and even an Arab horse, on the domain that had come down to him from the Saracens. When these bandits, who but yesterday dreaded my justice, learnt that they were sheltering the Duque de Soria—their master, a Henarez, at last, the first who had come near them since the days when the Moors held the island—from the vengeance of the King of Spain, their eyes flashed with wild joy and pride. Two-and-twenty carabines were instantly offered to make away with Ferdinand de Bourbon, that scion of a race unknown when the victorious Abencerages first appeared on the banks of the Loire. I thought I might have lived on the income of this huge property, upon which, unluckily, we have bestowed such scant attention. But my stay there has convinced me of my own mistake, and of the truthfulness of Quevedo's reports. The poor man had two-and-twenty human existences at my service, but not a single coin. There are savannas covering twenty thousand acres, but not a house of any kind: virgin forests, but not a stick of furniture. A million of piastres must be spent, and the owner must have made his home there for fifty years, before that splendid territory can be turned to profit. I will think it over. Vanquished men ponder as they flee, both on them-

The Memoirs of Two Young Brides

selves and on their lost cause. As I looked at that splendid corpse, already gnawed by monkish rats, tears swam in my eyes. I recognised the sad fate awaiting Spain. At Marseilles I heard of Riego's end, and reflected mournfully that my life, too, will end in martyrdom—but one that will be obscure and slow. Will life be life without the possibility of devoting it to one's country, or living it for a woman? Love, victory, these two aspects of the same idea, were the law graven on our sword-blades, written in letters of gold on the archways of our houses, repeated by the fountains that sprang in our marble basins. But in vain does my heart cling fanatically to the command. The sword is snapped, the palace lies in ashes, the fresh spring is swallowed up in barren sands! Here, then, is my last will.

Don Fernando, you will soon understand why I checked your eagerness and commanded you to continue faithful to the *Rey netto*. As your brother and your friend, I beseech you to obey me; as your master, I command you! You will go to the King, you will pray him to bestow my grandeeships and my possessions, my office and my titles, on yourself. He will hold back; he will make one or two royal faces, may be. But you will tell him that Maria Heredia loves you, and that Maria can marry nobody but the Duque de Soria. Then you will see him quiver with delight. The huge fortune of the Heredia family prevented him from accomplishing my ruin. He will think it complete then, and all I leave behind me will instantly

The Memoirs of Two Young Brides

be bestowed on you. You shall marry Maria. I had guessed the secret of the love against which you were both struggling, and I have prepared the old Count's mind for this exchange. We had bowed, Maria and I, to social rules and to our parents' will. You are as beautiful as any love-child; I, ugly as a Spanish grandee can be. You are beloved. I am the object of an unspoken aversion. You will soon overcome what little resistance my misfortunes may have inspired in the heart of the high-born Spanish maiden. Duque de Soria! your predecessor does not choose to cost you one touch of regret, nor to defraud you of a single maravedi. As Maria's jewels will replace the loss of my mother's diamonds to our family, you will send me those diamonds, which will suffice to insure me an independent livelihood, by my old nurse Urraca, the only person in my household whom I intend to keep about me . . . No other creature knows how to make my chocolate properly.

During our short-lived revolution, my constant labours had cut down the expenses of my life to the merest necessaries, and the salary of my office sufficed for them. You will find my income for those two years in your steward's keeping. This sum of money is my property. The marriage of a Duque de Soria entails a large outlay. So we will divide it between us. You will not refuse your bandit brother's wedding-present. And besides, such is my will. As the Barony of Macumer is not held under the King of Spain, it still remains with me; and I shall be able to assume a

The Memoirs of Two Young Brides

name and nationality if ever I should choose to become any one again. God be praised, this ends our business! The House of Soria is safe!

Just at this moment, in which I become Baron de Macumer and nothing more, the French artillery is booming out its greeting to the Duc d'Angoulême. You will understand, sir, wherefore I break off my letter.

October.

When I arrived here I had not ten double pistoles in the world. He must be a shabby statesman who, in the midst of misfortunes he has not averted, gives selfish thought to his own fortune. The vanquished Moor has his horse and the desert; the Christian whose hopes are shattered, the monastery and a handful of gold pieces. Yet, so far, my resignation is no more than weariness. I am not so near the cloister as to give no thought to life. Ozalga, on the merest chance, had given me a few letters of introduction, among them one for a bookseller, who, to our fellow-countrymen, is very much what Galignani is to the English here. This man has found me eight pupils at three francs a lesson. I go to each pupil every second day. So I give four lessons and earn twelve francs a day—a great deal more money than I need. When Urraca arrives, I shall make some Spanish exile happy by turning over my pupils to him. I live in the Rue Hillerin-Bertin, in the house of a poor widow who takes boarders. My room looks southward over a little garden. I hear no noise, I see green trees, and I

The Memoirs of Two Young Brides

don't spend more than a piastre a day. The calm and pure delights I discover in this existence are quite an astonishment to me.

From sunrise till ten o'clock, I smoke, and drink my chocolate, sitting by my window and looking at two Spanish shrubs—a broom, standing out against a mass of jessamine, gold on a white background, a sight that will always stir the soul of any descendant of the Moors. At ten o'clock I start forth to give my lessons until four. Then I come home to my dinner, and after that I smoke and read till bedtime. I can go on leading this life—in which solitude and company, labour and meditation, all bear a part—for a very long time. So, Don Fernando, you may be happy; my abdication is an accomplished fact, and there has been no backward glance, no after-regret as in the case of Charles V, nor any longing to play the old part again, as in Napoleon's. Five days and nights have gone by since I made my will. Seen through my meditations, they are like a thousand years. Greatness, titles, wealth, are to me as though they had never been. Now that the barrier of respect that parted us is broken down, I can open my heart to you, dear boy. That heart, hidden under its impenetrable mask of gravity, is full of tenderness and of a power of devotion which have found no outlet. But no woman—not even she who was destined from her cradle to be my wife—has ever guessed at their existence. There lies the secret of my feverish devotion to politics. Having no lady-love to worship, I worshipped Spain. And now Spain,

The Memoirs of Two Young Brides

too, has failed me. Now that I am nothing, I can contemplate the ruin of my individual existence, and I ask myself why life was ever bestowed on me, and when it will depart? Wherefore has the most chivalrous of all races transmitted its primitive virtues, its African passion, its burning poetry, to its last scion? Is the seed destined to die within its rough husk without sending up a single stalk, or scattering its Oriental perfume from even one tall bright-hued calyx? What crime was mine, as yet unborn, that I should never have inspired love in any human being? Was I, then, from my very birth but an ancient fragment, fated to be cast up on some barren shore? Within my own soul I discover my hereditary deserts, lighted by a sun so fierce that no plant can flourish on them. Here, more fittingly than in any other place, this proud remnant of a fallen race, this useless strength, this wasted love, this young man, old before his time, shall await the advent of that closing mercy—Death! Under these misty skies, alas! no spark will rekindle the flame buried deep beneath the ashes. Thus my last words may well be those of Jesus Christ, " My God, why hast thou forsaken me? " A terrible cry, truly, which no man has dared to fathom.

Imagine then, Fernando, what happiness I find in living afresh in Maria and in you. Henceforward I shall contemplate you with all the pride of a creator who glories in his work. Love each other faithfully. Give me no cause for sorrow. A storm between you two would hurt me more than it would hurt your-

The Memoirs of Two Young Brides

selves. Our mother had a presentiment that one of these days events would crown her secret hopes. Perhaps a mother's longing is a contract between her and the Almighty! And, then, she was surely one of those mysterious creatures who have the power of holding converse with Heaven, and of carrying some vision of futurity back to earth. How often have I read in the lines upon her forehead that she would fain see Fernando the possessor of Felipe's wealth and honours! If I said it to her, she would answer me with two great tears, and give me a glimpse of the wounds of a heart which should have belonged wholly to each one of us, but which an overmastering love had given to you alone. This being so, her spirit will surely hover over your heads as you bow them before the altar. Will there be one caress at last for Felipe, Doña Clara? Behold him: he gives you, best beloved, all, even the maiden you yourself have led unwillingly to his embrace. What I have done is pleasing in the sight of all women, of the dead, of the King. It is the will of God. Therefore, Don Fernando, lift no finger against it. Obey me and hold your peace.

P. S.—Desire Urraca never to call me anything but *Monsieur Henarez*. Not a word about me to Maria. You must be the only living being acquainted with the secret of the last converted Moor, in whose veins runs the blood of the mighty stock which sprang from the desert and is about to end in solitude. Farewell!

VII

FROM LOUISE DE CHAULIEU TO RENÉE DE MAUCOMBE

January, 1824.

WHAT! You are to be married at once! But was there ever such a surprise? Within one month you undertake to marry a man—without knowing him, without knowing anything about him. The man may be deaf—there are so many ways of being deaf. He may be sickly, tiresome, unendurable. Don't you see, Renée, what they want of you? You are necessary to them to carry on the splendid line of the De l'Estorades, and that's the whole story. You are going to turn yourself into a provincial lady. Was that what we promised each other? If I were you, I'd rather row round about the Isles of Hyères in a caique till some Algerine corsair carried me off and sold me to the Grand Signior. That way I'd be a Sultana first of all, and then Sultana Validé. I'd turn the seraglio upside down as long as I was young, and even when I was old. You are only leaving one convent to go into another. I know you; you are a coward, you'll enter the married state as submissively as a lamb. Be ruled by me. Come up to Paris, we'll drive all the men wild, and we shall end by reigning like two queens. Within

The Memoirs of Two Young Brides

three years, my dearest love, your husband will be able to get himself elected Deputy. I know now what a Deputy is. I'll explain it to you. You will play exceedingly well upon that instrument. You'll be able to live in Paris, and to become, as my mother says, " a fashionable woman." Oh, I'll certainly not leave you in your country-house!

For the last fortnight, my dear, I have been living the life of the gay world. One evening at the *Italiens*, the next at the Grand Opera, and on to a ball every night. Ah, society is like a fairy play. The music at the *Italiens* enchants me, and while my whole being floats in the most divine delight, I myself am admired, scanned through opera-glasses. But with one glance I make the boldest of the young men drop his eyes. I have seen some charming young men. Well, there is not one of them who takes my fancy, not one who inspires me with the emotion I feel when I hear Garcia sing his splendid duet with Pellegrini in Otello. Heavens, how jealous Rossini must have been to have expressed jealousy so admirably! What a passionate ring there is in *Il mio cor si divide*. All this is Greek to you, who haven't heard Garcia. But you know how jealous I can be! What a poor playwright is this Shakespeare! Otello falls in love with glory—he wins victories, he gives orders, he parades up and down, and goes hither and thither, leaving Desdemona alone in a corner, and she, who sees him preferring the inanities of public life to her own self, never grows angry! Forsooth, such a sheep deserves to be slaughtered!

The Memoirs of Two Young Brides

Let the man I condescend to love dare to do anything except love me back! I am all for the lengthy ordeals of ancient chivalry. I look on that churlish young nobleman who found fault because his sovereign lady sent him to fetch her glove out of the lion's den, as a very foolish and impertinent young fellow. I've no doubt she had reserved some exquisite blossom of love for him, and he lost it, insolent boy—after having earned it. But here I go on chattering as if I had not a great piece of news to give you. My father is to represent the King, our master, at Madrid. I say *our* master, for I am to be a member of the Embassy. My mother wishes to stay here, and my father will take me, so as to have a lady with him.

My dear, all this seems mighty simple to you—but there are huge matters underneath. In this fortnight, I've discovered all the secrets of the household. My mother would go with my father to Madrid if he could take M. de Canalis with him as secretary to the Embassy. But the King appoints all the secretaries. The Duke does not dare either to displease the King, who is very despotic, or to cross my mother, and this wily personage fancies he will solve the difficulties of the situation by leaving the Duchesse here behind him. M. de Canalis, the great poet of the day, is the young man who cultivates my mother's society, and, no doubt, studies diplomacy with her daily from three to five o'clock. Diplomacy must be an interesting subject, for he is as assiduous in his attendance as a gambler at the Stock Exchange. The Duc de Rhétoré, my eldest brother—a solemn, frigid, fanciful body—would be eclipsed by his father at Madrid. So he stays in Paris. Besides, Miss Griffiths knows Aphonse is devoted to an opera-dancer. How any man can fall in love with legs and pirouettes! We have noticed my brother is always present at the operas in which Tullia dances. He applauds the creature's performances, and departs when they are over. I believe two bad women work more harm in a household than an epidemic of the plague. As for my second brother, he is with his regiment, and I've not seen him yet. Thus it comes about that I am destined to be the Antigone of one of his Majesty's ambassadors. Perhaps I shall marry in Spain, and perhaps my father's idea is to marry me there without a portion, exactly as you are being married to that wreck of a former *Garde d'Honneur*. My father suggested that I should go with him, and offered to lend me his Spanish master.

"Do you want me to make Spanish marriages?" The only answer he vouchsafed me was a shrewd glance. For the last few days he has been pleased to tease me during breakfast; he studies me. I dissemble, and both as a parent and a future ambassador, I have imposed upon him cruelly. Didn't he take me for a fool? He would ask me what I thought of such a young man and of certain young ladies whom I had met in various houses. I replied by the most stupid dissertation on the colour of the hair, the figure, the expression of face of the young couple he men-

The Memoirs of Two Young Brides

tioned. My father looked disappointed to find me such a simpleton. He was blaming himself internally for having questioned me.

"However, father," I added, "I have not told you what I really think. Something my mother said to me a little time ago, makes me fear I may fall into some impropriety if I talk of my impressions."

"In your own family, you can speak openly and fearlessly," said my mother.

"Well, then," I said, "so far, the young men strike me as being more interested than interesting, more taken up with themselves than with us; but they certainly are far from artful. They instantly drop the expression they have put on when they speak to us, and they imagine, no doubt, that we don't know how to use our eyes. The man who speaks to us is the lover, the man who has just spoken to us is the husband. As for the young ladies, they are so false that the only sign by which one can possibly guess at their character is the way they dance. Their figures and their movements are the only truthful things about them. The thing that has most startled me is the brutality of smart society. When supper is in question things happen that give me—in a minor degree, of course—an idea of what a popular riot must be. The general selfishness is hidden under a very partial veil of politeness. I had fancied Society was quite a different thing. Women here count for very little. That, perhaps, is a remnant of Bonaparte's teachings."

The Memoirs of Two Young Brides

"Armande is making astonishing progress," said my mother.

"Mother," I said, "do you think I shall always ask you whether Mme. de Staël is dead?"

My father smiled, and rose from his chair.

Saturday.

My dear, I haven't told you all. This is what I have kept back for you. The love of which we dreamt must be very deeply hidden. I have discovered no trace of it anywhere. True, I have seen a few swift glances interchanged in drawing-rooms. But how cold they looked! *Our* love—that world of wonders, of fair dreams, of exquisite realities and suffering to match them, those smiles that light up all Nature, those words that enchant, that happiness ever given and received, the anguish of separation, the overmastering joys of the presence of the beloved—of these, not a sign! Where do the gorgeous flowers of existence bud? Who is it that lies, we or the world? I have seen young men by the hundred already, and not one has inspired me with the faintest emotion. They might have expressed all their admiration and devotion, they might have fought battles for me—I should have looked on with a callous eye. Love, my dear child, is so unusual a phenomenon that one may live out one's whole life without meeting the being on whom Nature has bestowed the power of making one happy. This consideration makes me shiver. For **if** the being in question is met late in life—what **then?**

The Memoirs of Two Young Brides

For the last few days I have begun to feel terrified at the thought of our fate, and to understand why so many women carry about sad faces under the layer of rouge which gives them a sham appearance of joy and festivity. Marriage is a mere chance, and such is yours. Whirlwinds of thought have passed over my soul. To be loved every day alike, yet with a difference, to be loved as fondly after ten years of happiness as on the opening day. Such a love must cover years. There must have been so long a period of ungratified longing. So many curiosities stirred, roused and then appeased. So many sympathies first excited and then satisfied. Are there laws that govern the creations of the heart, even as there are laws that rule the visible works of Nature? Can cheerfulness live on itself? In what proportion should the tears and the joys of love be mingled?

At such a moment the chilly regularity of the funereal, uniform, unchanging existence of the convent has seemed possible to me; whereas the riches, the splendour, the tears, the exquisite delights, the merriment, the joys, the pleasures of a well-matched, mutual, lawful love, have appeared to me impossible. I see no room in this town for the sweetness of love, for those blessed strolls beneath the branching arbour, while the full moon sheds her light on the waters and the tenderest entreaties are withstood. Young, rich, beautiful as I am, all I have to do is to fall in love. Love may become my life, my soul, my only occupation. Well, in these last three months which I have spent going to and fro with the most impatient curiosity, I have found, amid all these brilliant, greedy, vigilant eyes about me—nothing at all. Not a tone has touched me, not one look has flooded the world with light for me. Music alone has filled my soul, and been to me what our friendship is. Sometimes, at night, I have spent a whole hour at my window, gazing out on the garden, longing for something to happen, praying that events might spring from the unknown source which sends them forth. Sometimes I have driven to the Champs Élysées, fancying some man—the man destined to stir my slumbering soul—would surely appear, and follow me, and gaze at me. But on those days I have met mountebanks and ginger-bread sellers and conjurers, passers-by hurrying to their business, or lovers who fled the sight of every one. And I have been tempted to stop them, and cry: "You are happy; tell me what love is?" But I forced the wild fancy back and got me to my carriage, and vowed I would be an old maid. Love certainly is an incarnation, and how difficult are the conditions under which it must take place! We are not always certain of agreeing with ourselves. How will it be when there are two of us? God alone can solve the problem. I begin to think I will go back to my convent. If I remain in the world, I shall do things which will look like follies, for I cannot possibly accept the conditions I see around me. All these wound either my delicacy, my innermost proprieties, or my secret thoughts. Ah, my mother is the happiest woman in

The Memoirs of Two Young Brides

the world. Her tall young Canalis adores her. My dearest, I have a shocking longing, now and then, to know what my mother and that young gentleman may say to each other. Griffiths tells me she has had all these fancies. She has felt as if she could fly at the women she knew were happy. She has run them down, torn them to pieces. According to her, virtue consists in burying all these savage feelings at the bottom of one's heart. Then, what is the bottom of one's heart? A store-room full of all the worst things in us? I am very much humiliated at not having met any one to adore me. I am a young lady in search of a husband, but I have relations, brothers, parents, who are all touchy. Ah, if that were what kept the men back, they must be terrible cowards. The characters of Chimène and of the Cid, in Le Cid, delight me. What an admirable play! And now, good-bye.

VIII

FROM THE SAME TO THE SAME

January.

OUR Spanish master is a poor refugee, who has been driven into exile by the part he played in the revolution the Duc d'Angoulême has been sent to put down. We owe some fine entertainments here to his success in doing so. Though the man is a Liberal, and no doubt of the middle class, he has interested me. I fancy he must have been sentenced to death. I try to induce him to talk, so as to get at his secret. But he is as taciturn as any Castilian grandee, as proud as if he were Gonsalvo of Cordova, and for all that as gentle and patient as an angel. He does not wear his pride outside him like Miss Griffiths. It is hidden in his heart. He forces us to render him his due, by the manner in which he pays us his duty, and severs himself from us by the respect he shows us. My father will have it there is a great deal of the nobleman about this M. Henarez, whom among ourselves he jokingly denominates *Don* Henarez. When I ventured to call him by this name a few days since, he raised his eyes, which are generally dropped, and shot two shafts of lightning at me which quite abashed me. My dear, he certainly has the finest eyes that ever were seen. I asked him whether I had done anything to annoy him, whereupon he answered me in his own grand and majestic tongue:

"Señorita, I only come here to teach you Spanish!"

I felt humiliated, and the colour sprang into my face. I was just going to give him some thoroughly impertinent answer, when I remembered what our dear mother in God used to say to us, and then I replied:

"If you were to reprove me in any matter, you would be conferring an obligation on me."

He started, the blood rose to his olive skin, and he answered me in a gentle and touching voice:

"Religion must have taught you, far better than I could, how to respect misfortunes. If I were a *Don* in Spain, and I had lost everything when Ferdinand VII triumphed, your joke would have been cruel. But if I am nothing but a poor teacher, is it not a heartless jest? Neither of these are worthy of a high-born lady."

I took his hand as I said:

"Then I will appeal to religion to make you forget my fault."

He bowed his head, opened my Don Quixote and sat himself down.

This little incident threw me into greater confusion than all the looks, the compliments, the remarks of which I was the object the night when I was most admired. During the lesson I looked carefully at the man, who was quite unconscious of my scrutiny; he never raises his eyes to look at me. I then discovered that this Spanish master, whom we took to be forty, is quite young—not more than six or eight and twenty. My governess, to whose consideration I had hitherto left him, called my attention to the beauty of his black hair and of his teeth, which are like pearls. As for his eyes, they are at once as soft as velvet and as blazing as fire. There it ends—otherwise he is little and ugly. We used to be told that Spaniards were anything but cleanly. But this man is most careful of his person, his hands are whiter than his face; he is rather round-shouldered, his head is very large and rather oddly shaped; his ugliness—he is really very clever-looking in spite of it—is increased by his face being seamed with small-pox marks. The forehead is exceedingly prominent. His eye-brows meet and are too thick, they give him a severe look, which repels people. He has the sickly and crabbed countenance of a person who ought to have died in childhood, and whose life has only been preserved by dint of endless care—just like Sister Marthe. And altogether, as my father puts it, his face is the face of Cardinal Ximenes on a small scale. My father doesn't like him, he is not at his ease with him. There is a natural dignity about our master's manner which seems to make our dear Duke feel uneasy. He cannot endure any form of superiority in his own vicinity.

As soon as my father knows Spanish we are to start for Madrid. When Henarez came again, two days after my snubbing, I said to him, meaning it as a sort of sign of gratitude:

"I am quite certain you left Spain on account of some political matter. If my father is sent there, as we hear he will be, we should be able to be of some service to you, and to obtain your pardon, if any sentence has been pronounced on you."

"Nobody has it in his power to confer any obligations on me," he replied.

"How, sir?" I said. "Is that because you do not choose to accept any obligation, or is it a case of sheer impossibility?"

"It is both one and the other," he answered, with a bow, and there was something in his tone that reduced me to silence. My father's blood stirred in my veins. This arrogance roused my ire, and I left M. Henarez to himself. Yet, my dear, there is something fine in his refusal to accept anything from others. "He wouldn't even accept our friendship," thought I to myself, as I was conjugating a verb. Then I stopped short and I told him my thought, but in Spanish. Henarez answered very courteously that in such a case there must necessarily be an equality of feeling which was not possible under our circumstances, and that the question was therefore irrelevant.

"Do you mean," I asked, trying to break down his gravity which so provokes me, "that there must be equality as to mutual feeling, or equality of rank?"

Then he lifted those terrible eyes of his, and I

The Memoirs of Two Young Brides

dropped mine. My dear, this man is a hopeless riddle. He looked as if he were asking me whether my words were a declaration. There was an expression of delight and of surprise, and an agony of uncertainty in his voice that wrung my heart. I realized that things which in France are accepted at their proper value, take on a dangerous meaning when one has to deal with a Spaniard, and I retired into my shell, feeling rather foolish. When the lesson was over he bowed to me, with a look that was full of humble entreaty, and which said: " Don't make a sport of an unhappy man." This sudden contrast with his usual serious and dignified deportment made a lively impression upon me. Isn't that shocking to think of and to say. I am certain the man possesses depths of priceless affection.

IX

FROM MME. DE L'ESTORADE TO MLLE DE CHAULIEU

December.

ALL's said and done, dear child. 'Tis Mme. de l'Estorade who pens this letter to you. But nothing is changed between you and me. There is only one girl less in the world. Make your mind easy. I pondered what I did, and my consent was not given lightly. My life is settled now. The certainty that I must follow a clearly marked path suits both my temper and my mind. What we call the chances of life are permanently decided, for me, by a great moral force. We have lands to cultivate, we have a dwelling to embellish and adorn. I have a home to manage and enliven, there is a man whom I must reconcile with life. I shall no doubt have a family to care for, children to bring up. After all, life as a rule cannot well be anything very great or out of the common. Certainly those soaring desires which broaden soul and mind do not enter, apparently at least, into these plans. What is there to prevent me from letting the barks we launched on the ocean of the Infinite pursue their course thereon? Yet do not think that the humble objects to which I am devoting my existence cannot be touched by any passionate interest. To teach a poor fellow who has been the sport of many tempests to believe in his own happiness is a noble undertaking, and may well suffice to modify the monotony of my existence. I do not foresee that it need bring me sorrow, and I do see that there is good for me to do.

Between ourselves, I do not love Louis de l'Estorade with the love which makes a woman's heart throb when she hears a man's footstep, which makes her tremble with emotion at the very sound of his voice, or when his passionate glance falls upon her. But all the same, he is by no means displeasing to me. What am I going to do, you will inquire, with that instinctive feeling for the sublime, with those high thoughts we both of us nurse, and which are a bond between you and me? Yes, that has puzzled me. Well, after, all, will it not be a noble thing to hide them all, to use them unknown to others, for the good of the family—to turn them into means to serve the happiness of the beings confided to us, and to whose welfare we owe our best devotion? In us women, the period during which these faculties are at their best is a very short one. It will soon be over; and if my life has not been a wide one, it will have been calm, smooth, and free from vicissitudes.

We are born with an advantage all our own, we can choose between love and maternity. Well, I have made my choice. My children shall be my gods, this corner of the earth shall be my El Dorado. This is all I can tell you to-day. Thank you for all the things

The Memoirs of Two Young Brides

you have sent me. Look after those ordered in the list I inclose in this letter. I want to bring an atmosphere of luxury and elegance about me, with nothing of the province in it except its enchanting aspects. A woman who lives in solitude can never become provincial. She remains herself. I depend greatly on your goodness to keep me abreast of all the fashions. My father-in-law, in his rapture, does everything I ask, and is turning his house upside down. We are getting workmen from Paris and are modernizing the whole place.

X

FROM MLLE. DE CHAULIEU TO MME. DE L'ESTORADE

January.

Oh, Renée! You've saddened me for several days to come. So that exquisite form, that proud and lovely face, those manners instinct with natural elegance, that nature enriched with precious gifts, those eyes in which the soul may slake its thirst as in a living spring of love, that heart overflowing with exquisite tenderness, that great mind, all those rare powers, the growth of nature and of our mutual education, those treasures meant to crown love and longing with an unexampled wealth of poetry and passion—hours worth ordinary years, joys that with one graceful gesture should enslave a man forever—all are to be swallowed up in the dulness of a vulgar, commonplace marriage, lost in the emptiness of a life that will end by becoming a weariness to you. I hate the children you will bear already! They'll be ugly! Your whole life is mapped out beforehand. There is nothing left for you to hope, or fear, or suffer, and if, on some bright dazzling day you should find yourself face to face with the being fated to break the slumber into which you are now deliberately sinking. . . .

The Memoirs of Two Young Brides

Ah, the very thought makes me shiver! Well, at all events you have one woman friend. No doubt, you'll become the guardian spirit of your valley. You'll learn all its beauties, you'll commune with Nature, you'll fill your soul with the greatness of her works, the slow processes of vegetation, the swiftness of human thought; and as you gaze on all your gay flowers you'll turn your mind inwards and gaze into your own soul. Then, as your life flows onward between your husband and your children—he before and they behind you—they yelping, chattering, frolicking; he, silent, and content—I can tell beforehand what you'll write to me! Your misty valley and your hills, barren or crested with splendid trees; your meadow, that will be such a curiosity in Provence, the clear water divided into rivulets, the changeful play of the lights, all the wide landscape about you, which God has touched with infinite variety, will remind you of the infinite monotony within your heart! But at least I shall be there, my Renée, and you will have one friend whose heart will never be soiled by the smallest social pettiness—a heart that is yours utterly.

Monday.

My dear, my Spaniard is most entrancingly melancholy. There is something about him—a calmness, an austerity, a dignity, a depth—which interests me beyond all words. This invariable gravity and the silence in which the man wraps himself, challenge one's curiosity. He is mute and haughty as a fallen

The Memoirs of Two Young Brides

king. We puzzle over him, Griffiths and I, as if he were a riddle. How absurd it all is! A poor language teacher triumphantly rivets the interest which no other man—not all the well-born youths, the ambassadors and their *attachés*, the generals, the sub-lieutenants, the peers of France, or all their sons and nephews, the Court, the city—have been able to arouse. The man's reserve is most irritating. Pride overweening fills the gulf he strives, and successfully, to fix between himself and us. And further, he shrouds himself in darkness. The coquetry is his. The bold advances, mine. The queerness of the whole affair amuses me all the more because of its unimportance. What is a man—a Spaniard, and a language teacher? I don't feel the slightest respect for any man, not even for a king. I consider we are superior to every man in the world, even the most justly famous. Oh, how I would have ruled Napoleon! How he should have felt himself at my mercy, if he had cared for me!

Yesterday I launched a witticism which must have stung Sir Henarez to the quick. He made no answer. My lesson was just over. He took up his hat and bowed to me with a glance which made me think he is not coming back. That suits me very well. It would be rather a gloomy business to enact Jean Jacques Rousseau's Nouvelle Héloïse over again. I've just read it, and it has given me a horror of love. That sort of love, all talk and discussion, strikes me as odious. Clarissa, again, is much too pleased with herself when

The Memoirs of Two Young Brides

she has written her tedious little letters; but, on the other hand, my father tells me Richardson's book is an admirable representation of the ordinary Englishwoman. Rousseau's strikes me as being a philosophical disquisition in the form of letters.

I believe love is really a purely personal poem. Everything these authors write on the subject is at once true and false. Verily, my dear creature, as you, henceforth, will be able to talk to me about conjugal love, I believe it will be indispensable, for the sake, of course, of our dual being, that I should remain unmarried and have some mighty passion, so that we may arrive at the true essence of existence. Relate all your experiences with the animal I denominate a husband, especially those of the first few days, most faithfully. I promise I'll report everything just as faithfully to you, if anybody falls in love with me. Farewell, my poor wasted darling!

XI

FROM MME. DE L'ESTORADE TO MLLE. DE CHAULIEU

LA CRAMPADE.

You make me shiver, you and your Spaniard, my dear love! I write these few lines to beseech you to dismiss him. Everything you tell me about him marks him as belonging to the most dangerous species of that class of individuals who venture everything, because they have nothing to lose. The man must not be your lover, and cannot be your husband. I will write more fully as to the private incidents of my marriage, but not until my heart is relieved of the anxiety with which your last letter has filled it.

XII

FROM MLLE. DE CHAULIEU TO MME. DE L'ESTORADE

February.

MY DEAR LOVE: At nine o'clock this morning my father sent word that he was waiting to see me. I was already up, and dressed. I found him sitting solemnly beside the fire in my dressing-room, looking far more pensive than is his wont. He pointed to the arm-chair facing him. I understood him at once, dropped myself into it with a gravity which aped his own so thoroughly that he began to smile, though there was something serious and melancholy even about his smile.

"You're as clever as your grandmother, at all events," he said.

"Come, father," I replied, "pray don't play the courtier here. You have something to ask of me."

He rose to his feet in great agitation, and talked to me for a full half hour. That conversation, my dear, is worth preserving. As soon as he left me, I sat down to my table and tried to reproduce his words. This is the first occasion on which my father has revealed all his thoughts in my presence. He began by flattering me. It was anything but a foolish move on

The Memoirs of Two Young Brides

his part. I could not fail to be pleased with the manner in which he had understood me and appraised my value.

"Armande," he said, "you have deceived me strangely and surprised me delightfully. When you first came out of your convent I took you to be a girl like most other girls, ignorant, with no particular ability—the kind of girl who is easily bought over with fallals and trinkets, and who never thinks seriously about anything."

"I thank you, father, in the name of youth in general."

"Oh," he cried, with a sort of statesman-like gesture, "there's no such thing as youth nowadays! Your mind is astonishingly broad, you appreciate everything according to its value, you are exceedingly clear-sighted, you are excessively sly. People think you've seen nothing, when your eyes are already on the causes of the effects at which other folks are staring. You are a minister in petticoats, you are the only person in this house who is capable of understanding me, and therefore if I want to get any sacrifice out of you, the only thing for me to do is to use you against yourself. Therefore, I am about to explain to you, quite frankly, the plans I had formed, and in which I still persist. If I am to induce you to adopt them, I must demonstrate to you that they are suggested by a noble motive. I am, therefore, obliged to enter with you into political considerations which are of the highest importance to the mon-

The Memoirs of Two Young Brides

archy and which would very likely bore any one but yourself. When you have listened to me, you shall think over the matter for a long time—I'll give you six months if you must have them. You are your own absolute mistress, and if you refuse to make the sacrifice I ask of you, I shall accept your refusal, and give you no further trouble."

Listening to this exordium, my dear soul, I grew really and truly serious, and I said:

"Father, speak on."

Here is what the statesman said to me:

"My child, France is at present in a position the precariousness of which is known only to the King and to a few of the foremost intelligences in the country. But the King is nothing but a head without an arm. And the wise heads who are in the secret of this danger have no authority over the men who must be used, if a successful result is to be attained. These men, who have been cast upon the surface by the popular vote, do not choose to be used as instruments. Gifted though they are, they still carry on the work of social destruction, instead of helping us to strengthen and steady the edifice. In a word, there are only two parties left, the party of Marius and the party of Sylla. I fight for Sylla, and against Marius. This, roughly speaking, is the situation. Looking at it in detail, we see that the Revolution still pursues its course; it is implanted in the laws, it is written on the soil, it is still in the minds of men; it is all the more formidable because the majority of the councillors about the throne, seeing the Revolution has neither soldiers nor money at command, believe it therefore vanquished. The King has a great intelligence, he perceives everything clearly enough. But he is more and more influenced, every day, by his brother's party, who are all inclined to go too fast. He has not two years to live, and he is laying his plans so that he may die in peace. Do you know, my child, which act of the Revolution has worked the most destruction? You would never guess it. When the Revolution beheaded Louis XVI it beheaded the father of every family in France. There is no family nowadays, there is nothing but a horde of individuals. When Frenchmen insisted upon becoming a nation, they lost their chance of being an empire. When they proclaimed the right of equal succession to the paternal property they killed the family spirit, and they created the Exchequer. But they paved the way for the weakening of all superior forces, and for the advent of the blind rule of the mob, for the extinction of art and the supremacy of personal interest, and they opened the road to foreign conquest. We find ourselves between two systems. We must constitute the State either by means of the family, or else by means of personal interest. Democracy or aristocracy, discussion or obedience, Catholicism or religious indifference—there, in a few words, lies the question. I belong to that small party which desires to resist what is called 'the people'—in its own interests, of course. This is no longer a question of feudal rights, as the simple-minded are told, nor of aristocratic privilege. The matter affects the State, it affects the very life of France. No country which is not grounded in paternal power has any sure existence. There begins the ladder of responsibility and of subordination, which rises up to the King himself. The King stands for every one of us. To die for the King is to die for one's self, for one's family, which itself never dies, any more than does the monarchy. Every animal has its own instinct; the human instinct is the family spirit. A nation is a strong nation when it is composed of rich families, every member of which is interested in the defence of the common treasure, whether it be in money, glory, privilege, or enjoyment. A nation is weak when it is composed of individuals who have no community of interest, who care little whether they are ruled by seven men or one, by a Russian or a Corsican, so long as each man keeps his own field—and not one of the poor selfish wretches perceive that some of these days his field will be taken from him. We are tending towards a state of things which will become horrible, if any misfortune should overtake us. Nothing will be left us but penal laws, or fiscal laws— your money or your life. The most generous nation upon the face of the earth will cease to be influenced by feeling. Incurable sores will have been developed and fostered in its nature. Universal jealousy, in the first place. The upper classes will be all commingled, parity of desire will be taken for equality of capacity, the really superior men, who were formerly recognised and proved as such, will be engulfed in the floods of the '*bourgeoisie.*' There was some chance of choosing out one good man among a thousand. It will never be possible to find anything among three million, all nursing the same ambition and garbed in the same livery—that of mediocrity. This triumphant horde will not perceive that over against it will be ranged another and a redoubtable mob—that of the peasant proprietors. Twenty millions of acres, all living and moving and arguing, listening to nothing, ever asking for more, standing in the way of everything, with a whole force of brute power at its command."

"But," said I, interrupting my father, "what can I do for the State? I don't feel the smallest inclination to play Jeanne d'Arc for the family idea, and perish at the convent stake."

"You're a mischievous little wretch," said my father. "If I talk sense to you, you give me jokes, and when I jest, you talk to me as if you were an ambassador."

"Love lives on contrasts," quoth I.

And he laughed till he cried.

"You'll think over what I have just explained to you. You will notice how I prove my confidence and how honourably I treat you by speaking to you as I have spoken, and it may be that events will serve my plans. I know that, so far as you are concerned, these same plans are offensive and even iniquitous. And, indeed, it is less from your heart and your imagination than from your good sense that I hope for sanction. I have noticed more reason and good sense in you than I have seen in any other person."

"When you say that you praise yourself," I said with a smile, " for I really am your daughter."

"Well, well," he said, "I could not be inconsistent. The end justifies the means, and we have to set an example to every one else. Therefore you must not have any fortune until that of your younger brother is secured, and I desire to use all your capital to entail an income on him."

"But," I resumed, "you do not forbid me to live as I choose, and find my own happiness, if I leave my fortune to you?"

"Ah," he replied, "so long as the life you desire does no prejudice to the honour, the dignity and, I may add, the glory of your family!"

"Why," I exclaimed, "you're stripping me very promptly of that remarkable good sense of mine!"

"Nowhere in all France," said he bitterly, "shall we find a man who will marry a portionless girl of the highest birth and settle a fortune on her. If such a husband were to offer himself he would belong to the *parvenu* class. With regard to that point my ideas are those of the eleventh century."

"And mine, too," I answered. "But why do you dishearten me? Are there no old peers of France?"

"You're mighty advanced, Louise," he cried. Then, with a smile, he kissed my hand and left me.

I had received your letter that very morning, and

it had just made me think of that very abyss into which you declare I may possibly fall. A voice within me seemed to cry: "You will fall into it!" I had therefore taken my precautions. Henarez does dare to look at me, my dear, and his eyes disturb me. They give me a sensation which I can only compare to one of profound terror. One oughtn't to look at that man any more than at a toad. Like it, he is hideous and fascinating. For the last two days I have been debating whether I wouldn't tell my father simply, that I didn't choose to learn Spanish and have Henarez dismissed. But after all my bold resolutions I fear I want to be stirred by the horrible sensation I have when I see the man, and I say: "Just once more and then I'll speak." My dear, there's something most penetrating and sweet about his voice, his speech is like Fodor's singing. His manners are simple, without the slightest affectation, and what teeth! Just now, as he was about to leave me, he thought he noticed the interest that I take in him, and he made a gesture, most respectfully indeed, as if he would have taken my hand to kiss it. But he checked himself, as though startled by his own boldness and the gulf he would have crossed. Slight as the movement was I guessed its meaning. I smiled, for nothing is more touching than to see the impulse of an inferior nature which thus retires within itself. There is so much audacity in the love of a *bourgeois* for a highborn girl. My smile gave him courage; the poor man began looking for his hat without seeing it. He didn't want to find it, and I brought it to him very gravely. His eyes were wet with unshed tears. That short moment held a world of things—and thoughts. So well did we understand each other, that I held out my hand for him to kiss. Perhaps that told him love might bridge the abyss between us. Well, I don't know what moved me to do it. Griffiths had turned her back to us. I stretched out my white hand to him haughtily, and I felt the heat of his burning lips tempered by two great tears.

Ah, dearest angel, I sat on there, exhausted, in my arm-chair, thinking. I was happy, and I can't possibly explain how or why. What I felt was poetry. My condescension, of which I am ashamed now, seemed to me something noble. He had bewitched me—there's my excuse!

Friday.

The man really is very good-looking! His speech is cultured, his intelligence is remarkably superior. My dear, his explanation of the structure not only of the Spanish language, but of every other, and of human thought, is as masterly and as logical as though he were Bossuet himself. French seems to be his mother-tongue. When I expressed my surprise at this, he answered that when he was very young he had been brought to France, to Valençay, with the King of Spain. What change has taken place within this man's soul? He is quite altered; he came to me simply dressed, but looking exactly like some great gentleman out for his morning walk. All through the lesson his intellect flashed like a beacon, he displayed all his eloquence. Like some tired being whose strength had come back to him, he disclosed to me the inmost feelings he had so carefully hidden hitherto. He told me the story of a poor wretch of a serving-man who had let himself be killed for the sake of one glance from a Queen of Spain.

"All he could do was to die," I said.

This answer filled his heart with joy, and the look in his eyes absolutely terrified me.

That night I went to a ball given by the Duchesse de Lenoncourt. The Prince de Talleyrand was there. I made a charming young fellow, a M. de Vandenesse, ask him whether any one of the name of Henarez had been among the guests at his country-place in 1809. He answered:

"Henarez is the Moorish name of the Soria family, which claims descent from Abencerrages, who embraced Christianity. The old Duke and his two sons accompanied the King. The eldest son, the present Duque de Soria, has just been stripped of all his possessions, honours, and grandeeships by King Ferdinand, who thus wreaks an old-standing spite. The Duke made a huge mistake when he undertook to serve as Constitutional Minister with Valdez. Luckily, he escaped from Cadiz before the Duc d'Angoulême arrived, for in spite of all his good-will, the Duke would not have been able to save him from the King's fury."

This answer, which the Vicomte de Vandenesse

carried back to me word for word, gave me much food for reflection.

I cannot describe the anxiety in which I spent the time until my next lesson, which took place this morning. During the first fifteen minutes of this lesson I kept asking myself, as I watched him, whether he was a Duke or a *bourgeois*, without being able to make anything of it. He seemed to guess my thoughts as fast as they came into being, and to take delight in misleading them. At last I could bear it no longer. I suddenly put aside my book, and breaking off the translation I had been making, I said to him, in Spanish:

"You are deceiving us, sir. You are no poor liberal citizen; you are the Duque de Soria!"

"Mademoiselle," he answered, with a melancholy gesture, "unhappily I am not the Duque de Soria."

I understood all the despair he put into that word "unhappily." Ah, my dear, I am certain no other man will ever be able to impart so much passion and expression to a single word. He had dropped his eyes and dared not look at me again.

"M. de Talleyrand," I said, "in whose house you spent your years of exile, admits of no alternative for a Henarez, between being Duque de Soria in disgrace, or a servant."

He lifted up his eyes and showed me two black, shining furnaces, orbs that blazed and yet were filled with humiliation. At that moment the man seemed to me to be on the rack.

"My father," he said, "was, indeed, the servant of the King of Spain."

Griffiths could not comprehend this method of study; there were alarming silences between each question and answer.

"Well," I said, "are you a nobleman or a *bourgeois*?"

"You know, Señorita, that in Spain even the beggar is nobly born."

This reserve nettled me. Since the previous lesson I had prepared myself one of those entertainments which appeal to the imagination. I had written a letter in which I had formulated the ideal portrait of the man whom I should choose to be my lover, and I intended to ask him to translate it. Up to the present, I had been translating from Spanish into French, not from French into Spanish. I mentioned this fact to him, and then I asked Griffiths to fetch me the last letter I had received from one of my girl friends.

"By the effect my programme produces upon him," thought I to myself, "I shall find out what blood runs in his veins."

Taking the paper from Griffiths's hands, I said: "Let me see if I have copied it properly"—for it was all in my own handwriting. Then I laid the sheet, or if you choose, the snare, in front of him, and I watched him while he read.

"The man I could love, my dear, must be unbending and haughty with other men, but gentle with all women. His eagle glance will instantly quell

The Memoirs of Two Young Brides

anything that approaches ridicule. He will have a smile of pity for those who would joke at sacred things, more especially those things which constitute the poetry of the soul, and without which life would be nothing but a dreary reality. I have the deepest scorn for those who would cut us off from the spring of those religious sentiments which are so rich in consolation, and therefore his faith must have all the simplicity of a child's, together with the unalterable conviction of an intelligent man who has searched out the grounds of his belief. His mind, fresh and original, must be free from affectation and love of display. He will never say anything too much, nor anything inappropriate. It would be as impossible to him to weary others as to be weary with himself, for he will carry a wealth of interest within him. All his thoughts must be noble, high, chivalrous, without a touch of selfishness. Everything he does will be marked by a total absence of calculation or self-interest. His faults will spring from the very breadth of his ideas, which will be above those of his time. In every point I should desire to find him in advance of his epoch. Full of the delicate kindness due to all weak creatures, he will be good to every woman, but very slow to fall in love with any. He will consider that matter as one far too serious to permit of its being played with. Thus he might possibly spend his whole life without really loving any woman, although himself possessing all the qualities which should inspire the deepest passion. But if he should once meet with his ideal woman—the woman seen in those dreams a man dreams open-eyed—if he should find a being who will understand him, who will fill his heart, and cast a ray of gladness over all his life, and shine on him like a star athwart the clouds of the dark, chill, frozen world, who will impart an utterly new charm to his existence and strike chords within his being which have hitherto lain silent—be very sure that he will recognise and value his good fortune. And further, he will make that woman perfectly happy. Never, either by word or look, will he grieve the loving heart which will have committed itself to his care with the blind confidence of the child that slumbers in its mother's arms. For if this sweet dream of hers were to be broken, her heart and her whole being would be torn in twain forever. It never would be possible for her to embark upon that ocean without risking her whole future on the hazard.

"This man will necessarily possess the physiognomy, the appearance, the deportment and, in a word, the manner of doing things, small and great, peculiar to persons of a superior stamp, who are all simple and unpretending. His face may be ugly, but his hands beautiful. A faint smile, ironic and scornful, will curve his upper lip at the sight of those for whom he cares not, but on those he loves he will shed the bright and heavenly beam of a glance expressive of the soul within."

"Señorita," he said, in Spanish, and in a voice that shook with emotion, "will you allow me to keep

The Memoirs of Two Young Brides

this paper in memory of you? This lesson is the last I shall have the honour of giving you, and the teachings of this written sheet may become a rule of conduct to all eternity. I left Spain as a penniless fugitive, but my family has now remitted me a sum of money sufficient for my needs—I shall have the honour of sending some Spaniard to fill my place here."

It was as though he said to me, "The play is over." He rose to his feet with a gesture that had a wonderful dignity about it, and left me overwhelmed by the astounding delicacy peculiar to men of his class. He went downstairs and sent in to ask if he could speak to my father.

While we were at dinner my father said to me, with a smile:

"Louise, you have been taking Spanish lessons from a man who was formerly Minister to the King of Spain, and who has been sentenced to death."

"The Duque de Soria," said I.

"Duke!" replied my father; "he's that no longer. He now takes the title of Baron de Macumer, from a fief he still holds in Sardinia. He strikes me as being rather an oddity."

"Don't dishonour a man who is your equal, and who, I believe, has a noble heart, by applying to him a word which, as you use it, always implies derision and disdain."

"Baroness de Macumer!" exclaimed my father, with a mocking look.

The Memoirs of Two Young Brides

Instinctively I dropped my eyes.

"Why," said my mother, "Henarez must have met the Spanish Ambassador upon the doorstep."

"Yes," replied my father, "the Ambassador asked me whether I was conspiring against the King, his master, but he greeted the grandee of Spain with deep respect, and placed himself at his disposal."

All this, dear Mme. de l'Estorade, happened a fortnight ago, and for a whole fortnight I have not seen this man, who loves me—for the man does love me! What is he doing with himself? I wish I were a fly, or a mouse, or a sparrow. I wish I could see him alone, where he lives, without his seeing me. There is a man to whom I can say, "Go and die for me!" and he is capable of going—at least I think so. At last there is a man in Paris round whom my thoughts hover, and whose glance fills my innermost soul with brightness. Oh, but this is an enemy whom I must trample under foot! What! can there be a man without whom I cannot live, who is necessary to my existence? You are married, and I'm in love. Only four months, and these two turtle-doves who had soared so high have fallen down into the slough of reality!

Sunday.

Yesterday at the *Italiens* I felt somebody was looking at me. My eyes were drawn as by magic towards two shining orbs that blazed like two jewels out of a dark corner of the orchestra. Henarez never took his eyes off me; the wretch has sought out the only place in the theatre whence he could see me, and there he is established! I don't know what his political powers may be, but in love-making he is a genius.

"Voilà, belle Renée, à quel point nous en sommes," as the great Corneille says.

XIII

FROM MME. DE L'ESTORADE TO MLLE. DE CHAULIEU

LA CRAMPADE, *February.*

I WAS obliged to wait a little before writing to you, my dear Louise, but now I know, or I should rather say, I have learned, many things, and for the sake of your future happiness I must make them known to you. The difference between a young girl and a married woman is so great, that the girl is no more capable of conceiving it, than a married woman is capable of becoming a girl again. I preferred marrying Louis de l'Estorade to going back to the convent. That much is quite clear. After I had once guessed that if I did not marry Louis I should have to go back to my convent, I was obliged, in young girl's parlance, "to make up my mind to it." My mind once "made up," I set to work to consider my position, so as to turn it to the best possible account.

To begin with, the seriousness of the undertaking filled me with terror. Marriage is a matter of one's whole life; love is a matter of pleasure. But, then, marriage still endures after pleasure has passed away, and it gives birth to interests far dearer than those of the man and woman it binds together. It may be,

The Memoirs of Two Young Brides

then, that the only thing necessary to a happy marriage is that sort of friendship which, for the sake of the sweetness it brings, overlooks many a human imperfection. There was nothing to prevent my feeling affection for Louis de l'Estorade. Once I resolved never to seek in marriage those passionate delights on which we used to dwell so much and with such dangerous enthusiasm, I felt a sense of the sweetest calm within me. "If I cannot have love, why should I not seek for happiness?" said I to myself, "and besides, I am loved, and I will permit myself to be loved. There will be no servitude about my marriage, it will be a perpetual rule. What disadvantage can this state of things present to a woman who aspires to be absolute mistress of herself?"

This important point of being married, and yet not married, was settled in a conversation between Louis and myself, during which the excellence of his character and the goodness of his heart were both revealed to me. I greatly desired, my darling, to prolong that fair season of love and hope which, inasmuch as it involves no active enjoyment, leaves the virginity of the soul untouched. To grant nothing as a duty or in obedience to a law, to be a free agent, to preserve my own free-will—how sweet and noble that would be! A compact of this nature—one quite opposed to that of the law and even that of the sacrament—could only be arrived at between Louis and myself. This difficulty, the first on my horizon, was the only one that delayed the celebration of my marriage. Although from the very outset I had been determined to accept everything rather than go back to the convent, it is in our nature to ask for the greater advantage after we have obtained the least. And you and I, dear creature, are the sort of women who want everything. I kept watching my Louis out of the corner of my eye, saying to myself, Has misfortune made his heart good, or bad? By dint of study I discovered that his love for me amounted to a downright passion. Once I had obtained the status of an idol, when I saw him turn pale and tremble if I even glanced coldly at him, I realized that I might venture on anything. Of course I carried him off, far from the old people, to take long walks, during which I searched out his heart in the most prudent fashion. I made him talk; I made him tell me his ideas, his plans, his thoughts for our future. My questions revealed so much preconceived opinion, and made so direct an onslaught on the weak points of that hateful life *à deux*, that Louis, as he has since told me, was terrified at the thought that any maiden could know so much. As for me, I listened to his answers, the confusion of which proved him one of those people whom terror renders helpless. I ended by perceiving that chance had given me an adversary, whose inferiority was deepened by the fact that he had an inkling of what you so proudly denominate " the greatness of my mind." Broken down by suffering and misfortune, he looked upon himself as something not far from a wreck, and was torn by hideous fears. To begin with, he is thirty-

The Memoirs of Two Young Brides

seven and I am seventeen, and he could not survey the twenty years between us without alarm. Then, as you and I have agreed, I am very beautiful, and Louis, who shares our opinion on this subject, could not realize how sorely suffering had robbed him of his youth without a sensation of bitter regret. Finally, he felt that I, as a woman, was much superior to himself as a man. These three patent items of inferiority had undermined his confidence in himself. He feared he might not make me happy, and believed I had accepted him to avoid a worse fate. One evening he said shyly, that but for my dread of the convent I would not have married him.

"That is true," I answered gravely.

My dear friend, he made me feel the first throb of emotion with which a man can inspire us women. My very heart was wrung by the two great tears that rose to his eyes.

"Louis," I went on consolingly, "it rests with you to turn this marriage of convenience into a marriage to which I could give my full consent. What I am going to ask of you demands a much greater sacrifice on your part than the so-called 'servitude of love'—when that is sincere. Can you rise to the level of friendship, as I understand it? A man has only one real friend in his life, and I would be that friend to you. Friendship is the bond between twin souls, one in their strength, and yet independent of each other. Let us be friends and partners, to go through life together. Leave me my absolute independence. I do not forbid you to inspire me with the love you say you feel for me, but I do not desire to be your wife except of my own free-will. Make me desire to give over my free-will to you, and I will sacrifice it to you that instant. You see, I do not forbid you to import passion into our friendship, nor to disturb it with words of love, and I, on my part, will strive to make our affection perfect. Above all things spare me the discomfort the rather peculiar position in which we shall find ourselves might bring upon me in the outer world. I do not choose to appear either capricious or prudish, for I am neither, and I believe you to be so thorough a gentleman that I hereby offer to keep up the outward appearance of married life."

My dear, never did I see a man so delighted as Louis was with this proposal. His eyes began to shine—happiness had dried up all his tears.

"Consider," I said, as I closed the conversation, "that there is nothing so very extraordinary about what I am asking you to do. The condition I propose arises out of my intense desire to possess your esteem. Supposing you were to owe your possession of me merely to the marriage service, would it be a great satisfaction to you, in later days, to reflect that your longings had been crowned by legal or religious formalities, and not by my free-will? Supposing that while I did not love you, and owing simply to that passive obedience the duty of which my much-honoured mother has just impressed upon me, I should bear a child.

The Memoirs of Two Young Brides

Do you believe that I should love that child as dearly as one that was born of a mutual desire? Even if it be not indispensable that there should be love like the passion of a pair of lovers between a husband and wife, you will surely admit, sir, that it is indispensable there should be no dislike. Well, we shall soon be placed in a very perilous position. We are to make our home in the country. Should we not consider how unstable all passion is? May not wise folk arm themselves against the misfortunes arising from such changes?"

He was wonderfully taken aback to find me so reasonable and so full of sound reasoning, but he gave me his solemn promise, and thereupon I took his hand and squeezed it affectionately.

We were married at the end of that week. Once I was sure of my freedom, I applied myself with the greatest cheerfulness to the dull details of all the various ceremonies. I was able to be my own natural self, and I may, indeed, have been considered what would have been called in the language we used at Blois, "a very knowing little body." Onlookers took a young girl, delighted with the novel and promising position in which she had contrived to place herself, for a notable woman of the world. My dear soul, I had beheld, as in a vision, all the difficulties of my future life, and I was sincerely bent on making this man happy. Now, in the solitude in which we are to live, if the woman does not rule, the marriage state must soon become unendurable. The woman in such a case should possess all the charms of the mistress and all the good qualities of the wife. Does not the uncertainty which hangs about enjoyment prolong the illusion and perpetuate those flattering delights to which every human creature clings, and so rightly clings? Conjugal love, as I understand it, drapes the woman in a robe of hope, endues her with sovereign power, inspires her with exhaustless strength and with a vivifying warmth which causes everything about her to blossom. The more completely she is mistress of herself, the more certain she is to bring love and happiness into being. But I have specially insisted that all our private arrangements shall be veiled in the deepest mystery. The man who is subjugated by his wife is deservedly covered with ridicule. A woman's influence must be altogether secret. In our sex, charm and mystery are synonymous in all things. Though I set myself to raise up this crushed nature and bring back their lustre to the good qualities I have discovered in it, I intend it all to seem the spontaneous growth of Louis's character. This is the task, a not ignoble one, I have set before me. The glory of it may well suffice a woman. I am almost proud in my possession of a secret that fills my life, a plan which shall absorb all my efforts, which shall be hidden from every one, save yourself and God.

Now I am nearly happy, and perhaps I should not be altogether so, if I could not tell all I feel to one loving heart. For how can I say it to him? My happiness would wound him, I have been obliged to hide it from him. My dear, he is as delicate in feeling as any woman, like all men who have suffered acutely. For three months we lived just as we had lived before we married. As you will easily believe, I studied numberless little personal questions which have much more to do with love than any one would believe. In spite of my coldness, his heart unfolded as he grew bolder. I saw the expression of his face change and grow younger—the refinement I introduced into the household began to be reflected in his person. Gradually I grew accustomed to him, I made him my second self. By dint of looking at him, I discovered the agreement between his nature and his physiognomy. The "animal we call a husband," as you express it, disappeared from sight. One balmy evening I perceived a lover whose words touched my very heart, and on whose arm I leant with an unspeakable delight. And, last of all—to be as truthful with you as I would be with God, whom no man can deceive—curiosity, stirred, it may be, by the admirable faithfulness with which he kept his oath, rose up within my heart. Horribly ashamed, I fought against myself. Alas! when dignity is the only thing that holds one back, the intellect soon pitches on some compromise. All then was secret, as though we had been lovers, and secret it must remain between us two. When your own marriage comes, you will applaud my discretion. Yet nothing, be sure, was lacking that the most exquisite passion could desire, nor the unexpectedness, which is, in a manner, the glory of that special moment. The mysterious charm for which our imagination longs, the impulse which is our excuse, the half-extorted consent, the ideal delights over which we have dimly dreamt, and which overwhelmed our being before we yield to their reality, every one of these seductions, in all their most enchanting forms, was there.

I will confess to you that in spite of all these glories I have once more stipulated for my freedom, and I will not tell you all my reasons for so doing. You will certainly be the only creature upon whom even this half confidence shall be bestowed. The woman who gives herself to her husband, whether he adores her or not, would, I think, act very foolishly were she not to conceal her feelings and her personal judgment concerning marriage. The sole delight I have known, and it has been a heavenly joy, comes from the certainty that I have restored life to that poor fellow, before I give life to his children. Louis has recovered his youth, his strength, and his spirits. He is a different man. Like some fairy, I have wiped out the very memory of his misfortunes. I have metamorphosed him; he has become a charming fellow. Now that he is sure I care for him, he displays his mental powers and constantly reveals fresh qualities. To be the constant spring of a man's happiness— when that man knows it, and mingles gratitude with his love—ah, my dear, this certainly develops a force within the soul far surpassing that of the most absorbing passion. This force, impetuous and lasting, uniform yet varied, evolves the family—that splendid work of womanhood which I can realize now in all its fruitful duty. The old father is not stingy any more. He gives everything I ask, unquestioningly. The servants are light-hearted; it seems as though Louis's happiness were reflected over the whole of this household which I rule by love. The old man has brought himself into harmony with all the improvements. He would not let himself be a blot upon my dainty arrangements. To please me, he has assumed the dress, and with the dress, the habits of the present day. We have English horses, we have a brougham, a barouche and a tilbury. Our servants are simply but carefully turned out, and we have the reputation of being spendthrifts. I apply my wits (joking apart) to keeping my house economically and giving the greatest possible amount of enjoyment for the smallest possible expenditure. I have already shown Louis how necessary it is for him to build roads, so as to gain a reputation of a man who takes an interest in the welfare of his neighbourhood. I am making him fill up the gaps in his education. I hope soon, by the influence of my family and his mother's, to see him elected to the Conseil Général of his department. I have told him quite frankly that I am ambitious, and that I do not think it at all a bad thing that his father should continue to look after our property and save money, because I want him to apply his whole mind to politics; that if we have children I desire to see them all comfortable and well provided for under Government; that under pain of losing my regard and affection, he must become Deputy for this department at the next election; that my family will back up his candidature, and that we shall then have the pleasure of spending all our winters in Paris. Ah, my angel, the fervour of his obedience showed me how deeply I was loved! And, to conclude, he wrote me this letter yesterday from Marseilles, whither he has gone for a few hours:

"When you gave me leave to love you, my gentle Renée, I believed in happiness. But now I see no end to it. The past is nothing but a vague memory, a shadow, the necessary background to the brightness of my felicity. The transports of my love are so intoxicating, when I am near you, that they deprive me of power of expressing it. All I can do is to admire and worship you. It is only when I am far away that words come back to me. You are perfectly beautiful, and with a beauty so grave, so majestic, that time will scarcely change it. And though the love between man and wife depends not so much on beauty as on feeling (and how exquisite is yours!), let me tell you that this certainty that you will always be beautiful gives me a joy that deepens with every glance I cast upon you. The harmonious and dignified lines of your noble face show that there is something ineffably pure under the warm colour of the skin.

"The radiance of your dark eyes and the bold outlines of your brow reveal how lofty are your virtues, how steadfast your loyalty, how strong your heart to face the storms of life, if they should burst upon us. Nobility is your distinctive quality. I am not so vain as to think I am the first to tell you this, but I write the words so that you may clearly know I realize the full value of the treasure I possess. The little you may grant me will always make my happiness—a long time hence, even as now. For I feel all the grandeur of our mutual promise to preserve our freedom. We shall never owe any token of tenderness to anything but our own will. We shall be free, in spite of the closest chains. I shall be all the prouder of winning you afresh, now that I know the value you set upon that conquest. Never will you be able to speak, or breathe, or act, or think without increasing my admiration for your physical charms and mental graces! There is a something in you, I scarce know what, a something divine, wise, enchanting, which reconciles reason, honour, pleasure, and hope, and gives love a horizon wider than life itself. Oh, my angel, may the spirit of love be faithful to me, and may the future be filled with that exquisite delight wherewith you have embellished everything about me! When will motherhood come to you, that I may see you rejoice in the fulness of your life?—that I may hear that sweet voice of yours and those delicate thoughts, so fresh and so strangely well expressed, bless the love which is my glory, and from which, as from a magic spring, I have drawn new life. Yes, I will be all you desire. I will become one of the useful men of my country, and all the glory of my success shall be yours, since its sole and quickening essence lies in your satisfaction!"

This, my dear, is how I am training him up. His style is somewhat unformed; it will be better in another year. Louis is still in his first transports. I await that regular and continuous sensation of happiness which must result from a well-assorted marriage, when the woman and the man, sure of each other and thoroughly acquainted, have discovered the secret of varying the infinite, and touching the very groundwork of existence with a magic spell. I have a glimpse of the glorious secret of truly wedded spouses, and I am determined to possess it fully. This coxcomb, you observe, fancies he is as much loved as if he were not my husband. So far I have not reached that point of material attachment which enables one to endure many things. Still, Louis is likeable. He has an exceedingly equal temper, and he does things of which most men would boast in very simple fashion. In fact, though I am not in love with him, I feel I am capable of growing fond of him.

So here you perceive my dusky hair, those black eyes, the lashes of which, so you say, " unfold like sun-blinds," my imperial port, and my whole person, raised to the dignity of sovereign power. We shall see, ten years hence, my dear, whether we are not both of us very merry and very happy in that great Paris, whence I shall carry you now and then to my

The Memoirs of Two Young Brides

lovely oasis in Provence. Ah, Louise, don't risk the fair future that lies before us both. Don't commit the follies with which you threaten me. I have married an old young man—do you marry a young old man in the House of Peers! There is real sense in that idea of yours!

XIV

FROM THE DUQUE DE SORIA TO THE BARON DE MACUMER

MADRID.

MY DEAR BROTHER: You have not made me Duque de Soria for me to act otherwise than as Duque de Soria. If I felt that you were a wanderer and deprived of the comforts which money insures in every place, you would make my own happiness unendurable. Neither Maria nor I will consent to marry until we know you have accepted the sum of money we have made over to Urraca for your use. These two millions are your own savings, and Maria's. Kneeling side by side before the same altar, we have prayed—how fervently God alone knows—for your happiness. Oh, my brother, surely our prayers will be granted! The love which you seek, and which would be the consolation of your exile, will be sent down to you from Heaven. Maria read your letter with tears, and you possess her deepest admiration. As for me, I have accepted for our house—not for myself. The King has fulfilled your expectations. Ah! there was such scorn in the fashion in which you cast his gratification to him, just as a man casts prey to wild beasts, that I longed to avenge you by telling him how your great-

The Memoirs of Two Young Brides

ness has abased him. The one thing I have accepted for myself, my dearly loved brother, is my happiness —is Maria. For that boon, I shall always be to you even as the creature at the feet of its Creator. There will be a day in my life, and in Maria's, as bright as our own happy marriage—the day on which we learn that your heart is appreciated, that a woman loves you as you deserve and desire to be loved. Never forget that if you live for us, we, too, live for you. You can write to us in perfect safety, under cover of the Nuncio, and sending your letters round by Rome. The French Ambassador in Rome will, no doubt, undertake to forward them to the State Secretary, Monsignor Bemboni, with whom our Legate has probably communicated already. No other method would be safe. Farewell, dear despoiled brother, beloved exile! Be proud, at all events, of the bliss you have given us, even if you cannot be happy in it. God will surely hearken to our prayers, which are full of you.   FERNANDO.

XV

FROM LOUISE DE CHAULIEU TO MME. DE L'ESTORADE

March.

AH, my angel, marriage teaches philosophy. . . . Your dear face must have been yellow with envy while you were writing me those terrible sentiments about human life and feminine duty. Do you really think you'll convert me to marriage by your programme of subterranean toil? Alack! is this whither our too learned reveries have led you? We left Blois, robed in all our innocence and armed with the sharp arrows of thought, and now the darts of our purely theoretical experience have turned against your own bosom. If I did not know you for the purest and most angelic creature upon earth, I should say that all these calculations of yours smacked of depravity. How, my dear, in the interest of this country life of yours, you mark out your pleasures in regular fellings. You treat love just as you would treat your woods. Oh, I would rather perish in the wild whirlwinds of my own heart than live in the barrenness of your learned arithmetic! You and I were the two wisest of the girls, because we had given a very great deal of thought to a very few things. But, my child, a loveless philosophy

The Memoirs of Two Young Brides

or the philosophy of a sham love, is the most hideous of all conjugal hypocrisies. Surely now and again the greatest rule in the world would discover the owl of wisdom crouched beneath your roses—an anything but entertaining discovery that, and one which may well put the most fervent passion to flight. You are concocting your fate, instead of being its plaything. We are each of us taking a very unusual course. A great deal of philosophy and very little love, there's yours. A world of love and mighty little philosophy, there's mine. Jean Jacques' *Julie*, whom I took for a professor, is a mere student beside you. By all that's virtuous, you've taken stock of life pretty thoroughly!

Alack, I laugh at you, and maybe it is you who are right! You have sacrificed your youth in a single day, and you have grown miserly before your time. Your Louis will no doubt be a happy man. If he loves you, and I am sure he does, he'll never discover that you are behaving in the interest of your family, just as the *courtesans* behave in the interests of their pockets. And they certainly do make men happy, if we may judge by the wild expenditure lavished on them. No doubt a clear-sighted husband might retain this passion for you, but would he not end by feeling himself relieved from any necessity for gratitude toward a woman who treats falsehood as sort of a moral corset, as indispensable to her existence as the other sort is to her body? Why, my dear, love, in my eyes, is the principle of every virtue, summed up into the image of the Divine Love. Love, like every other principle, is no matter of calculation. It is the infinite ether of the soul. Have you not been making an effort to justify in your own sight the horrible position of a girl who is married to a man for whom she cannot feel anything beyond esteem? Duty—there's your rule and measure. But is not action spurred by necessity the social teaching of Atheism? Is not action arising out of love and feeling the hidden law of woman? You have turned yourself into the man, and your Louis will find himself the woman. Ah, dearest, your letter has plunged me into endless meditations. I perceive the convent can never replace the mother to young girls. I beseech you, my noble dark-eyed angel, so pure, so haughty, so grave, so exquisite, think over this first outcry extorted by your letter. I have consoled myself by considering that even while I lament, love has probably overthrown all the edifice your arguments had built up. I shall perhaps be worse than you, without either reason or calculation. Passion is an element whose logic must be as merciless as your own.

Monday.

Yesterday evening, just as I was going to bed, I went to my window to admire the sky, which was magnificently clear. The stars were like silver nails holding up a blue curtain. In the silence of the night I heard somebody breathing, and by the dim light of the stars I beheld my Spaniard perched like a squirrel on the branches of one of the trees on the sidewalk of the boulevard, no doubt gazing at my window. The

The Memoirs of Two Young Brides

first effect of this discovery was to send me back into my room, feeling as if all the strength had gone out of my hands and feet. But beneath this sensation of terror I was conscious of a most exquisite delight. I was crushed, and still I was happy. Not one of those witty French gentlemen who desire to marry me has had the wit to come and spend his nights in an elm tree and risk being caught by the watchman. My Spaniard, of course, had been there for some time. Aha! he doesn't give me lessons; he wants some one to give them to him. Well, he shall have them. If he only knew all I have said to myself about his apparent ugliness! I've talked philosophy, Renée, as well as you. I've considered that there would be something horrible about loving a handsome man. Isn't that to acknowledge that love, which should be divine, is three parts a matter of the senses? When I had got over my first alarm, I stretched my neck behind the window-pane to see him again, and, just like my luck, he blew a letter, cunningly wound round a good-sized bit of lead, into the window, through an air-gun.

"Good heavens," said I to myself, "will he think I left my window open on purpose? If I shut it suddenly now, I shall look like his accomplice."

I did better than that. I came back to the window as if I had never heard the nosie of his note falling, as if I had not noticed anything at all, and I said aloud: "Do come and look at the stars, Miss Griffiths."

Now Griffiths was sound asleep like a respectable old maid. When the Moor heard me he disappeared as swiftly as a shadow. He must have been nearly as dead of fright as I had been, for I never heard him go away, and he no doubt remained some time at the foot of the tree. After a full quarter of an hour, which I spent soaring to the blue vault of Heaven and swimming over the wild ocean of curiosity, I shut up my window and got into bed, there to unfold the thin paper with all the carefulness of a restorer of antique books at Naples. It burnt my fingers. "What a horrible power this man has over me!" said I to myself, and instantly I held the paper to the light, meaning to burn it unread. . . . An idea made me hold my hand. "What can he write to me in secret?" Well, my dear, I burnt the letter up, for I thought that though every other girl upon the earth would have devoured it, I, Armande Louise Marie de Chaulieu, ought not to read it.

The next day he was at his post at the *Italiens*. But Constitutional Prime Minister though he may have been, I do not believe he read the smallest sign of internal agitation in my demeanour. I behaved absolutely as if I had neither seen nor received anything on the previous night. I was pleased with myself, but he was very melancholy. Poor man! in Spain it seems so natural that love should come in by the window. During the *entr'acte* he came and walked about the corridors. This was told me by the first Secretary of the Spanish Embassy, who also related an action of his which really is sublime. When he was Duque de Soria he was to have married one of the richest heiresses in Spain, the young Princess Maria Heredia, whose wealth would have softened the misery of his exile. But it seems that in defiance of the desire of the two fathers who had betrothed them in their childhood, Maria loved the younger de Soria, and my Felipe gave up the Princess Maria when he allowed himself to be stripped of everything by the King of Spain.

"I am sure he did that great thing very simply," said I to the young man.

"Why, do you know him?" he answered artlessly.

My mother smiled.

"What will become of him, for he is condemned to death?" I said.

"Though he's dead in Spain, he has the right to live in Sardinia," he replied.

"What, are there tombs in Spain, too?" I rejoined, so as to seem to take the thing as a joke.

"In Spain there is everything—even Spaniards of the old type," answered my mother.

"The King of Sardinia," continued the young diplomat, "has granted the Baron de Macumer a passport, somewhat against the grain. But, after all, he has become a Sardinian subject. He owns magnificent fiefs in Sardinia, within which he has powers of life and death. He has a palace at Sassari. If Ferdinand VII were to die, Macumer would probably enter the diplomatic service, and the Court of Turin, in spite of his youth, would give him an Embassy."

"Ah, he is young, then?"

"Yes, mademoiselle . . . in spite of his youth, he is one of the most distinguished men in Spain."

All the while the Secretary was talking I was looking about the theatre through my opera-glass and apparently paying him scant attention, but between ourselves I was in despair at having burnt that letter. How does such a man express himself when he is in love? And he does love me! To be loved and adored in secret, to feel that in that building, where all the most important folk in Paris were gathered together, there was one man who was my property, though not a soul knew it! Oh, Renée, then I understood this Paris life with its balls and fêtes! Everything appeared to me in its true colours. When one loves one needs the presence of others, if it be only for the sake of sacrificing them to the object of one's love. Within my being I felt another happy being. Every feeling of vanity, my pride, my self-love, all were flattered. God alone knows what sort of glance I cast upon the world about me.

"Oh, little rogue," whispered the Duchess, smiling, in my ear.

Yes, my crafty mother had discovered some symptom of secret delight in my attitude, and I hauled down my flag before that clear-sighted woman. Those three words of hers taught me more knowledge of the world than I had picked up in a year—

for it is March again. Alas! in another month the *Italiens* will be closed. How are people whose hearts are full of love to live without that delicious music?

My dear, as soon as I got home, with a resolve that was worthy of a Chaulieu, I opened my window wide to admire a shower of rain. Oh, if men only knew the seductive power of heroic actions over women, they would all be very noble—the veriest cowards would turn into heroes. The story I had heard about my Spaniard had fevered my blood. I felt certain he was there, ready to throw me another letter. And this time I burnt nothing—I read it all. Here, then, sweet Madam Argument, is my first love-letter—we each have one now:

"Louise, it is not for your splendid beauty I love you. It is not for your brilliant mind, your noble feelings, the infinite charm you give to every action, nor is it for your pride, your royal scorn of everything that does not belong to your own sphere—a scorn which does not affect your goodness, for your charity is like an angel's. I love you, Louise, because in all your pride and grandeur you have condescended to comfort a poor exile; because by a gesture, by a look, you consoled one man for being so far below you that he had no claim on anything save your pity, but that a generous pity. You are the only woman in the world whose eyes have softened as they looked on me, and since, when I was nothing but a grain of dust, you cast that beneficent glance on me, and thereby gave me what I never obtained, when I had all the power to which any subject can aspire—I would fain tell you, Louise, that you have grown dear to me, that I love you unreservedly and for yourself, in a measure far surpassing the conditions you yourself have formulated to define a perfect love. Know then, my idol, whom I have set in my highest heaven, that the world contains one scion of the Saracen race whose life is yours, whom you may command, as though he were your slave, and whose glory it will be to do your will. I have given myself to you forever—for the mere joy of doing it—for the sake of one glance of yours, for the sake of the hand you stretched out one morning to your Spanish master. You have a henchman, Louise, and nothing more. No, I dare not think I ever can be loved, but perhaps I may be endured, if only for the sake of my devotion. Ever since that morning when you smiled on me, like a noble maiden who guessed the misery of my betrayed and solitary soul, I have enthroned you in my heart. You are the absolute sovereign of my life—the queen of all my thoughts, the goddess of my soul, the light that brightens my dwelling, the flower of all my flowers, the perfume of the air I breathe, the strength of my blood, the soft ray beneath which I slumber. One thought alone has troubled my happiness. You dreamt not you possessed a limitless devotion, a faithful arm, an unquestioning slave, a silent servitor, a treasury—for I am nothing now but the depository of all I own. You knew not there was a heart to which you might confide all things, the heart of an aged grandparent of whom you might ask what you will, of a father whose protection you might claim, the heart of a friend, a brother—all these are lacking about you, as I know. I have found out your secret loneliness. My boldness springs now from my longing to make you know how much you do possess. Accept it all, Louise, and you will give me the only life that is possible for me in this world— a life of devotion. You run no risk when you clasp the slave's collar about my neck. I will never ask for anything save the delight of knowing I belong to you. Do not even tell me you will never love me. That must be so, I know. I must love you from afar, without hope, and for myself alone. I greatly long to know if you will accept my service, and I have searched about to discover some proof which may convince you there would be no loss of dignity in your granting this prayer of mine, seeing I have been your property for many a day, now, although you knew it not. You would give me my answer, then, if, some evening at the *Italiens*, you were to carry a nosegay consisting of two camellias, a white one and a red—the type of a man's life blood, wholly devoted to the service of the purity he adores. That would settle it all forever. Ten years hence—even as tomorrow—whatever you may desire that man can do will be performed as soon as you choose to lay your commands on your happy servant,

"Felipe Henarez."

The Memoirs of Two Young Brides

P. S.—My dear, you must confess that these great gentlemen know how to love. Isn't that the spring of the African lion? What restrained passion! What trust! What sincerity! What noble-mindedness, even in his humility! I felt very small, indeed, and I asked myself, half stunned, " What am I to do? " The peculiarity of a great man is that he throws all ordinary calculations out. He is sublime and touching at once, artless and still gigantic. In one single letter, he rises higher than Lovelace and Saint Preux, in a hundred. Ah, this is genuine love, with nothing petty about it. Love may exist or it may not, but when it does it must appear in all its vastness. This puts a stop to all my coquetting. Refusal or acceptance—I stand between the two, without the ghost of a pretext to shelter my irresolution. There's an end to all discussion. This isn't Paris; it is Spain, or the East. It is the Abencerrage who speaks and kneels to the Catholic Eve, laying his scimitar, his horse, and his own head at her feet. Am I to accept this remnant of the Moors. Read my Spanish-Saracen letter over and over again, my Renée, and you'll see that love wipes out all the stipulations of your philosophy. Hark ye, Renée, your letter shocks me; you've made life look vulgar to me. Why should I shuffle? Am I not mistress to all eternity of this lion who has softened his roar to submissive and obedient sighs? Heavens, how he must have roared in his lair in the Rue Hillerin-Bertin! I know where he lives, I have his card—*F. Baron de Macumer.* He has made it impossible for me

The Memoirs of Two Young Brides

to send him any answer. All I can do is to throw two camellias in his face. What fiendish cleverness there is in a real, pure, simple love! Here, then, is the greatest event in the history of a woman's heart reduced to an easy and simple action. O Asia, I've read the Arabian Nights and here's their meaning—two blossoms, and that ends it all! We sum up the fourteen volumes of Clarissa Harlowe in a posy. His letter makes me writhe just as a cord twists in the fire. Will you take those two camellias or will you not? Yes or no? Kill me or give me life. Then I hear a voice cry: "Put him to the test." And I am going to do it.

XVI

FROM THE SAME TO THE SAME
March.

I AM dressed all in white. I have white camellias in my hair and a white camellia in my hand. My mother has red camellias in hers. I can take one from her, if I like. I have a sort of longing to make his camellia cost him dearer, by dint of a little hesitation, and not to make up my mind till I am on the spot. I really look lovely. Griffiths begged me to let her gaze at me for a moment. The solemnity of the occasion and the dramatic nature of the consent I am giving have heightened my colour—each of my cheeks is a camellia blooming red on white.

One o'clock in the Morning.

Every soul admired me—only one knew how to worship me. He dropped his head when he saw the white camellia in my hand, and I saw him turn as white as the flower after I had taken a red one from my mother's bouquet. To have appeared with both might have been an accident. But my action gave him a direct reply, so I enlarged my acknowledgment. The opera was Romeo and Juliet, and as you do not know the duet between the two lovers, you can't realize the bliss it was for two neophytes in love to listen to that divine expression of the tender passion. As I went to bed I heard steps resounding on the pavement of the sidewalk. Oh, dearest, my heart is on fire, and my brain as well. What is he doing? What is he thinking about? Has he one thought, one single thought, to which I am a stranger? Is he the ever-ready slave he has declared himself to be? How am I to make sure of it? Has he the very slightest feeling that my acceptance involves a censure, a change of any kind, an expression of thanks? I am a prey to all the minute hair-splittings of the female character in Cyrus, and Astrea, to the subtleties of the Courts of Love. Does he know that where love is concerned, a woman's smallest actions are the outcome of a whole world of thought, internal struggle, and wasted victories? What is he thinking about? How am I to give him orders to write me all the details of the day every evening? He is my slave! I must give him something to do, and I mean to overwhelm him with labour.

Sunday Morning.

I only slept a very little, toward morning. It is midday now. I have just made Griffiths write the following letter:

"To the Baron de Macumer: Mlle. de Chaulieu desires me, sir, to ask you for the copy of a letter from one of her friends, in her own hand, which you have taken away with you. Believe me, etc.,

"Griffiths."

The Memoirs of Two Young Brides

My dear, Griffiths put on her bonnet, she went to the Rue Hillerin-Bertin, she sent up this love-letter to my slave, and he returned me my programme, damp with his tears, in an envelope. He has obeyed me! Ah, my dear soul, it must have cost him something. Another man would have written me a letter crammed with flattery and refused. But the Saracen has been what he promised he would be. He has obeyed! This has touched me even to tears.

XVII

FROM THE SAME TO THE SAME
April 2d.

YESTERDAY the weather was glorious. I dressed myself like a girl who is loved and desires to be loved. My father, at my request, has given me the prettiest turnout to be seen in Paris—two dapple-gray horses, and the most elegant carriage you can conceive. I went out in it for the first time. I looked like a flower under my sunshade lined with white silk. As I drove up the Champs-Elysées I saw my Abencerrage coming towards me on the most magnificent horse. The men, who are nearly all of them first-class horse-jockeys nowadays, were all stopping to look at him and watch him. He bowed to me, and I made him a friendly and encouraging gesture. He slackened his horse's pace, and I was able to say to him:

"You will not be vexed with me, Baron, for having asked you to let me have my letter back. It was useless to you. You have outstripped that programme already," I added, in a low voice. Then I said:

"That horse of yours attracts a great deal of attention."

"My agent in Sardinia sent it to me out of

sheer pride, for this Arab horse was born in my *mâquis*."

This morning, my dear, Henarez was riding an English chestnut, a very fine horse, indeed, but which did not attract every eye. The touch of jesting criticism in my words had been enough for him. He bowed to me, and I bent my head slightly in response. The Duc d'Angoulême has bought Macumer's horse. My slave understood that when he attracted the attention of the loungers in the street he lost something of the simplicity I desire for him. A man should be remarked on account of himself, not because of his horse or any other thing about him. To have too fine a horse seems to me as absurd as to wear a huge diamond in your shirt-front. I was delighted to catch him in fault, and there may have been a touch of vanity such as may well be allowed a poor exile in what he did. All this childishness delights me. Oh, my aged Arguer, do my love affairs enchant you as much as your dreary philosophy depresses me? Dear Philip II in petticoats! Do you find it pleasant driving in my carriage? Do you note that velvet glance, humble yet full, proud of his servitude, cast on me as he passes by, by that truly great man who has donned my livery and always wears a red camellia in his buttonhole, just as I always carry a white one in my hand? How love clears up everything! How well I understand Paris! Now everything I see full of meaning. Yes, love is fairer here, nobler, more fascinating than in any other place. I have come to the

The Memoirs of Two Young Brides

absolute conclusion that I could never tease nor disturb a fool, nor wield the slightest influence over one. Superior men are the only beings capable of understanding us thoroughly, and on whom we can produce any effect. Oh, my poor dear, I forgot l'Estorade. But then didn't you tell me you were going to turn him into a genius? I know why! You're bringing him up tenderly, so that some day he may appreciate you! Good-bye. I'm rather wild, and I'd better not go on.

XVIII

FROM MME. DE L'ESTORADE TO MLLE. DE CHAULIEU

April.

SWEET angel, or should I not rather say, sweet fiend! Without intending it, you have grieved me, and if we were not one in heart I should say you had wounded me—but does one not wound one's self sometimes? How clear it is that you have never yet fixed your thoughts on that one word *indissoluble* as applied to the compact that binds the woman to the man! I will not attempt to gainsay philosophers and legislators. They are surely well enough able to gainsay each other. But, my dearest, though marriage has been made irrevocable by the imposition of an unvarying and pitiless formula, each union is thereby rendered utterly different—as different as are the individuals bound together. Every marriage has its special private laws. The laws that govern a country couple, the members of which are to remain perpetually in each other's presence, are not those which govern a city household in which existence is more diversified by pleasure. And the laws that rule a couple settled in Paris, where life roars by like a torrent, can never resemble those that guide a married pair in the provinces, where life is so infinitely quieter. While

The Memoirs of Two Young Brides

conditions vary with surroundings, they vary much more with characters. The wife of a man of genius has only to permit herself to be guided; and the wife of a fool, unless she is prepared to face the most hideous misfortune, takes the reins into her own hands if she feels herself to be cleverer than her husband. It may be, after all, that argument and reason land us in what some would call depravity. What is this so-called feminine depravity but a calculation of feelings? A reasoning passion is a depraved thing. Passion is beautiful only when it is involuntary and full of those noble outbursts in which selfishness has no place. Ah, sooner or later, my dear, you'll say to yourself: "Yes, deception is as necessary to every woman as her corset—that is, if deception means the silence of the woman who has courage to hold her peace—if deception means the calculation on which our future happiness necessarily depends." At her own cost, every woman must learn the social law, a law incompatible in many respects with the law of Nature. Women marrying at our age may bear a dozen lawful children, but if we were to bear them we should commit a dozen crimes, we should engender a dozen miseries—for should we not doom twelve beloved beings to poverty and despair? Whereas two children are two joys, two blessings, two creations that harmonize with our existing laws and customs. The natural law and the Code are at war, and we ourselves are the field on which they fight. Would you call the wisdom of the wife who takes care the family shall not be brought to ruin through her, depravity? Whether we calculate once or a thousand times, all's lost in matters of the heart. But you'll make this hideous calculation one of these days, my lovely Baronne de Macumer, when you are the proud and happy wife of the man who adores you—or rather that great-minded man will save you from making the calculation, for he will do it himself. You perceive, dear giddy creature, that we have studied the Code in its relations to conjugal love. You must know that it is only to God and to ourselves that we owe any account of the means we use for the perpetuation of happiness in the bosom of our households. And the deliberate calculation which succeeds in that is better than the unthinking love that brings sorrow, wrangling, and separation in its train. I have given painful study to the part assigned to the wife and mother. Yes, my dear love, some sublime deception she must practise in order to become the noble creature she is, when she fulfils all her duties. You tax me with duplicity because I desire to measure out Louis's knowledge of myself to him in daily doses. But is it not too intimate an acquaintance that brings about most separations? My object is to keep him very busy, to distract his thought from me, for the sake of his own happiness, and this desire has nothing in common with a calculating passion.

The spring of love is not inexhaustible, though that of affection may be, and it is a great undertaking for any good woman to distribute her allotted portion wisely over the span of life. I will risk the

The Memoirs of Two Young Brides

chance of horrifying you, and I will tell you that I adhere to my principles, and continue to consider myself a very noble-minded and very generous person. Virtue, my darling, is a principle which manifests itself variously in various surroundings. It produces absolutely different effects in Provence, in Constantinople, in London, in Paris—but virtue it still remains. The tissue of each human existence is full of the most irregular combinations. Yet viewed from a certain altitude, every life looks like the rest. If I wanted to see Louis an unhappy man and to bring about a regular separation between us, I should only have to allow him to lead me by the nose. I have not, like you, had the good luck to meet with a superior being. But I may have the happiness of turning him into one; and I summon you to meet me in Paris five years hence. You will be deceived yourself, and you'll tell me I was quite mistaken, and that M. de l'Estorade is by nature a remarkable man. As for those fair delights, those deep emotions that I only feel through you; as for those tarryings on balconies under starlight nights, as for the excessive adoration that turns us into divinities, I have known from the first that I must give all that up. In your life you blossom freely as you choose. Mine is circumscribed, hemmed in by the walls of La Crampade—and you find fault with the precautions that are necessary, if this fragile, secret, weakly happiness of mine is to grow lasting, rich, and mysterious? I fancied I had discovered the charms of a mistress in my married state, and you have driven me almost to blush for myself.

Which of us is right? Which wrong? It may be that each of us is wrong and right as well. And it may be, also, that society makes us pay very dear for our laces and our titles and our children. I have my red camellias, too. They are on my lips, that shed smiles on the two men, father and son, to whom I devote myself—at once their mistress and their slave. Still, my dearest, your last two letters have made me realize how much I have missed. You have taught me the extent of the sacrifice a married woman makes. I had hardly time to cast a glance at the splendid wild steppe over which you are careering, and I will not enlarge on the few tears I wiped away as I read your letters. But regret is not remorse, though they are closely akin. You tell me "marriage breeds philosophy." Ah, no! I was very sure of that, when I sat crying, and thought of you swept away on the torrent of love! But my father has given me the works of one of the most learned authors of these parts, one of Bossuet's heirs, one of those merciless reasoners whose pages carry conviction to their readers' souls. While you were reading Corinne I was reading Bonald, and there lies the secret of my philosophy—the family rose up before me in all its holiness and might. According to Bonald, your father was perfectly right in all he said.

Farewell, my dear imagination, my friend, you who are all the frolic of my life!

XIX

FROM LOUISE DE CHAULIEU TO MME. DE L'ESTORADE

WELL, well, you are the dearest of women, my Renée, and I am convinced now that deceit is an honest thing. Are you pleased with me? Besides, the man who loves us belongs to us. We have the right to turn him either into a fool or a man of genius, though between ourselves we do generally make a fool of him. You'll make yours into a man of genius, and you'll keep your own secret—two noble actions. Ah, if there were no Paradise, you would be properly hoaxed, for you are certainly devoting yourself to a deliberate martyrdom on earth. You want to make him ambitious and to keep him in love with you. But, child that you are, it would be quite enough to go on feeding his passion. Up to what point is calculation virtue, or virtue calculation—eh? We won't lose our tempers over this question, since Bonald is of the party. We are and we intend to be virtuous, but in spite of all your delightful knaveries I believe you to be less wicked at this moment than I am. Yes, I'm a horribly deceitful girl! I love Felipe, and I conceal the fact from him with the most infamous hypocrisy. I would like to see him leap from his tree on to the top of the wall, and from the top of the wall on to my balcony—and if he were to do as I desire, I should crush him with my disdain. I am hideously frank, you see. What stops me? What mysterious power is it that prevents me from letting that dear Felipe know the happiness his pure, perfect, noble, secret, all-abounding love pours out upon me? Mme. de Mirbel is painting my picture, and I mean to give it him, my dear. A thing that surprises me more and more every day is the activity with which love inspires life. What fresh interests one finds in seasons and actions, and the very smallest things, and how delightfully past and future are confused together! Every verb seems to have three tenses at once. Are things still like this after happiness has come to one? Oh, answer me quickly, tell me what happiness is— whether it calms or whether it excites. I am in a state of mortal anxiety. I no longer know how to act. There is some force in my heart that sweeps me towards him, in spite of reason and propriety. In short, I understand your curiosity about Louis—now are you pleased? Felipe's content in the thought that he belongs to me, his distant love and his obedience provoke me as much as his profound respect used to exasperate me when he was only my Spanish master. I feel inclined to shriek out at him as he goes by: "Idiot, if you love my picture, what would it be if you knew myself?"

Oh, Renée, you burn all my letters, don't you? I'll burn all yours. If any eyes but your own were to

The Memoirs of Two Young Brides

read these thoughts we pour into each other's hearts, I would tell Felipe to go and put them out, and kill a few people, so that we might be safer.

Monday.

Ah, Renée, can a woman fathom a man's heart? My father is to present your M. Bonald to me, and since he is so wise, I'll ask him to tell me. Would that I had the divine power of reading the secrets of all hearts. Am I still an angel in that man's sight? There's the whole question.

If ever, in a gesture, a look, the accent on a word, I were to detect any falling off in the respect he had for me when he gave me Spanish lessons, I feel I should have strength to forget everything. "Wherefore these fine words and mighty resolutions?" you will say. Ah, here it is, my dear. My delightful father, who treats me as if he were an elderly *Cavaliere Servente*, and I an Italian lady, has, as I told you, had my picture painted by Mme. de Mirbel. I have contrived to have a copy made, and such a good one that I have been able to give it to the Duke, and send the original to Felipe. This I did yesterday, and these four lines went with it:

"Don Felipe: In response to your absolute devotion, a blind confidence is bestowed on you. Time will prove whether any man can rise to the height of nobility required."

It is a great reward. It looks like a promise and, what is horrible, like an invitation. But what will seem still more horrible to you is that I intended the reward to express a promise and an invitation, without going so far as to be an offer. If in his answer he writes " My Louise," or even " Louise," he is lost.

Tuesday.

No, he's not lost. This Constitutional Minister is a most adorable lover. Here is his letter:

" Every moment spent without seeing you was filled with the thought of you. My eyes, blind to all else, were fixed in meditation on your figure, which would never stand out swiftly enough in that palace of darkness, peopled with dream figures, on which brightness is shed by you alone. Henceforward my eyes will feed on this wonderful ivory, this talisman, I may call it, for when I look at it, life stirs your blue eyes and the portrait instantly turns to a reality. My letter has been delayed by my eagerness to indulge in this contemplation, in the course of which I have been telling you all those things concerning which I am forced to hold my peace. Yes, ever since yesterday, shut up alone with you, I have given myself over, for the first time in my life, to a full, complete, and infinite happiness. If you could see yourself where I have set you, between the Blessed Virgin and God himself, you would understand the agony of agitation in which I have spent the night. But I would not offend you by speaking of this— I should suffer so frightfully if one glance of yours were stripped of the angelic kindness on which I live, that I crave your pardon beforehand. Ah, queen of my

The Memoirs of Two Young Brides

life and of my soul, if you should be pleased to grant me the thousandth part of the love I bear you!

"The *if* of this ceaseless petition wrung my soul. I stood between belief and error, between life and death, between darkness and light. No criminal is more anguished during the decision of his fate than I, as I acknowledge this audacity to you. The smile upon your lips, which I turn back to gaze at every other moment, has calmed the tempest stirred by my terror of displeasing you. In all my life no one, not even my mother, has smiled upon me. The fair young girl who was my destined bride refused my heart and fell in love with my own brother. In politics my efforts met with failure. I never read aught but a thirst for vengeance in the eyes of my King, and from our youth up the enmity between us has been so deep that he regarded the vote whereby the Cortes called me to power as a deadly insult to himself. However steadfast a man's heart may be, some doubt will creep into it. And besides, I am just to myself, I know my own ugliness, and I comprehend how difficult it must be to realize the nature of the heart that beats beneath an exterior such as mine. When I first saw you, the thought of being loved had grown to be nothing but a dream to me, and when I first set my heart on you, I understood that my affection could only be excused by my devotion. But as I gaze upon this portrait, and listen to the divine promise of that smile, a hope I had not dared to permit myself has sprung up in my soul. The gloom of doubt fights with this tender dawn, and the fear of your displeasure overshadows it. No, you cannot love me yet. I feel it. But as you test the strength, the durability, the extent of my inexhaustible affection, you will give it a tiny foothold in your heart. If my ambition is an insult to you, you will tell me so without anger, and I will go back to my place. But if you will indeed try to love me, do not make it known without minute precautions to the man who had built all the happiness of his life solely on being your slave."

My dear, when I read those last words, I fancied I saw him, white, as he was that night when I showed him by the camellia that I accepted the treasures of his devotion. Those submissive sentences of his were anything but a mere flower of lovers' rhetoric in my eyes, and I felt a sort of great emotion in my soul—the breath of happiness.

The weather has been horrible. It has been impossible for me to go to the Bois without giving rise to all sort of strange suspicions; for my mother, who often goes out in spite of the rain, has stayed at home alone.

Wednesday Evening.

I have just seen *him* at the Opera. My dear, he is quite a different man. He came to our box and was introduced by the Sardinian Ambassador. After he had read in my eyes that his boldness had not displeased me, he seemed to me to grow suddenly shy, and said "Mademoiselle" to the Marquise d'Espard. His eyes flashed glances more brilliant than the light

The Memoirs of Two Young Brides

from the chandeliers. At last he departed, like a man who was afraid of doing something foolish.

"The Baron de Macumer is in love," said Mme. de Maufrigneuse to my mother.

"And that's all the more extraordinary," replied my mother, "because he is a fallen Minister."

I kept sufficient command of myself to look at Mme. d'Espard, Mme. de Maufrigneuse, and my mother with the curiosity of a person who doesn't understand a foreign language and wonders what is being said. But within me raged a voluptuous joy in which my very soul seemed steeped. There is only one word to express what I feel, it is rapture. Felipe's love is so great that I feel he is worthy to be loved. I am literally the principle of his existence, and I hold the thread of all his thoughts in my hand. Indeed—as we are to tell each other everything—I feel the most violent longing to see him break down every obstacle between us and beseech me to bestow myself upon him, so that I may discover whether this fierce love will grow calm and submissive again at a single glance from me.

Ah, my dear, I broke off here and I am still trembling from head to foot. As I sat writing I heard a little noise outside and left my chair. Out of my window I saw him coming along the top of the wall at the risk of his life. I went to the window and I only made him one sign. He leapt off the wall, which is ten feet high; then he ran out upon the road until I could see him so as to show me he was unhurt.

The Memoirs of Two Young Brides

This consideration, just at the moment when he must have been half stunned by his fall, touched me so much that I am still crying without well knowing why. Poor ugly fellow! What was he coming for? What did he want to say to me?

I dare not set down my thoughts, and I am going to bed happy, thinking of all we would say to each other if we were together. Farewell, my silent beauty. I have no time to scold you, but it is more than a month since I have had news of you. Is it, perhaps, that happiness has come to you? Can it be that you have lost that independence of will of which you were so proud, and which so nearly slipped from my grasp to-night?

XX

FROM RENÉE DE L'ESTORADE TO LOUISE DE CHAULIEU

May.

IF love is the life of the world, why do austere philosophers eliminate it from marriage? Why does society make the sacrifice of woman to the family the chief law of its existence, thus necessarily sowing secret discord between every married couple?—a discord so dangerous and so amply foreseen that special powers have been devised to strengthen men against women, who, as they feel, are able to wipe out all things either by the might of love or by the persistence of a hidden hate? At this moment I behold in the married state two warring forces, which the legislator should have brought into alliance. When will they be joined in one? That is what I ask myself as I read your letter. Ah, dearest, one letter of yours has overthrown that edifice built up by the great writer of the Aveyron, in which I had taken up my abode with such a sense of sweet content. These laws were made by old men. We women find that out. They have most wisely decreed that conjugal love which is devoid of passion does not degrade us, and that it is the woman's duty to yield, once the law permits the man to possess her. Their sole thought has been for the family, and they have followed Nature, whose sole object is to perpetuate the race. A while ago I was a living being. Now I am nothing but a chattel. Many a lonely tear have I gulped down— many a tear that I have longed to barter for a consoling smile. Why are our fates so different? A lawful love ennobles your whole soul. Virtue, for you, is bound up in enjoyment. You will not suffer except as you may choose. Your duty, if you marry your Felipe, will be found in the sweetest, the most unreserved of all your feelings. Our future is big with the answer to my cry, and I await it with most agonizing anxiety.

You love and you are adored. Oh, dear one, yield up your whole being to that exquisite poetry of which we have so often dreamt. Woman's beauty, so dainty and so spiritualized in your person, was designed by God that it might charm and delight man's soul. Yes, my beloved, keep the secret of your love well hidden, and put Felipe to the subtle tests we used to invent to discover whether the lover of your dreams would be worthy of us. But make more certain that you love him than that he loves you. Nothing is more deceptive than that mirage of the heart called into being by longing, desire, or faith in one's own happiness. You, who are the one of us two that yet remains intact, don't, I beseech you, risk everything on so perilous an adventure as an irrevocable marriage without some preliminary safeguard. A gesture, a word, a look during one of those *tête-à-tête* conversations, in which worldly hypocrisies drop off a man's soul, will often shed a light over a yawning gulf. You are sufficiently noble-hearted of yourself to permit of your treading boldly in paths where other women lose their footing. You cannot conceive my state of anxiety. In spite of the distance that parts us, I see you and feel everything you feel. So don't fail to write to me and to tell me everything. Your letters fill my life with passion in the midst of this household existence of mine—so simple, so peaceful—as dull as a high-road on a sunless day. The only incidents here, my dear love, are the succession of bickerings with my own self, concerning which I will keep silence for the present. At some later time I will tell you of them. I yield, and then I retake possession of myself with a sort of dreary obstinacy, sometimes discouraged, sometimes full of hope. Perhaps I have asked more happiness of life than life really owes me. In our youth we are rather apt to insist that our own ideal and the real essence of things must agree. My meditations, and I ponder alone, now, sitting at the foot of a great rock in my pleasure-grounds, have led me to the conviction that love in the married state is an accident on which one cannot found any unvarying law. My philosopher was right when he looked at the family as the only social unit, and made woman subservient, as she has been from time immemorial, to the family. The solution of this great question, one that is almost terrible to us women-folk, depends on the

The Memoirs of Two Young Brides

first child we bear. And I long to be a mother, were it only to give scope to the consuming activity of my being.

Louis is still a pattern of the most exquisite kindness. His love is active, and my affection passive. He is happy. He gathers the blossoms for himself alone, and never gives a thought to the effort of the soil that brings them forth. Blessed is his self-absorption. Whatever it may cost me, I favor his illusions, just as a mother, as I conceive her, wears herself out to give her child a pleasure. His happiness is so deep that it blinds him and even casts a reflected glamour back upon me. My smile and my glance, both bright with the satisfaction born of the certainty of the happiness I inspire, deceive him thoroughly. And the affectionate epithet I use in speaking to him between ourselves is, "My child." I await the reward of all this sacrifice, which will remain a secret between yourself and me, and God. Maternity is an undertaking on which I have staked huge hopes. So much does it owe me now, that I fear I may never recover all I have risked. It must unfold my energies, it must enlarge my heart, and make good many things by the boundless joy it brings. O Heaven, grant that I be not disappointed! All my future hangs on that, and—what a terrifying thought!—all my virtue, too.

XXI

FROM LOUISE DE CHAULIEU TO RENÉE DE L'ESTORADE

June.

DEAR MARRIED DARLING: Your letter came at the very moment when I needed it to justify in my own eyes a piece of boldness I have been cogitating all day and all night. I am possessed with the strangest longing after unknown or, if you will, forbidden things—a longing that alarms me and warns me that the laws of Society and the laws of Nature will yet fight a desperate battle within my soul. I know not whether Nature is stronger than Society in my case, but I catch myself planning compromises between the two powers. In short, to put it plainly, I pined to spend an hour in the dark under the lime-trees at the foot of our garden, talking to Felipe all alone. No doubt this desire is characteristic of a girl on whom the title of "sprightly rogue," with which my mother has dubbed me, and which my father has confirmed, is deservedly bestowed. Nevertheless, the misdeed appears to me both wise and prudent. While I shall thereby reward Felipe for the many nights he has spent at the foot of my wall, I shall also find out what view he takes of my escapade and judge him by his behaviour at such a crucial moment. If he treats my fault as something divine, I will make him my adored husband; or if he should not prove more respectful and more overcome than when he bows as he rides past me in the Champs-Élysées, I will never look upon his face again. As far as society is concerned, I risk less by seeing my lover in this fashion than if I were to smile upon him in the drawing-room of Mme. de Maufrigneuse or the old Marquise de Beauséant, for there are spies all about us now, and Heaven alone knows what strange looks are cast at a girl who is suspected of bestowing her attention on a monster such as Macumer. Oh, if you only knew the tumult within me, as I dream over this plan of mine, and if you could realize how I have striven to discover how it was to be carried out! I have often longed for you. We would have spent many a pleasant hour chattering to each other, lost in the labyrinths of doubt and enjoying the foretaste of all the good things, or the bad, that may come of a first lovers' meeting after nightfall in the shadow and silence under the beautiful lime-trees of the Hôtel de Chaulieu, athwart whose branches the moon casts a thousand shafts of tender light. I fairly panted as I sat alone, saying to myself, "Ah, Renée, where are you?" Well, your letter fired the train, and my last scruples were blown to atoms. Out of my window I cast to my astounded worshipper a careful drawing of the key that opens the small door at the end of the garden, and with it the following note: "You must be prevented from doing mad things. If you were to break your neck, you would destroy the reputation of the person you claim to love. Are you worthy of a fresh proof of esteem, and do you deserve an interview at the hour when the moon leaves the lime-trees at the foot of the garden in deep shadows?"

At one o'clock yesterday morning, just as Griffiths was departing to her bed, I said to her:

"Put on your shawl and come with me, my dear. I want to go to the end of the garden, and nobody must know it."

She didn't say a word, and followed me. What a sensation, my Renée! For after watching with a delicious feeling of anxiety for his arrival, I had seen him slip in like a shadow. We reached the garden unhindered, and then I said to Griffiths:

"Don't be astonished. The Baron de Macumer is over there, and it is on his account that I have brought you with me."

She didn't speak.

"What do you want with me?" said Felipe to me, in a voice that told me the rustle of our gowns in the stillness and the noise of our steps on the gravel, slight as they were, had almost driven him wild with emotion. "I want to tell you what I cannot well write," I answered. Griffiths moved a dozen paces away from me. It was one of those soft nights when the air is laden with the scent of flowers. I felt a sort of intoxication of delight at finding myself thus

The Memoirs of Two Young Brides

almost alone with him, in the soft shadow of the lime-trees, beyond which the garden shone all the brighter because the moonlight gleamed from the white façade of the house. The contrast was a dim image of the mystery of our love, destined to end in the garish publicity of marriage. After enjoying for a moment the delight of a position which was new to each of us, and equally surprised us both, I recovered the use of my tongue.

"Though slander does not terrify me," I said, "I do not wish you to go on climbing that tree" (pointing to the elm), "nor yet that wall. You and I have behaved like school children long enough. Let us lift our minds now to the level of our destiny. If you had been killed by your fall, I should have died dishonored."

I looked at him; his face was ghastly white.

"And if any one saw you thus, suspicion would fall either on my mother or on me."

"Forgive!" he said, in a faint voice.

"Walk along the boulevard, I shall hear your footstep, and when I want to see you I will open my window. But I will neither allow you to run that risk nor run it myself, except for a serious reason. Why have you forced me by your imprudence to commit another on my own part, and drive you to think ill of me?"

In his eyes I saw tears, and I thought them the noblest answer in the world.

"You must think my behaviour exceedingly for-

The Memoirs of Two Young Brides

ward," I went on, with a smile. We walked up and down under the trees, once or twice, in silence. Then words came back to him.

"You must think me utterly stupid. And indeed I am so drunk with happiness, that I have neither strength nor wits left in me. But be sure, at all events, that the very fact that you do a thing makes it holy in my eyes. The reverence I feel for you can only be compared with my reverence for God himself. And besides, Miss Griffiths is here——"

"She is here on other folks' account, not on ours, Felipe," I said hastily. That man understood me, my dear soul.

"I know very well," he rejoined, with the most submissive of glances at me, "that even if she were not here, everything between us two would be just as though she saw us. Even if we are not in men's sight, we are always in the sight of God, and we stand as much in need of our own self-respect as of the respect of others."

"I thank you, Felipe," said I, holding out my hand to him with a gesture which I have no doubt you can imagine. "A woman, and I am a true woman, is always inclined to love a man who understands her. Oh, no more than inclined," I added, laying one finger on my lips. "I do not wish you to have more hope than I choose to give you. My heart will never belong to any one but the man who is able to read it and know it thoroughly. Our feelings, without being exactly similar, must have the same

The Memoirs of Two Young Brides

scope and the same level. I make no attempt to make myself appear greater than I am, for no doubt such qualities as I think I possess carry their own faults with them. Still I should be very unhappy if I did not possess them."

"First of all, you accepted me as your servant, and then you gave me leave to love you." He trembled as he spoke, and looked at me between every word. "I have more than I sued for at first."

"But," I answered quickly, "your lot seems to me happier than my own. I should not be sorry to alter mine—and that is in your hands."

"It is my turn to thank you now," he answered. "I know the duty of a loyal lover. I must prove that I am worthy of you, and you have the right to test me as long as it may please you. You have even power, God help me, to cast me off, if you should be disappointed in me."

"I know you love me," I replied. "Up to the present"—I laid merciless emphasis on this last word—"you are the suitor I prefer, and that is why you are here to-night."

We took a few more turns up and down, talking as we walked, and I must confess that once my Spaniard's mind was set at ease, he expressed, not his passion, but his tender affection with the most artless eloquence, illustrating his feeling for me by an exquisite comparison of the divine love. That thrilling voice of his, which imparted a special value to ideas that were already so full of delicacy, was like a night-

The Memoirs of Two Young Brides

ingale's. He spoke in an undertone, pouring out his words eagerly like a gushing spring, the overflowing of his full heart.

"Hush!" I said at last, "or I shall stay here longer than I ought," and with a gesture I dismissed him.

"So now you are plighted, mademoiselle," quoth Griffiths to me.

"That might be so in England," I answered carelessly, "but not in France; I intend to marry for love, and not to be deceived—that's all."

You see, my dear, love did not come to me, and so I have done as Mahomet did with his mountain.

Friday.

I have seen my slave once more. He has grown timorous, he has assumed an air of mystery and devotion, which I like. He seems to be imbued with a deep sense of my power and glory. But nothing, either in his look or manner, would lead the soothsayers of smart society to suspect the infinite adoration I perceive in him.

Nevertheless, my dear, I am not swept away, nor ruled, nor mastered. On the contrary, it is I who conquer, who rule, and who prevail. In other words, I can reason. Ah, how I wish I could recover that sensation of fear I felt, under the fascination of the teacher, the plain citizen, to whom I would not yield. There are two kinds of love—the love which commands, and the love which obeys. They are distinct,

The Memoirs of Two Young Brides

and they give birth to two separate passions, the one quite different from the other. Perhaps, if a woman is to have her full due from life, she ought to feel them both. Can these two passions ever blend together? Can the man, in whom we inspire love, inspire us with the same feeling? Will Felipe be my master one of these days? Shall I ever tremble as he trembles now? These questions thrill me through and through. He's very blind. In his place, under the lime-trees, I should have thought Mlle. de Chaulieu a very cold coquette, starched and calculating. No, that kind of thing is not love; that is mere playing with fire. I care for Felipe still, but I am calm now, and at my ease. There are no more obstacles between us—distressing thought! I feel everything within me droop and collapse, and I am afraid to question my own heart. He should not have hidden the vehemence of his love from me. He has left me mistress of myself. Certainly this sort of blunder brings me no benefit. Yes, my dearest, delightful as is the memory of that half hour spent under the trees, the pleasure it gave me seems to me far inferior to my sensations while I was wondering, "Shall I go, or shall I not? Shall I write to him, or shall I not?" Can it be the same with all pleasures? Would it be better to put them off than to enjoy them? Is anticipation really superior to possession? Are the rich really the poor? Have we both of us over-exaggerated our feelings by developing the strength of our imagination out of all measure? There are moments when this idea strikes cold

The Memoirs of Two Young Brides

to my heart. Do you know why? I am thinking of returning to the bottom of the garden without Griffiths! Whither shall I go at this rate? Imagination may know no bounds, but enjoyment has its limits. Tell me, sweet doctor in petticoats, how I am to reconcile these two goals of our feminine existence?

XXII

FROM LOUISE TO FELIPE

I AM not pleased with you. If you have wept over Racine's Bérénice, if you have not thought it the most hideous of all tragedies, you will not understand me, and we shall never understand each other. Let us part—let there be an end to our meetings—forget me —for if you do not give me a satisfactory answer, I shall forget you. You will become the Baron de Macumer to me, or rather you will become nothing at all—as far as I am concerned, it will be as though you had never existed. At Mme. d'Espard's yesterday you wore a sort of air of satisfaction which was excessively displeasing to me. You seemed to be certain that you were loved. Altogether your self-possession horrified me, and I failed to recognise in you at that moment the servitor you described yourself as being in your first letter. Far from being absent, as a man in love should be, you made witty remarks. This is not the behaviour of the true believer—he is always bowed down in the presence of the divinity. If I am not a being superior to all other women, if you do not look on me as the spring of your existence, I am less than a woman—because then I am merely a woman in

The Memoirs of Two Young Brides

your sight. You have sowed distrust in my soul, Felipe, and its murmur has drowned the voice of affection. When I look back over our past, I see I have a right to be distrustful. Learn, Sir Constitutional Minister of all the Spains, that I have pondered deeply over the parlous condition of my sex. My innocence has held flaring torches without burning its fingers. Lend an attentive ear to that which my young experience has taught me, and which I now repeat to you. In all other matters, duplicity, lack of faith, broken promises, meet their judges, and those judges inflict punishments. But it is not so with love. Love must be at once victim, accuser, advocate, judge and executioner. For the most hideous of perfidies, the vilest of crimes, are those which remain unknown. They are committed between human hearts, they have no witnesses, and it is in the interest of the murdered heart, of course, to hold its peace. Love, then, has its own code and its own vengeance—the world has no part in them. Now I have made a vow that I will never pardon a crime, and in matters of the heart there is no such thing as a trivial offence. Yesterday you looked like a man who was certain he was loved. If you were not certain of this, you would be wrong. But it would be criminal on your part if that certainty were to rob you of the ingenuous charm with which the fluctuations of hope have hitherto endowed you. I do not desire to see you either a faint heart or a fop. I will not have you tremble lest you should lose my affection, because that would be an insult. But

The Memoirs of Two Young Brides

neither do I choose that a sense of security shall permit you to carry your love lightly. You must never seem more self-possessed than I appear myself. If you do not know the anguish a single idea of doubt stirs in the soul—tremble lest I should teach it you. By one single glance I yielded up my heart to you, and you have read it. You possess the purest feelings that ever sprang in a young girl's breast. The thought and meditation of which I have spoken have only enriched the brain; but if a wounded heart be driven to take counsel with the intellect, that girl, believe me, will be something like the angel who knows all things, and is capable of all. I swear to you, Felipe, that if you love me, as I believe you do, and if you allow me to suspect the slightest diminution in those feelings of fear, obedience, reverent expectation, and submissive longing, of which you have given me indications; if any day I come to perceive the smallest slackening in that first and noble love which has passed from your heart into mine, I will say nothing to you. I will not weary you with any letter, more or less dignified, more or less proud or angry, or even grumbling, like this one of mine. I will not say one word, Felipe. You would see me sad, with the sadness of one who watches the approach of death. But I would not die without having set the most horrible blight upon you, without having dishonoured the woman you have loved in the most shameful manner, and implanted an eternal regret within your heart; for you would see me lost in the eyes of men on earth, and damned forever in the life beyond.

Do not make me jealous, then, of another, and a happy Louise, of a Louise who was loved with a holy adoration, of a Louise whose heart was gladdened by a love that knew no shadow, and who, as Dante so sublimely puts it, possessed

"Senza brama, sicura ricchezza."

Let me tell you that I have sought all through his Inferno to discover the most agonizing of tortures, a frightful moral punishment, to which would be added the eternal vengeance of the Most High.

Yesterday, then, thanks to your behaviour, the cold and cruel dagger of suspicion entered my heart. Do you understand me? I doubted you, and it was such agony that I desire to be relieved of future doubt. If you find my service too hard for you, leave it—and I shall bear you no malice. Am I not well aware that you are a clever man? Keep all the blossoms of your soul for me. Let your eyes seem dim to the outer world. Never place yourself in a situation which may expose you to flattery, or praise, or compliment from any other being. Come to me, bowed with hate, the object of a thousand slanders, or loaded with scorn. Tell me that women do not understand you, that they pass close beside you without seeing you, and that not one of them will ever love you. Then you will learn what the heart and the love of Louise hold for you. Our treasure must be so safely buried that the whole world may tread on it, and never guess it. If you had been a handsome man I should, no doubt, never have bestowed the least attention on you, and so should never have discovered in your person that world of causes which lie at the root of love; and although we know no more about these causes than we know how it is the sun makes the flowers bloom or the fruit ripen, there is one, nevertheless, which I do know and which is my delight. Your noble face keeps its character, its language, its expression for me alone. It is I alone who possess the power to transform you and turn you into the most lovable man on earth. Therefore I do not choose that your intellect should slip out of my hand. It must not be revealed to others, any more than your eyes, your charming mouth, and all your features may speak to them. The light of your intelligence, like the brightness of your glance, must be kindled by me alone. Remain the gloomy, cold, sullen, and disdainful grandee of Spain you have been. Then you were like some untamed though shattered power, amid the ruins of which no man dared venture; they watched you from afar. Now, I see you opening up convenient paths, so that all may enter, and before long you will be transformed into a mere polite Parisian. Have you forgotten my programme? Your love was a little too clearly evident in your joy. My glance was needed to prevent you from letting the occupants of the most clear-sighted, the most satirical and the wittiest drawing-room in Paris into the secret that you

The Memoirs of Two Young Brides

owed your brilliancy to Armande Louise Marie de Chaulieu. I think you too great-minded to adopt any political artifice in connection with your love; but if you were not to treat me with all the simplicity of a child, I should be sorry for you; and in spite of this first mistake, you are still an object of deep admiration on the part of

LOUISE DE CHAULIEU.

XXIII

FROM FELIPE TO LOUISE

When God sees our shortcomings, he sees our repentance too. You are right, my dear mistress. I felt I had displeased you, without being able to discover the cause of your displeasure. But you have made that clear to me, and you have given me fresh reason to adore you. That jealousy of yours, so like the jealousy of the God of Israel, has filled me with delight. There is nothing more sacred nor more holy than jealousy. Oh, my fair guardian angel, jealousy is the sentinel who never slumbers; jealousy is, to love, what suffering is to man—a truthful monitor. Be jealous of your servant, Louise. The oftener you strike him, the more humbly, submissively, pitifully, he will caress the rod, knowing your severity proves how much you care for him. But alas! my dear one, if they escaped you, will God himself give me credit for all the efforts I have made to overcome my own timidity and subdue the feelings you have taken to be weak in me. Ah, it was a mighty effort that I made to show you what I had been before I began to love you. At Madrid my conversation was considered agreeable, and I

The Memoirs of Two Young Brides

wanted you to find out for yourself whatever powers I possessed. If this is vanity, you have punished it very thoroughly. That last look of yours set me trembling as I have never trembled before—not even when I saw the French troops before Cadiz—not even when my life hung on a deceitful sentence spoken by my King. Vainly had I sought the cause of your displeasure, and the disunion of our souls drove me to despair, for I must act on your will, think with your thought, see through your eyes, joy in your delight, suffer by your pain, as surely as I feel the sensations of heat and cold. To me the crime and the anguish lay in the lack of simultaneity in that heart-life of ours, which you have made so beautiful. I have displeased her, said I to myself a thousand times over, like a madman. My beautiful, noble Louise, if anything could have increased my absolute devotion to you, and my unshakeable belief in your pure conscience, it would be your teaching, which has fallen on my heart like a new light. You have explained my own feelings to me. You have cleared up things that have appeared confusedly to my mind. . . . Oh, if this be your idea of punishment, what are your rewards? But to have been accepted as your servant already fulfilled all my desire. To you I owe an unhoped-for life. I am vowed to you. I do not draw my breath in vain. My strength has found employment were it only in suffering for your sake. I have told you before, I say it now again, you will always find me what I was when I offered you my humble and modest service. Yes, even

The Memoirs of Two Young Brides

lost and dishonoured, as you say you might become, my adoration would be deepened by your self-sought misfortunes. I would cleanse your wounds, I would heal them up, my prayers should convince the Almighty of your innocence and that your shortcomings are another's crimes. Have I not told you that my heart holds all the diverse affections that a father, a mother, a brother, a sister, would feel for you? That above and beyond all things, I am your family—everything or nothing, just as you may choose? But is it not you who have imprisoned so many hearts within the heart of this one lover? Forgive me, then, if, now and then, the lover overrides the father and the brother, when you remember that beneath the lover the father and the brother still remain. If you could read my heart, when I see you, radiant in your beauty, calmly seated, the cynosure of every eye, in your carriage at the Champs-Élysées, or in your box at the opera. . . . Ah, if you knew how little personal feeling there is in the pride with which I listen to the praise extorted by your beauty and your dignity, and how I love the unknown strangers who gaze at you in admiration. When you chance to rejoice my soul by a greeting, I am proud and humble, both at once. I go on my way as though God had blessed me. I come home rejoicing, and my joy leaves a long furrow of light within my soul. It shines even in the clouds of smoke from my cigarette, and makes me feel more sure than ever that every drop of the blood that courses in my veins is yours alone. After I have seen

The Memoirs of Two Young Brides

you, I come back to my study, decked with a Moorish splendour, utterly eclipsed by the beauty of your portrait, the instant I touch the spring that keeps it hidden from every eye. And then I lose myself in labyrinths of contemplation. I live over whole poems of bliss. Soaring on high, I gaze over the course of a whole future existence on which I dare to set my hope. Has it ever happened to you in the silence of the night, or athwart the clatter of the gay world, to hear a voice whispering in the dear dainty little ear I worship? Do you know nothing of the endless supplications I make to you? By dint of gazing at you in the silence, I have ended by discovering the reason of your every feature, and how each corresponds with some perfection of your inner being. Then I make Spanish sonnets—sonnets of which you know nothing, for my verses are too far below my subject, and I dare not send them to you—on the agreement between these two exquisite natures. So utterly is my heart absorbed in yours, that I am never a moment without thinking of you; and if you ceased to quicken my life, after this fashion, I should be full of suffering. Now, Louise, do you understand the anguish I endured at having, most unwittingly, roused your displeasure, and being unable to discover its cause? This fair dual existence was checked, and I felt an icy chill upon my heart. At last, in my utter inability to account for the discord, I began to think you had ceased to care for me. I was turning back, very sadly but still thankfully, to my station as your servant, when the arrival

The Memoirs of Two Young Brides

of your letter filled my heart with joy. Oh, chide me like this forever!

A child who had fallen down, raised himself up, and, hiding his suffering, said to his mother, " Forgive me." Yes, he craved her pardon for having given her pain. Well, I am as that child. I have not changed, I give you the key to my nature with all the submission of a slave. But, dear Louise, I will make no more false steps. See to it that the chain which binds me to you is always kept so taut that a touch may impart your slightest wish to the man who will always be your slave,

FELIPE.

XXIV

FROM LOUISE DE CHAULIEU TO RENÉE DE L'ESTORADE

October, 1825.

DEAR FRIEND: You who were married within two months to a poor ailing body into whose mother you have turned yourself, can know nothing of the frightful vicissitudes of that drama played out in human hearts which we call love—wherein everything in one moment turns to tragedy, with death in a look or in a careless answer. I have kept back a cruel but a decisive test, which shall be Felipe's final ordeal. I was resolved to find out whether I am loved "*in spite* of all," that noble and sublime motto of the Royalists, and why not of Catholics as well?

He walked up and down with me under the lime-trees in our garden the whole night long and not even the shadow of a doubt was in his heart. The next morning he loved me better, and I was just as pure and noble and maidenly in his eyes as I had been before. He had not taken the smallest advantage of me. Oh, he is a true Spaniard; a true Abencerrage. He climbed my wall in the dark to kiss the hand I held out to him from my balcony. He nearly killed himself. But how many young men would have done the

The Memoirs of Two Young Brides

same! All that is nothing. Christians will endure the most frightful martyrdom for the sake of reaching Heaven.

The day before yesterday, in the evening, I drew the King's future Ambassador to the Spanish Court, my much-honoured father, apart, and said to him, with a smile:

"Sir, a few of your friends believe you are about to marry your beloved Armande to the nephew of an Ambassador, who, in his desire for this alliance, which he has long been seeking, settles his fortune and his titles on the young couple after his death, and at once insures them an income of a hundred thousand francs, besides settling a dowry of eight hundred thousand francs upon the bride. Your daughter weeps, but bows to the resistless authority of your majestic and paternal will. Some spiteful folk are saying that her tears cloak a selfish and ambitious nature. We are going to the noble's box at the opera to-night, and the Baron de Macumer will be there."

"A hitch in the negotiations?" said my father, as if I had been an ambassadress.

"You are taking Clarissa Harlowe for Figaro," I replied, with a glance full of scorn and irony. "When you see my right hand ungloved, you'll contradict this impertinent tale, and let it be seen that it offends you."

"I need have no anxiety about your future. You have no more the mind of a young girl than Jeanne d'Arc had a woman's heart. You'll be quite happy.

The Memoirs of Two Young Brides

You'll never love any one, and you'll let yourself be loved."

This time I burst out laughing.

"What's amiss with you, little coquette?" he said.

"I tremble for the interests of my country," quoth I, and seeing he did not understand, I added, "at Madrid."

"You have no idea," said he to the Duchesse, "how this young lady has learnt to laugh her father to scorn in one short year."

"Armande laughs everything to scorn," said my mother, looking full at me.

"What can you mean?" I cried.

"Nothing daunts you, not even the night damps, which might give you rheumatism," she replied, with another look.

"The mornings are so burning hot," I answered.

The Duchesse dropped her eyes.

"It is high time she were married," said my father. "It will be done, I hope, before I leave Paris."

"Yes, if you choose," I answered simply.

Two hours later we were blooming like four roses in the front of the box—the Duchesse de Maufrigneuse, Mme. d'Espard, my mother, and myself. I sat sideways, with one shoulder turned to the audience, so that I could see everything, without being seen, that happened in that roomy box, which fills up one of the corners cut off the back of the theatre, between the pillars. At the first *entr'acte* a young man of feminine beauty, whom I always call *Le Roi des Ribauds*, made his appearance. Comte Henri de Marsay entered the box with an epigram in his eyes, a smile on his lips, and a general air of joy and delight. He paid the preliminary civilities to my mother, to Mme. d'Espard, to the Duchesse, and to M. de Canalis, and then he said to me:

"I wonder whether mine will be your first congratulations on an event which will make you the object of much envy."

"A marriage?" I replied. "Must a young person just out of her convent remind you that the marriages that are talked about never come to pass?"

M. de Marsay had leant over to whisper in Macumer's ear, and by the mere motion of his lips I knew exactly what he was telling him.

"Baron, you may have fallen in love with that little flirt, who has been making use of you. But as it is with you a question of marriage and not of a mere passion, 'tis always just as well to know what is going on."

Macumer shot one of those glances of his, which to me are a perfect poem, at the officious scandalmonger, and cast him back some such rejoinder as "I love no little flirt," with a look which so delighted me that the instant I saw my father I took off my glove. Felipe had not felt the slightest fear, nor the tiniest suspicion. He has thoroughly realized all my expectations of his nature. All his belief is solely centred in me alone, the world and its lies have no hold upon him. The Abencerrage never moved a muscle, his blue blood never tinged his olive cheek. The two young Counts went out together. Then I said to Macumer laughingly, "M. de Marsay has been making you some epigram about me."

"Much more than epigram," he answered, "an epithalamium."

"You are talking Greek to me," I answered with a smile, and I rewarded him with a certain look which always puts him out of countenance.

"I hope so, indeed," cried my father, turning to Mme. de Maufrigneuse. "Society is full of the vilest gossip. The moment a young lady begins to go out, everybody is wild to see her married, and the most absurd stories are invented. I will never ask Armande to marry against her own inclination. I shall go and take a turn in the crush-room, for people may think I am allowing this story to get about so as to put the idea of this marriage into the Ambassador's head, and Cæsar's daughter must be even less doubted than his wife, who must be above all suspicion."

The Duchesse de Maufrigneuse and Mme. d'Espard glanced, first at my mother, and then at the Baron, with an expression at once eager, mocking, sly, and full of suppressed inquiry. The wily creatures had guessed something at last. Of all hidden things love is the most public, and I really believe we women exhale it from our persons; the woman, indeed, who could conceal it must be a perfect monster. Our eyes reveal even more than do our tongues. After I had enjoyed the exquisite delight of finding Felipe as noble as I could wish him to be, I naturally began to long for something more. I made him the preconcerted signal which was to bring him to my window by the dangerous road already known to you. A couple of hours later I found him there, erect as a statue, standing against a wall, his hand resting on a corner of my balcony and his eyes fixed upon the glimmer of the lights within my room.

" My dear Felipe," I said, " you have done well tonight. You have behaved as I should have behaved myself, if I had been told you were going to be married."

" I thought you would have told me of such an intention before any one else," he replied.

" And what is your right to that privilege? "

" The right of a devoted servant."

" Are you that really? "

" Yes," he answered, " and I shall never change."

" Well, then, if this marriage were necessary—if I were to make up my mind———"

The soft light of the moon was brightened, as it were, by the two glances he shot, first on me and then at the abyss below the wall. It was as though he were asking himself whether we might not die there together in one crash. But the thought which flashed like lightning over his face and eyes was instantly mastered by a mightier force than that of passion.

The Memoirs of Two Young Brides

"An Arab has only one oath," said he, in a voice that choked. "I am your servant; I belong to you; I will live my whole life for you."

The grasp of his hand on the balcony seemed to weaken. I laid my hand on his, and said:

"Felipe, my friend, from this moment I am your wife, by my own free-will. Go to my father in the morning and ask him for my hand. He desires to keep back my fortune, but you will undertake to settle it on me, without having received it, and your suit will most certainly be accepted. Now I am not Armande de Chaulieu any more. Depart at once! Louise de Macumer must not be guilty of the slightest imprudence."

He turned pale, his knees bent under him. He sprang to the ground, a full ten feet, without hurting himself in the least. Then, after having caused me the most horrible alarm, he waved his hand to me and disappeared.

"So I am loved," said I to myself, "as never woman was loved before." And I fell asleep as happy as a child. My fate was settled forever. Toward two o'clock my father sent for me to his study, where I found the Duchesse and Macumer. There was a short exchange of civil speeches. I answered very simply that if M. Henarez and my father were agreed, I had no reason to oppose their wishes. Thereupon my mother kept the Baron to dinner, after which meal we all four went out to drive in the Bois de Boulogne. I cast a very satirical look at M. de Marsay as he

The Memoirs of Two Young Brides

rode past us, for he noticed Macumer and my father in the front of the carriage.

My dearest Felipe has had his cards printed again, thus:

HENAREZ,

Des Ducs de Soria, Baron de Macumer.

Every morning he brings me the most delicious and magnificent bouquet. In the midst of it I always find a letter containing a Spanish sonnet in my honour which he has written during the night.

To avoid making this packet too heavy, I send you, as specimens, the first and the last of these sonnets, which I have translated for you word for word and line by line.

FIRST SONNET

"More than once, dressed in a thin silk vest—
  With my sword drawn, and a pulse that throbbed **no whit the faster—**
  I have awaited the onslaught of the furious bull
  Whose horns are sharper than the crescent moon.

"Humming an Andalusian seguidillo, I have climbed
  The slope of a redoubt, under a hail of lead;
  I have wagered my life on the green cloth of chance,
  With no more care for it than for a gold doubloon.

"Once I would have snatched the ball from a cannon's mouth,
  But I believe I have grown more timid than a frightened hare—
  Or a child that sees a ghost in the fold of his window curtain.

"For when your gentle eyes are turned on me—
  A cold sweat stands on my brow, my knees bend **under me—**
  I tremble, I shrink, and all my courage fails."

The Memoirs of Two Young Brides

SECOND SONNET

"Last night I longed for sleep that I might dream of thee—
But jealous slumber fled my eyes—
I drew near the balcony and gazed upon the sky:
For when I think of thee my eyes look always upwards.

"Then came a strange phenomenon, which love alone can explain—
The firmament had lost its sapphire tinge—
The stars like lustreless diamonds in their golden setting
Looked down with dim eyes, shedding chilly rays.

"The moon, no longer painted with silver and lily white,
Travelled mournfully across the dreary sky,
For thou hast robbed the heavens of all their splendour!

"The whiteness of the moon gleams on thy lovely forehead—
All the blue of heaven shines in thine eyes,
And thy lashes are all star-beams!"

Could any young girl be assured she fills all her lover's thoughts in more delightful fashion? What think you of this love which lavishes all the flowers of intelligence, and all the flowers of earth, on the expression of his fervour? For the last ten days I have been making acquaintance with the far-famed Spanish gallantry of bygone times.

Well, my dear, and how do things go with you at La Crampade, where I so often take my walks abroad and watch the progress of our agricultural operations? Haven't you a word to tell me about our mulberry trees and all the things we planted last winter? Does everything succeed after your heart's desire? Have the flowers blossomed in your wifely bosom even as they have bloomed in our shrubberies—I dare not say our garden-beds. Does Louis still sing you madrigals? Do you get on well together? Is the gentle murmur of your streamlet of conjugal affection a better thing than the turbulent torrent of my love? Is my sweet doctor in petticoats vexed with me? I can hardly believe it, and if I did I would send Felipe to cast himself at your feet and bring me back forgiveness or your head. My life here, dear love, is exquisite. I would fain know how life goes with you in Provence. We have just increased our family by the addition of a Spaniard, as brown as a Havana cigar, and I am still awaiting your congratulations.

Seriously, my sweet Renée, I am uneasy. I am afraid you may be gulping down some misery of your own for fear it should sadden my rapture. Write me without delay. Send me several pages describing all the tiniest incidents of your life, and mind you tell me if you are still holding out, if your " free-will " is still erect, or on its knees, or sitting meekly down —which would be serious. Do you fancy the events of your married life do not occupy my thoughts? Sometimes all you have written me sends me into a reverie. Often when people have thought I was watching the ballet twirl at the opera, I have been saying to myself: " Half past nine o'clock now, perhaps she is going to bed. Is she all alone with her free-will? or has her free-will gone to join all the other free-wills whose owners have ceased to value them? "

A thousand loves to you!

XXV

FROM RENÉE DE L'ESTORADE TO LOUISE DE CHAULIEU

October.

IMPERTINENCE: Why should I have written to you? What was there for me to tell? While you are leading your life crammed with love's joys and terrors, the furies and the blossoms of delight you have described to me—a life at which I look on as though it were some well-acted play—my existence follows a course as regular and monotonous as that of any convent. We are always in our beds by nine o'clock at night. We are always up with the sun. Our meals are always served with the most exasperating punctuality. Never does the most trifling accident break the calm. I have grown accustomed, and without much difficulty, to this regular arrangement of my time. This may be natural. What would life be, unless it were ruled by fixed laws, which, so Louis and the astronomers declare, rule every sphere. Orderliness never wearies one, and besides, I have made myself rules, as to my toilet, which fill up all my time between the hour at which I rise and that of breakfast. My sense of feminine duty makes me desire to look charming at the meal. It is a satisfaction to myself, and a very keen pleasure to the kind old father and to Louis. After breakfast we go out of doors. When the newspapers make their appearance I retire to see after my household duties, to read—for I read a great deal—or to write to you. I reappear an hour before we dine, and after that we play cards, or pay visits or receive them. Thus my days are spent, between a happy old man, who has no wish ungratified, and a younger one, whose whole bliss is centred in me. Louis's happiness is so immense that his joy has warmed my heart at last. Our happiness, of course, is not exactly pleasure. Sometimes of an evening, when I am not wanted for the game and lie back quietly in an arm-chair, my meditation grows so deep that I pass into your very being. Then I share your beautiful existence—so full of incident and colour and mighty stir—and I wonder whither this turbulent preface will lead you. Will it not kill the book? You may have all the illusions of love, dear child, but the realities of the married state are all that is left to me. Yes, your love passages sound to me like a dream. And I find it quite difficult to comprehend wherefore you make them so romantic. You want a man with a heart stronger than his sense, with more virtue and nobility than love. You want the embodiment of every young girl's dream. You ask for sacrifice that you may reward it; you put your Felipe to the test to discover whether hope, longing, curiosity, will endure. But, simple child, behind all your fanciful adornments stands an altar, before which an eternal

The Memoirs of Two Young Brides

bond is preparing for you. On the very morrow of the wedding day, the grim fact whereby the maid becomes a woman, and the lover a husband, may overthrow the whole of the dainty edifice your cunning foresight has built up. Learn, once for all, that two lovers, every whit as much as a couple married as Louis and I have married, go forth, as Rabelais puts it, "to meet, beneath their wedded joys, a great *Perhaps.*"

I do not blame you—though it was a giddy thing to do—for talking to Don Felipe in your garden, for asking him questions, for spending a night on your balcony while he stood on the wall. But, child, this is trifling with life, and I dread lest life should trifle with you. I dare not advise you to do what my experience tells me would be best for your own happiness. But let me tell you once more, out of my distant valley, that the secret of a successful marriage lies in these two words: Resignation and Sacrifice. For I see plainly that in spite of all your tests, your coquettish ways, and your cautious reconnoitring, you will marry, in the end, just exactly as I have married. By sharpening desire you deepen the precipice a little—that is all!

Oh, how I wish I could see the Baron de Macumer and have a couple of hours' talk with him—so intensely do I desire your happiness!

XXVI

FROM LOUISE DE CHAULIEU TO RENÉE DE L'ESTORADE

March, 1825.

As Felipe, with true Saracen generosity, has realized all my parents' plans, and settled my fortune on me, without receiving it from them, the Duchesse is even more good-natured to me than before. She calls me "little sly-boots," "little rogue"; she vows I have "a sharp little nose."

"But, dear mamma," said I, the night before the signature of the marriage contract, "you are writing down the effect of the truest, the simplest, the most disinterested, the most absorbing love that ever existed to policy, to cunning, and to clever management. Please understand that I am not at all the 'rogue' for whom you do me the honour to take me."

"Come, come, Armande," she said, as she threw her arm around my neck and drew me near her to kiss my forehead. "You didn't choose to go back to your convent, you didn't choose to live unmarried, and like the noble and beautiful daughter of the Chaulieus you are, you realized the necessity of raising up your father's house." . . . If you only knew, Renée,

The Memoirs of Two Young Brides

what flattery lay in those last words for the Duke, who was listening to our talk! " I have watched you for a whole winter, poking your little nose into every corner, weighing men well and truly, and recognising the real nature of French society as it now exists. And then you pitched on the one and only Spaniard who was capable of insuring you the delightful existence led by a wife who rules supreme within her home. My dear child, you have managed him, just exactly as Tullia manages your brother."

" What a school my sister's convent is! " cried my father.

I cast a look at him that struck him dumb. Then I turned to the Duchesse, and I said:

" Madame, I love my *fiancé*, Felipe de Soria, with all the strength of my heart. Although this love was quite involuntary, and although I fought against it when it first rose up in my heart, I can swear to you that I never gave way to it till I was sure the Baron de Macumer possessed a heart worthy of mine, and that the delicacy, the generosity, the devotedness, the whole character and feeling of his nature, coincided with my own."

" But, my dear child," she broke in, " he is as ugly as———"

" As you choose," I answered swiftly, " but I love his ugliness."

" Listen, Armande," said my father. " If you love him, and if you have had strength to master your passion, you mustn't imperil your future happiness.

The Memoirs of Two Young Brides

Now happiness largely depends on the first days of married life."

"Why not say the first nights," cried my mother. "Leave us, sir," the Duchesse added, looking at my father.

"In three days, little one, you are to be married," whispered my mother in my ear. "So it behoves me now to give you, without any vulgar snivelling, the weighty counsel every mother gives her child in such a case. You love the man you are about to marry, therefore I need waste no pity either on you or on myself. You have only been with me for a year. If that has been long enough for me to grow fond of you, it is not a length of time that would warrant my bursting into tears over the loss of your company. Your wit has been even greater than your beauty. You have flattered my maternal vanity, and you have behaved like a good-tempered and lovable daughter, and you will always find me an excellent mother. You smile? . . . Alas! often when a mother and daughter have got on well together, the two married women will fall out. I want you to be happy. Therefore listen to me. The love you now feel is a childish love—the love that is natural to every woman, all women being born to cling to some man. But, my child, the sad thing is that there is only one man in the world for each of us—one, not two. And the man we are destined to cherish is not always the man we have chosen to be our husband, believing that we loved him. Strange as these words may seem to you, I beseech you to ponder them. If we do not love the man we have chosen, that may be our fault or his, or the fault of circumstances over which neither he nor we have any control at all. Yet none of these things need prevent the man our family chooses for us, the man to whom our heart turns, from being the man of our love. The barrier that rises later between him and us is often the outcome of a lack of perseverance on the husband's part, or ours. To turn a husband into a lover is as delicate an undertaking as to turn a lover into a husband, and this last task you have just performed most admirably. Well, I say again, I want you to be happy. So remember, henceforward, that your first three months of wedlock may bring you great unhappiness, unless you on your part submit yourself to the married state, with all the obedience, the tenderness, and the wit you have displayed in your love-making.

"For, my little rogue, you have indulged in all the innocent delights of a clandestine love affair. If the beginnings of your happy love are clouded by disappointment, dissatisfaction, and even by suffering, then come to me. Don't hope too much from marriage at the outset. It may very possibly bring you more pains than pleasures. Your happiness will need as much careful cultivation as your love has needed. Even if you were by chance to love your lover, you would always have the father of your children. There, dear child, lies the whole of our social life. Sacrifice everything to the man whose name is yours, the very slightest hurt to whose honour and reputation must inflict a frightful breach upon your own. This sacrifice of everything to the husband is not merely an absolute duty to all women of our condition, it is also the wisest course in our own interest. The noblest prerogative of the great principles of morality is that they are true and profitable whatever may be the point from which we study them. I have said enough of all this. Now, I think you are disposed to be jealous; and I, too, my dear, am jealous! . . . But I would not have you foolishly jealous. Listen to me again. Jealousy which lets itself be seen is like a policy in which all the cards are laid upon the table. To acknowledge jealousy, to betray it, is surely to show one's hand, and that when one knows nothing of one's adversary's cards. In every circumstance we must know how to suffer in silence. However, I shall have some serious talk with Macumer about you the night before you are married."

I took hold of my mother's beautiful arm and kissed her hand, leaving upon it a tear, which the tone of her voice had brought to my eyes. In that lofty teaching, worthy alike of herself and of me, I recognised a deep wisdom, an affection untouched by any social bigotry, and, above all, a real esteem for my own character. Those simple words of hers summed up the precepts life and experience had taught her—it may be at a bitter cost. She was touched, and said, looking at me:

"Dear little girl, you have a terrible crossing before you; and most women, if they are ignorant or bereft of their illusions, are capable of doing like Lord Westmoreland."

At that we both began to laugh. To explain the joke, I must tell you that at dinner the night before, a Russian Princess had been telling us that Lord Westmoreland, who had suffered frightfully when he crossed the Channel on his way to Italy, turned back when he heard that he had to cross the Alps as well. " I've had enough of crossings," said he. You'll understand, Renée, that your dreary philosophy and my mother's lecture were calculated to reawaken all the terrors that used to disturb our souls at Blois. The nearer my wedding day approached, the more I gathered up my strength and will and all my feelings to face the terrible transition from girlhood into womanhood. All our talks came back to me. I read all your letters over again, and found them full of a sort of hidden melancholy. These alarms had the good effect of turning me into the ordinary commonplace *fiancée* known to engravers and the public. And every one thought me charming and most correct when the contract was signed. This morning at the Mairie, whither we went quite quietly, nobody was present but the necessary witnesses. I am finishing off this scrap while the preparations for dressing me for dinner are being made. We are to be married at the Church of Ste. Valère at twelve o'clock to-night, after a great party here. My terrors, I must confess, have given me a victim-like appearance and a sham modest air, which will insure me an admiration I do not in the least comprehend. I am delighted to see my poor dear Felipe is just as much abashed as I am. Society is hateful to him. He is like a bat in a glass-shop.

"Happily this day will have a morrow," he whispered in my ear just now, without an idea he was saying anything peculiar.

So shy and ashamed of himself is he, that he would prefer not to see a soul. When the Sardinian Ambassador came to sign our marriage contract, he took me aside and handed me a pearl necklace, the clasp composed of six magnificent diamonds. It was a present from my sister-in-law, the Duchesse de Soria. With the necklace there was a sapphire bracelet, within which is engraved the legend, "*I love thee, though I know thee not.*" Two charming letters were inclosed with these two presents, which I would not accept until I knew I had Felipe's permission. "For," said I to him, "I should not like to see you wear anything I had not given you."

He was quite moved, and kissed my hand, saying:

"Wear them for the sake of the motto and of the affection of the givers, which is genuine."

Saturday Night.

Here then, my poor Renée, you behold the last lines this maiden will ever write you. After the midnight mass we start for a country-place which Felipe,

The Memoirs of Two Young Brides

with the most delicate consideration, has bought in the Nivernais, on the road to Provence. My name is Louise de Macumer even now, but I shall still be Louise de Chaulieu when I leave Paris, a few hours hence. Well, whatever I may be called, I shall never be anything to you except

LOUISE.

XXVII

FROM THE SAME TO THE SAME

October, 1825.

I HAVE never written you a line, my dearest, since we were married at the Mairie, and that is nearly eight months ago, and not a word from you either. This, madame, is too bad!

Well, we started off with post-horses for Chantepleurs, the country-place Macumer had bought in the Nivernais, on the banks of the Loire, some sixty leagues from Paris. Our servants, except my maid, had gone before us to await our coming, and we travelled very rapidly, arriving the following evening. I slept all the way from Paris to the other side of Montargis. The only freedom my lord and master permitted himself was to put his arm around my waist and make me rest my head on his shoulder, on which he had laid several handkerchiefs. This almost maternal solicitude on his part, which prevented him from going to sleep himself, filled me with the strangest and deepest emotion. I fell asleep under the blaze of his dark eyes. I woke, and they were still shining on me with the same fervour, the same love. But what thousands of thoughts had passed through his brain. He had kissed my forehead twice over.

We breakfasted in our carriage at Briare. At half past seven that evening, after we had talked, as you and I have talked at Blois, and admired the Loire as you and I used to admire it together, we passed into the long and splendid avenue of lime, acacia, sycamore and larch trees, that leads up to Chantepleurs. At eight o'clock we were sitting at dinner. At ten we were in a charming Gothic chamber, embellished with everything that modern luxury can invent. My Felipe, whom every one else thinks ugly, seemed to me full of a great beauty—the beauty of goodness, of charm, of tenderness, of the most exquisite refinement. Of passionate desire I did not perceive a trace. All through our journey he had behaved like some friend of fifteen years' standing. He had described, as he so well knows how to do it (he is still the man depicted in his first letter), the frightful tempests he had curbed and forced to die away on his face, as on the surface of the waters.

"There is nothing very terrifying in marriage so far," said I, as I went over to the window and looked out over a beautiful park bathed in the loveliest moonlight and redolent of balmy odours.

He came close to me, put his arm about me again, and said:

"And why should it terrify you? Have I failed in my promises even by one look or gesture? Shall I ever fail in them?"

Never did look or tone wield so mighty a power. His voice stirred every fibre and woke every feeling in me. His glance burnt me like the sun.

"Oh," I cried, "what Moorish perfidy lies beneath this perpetual slavery of yours?"

Dear, he understood me. Therefore, my darling, if I have not written for months, you will guess why, now. I am forced to remind myself of the young girl's strange past, so that I may explain the woman to you. Renée, I understand you now. Neither to her close friend, nor to her mother, nor perhaps even to herself, can a happy young wife speak of her happy marriage. That memory must be buried within her soul, yet another of those feelings which are hers alone, and which can never be described. What! the exquisite fooleries of the heart, the overwhelming impulses of passionate desire, have been dubbed a duty! What monstrous power conceived the notion of forcing woman to trample every refinement and all the instinctive modesty of her nature under foot, by turning these delights into a *duty*? How can these blossoms of the soul, these roses of existence, these poems of intense feeling, be a duty owed to a being she does not love? Rights! and in such sensations! Why, they sprout and blossom under the sun of love; or else their germs are killed by the chill of repugnance and aversion! Love alone can wield such spells. Ah, my noble Renée, you have grown very great in my eyes. I bend the knee before you. Your penetration and clear-sightedness amaze me. Yes, the woman who does not, like me, hide some secret love marriage beneath her legal and public vows, must throw herself on motherhood just as a soul that has lost everything in this life casts itself on the next. One merciless fact is the outcome of everything you have written me—none but superior men really know how to love. I know why now. Man is impelled by two principles. These are desire and feeling. Weak or inferior natures take desire for feeling; whereas in superior natures the effect of their exquisite feeling conceals desire. This feeling, by its excessive strength, inspires them with extreme reserve and, at the same time, with an adoration for the woman. A man's power of feeling naturally coincides with the strength of his mental organization, and thus the man of genius is the only man whose delicacy can approximate to ours. He knows, divines, understands the woman's nature. He bears her on the wings of a passion chastened by the reticence of his own feeling. And when we are swept away by the simultaneous intoxication of mind, heart and senses, we do not fall down to earth; we rise to the celestial spheres, and, unhappily, we have to leave them all too soon. Here, my dear soul, you have the philosophy extracted from my first three months of married life. Felipe is an angel. I can think aloud in his presence. Rhetoric apart, he is my second self. His noble-heartedness is something singular. Possession makes him cling still closer to me. In his very happiness he finds fresh cause to love me. To him

The Memoirs of Two Young Brides

I am the fairest part of his own being. I can see plainly that, far from revealing any deterioration in the object of his delight, the lapse of our married years will only increase his trust, evoke fresh feeling, and strengthen the bond between us. What a blessed frenzy! I am so constituted that happiness leaves a bright glow within me—it warms my soul, it saturates my inner being. The intervals between each delight are like the short nights between summer days. The sun that gilded the heights as it sank to rest finds them scarce cooled when it rises in the sky once more. By what fortunate chance did this come to me from the very outset? My mother had stirred a thousand fears within me. Her forecasts—which struck me as being full of jealousy, though quite free from the slightest pettiness—have been falsified by the event; for your alarms and hers and mine have all been scattered to the winds.

We spent seven and a half months at Chantepleurs, like a pair of runaway lovers who were fleeing from their parents' wrath. Our love has been crowned with flowers of delight, and all our mutual existence is decked with them. One morning when I was particularly happy, my thought, by a sudden revulsion, flew to my Renée and her prudent marriage. And then I divined the nature of your life and fathomed it. Oh, dearest angel, why do we speak a different tongue? Your purely social marriage, and mine, which is nothing but a happy passion, are no more intelligible to each other than the infinite is to the finite. You are

The Memoirs of Two Young Brides

down on the earth; I am in heaven. You are in the human sphere; I in the divine. I **rule by love;** you rule by forethought and duty. I soar so high that if I were to fall I should be shivered into atoms. But I must hold my peace, for I should be ashamed to tell you of all the brightness, the wealth, the ever-fresh delights of such a springtide of love as mine.

We have been in Paris for the last ten days, in a charming house in the Rue du Bac, remodelled by the architect whom Felipe employed to remodel Chantepleurs. I have just been hearing that heavenly music of Rossini's, to which I listened some months since with disquiet in my soul—vexed, although I knew it not, by the curiosity that love brings in its train. Now it is gladdened by the lawful joys of a happy marriage. Every one thinks I have improved in looks, and I take a childish pleasure in hearing myself called Madame.

Renée, my sweet saint, my own happiness brings my thought back perpetually to you. I feel I care for you more than I ever did. I am so devoted to you. I have studied your conjugal existence so deeply by the light of the beginning of my own, and I see you to be so great, so noble, so sublimely virtuous, that I hereby declare myself not your friend only, but your inferior, your sincere admirer. Looking at what my own marriage is, it is almost clear to me that I should have died if it had been otherwise. And yet you live! On what feeling? Tell me that? And, indeed, I will not say one jesting word to you. Derision, my dearest, is the daughter of ignorance. People make a jest of that which they do not understand. "When the recruits begin to laugh, tried soldiers look grave," said the Comte de Chaulieu to me—he, a mere cavalry captain, who had never travelled farther than from Paris to Fontainebleau, and back again from Fontainebleau to Paris. And I have guessed too, my dear love, that you have not told me everything. Yes, you have hidden some wounds from me. You suffer; I can feel it. I have dreamed whole novels about you, far from you as I am, and with nothing to go on but the little you have told me about yourself, to discover the reasons of your conduct.

"She has given wedded life a trial," thought I one evening, "and that which has been bliss to me has been nothing but a misery to her. She has gained nothing by the sacrifices she has made, and she would fain limit their number. She has cloaked her sorrow under the pompous axioms of social morality." Ah, Renée, one admirable thing about enjoyment is that it needs neither religion, nor fuss, nor fine words. It is everything in itself. Whereas men, to justify the vile ingenuity which has compassed our slavery and vassalage, have heaped up theories and maxims. If your self-immolation is noble and sublime, can my bliss, sheltered by the white and gold canopy of Mother Church, and signed with due flourish by the grumpiest of Mayors, be a monstrosity? For the honour of the law, for your own sake—but, above all, to complete my own happiness—I would have you happy, my

The Memoirs of Two Young Brides

Renée. Oh, tell me you feel a little love creeping into your heart for the Louis who worships you! Tell me that Hymen's solemn and symbolic torch has served to do something more than reveal the darkness about you. For love, my darling, is to our moral being just exactly what the sun is to the earth. I can not help reverting to the blaze that shines on me, and that will end, I fear, by burning me quite up. Dear Renée, you who in the ecstasy of your friendship would say to me under the vine arbour at the convent, "I love you so dearly, Louise, that if God were to make himself manifest to me I would ask him to give me all the sorrows of life and you all its joys. Yes, I have a passionate longing to suffer." Well, my darling, I feel like that for you now, and I implore the Almighty to bestow half my joys on you.

Listen to me! I have guessed that under the name of Louis de l'Estorade you hide an ambitious woman. So see he is elected Deputy at the next elections. He will be nearly forty then, and as the House will not meet till six months after that, he will be just the right age for a political man. Come to Paris, and you will see.

My father and the friends I shall make for myself will recognise your value, and if your old father-in-law chooses to entail his estate, we'll get Louis created a Count. That will be something gained; and then, besides, we shall be together!

XXVIII

RENÉE DE L'ESTORADE TO LOUISE DE MACUMER

December, 1825.

My Blissful Louise: You have made me dizzy. I have been sitting here for a moment alone on a bench at the foot of a small bare rock, my arms dropping wearily down, holding your letter, on which a few tears have lain glistening in the setting sun. In the distance the Mediterranean glitters like a steel sword-blade. Two or three sweet-scented trees shadow the seat, about which I have planted a huge jasmine bush, some honeysuckles, and Spanish broom. Some of these days the boulder will be all covered with climbing plants. There is Virginia creeper on it already. But winter is upon us, and all the greenery has grown like a shabby hanging. When I am sitting here nobody ever comes near me, for every one knows I want to be alone. The bench goes by the name of "Louise's seat." Does not that tell you that even when I am here alone, I am not alone?

When I tell you all these details, which will seem so trivial to you, when I describe the verdant hope that already clothes this bare steep rock, which some whim of Nature has crowned with a splendid um-

The Memoirs of Two Young Brides

brella pine, I do it because here thoughts and ideas have come to me, to which I cling.

Even as I rejoiced in your happy wedlock, and (why should I not acknowledge all the truth to you?) even as I envied it with all my might, I felt within me the first stirrings of my unborn child, and that throb in the depths of my physical existence straightway found its answer in my inmost soul. This obscure sensation—a premonition, a delight, a pain, a promise, a reality, all in one—this happiness which belongs to me alone in all the world and lies a secret betwixt me and God—this strange mystery, told me that my rock should some day be carpeted with flowers, that the joyous laughter of children should ring about it, that my womb was blessed at last, and that I was destined to bring forth life in full measure. I knew then that I was born for motherhood, and this first certainty that I bore another life within my own brought a most blessed consolation to me. An infinite joy had crowned all the long days of sacrifice which have already made Louis so happy.

"Sacrifice," said I to myself, "art thou not greater than love? Art thou not the deepest bliss of all, because thou art an abstract, a life-giving bliss? Art thou not, O Sacrifice! that creative power far greater and higher than its own effects? Art thou not the mysterious, untiring divinity hidden behind all the innumerable spheres, in some undiscovered spot through which each world must pass in turn? Sacrifice! alone with its secret full of silent joys which none suspect, and on which no profane eye ever rests. Sacrifice! that jealous and overwhelming, that mighty and victorious deity—exhaustless because he is bound up with the very nature of things, and therefore immutable in spite of all the outpourings of his strength. Sacrifice! that is the watchword of my life."

Your love, Louise, is the result of Felipe's effort upon you. But the radiance I cast over this family will be perpetually reflected back from my little circle upon me. Your fair, golden harvest is short-lived. But will not mine be all the more enduring because it has ripened late? It will be constantly renewed. Love is the daintiest theft Society has ever contrived to practise upon Nature. But is not maternity Nature's own joy? My tears change to a smile of happiness. Love makes my Louis a happy man. But marriage has brought me motherhood, and I am determined to be happy too. Then I came slowly back to my green-shuttered house to write this letter to you.

So, my dearest, the most natural and the most surprising event in a woman's life took place in mine five months ago. But I may tell you, in an undertone, that neither my heart nor my intellect have been one whit stirred thereby. I see all those about me are delighted. The future grandfather encroaches on his grandson's rights—he has grown like a child himself. The father assumes a serious and anxious air. They all overwhelm me with attentions, and they all talk about the bliss of being a mother. Alack! I alone feel nothing at all, and dare not betray the state of utter indifference in which I am. I am constrained to fib a little so as not to sadden their joy. As with you I can be perfectly frank, I will confess that, as far as I have gone, my maternity has no existence, except in my imagination.

The news of my condition was as great a surprise to Louis as it was to me. Is that not enough to show you the child came of its own accord, on no other summons than its father's impatient and eagerly expressed desire? Chance, my dear soul, is the God of maternity. Although, so our doctor declares, these same chances harmonize with the will of Nature, he does not attempt to deny that the children so appropriately described as "love-children" probably turn out both beautiful and clever, and that their lives often seem sheltered, as it were, by the happiness which shone like a beaming star over the moment of their conception. So it may be, my Louise, that motherhood will bring you delights which I shall never know. Perhaps a woman loves the child of a man she adores, as you adore your Felipe, better than she can love the child of a husband whom she has married in cold blood, to whom she gives herself as a duty and for the sake, in fact, of reaching woman's full estate. These thoughts, which I keep in the bottom of my heart, increase the seriousness with which I look forward to becoming a mother. But, as there can be no family unless there are children, I long to hasten the time when those family joys, which are to be my whole existence, shall begin for me. At

The Memoirs of Two Young Brides

the present moment my life is one of mystery and expectation, the nauseating discomfort of which no doubt prepares a woman to endure still greater suffering. I watch myself. In spite of all Louis's efforts—his love showers care, and gentleness, and affection, on me—I have some dim alarms with which are mingled the distaste, the uneasiness, the strange fancies, peculiar to my condition. If I am to tell you the things just as they are, and risk inspiring you with some aversion for my present employment, I will confide to you that I have the most inexplicable fancy for a certain sort of orange—an eccentric taste, which nevertheless comes quite naturally to me. My husband goes over to Marseilles to procure me the finest oranges to be had. He has had them sent from Malta, from Portugal, from Corsica. But all those oranges I leave untouched. I hurry off to Marseilles, sometimes I even walk there, and there I devour vile, half-rotten things that are sold four for a sou, in a little street running down to the port, close to the Hôtel de Ville. The blue and green mould upon these oranges shines like diamonds to my eyes. They are like flowers to me. I remember nothing of their deathly odour, and only feel that their flavour excites my palate, that their warmth is wine-like, and their taste delicious. Well, dear soul, there you have the first amorous sensation I have known. Those disgusting oranges are my joy. You do not long for Felipe more than I long for that rotten fruit. I even slip out on the sly, I tear off, with active step, to Marseilles. I shiver with voluptuous expectation as I approach the street. I am in terror lest there should be no more over-ripe oranges in the shop. I fly at them, I eat them up, I devour them in the open street. To me they are fruits grown in Paradise, and their pulp the most exquisite of all foods. I have seen Louis turn his head away to avoid the stench they exhale. I have recalled Obermann's terrible saying in that dreary elegy which I am sorry I ever read, "*Les racines s'abreuvent dans une eau fetide.*" "The roots quench their thirst in a fetid pool." Since I have begun to eat these oranges the nausea from which I suffered has disappeared and my health is quite restored. These depraved longings must have some meaning, since they are a natural symptom, and quite half of the sex is subject to such fancies, some of them really monstrous. When my condition becomes very apparent, I shall never go outside this place. I should not like any one to see me under such circumstances.

I am longing eagerly to know at what moment of one's life maternity begins. It can hardly be in the midst of the frightful suffering I so greatly dread.

Farewell, my happy creature! Farewell, friend, in whom I live again and in whose person I am able to conceive those exquisite delights, that jealousy over a single look, those whispered words, and all those joys that wrap us round as though in a different atmosphere, a different state of being, a different light, a different life. Ah, pretty one, I know what love is too. Never tire of telling me everything. Let us keep our agreement faithfully. I will spare you nothing. And, to close this letter seriously, I will tell you that as I read yours over again, a deep and unconquerable terror fell on me. It seemed to me as though this insolent love of yours were setting God at defiance. If sorrow, that sovereign lord of the whole earth, finds no place at your festive board, will not his rage be stirred against you? Show me the glorious fortune he has not overthrown? Ah, Louise, don't forget your prayers in the midst of all your happiness. Do good to others, be kind and charitable. Let your modesty ward off adversity from you. Since my marriage I have grown even more religious than I was in the convent. You tell me nothing about religion in your Paris letters. It strikes me that in your worship of Felipe you look (contrary to the proverb) more to the saint than to God himself. But these terrors of mine spring from my too great love. You do go to church together, don't you? And you do good by stealth? You'll think this last bit of my letter very countrified, perhaps. But consider that my fears are dictated by my extreme affection—an affection, as La Fontaine understood the feeling, that grows uneasy and takes fright over a dream, an idea that is no more than a shadow. You deserve to be happy, seeing that in the midst of all your happiness you think of me, just as in my monotonous existence —a trifle dull, but full enough; sober, but fruitful— I think of you. All blessings go with you, then!

XXIX

M. DE L'ESTORADE TO THE BARONNE DE MACUMER

December, 1825.

MADAME: My wife is anxious you should not be informed of the joyful event which has just occurred through the commonplace medium of a formal announcement. She has just been confined of a fine boy, and we shall defer his christening until the period of your return to your country-house at Chantepleurs. We are in hopes, Renée and I, that you will push on as far as La Crampade, and stand godmother to our first-born son. In this hope I have registered the child under the names of Armand Louis de l'Estorade. Our dear Renée has suffered horribly, but with the patience of an angel—you know her nature. She has been supported through this first maternal trial by the certainty that she was conferring happiness on us all. Without indulging in the somewhat absurd exaggeration of a father who enjoys his paternal dignity for the first time, I may assure you that little Armand is a splendid fellow; but you will have no difficulty in believing that, when I tell you he has Renée's face and Renée's eyes. This proves his sense already. Now that the doctor and the *accoucheur* have both assured us that Renée is not in the slightest danger—for she is nursing the child, he thrives apace, and his mother's vigorous nature insures a liberal supply of nourishment—we are free, my father and I, to luxuriate in our happiness. So great is our joy, madame, so deep, so full, it has so stirred our household, it has so altered my dear wife's existence, that, for your own sake, I wish you may soon be in her case. Renée has prepared a set of rooms which I wish I could make worthy of our guest. You would be welcome to them with fraternal cordiality, at all events, though splendour may be lacking.

Renée has told me, madame, of your intentions with regard to us, and I seize this occasion of thanking you for them, all the more eagerly because nothing could be more seasonable. The birth of my boy has reconciled my father to sacrifices such as an old man is somewhat loath to face. He has just bought two properties. La Crampade will now bring in some thirty thousand francs a year. My father is about to solicit the King's permission to entail this estate, but if you obtain him the title you mentioned in your last letter, you will already have done something for your godson.

As for myself, I will follow your advice with the sole object of enabling you and Renée to be together during the Parliamentary session. I am studying hard, and endeavouring to become what is known as "a specialist." But nothing will give me more courage than to know that you will protect my little

The Memoirs of Two Young Brides

Armand. So give us your promise, pray, that you will come, in all your beauty and your grace, your grandeur and your wit, to play the part of fairy godmother to my eldest boy. Thus, madame, you will add eternal gratitude to those feelings of respectful affection with which I have the honour to remain, your very humble and obedient servant,

LOUIS DE L'ESTORADE.

XXX

FROM LOUISE DE MACUMER TO RENÉE DE L'ESTORADE

January, 1826.

MACUMER woke me up just now, and brought me your husband's letter, my dear love. The first thing I say shall be " yes." We shall be going to Chantepleurs toward the end of April. To me it will be pleasure heaped on pleasure to travel to see you, and to stand godmother to your first child. Only I must have Macumer for the godfather. A Catholic alliance with any other sponsor would be hateful to me. Ah, if you could have seen the expression on his face when I told him that, you would know how deeply the darling loves me.

"I am all the more anxious that we should go to La Crampade together, Felipe," said I, "because perhaps a child will come to us there. I want to be a mother, too, . . . although, indeed, I should be sorely divided between a child and you. To begin with, if I were to see you prefer any creature, even my own son, to me, I don't know what would happen! Medea may have been right after all, the ancients had their good points."

He burst out laughing. So, dear soul, you have

The Memoirs of Two Young Brides

the fruit without having had the flowers, and I have the flowers without the fruit. The contrast between our fates is still kept up. There is enough philosophy in us to make us cast about, one of these days, for the meaning and moral of it all. Pshaw! I have only been married ten months; you must admit there's not much time lost as yet.

We are living the life—dissipated, and yet full—of a happy couple. Our days always seem to us much too short. Society, to which I have returned in the garb of a married woman, admires the Baronne de Macumer more than it admired Louise de Chaulieu. A happy love imparts a beauty of its own. As we drive together, Felipe and I, on one of these sunny, frosty January days, when the trees of the Champs-Elysées are laden with white starry clusters—united now, in the face of all Paris, on the very spot where we were parted only a year ago—thoughts crowd on me in thousands, and I am afraid lest, as you foresaw in your last letter, my insolence may grow too great.

If I know nothing of the joys of maternity, you shall describe them to me, and through you I will be a mother, too—but, to my thinking, nothing can be compared to the delights of love. You'll think me very odd, but ten times certainly in the last ten months I have caught myself wishing I might die when I was thirty, in all the glory of my life, crowned with the blossoms of love and lapped in its delights; to go my way, satisfied, without a shadow of disappointment, having lived in the sunshine, in the blue

The Memoirs of Two Young Brides

ether, even to die, in part, perhaps, of love, my garland intact, even to every leaf, and all my illusions with me still. Just think what it must be to have a young heart in an old body; to meet dull, cold faces where every one, even those for whom we cared not, used to smile upon us; to be, in fact, a venerable woman—oh, that must be hell on earth!

We have had our first quarrel on this very subject, Felipe and I. I wanted him to have courage, when I was thirty, to kill me in my sleep, without my knowing it, so that I might pass out of one dream into another. The wretch wouldn't do it! I threatened to leave him alone in the world, and he turned white, poor boy! This mighty Minister has become a regular baby, my dear soul. You would never believe how much youth and simplicity have lain hidden in his heart. Now that I think aloud with him, just as I do with you, and have taken him thoroughly into my confidence, we are full of admiration for each other.

My dear, the two lovers, Felipe and Louise, are anxious to send a present to the young mother. We should like to send something that would please you, so tell me frankly what you want, for we don't at all cling to the ordinary system of giving a surprise.

What we should like is to send you something which may recall us to you constantly by a pleasant memory, and by something for daily use, and which will not easily wear out. Our cheeriest, most familiar, most lively meal, because it is that at which we are always alone, is our breakfast. I have there-

The Memoirs of Two Young Brides

fore planned to send you a special service called a breakfast service, which shall be ornamented with figures of children. If you approve of my idea, answer me quickly. For if I am to bring it to you, I must order it, and these Paris artists are so many "*Rois fainéants.*" This shall be my offering to Lucina.

Farewell, dear nursing mother! I wish you all maternal happiness, and I wait longingly for your first letter, which will tell me everything, will it not? That "*accoucheur*" made me shudder—the very word in your husband's letter, struck, not my eyes, but my heart. Poor Renée, a child costs a heavy price, doesn't it? I'll tell that godson of mine how much he ought to love you.

A thousand tender loves, my dear one!

XXXI

FROM RENÉE DE L'ESTORADE TO LOUISE DE MACUMER

It is almost three months now since my child was born, and I have never been able to find a single tiny moment to write to you, my dear soul. When you have a child of your own you will forgive me this, even more freely than you do at present—for you have punished me a little by sending me so few letters. Write to me, my dear love. Tell me about all your gaieties, paint your happiness to me in the brightest hues; don't spare the ultramarine for fear of distressing me, for I, too, am happy—happier than you would ever imagine.

I went in great state, according to the custom of our old Provençal families, to return thanks for my safe delivery at the parish church. The two grandfathers, Louis's father and my own, supported me on either side. Ah, never did I bend the knee before God in such a passion of gratitude. There are so many things for me to tell you, so many feelings to describe, that I know not where to begin. But out of the midst of the confusion one radiant memory rises, the thought of the prayer I offered in that church.

The Memoirs of Two Young Brides

When I felt myself transformed into a rejoicing mother, on the very spot where as a girl I had doubted of life and of my future, I fancied I saw the Virgin on the altar bowing her head to me and showing me the Divine Child, who seemed to smile upon me. What a blessed overflowing of heavenly love I felt as I held out our little Armand to receive the benediction of the priest, who touched him with the chrism, until he can be fully baptized!

But you will see us together, my Armand and me. My child—why now I've called you my child!—but indeed it is the sweetest word that ever rises to a mother's heart, and mind, and lips—well then, dear child, I dragged myself about our garden, wearily enough all through those last two months, weighed down by the discomfort of my burden. I did not know how dear and tender it was, in spite of all the misery it was costing me. I felt such terrors, such deadly presentiments, that no amount of curiosity could overcome them. I reasoned with myself, told myself there was nothing to dread in any natural event—I promised myself the joys of motherhood. But alas! I felt no stir at my heart, even when I thought of the child, which stirred so briskly within me; and, my dear, that kind of stir may be pleasant to a woman who has already borne children, but in the first instance the griever of an unseen life brings one more astonishment than satisfaction. I give you my own experience, you know me to be neither insincere nor theatrical, and my child was more the gift of God—for it is God who sends us children—than that of a beloved husband. Let us bid farewell to these bygone sorrows, which, as I think, I shall never know again.

When the awful moment came upon me I had gathered up such powers of endurance and I had expected such cruel anguish that, so I am told, I bore the hideous torture in the most astounding fashion. For about an hour, dear love, I was sunk in a condition of prostration which was something like a dream. I felt as if I were two persons. An outer husk, torn, tortured, agonized; and an inner soul that was all calm and peace. While I was in that strange condition my sufferings seemed to blossom like a crown of flowers above my head. It was as though a huge rose that sprang upward out of my skull grew larger and larger, and wrapped me all about. The rosy colour of the blood-stained blossom was in the very air, and everything was red to me. Then, when I had reached a point at which body and soul seemed ready to part company, I felt a pang that made me think I was going to die that instant. I screamed aloud, and then I found fresh strength to bear fresh pains. Suddenly the hideous concert was hushed within me by the delicious sound of the little creature's shrill wail. No words of mine will ever express that moment to you. It seemed to me that the whole world had been crying out with me, that everything that was not pain was clamour, and then that my baby's feeble cry had hushed it all. They laid me back in my great bed. It was like entering Paradise to me, in spite of my excessive weakness. Then two or three people with joyful faces and tearful eyes held out the child to me. My dear, I cried out in horror:

"What a little monkey!" I said. "Are you sure it is a baby?" I asked. And I lay back once more, rather grieved at not feeling more maternal.

"Don't distress yourself, my dear," said my mother, who had constituted herself my nurse, "you've borne the finest child that ever was seen. Take care not to excite yourself; you must apply your whole mind now to growing dull; you must be just exactly like the cow that grazes for the sake of having milk."

So I went to sleep, firmly resolved to do as Nature bade me. Ah, dearest, the waking up out of all that pain, those confused feelings, those first days during which everything is dim and painful and uncertain, was something divine. The darkness was lightened by a sensation the delights of which surpassed that of my child's first cry. My heart, my soul, my being, an individuality hitherto unknown was roused out of the shell in which it had been lying suffering and dull, just as the flower springs from the root at the blazing summons of the sun. The little rogue was put to my breast; that was my "*fiat lux.*" Of a sudden I knew I was a mother. Here was happiness, delight—ineffable delight, although it be one which involves some suffering. O my beautiful, jealous Louise, how you will prize a pleasure which lies between ourselves, the child, and God! The only earthly thing the little creature knows is his mother's breast, that is the only spot that shines to him in all the world. He loves it with all his strength; he thinks of nothing but the fountain of his life; he comes to it, and goes away to sleep, and wakes to come back to it again. There is an ineffable love in the very touch of his lips, and when I feel them, they give me pain and pleasure at once—a pleasure that becomes an actual pain—a pain that ends in delight. I can give no explanation of the sensation I feel radiate from my breast to the very springs of my life—for it seems as though it were the centre of a thousand rays, that rejoice my heart and soul. To bear a child is nothing, but to nurse it is a perpetual maternity. O Louise, no lover's caress can equal that of the little pink hands that move about so softly and try to cling to life. What looks the child casts, first at its mother's breast, and then at her eyes. What dreams she dreams, as she watches his lips clinging to his precious possession. All one's mental powers, as well as all one's bodily strength, are called into action. One's corporal life and one's intelligence are both kept busy. Every desire is more than satisfied.

That heavenly sensation of my child's first cry—which was to me what the first sunbeam must have been to the earth—came back to me when I felt my milk flow into his mouth, and it came back to me again just now, when I read his first thought in his first smile. He laughed, my dear. That laugh, that look, that pressure, that cry, those four delights are infinite—they stir the very bottom of one's heart and

The Memoirs of Two Young Brides

touch strings which nothing but they can reach. The spheres must be bound to the Deity, even as a child is bound to every fibre of his mother's being. God must be one great mother's heart. There is nothing visible, nor perceptible, in conception, nor even in the months of waiting; but to nurse a child, Louise, is a constant happiness. You watch the daily progress of your work, you see the milk grow into flesh, and blossom in the dainty fingers, so like flowers and quite as delicate—you see it form slender and transparent nails, and silky hair, and little restless feet. A child's feet—why, they have a language of their own—a child's first expression lies in them. To nurse a child, Louise, is to watch with astonished eye an hourly process of transformation. When the baby cries, you do not hear it with your ears, but with your heart. When its eyes smile, or its lips, or it kicks with its feet, you understand all it means as though God wrote it for you on space in letters of fire. Nothing else in the world possesses the smallest interest for you. The father . . . you are ready to kill him if he dares wake the child. The mother by herself is the whole world to her babe, just as the babe is the whole world to its mother. She feels so certain that her existence is shared by another, she is so amply rewarded for her care and suffering—for there is suffering . . . as every nursing mother finds out for herself.

In these five months my young monkey has grown into the prettiest creature that any mother ever

The Memoirs of Two Young Brides

bathed with her happy tears, washed, brushed, combed, and adorned, for God himself only knows the unwearying delight with which a mother dresses, and undresses, brushes and washes and kisses her little blossom. My monkey, then, is not a monkey any longer, but a baby, as my English nurse calls him, a pink-and-white baby, and feeling himself loved, he doesn't scream so very much—but the real truth is that I hardly ever leave him, and I try to pervade his very soul with mine.

Dearest, I feel something in my heart for Louis now which is not love, but which must complete the feeling in the case of a woman who does love. I am not sure that this tender regard, this gratitude, which is quite free from any interested feeling, is not something beyond love. According to all you have told me about it, my darling, there is something frightfully earthly about love, whereas there is something very religious and divine in the affection of a happy mother for the man who has given her these endearing and never-ending joys. A mother's joy is a light shining over and illuminating the future, and reflecting back over the past, which it fills with delightful memories.

And indeed old M. de l'Estorade and his son are kinder than ever to me. I have become a new person in their eyes. Their words and looks go to my very heart, for they rejoice over me afresh each time they see or speak to me. The old grandfather is growing childish, I think; he gazes upon me with admiration. The first time I came downstairs to breakfast and he

The Memoirs of Two Young Brides

saw me eating with them and nursing his grandson, he began to cry. Those tears in the dry eyes which rarely shine with anything save thoughts of money, were an inexpressible delight to me—they made me feel as if the old fellow understood my joy. As for Louis, he was ready to tell the very trees and stones on the high-road that he had a son. He spends whole hours watching your godson asleep; he says he doesn't know if he will ever grow accustomed to seeing him. These demonstrations of excessive delight have revealed the extent of their fears and terrors to me, and Louis has ended by confessing that he had grave doubts, and indeed believed, he was fated never to have a child at all. My poor Louis has suddenly and vastly improved. He studies still harder than before. As for me, dear soul, I grow happier and happier every moment. Every hour adds some fresh bond between a mother and her child. The feeling within my heart convinces me that this maternal sentiment is imperishable, natural, and unfailing—whereas I strongly suspect that love has its intermissions. People do not love each other in the same fashion at every moment —the flowers embroidered into the tissue of this life are not always of the brightest colours. And then, love may and must come to an end. But motherhood need fear no decline; it deepens with the child's needs and develops with its growth. Is it not a passion, a need, a feeling, a duty, a necessity, and happiness, all at once? Yes, my dearest; this is the woman's own special life. It satisfies our thirst for sacrifice, and it is free from the disturbing effects of jealousy. And perhaps it is the only point, so far as we are concerned, on which Nature and Society are agreed. In this matter Society certainly has enriched Nature, for it has strengthened the maternal sentiment, by the addition of the family spirit, with its continuity of name and race and fortune. What love must a woman lavish on the beloved being who has first acquainted her with such delights, has called the strength of her being into action, and taught her the great art of motherhood! The birthright of the elder son, which is as old as the world itself, and is mingled with the origin of every society, seems to me not open to question. How many things does a child teach its mother! We give so many hostages to virtue by the incessant protection we owe to the feeble creature born of us, that no wife has reached her true sphere unless she is a mother. Then alone does she unfold all her strength, perform the full duties of her life, and enjoy all its happiness and all its pleasures. A wife who is not a mother is an incomplete being—a failure. Make haste to be a mother, my dear one, then will your present happiness be multiplied by all my joys. . . .

I broke off writing because I heard your godson cry. I can hear him crying from the bottom of the garden. I cannot send this letter without saying one word of good-bye to you. I have just read it over, and I am startled by the commonplaceness of the feeling it expresses. I fear, alas! that every mother has felt what I feel, and must express it in the same

The Memoirs of Two Young Brides

fashion. And I fear you'll laugh at me, just as people laugh at the simplicity of every father who talks about the beauty and intelligence of his children and thinks each one of them has something very remarkable about it. Well, dearest love, here is the great point of my letter—I will say it again: I am as happy now as I was unhappy before. This country-house, which is now to be a property settled on my eldest son, is my Promised Land. I have crossed my desert at last. A thousand loves to you, my dearest love! Write to me. I can read your description of your happiness and your love without shedding tears, now. Farewell!

XXXII

FROM MME. DE MACUMER TO MME. DE L'ESTORADE

March, 1826.

How's this, my love? For three months I have not written a line to you nor heard of you. . . . I'm the most guilty of the two, for I owe you a letter. But still I have never known you to be huffy.

We took your silence, Macumer and I, to mean consent as to the breakfast service with the figures of children, and the pretty things will be sent off to Marseilles this very day. These Paris people have taken six months to make them. And it really woke me with a shock when Macumer suggested we should go and look at the service before the silversmith packed it up. Suddenly it struck me we had never exchanged a word since that letter of yours that made me feel myself a mother in your person.

Dearest, this dreadful Paris—there's my sole excuse. I am still waiting to hear yours. Oh, what an abyss Society is! Didn't I tell you long ago that in Paris one has no chance of being anything but a *Parisienne*? The life here destroys all sentiment. It eats up all your time. It would eat up your very heart if you were not careful. What a wonderful master-

The Memoirs of Two Young Brides

piece is that character of Celimène in Molière's Misanthrope! She is the woman of fashion of Louis XIV's time, and of ours—the woman of fashion of all times, in short. What would become of me without my buckler—in other words, my love for Felipe? And indeed only this morning, thinking of it all, I told him he was my salvation. Though my evenings are all taken up with parties, balls, concerts, theatres, I can come back from them to the delights of love, to the sweet follies that gladden my heart and heal the stings the world inflicts upon it. I have never dined at home except on the days when we have entertained what are called one's friends, and I have never sat at home except on my reception days. I have a day of my own, the Wednesday, on which I receive my company. I have entered the lists with Mme. d'Espard, and Mme. de Maufrigneuse, and the old Duchesse de Lenoncourt. My house is considered a very pleasant one. I allowed myself to be made the fashion when I saw how happy my Felipe was in my success. My forenoons I devote to him—for from four o'clock in the afternoon till two o'clock in the morning I belong to Paris. Macumer is a most perfect host, so witty and yet so serious, so genuinely noble and so absolutely gracious—he would make himself loved even by a woman who had married him in the first place for her own convenience. My father and mother have departed to Madrid. Once Louis XVIII was dead the Duchesse easily persuaded our good-natured King Charles X to appoint her charming poet to the Embassy, and she has carried him off as an *attaché*. My brother, the Duc de Rhétoré, condescends to consider me a superior woman. As for the Comte de Chaulieu, that carpet-knight owes me undying gratitude. Before my father's departure my fortune was applied to settling a landed property worth forty thousand francs a year upon him, and his marriage with Mlle. de Mortsauf, a great heiress from Touraine, is quite a settled thing. To avoid the extinction of the titles of Lenoncourt and Givry, the King is about to grant my brother the succession to the names, titles, and arms of these two houses. How, indeed, could his Majesty permit two such splendid names and their proud motto, *Faciem semper monstramus,* to drop out of existence? Mlle. de Mortsauf, who is the grandchild and sole heiress of the Duc de Lenoncourt—Givry will, I hear, have over a hundred thousand francs a year. My father has only made one stipulation—that the Chaulieu arms should be borne in an escutcheon of pretense on those of Lenoncourt. So my brother will be the Duc de Lenoncourt. Young M. de Mortsauf, to whom the whole of this fortune should have passed, is in the last stage of consumption; his death is expected at any moment. Next winter, when the mourning for him is over, the marriage will take place. I am told I shall find Madeleine de Mortsauf a most delightful sister-in-law. Thus, as you see, my father's argument was sound. This result has gained me the admiration of many people, and my marriage is now accounted for. Out of affection

The Memoirs of Two Young Brides

for my grandmother, the Prince de Talleyrand makes a great deal of Macumer, and thus our success is quite complete. Society, which began by finding fault with me, now lavishes approval on me. In short, I am now a power in this very Paris where, less than two years ago, I was so insignificant a person. Macumer sees his good fortune envied by every one about him, for I am " the wittiest woman in Paris." You know there are a score of " the wittiest women in Paris " in this city. The men coo words of admiration in my ear, or content themselves with expressing it by hungry glances. Really this concert of longing and admiration brings such a never-ending satisfaction to one's vanity, that I am now able to understand the excessive expenditure into which some women fall in their desire to enjoy these frail and fleeting joys. Such triumphs intoxicate one's pride, one's vanity, one's conceit, and every feeling, in short, that has to do with self. The perpetual worship so gets into one's head, that I never wonder when I see a woman grow selfish, forgetful, and frivolous in the midst of all her gaities. Society does certainly affect the brain. We shower the blossoms of our heart and intellect, our most precious hours, our most liberal efforts, on people who repay us with jealousy and empty smiles, and exchange the base coin of their empty phrases, their vain compliments and adulation, for the gold ingots of our courage, our sacrifice, and all the ingenuity we use to be beautiful, well dressed, witty, affable, and unfailingly delightful. We know what a costly game it is, we know we are cheated, and yet, in spite of all, every one of us is devoted to it. Ah, dearest love, how one longs for a faithful heart, how precious are my Felipe's love and devotion, how dear you are to me! With what delight am I now preparing to turn my back on the play-acting here in the Rue de Bac, and in every Paris drawing-room, and to seek repose at Chantepleurs. In fine, after reading over your letter, I feel I shall have described this infernal paradise called Paris most truly when I tell you it is impossible for any woman of fashion to be a mother.

I shall see you soon, my darling. We shall not delay more than a week at Chantepleurs, and we shall be with you toward the tenth of May. So we are to meet again, after two years' separation. How things have changed! We are both of us women, now. I am the happiest of Mistresses; you the happiest of Mothers. Though I have not written, my dearest love, it is not because I have forgotten you. And that monkey of a godson of mine—is he still pretty? Does he do me credit? I should like to have seen him take his first step in the world—but Macumer tells me even the most precocious children can hardly walk at ten months old. Well, we'll have a rare gossip, as they say at Blois, and I shall see whether, as many people declare, a baby spoils one's figure.

P. S.—If you send me an answer, most noble mother! address your letter to Chantepleurs. I am just starting.

XXXIII

FROM MME. DE L'ESTORADE TO MME. DE MACUMER

ALACK, my child, if ever you have a baby of your own, you'll find out whether there's any possibility of writing during the first two months of one's nursing. We are fairly worn-out, my English nurse, Mary, and I. But I know I haven't told you that I insist upon doing everything myself. Before the child was born I made all his clothes, and embroidered and trimmed all his caps myself. I am a slave, my dear, a slave all day and all night. First of all, Armand-Louis must be nursed whenever he chooses, and he always chooses. Then he has to be perpetually washed and tidied up, and dressed, and his mother so delights in watching him when he is asleep, and singing songs to him, and carrying him about in her arms when the weather is fine, that there is no time left for her to attempt to attend to herself. Well, while you had the gay world, I had my child—our child. How rich and full my life is! Oh, my dear, I am looking for your coming—you shall see. But I'm afraid his teething is beginning, and that you'll think him very noisy and fretful. He has not cried much as yet, for

The Memoirs of Two Young Brides

I am always by. Children only cry because they feel a want which nobody guesses, but I am perpetually on the track of his. Oh, my dearest, how my heart-life has widened, while you have been narrowing yours down by setting it to serve the gay world. I am expecting you with all the eagerness of a hermit. I am longing for your opinion of l'Estorade, just as you, I am sure, long to know mine of Macumer. Write me your last stopping-place—my two men would like to go out to meet our illustrious guests. Come then, my Queen of Paris! come to our poor country-house, where you will be most lovingly **welcomed**.

XXXIV

MME. DE MACUMER TO VICOMTESSE DE L'ESTORADE

April, 1826.

DEAREST: The address on this letter will inform you of the success of my endeavours. Your father-in-law is now the Comte de l'Estorade. I was determined not to leave Paris without having obtained your wish for you, and I write this in the presence of the Garde des Sceaux, who has just come to tell me the decree is actually signed.

We shall meet before long.

XXXV

THE SAME TO THE SAME

MARSEILLES, *July*.

My sudden departure will have astonished you, and I am ashamed of it. But since I am always truthful, and since I love you just as much as ever, I am going to tell you the whole thing frankly in two words—I am horribly jealous. Felipe looked at you too much, you used to have little conversations at the foot of your rock that put me to torture, soured my temper, and were altering my whole nature. That Spanish beauty of yours must have reminded him of his own country, and of that Maria Heredia, of whom I am jealous—for I am jealous of his past. Your magnificent black hair, and your splendid dark eyes, your brow, eloquent of the joys of motherhood—the shadows of bygone anguish just touching their radiant light, the bloom of your Southern skin, whiter even than that which goes with my fair hair, your noble outline, your white bosom, shining under your laces as though it were some exquisite fruit to which my pretty godson clings—all these things pain my eyes and pain my heart. In vain did I put corn-flowers in my hair, or brighten the dulness of my fair tresses with cherry-coloured ribbon—everything paled before a Renée such as I had not dreamt I should find in the oasis of La Crampade.

Besides, Felipe was too covetous of the child, and I was beginning to hate it. Yes! I envied the insolent baby-life that fills your house and peoples it with laughter and with noise.

I read regret in Macumer's eyes, and cried over it two whole nights in secret. I suffered agonies while I was with you. You are too beautiful a woman and too happy a mother for me to be able to stay with you. Ah, hypocrite—and you complained! To begin with, your l'Estorade is a charming fellow; he talks very well; his black hair streaked with white is good to look at; he has fine eyes, and his manners have just that Southern touch which is attractive. From what I have seen, I am certain he will sooner or later be elected Deputy for the Bouches du Rhône, and he will make his way in the Chamber—for I shall always be ready to serve you in everything that concerns your ambition. The sufferings of his exile have given him that air of calm and steadiness which always seems to me to be half the battle in politics. In my view, my dear, the greatest thing in political life is to look solemn. And indeed I am always telling Macumer he must be a very great statesman.

To sum it up, now that I am quite certain of your happiness, I am off at full speed to Chantepleurs, where I expect Felipe to make me, too, a mother. I will not have you there till I am nursing a child as beautiful as yours. I deserve every name you choose to call me—I am absurd and vile—I have no sense. Alas! all that comes to a woman when she is jealous. I bear you no ill-will, but I was in misery, and you will forgive me for having fled my suffering. In another two days I should have done something foolish—oh, yes, I should have committed some sin against good taste. In spite of the rage that tore my heart, I am glad to have been with you, I am glad to have seen you—so beautiful in your fruitful motherhood, and my friend still, amid your maternal joys, just as I still am yours, in the midst of all my love. Why, even here at Marseilles, a few steps from you, I am proud of you already—proud of the noble mother of children you will be. How truly you have divined your own vocation—for you seem to me to be born more of the mother than the mistress, just as I am born for love rather than for maternity. There are some women who can neither be the one thing nor the other; they are either too ugly or too stupid. A good mother, and a wife who is her husband's mistress, must be perpetually exerting their intelligence and their judgment, and must know how to bring all the most exquisite feminine qualities to bear at any moment. Oh, I have watched you well. And does not that tell you, my darling, that I have admired you? Your children will be happy, they will be well brought up, lapped in your tenderness, warmed by the beams of your heart's love.

You can tell your Louis the truth about my de-

The Memoirs of Two Young Brides

parture, but present it in some creditable light to your father-in-law, who seems to be your man of business, and especially to your own family, so exactly like that of Clarissa Harlowe with its own Provençal wit thrown in. Felipe does not know why I have left you yet, and he will never know. If he inquires, I shall contrive to find some reason that will satisfy him. Probably I shall tell him you were jealous of me. You will permit me that little semi-official fib. Farewell! I am writing hurriedly so that you may have this letter at breakfast-time, and the postillion, who has undertaken to deliver it to you, is drinking below while he awaits it. Mind you kiss my dear little godson for me. Come to Chantepleurs in October; I shall be there alone all the time that Macumer is in Sardinia, where he intends to make great alterations on his estates. Such, at least, is his plan at this moment, and it is a piece of conceit on his part to have a plan. He fancies he is independent. So he is always very nervous when he mentions it to me. Farewell!

XXXVI

THE VICOMTESSE DE L'ESTORADE TO THE BARONNE MACUMER

Words fail to express our astonishment, my dear, when we heard at breakfast-time that you were gone, and especially when the postillion who had taken you to Marseilles brought me back your mad letter. Why, naughty creature, all those conversations on "Louise's seat" at the foot of the rock only concerned your happiness, and you did very wrong to take offence at them. Ingrate! my sentence is that you must return at my very first summons. That hateful letter, scrawled on the innkeeper's paper, does not give me any of your stopping-places, so I am obliged to send my answer to Chantepleurs.

Listen to me now, dear sister of my choice, and be sure, above all things, that my sole object is your happiness. There is a depth, my Louise, in your husband's soul and mind that overawes one as much as his natural gravity and his noble countenance. Further, his expressive ugliness and his soft glance have a real power about them. Therefore it was some time before I could reach that point of familiarity without which no thorough observation is possible. Besides,

The Memoirs of Two Young Brides

this *ci-devant* Prime Minister worships you even as he worships God. Hence he necessarily practises a profound dissimulation. And to lure the diplomat's secrets from beneath the rocks sunk deep down in his heart, I was fain to use all the skill and cunning I possessed. But I ended, at last, without any suspicion on the good man's part, by discovering many things of which my darling does not dream. Of us two, I stand for Reason, even as you stand for Imagination. I am grave Duty; you are giddy Love. Fate has willed that this moral contrast, originally confined to our two persons, should be continued in our destinies. I am a humble provincial Vicomtesse, exceedingly ambitious, whose mission it is to guide her family on the road to prosperity. Whereas every one knows that Macumer was once the Duque de Soria, and you who are by right a Duchesse, are a Queen in Paris, where even kings find it so difficult to reign. You have a great fortune, which Macumer will double if he carries out his plans for working his huge properties in Sardinia, the value of which is a matter of common knowledge in Marseilles. You must confess that if one of us were to be jealous, it should be me. But let us thank God that we are both too noble-hearted for our friendship ever to descend to vulgar pettiness. I know you well. You are ashamed of having left me. For all your flight, I will not spare you one word of what I had made up my mind to say to you to-day at the foot of my rock. So read this letter carefully, I beseech you, for it concerns you even more than it concerns Macumer, although he is of great importance to my argument. In the first place, my darling, you don't love him. Before two years are out you will be weary of his adoration. You will never look upon Felipe as a husband, but always as a lover, with whom you will trifle quite unconcernedly, as every woman trifles with her lover. You stand in no awe of him, you have not that profound respect, that tenderness touched with fear which a truly loving woman feels for the man who is as a god to her. Oh, I've studied this matter of love, my child, and more than once I have sounded the depths of my own heart. Now that I have watched you well, I can say it to you—you do not love. Yes, dear Queen of Paris, you will long some day, like every other queen, to be treated like a "grisette." You will pine to be mastered and swept along by some strong man, who, instead of adoring you, will snatch at your arm and bruise it in the heat of a jealous quarrel. Macumer loves you too much ever to be able to rebuke or resist you. One look from you, one coaxing word, melts his strongest will to water. Sooner or later, you will despise him for loving you too much; he spoils you, alas! just as I spoiled you in the convent—for you are one of the most seductive of women, with the most enchanting intelligences that can ever be conceived. Above all things, you are genuine, and our own happiness often exacts social falsehoods to which you will never condescend. Thus, Society demands that a woman should never allow the influence she exerts over her husband to appear. Socially speaking, a husband should no more seem to be his wife's lover, if he should love her in that fashion, than a wife should play the part of a mistress. Now you both transgress this law. In the first place, my child, if I am to judge the world by what you have told me of it, the last thing it will forgive is happiness—that must be hidden from its sight. But this is nothing. There is an equality between lovers which, to my thinking, can never be apparent between wife and husband, except under pain of a social upheaval, and of irreparable woes. A man who is a cipher is a frightful thing, but there is something worse—a man who has been turned into a cipher. Within a certain time, you will have reduced Macumer to nothing but the shadow of a man. His power of volition will have passed from him, he will not be himself, but something you have shaped to your own uses. So completely will you have assimilated him, that instead of two persons in your household, there will be only one, and that a being which must necessarily be incomplete. This will bring suffering on you, and by the time you condescend to open your eyes, there will be no remedy for the evil. However we may strive, our sex will never possess the peculiar qualities of men, and these qualities are more than necessary, they are indispensable to the family. At this moment, and in spite of his blindness, Macumer has a glimpse of the future; he feels he is lowered by his love. His proposed journey to Sardinia convinces me of his desire to recover himself by means of that temporary separation. You never hesitate to wield the power love gives you. Your authority is evident in your gestures, your looks, your voice. Oh, dearest, as your mother used to tell you, you behave like a giddy courtesan.

You are quite convinced, darling, that I am vastly Louis's superior; but did you ever hear me contradict him? Do I not always behave in public as the wife who respects in him the ruler of the family? "Hypocrisy!" you'll cry. In the first place, the advice I think it well to give him, my opinions, my ideas, are never offered except in the silence and retirement of our own bed-chamber. But I can swear to you, my dearest, that even then I never affect any superiority over him. If I did not continue to be his wife in secret just as I am in public, he would have no confidence in himself. My dear, the perfection of beneficence is so thoroughly to efface one's self that the person on whom the benefit is conferred does not feel himself inferior to the person who confers it, and this self-suppression is full of endless sweetness. Thus, my chief glory has been that I deceived even you—for you have paid me compliments about Louis. And indeed, prosperity, happiness, and hope, have helped him, in these two years, to recover everything of which misery, suffering, loneliness, and doubt, had robbed him. At present, then, according to what I have observed, you seem to me to love Felipe for your own sake, and not for his. There is truth in what your father said to you. The selfishness of the great lady is but masked

The Memoirs of Two Young Brides

by the blossoms of your early loves. Ah, child! if you were not so very dear to me, I could not tell you such cruel truths. Let me relate the close of one of our conversations, on condition that you never breathe a word of it to the Baron. We had been singing your praises in every key, for he saw, of course, that I loved you as a beloved sister, and after having led him on to confide in me unconsciously, I said to him:

"Louise has never yet had to struggle with life. Fate has treated her like a spoilt child, and perhaps she might grow unhappy, if you did not know how to be a father to her as well as a lover."

"Ah! am I capable of that?" he said.

He stopped short, like a man who sees the chasm into which he is about to slip. That exclamation was enough for me. If you had not departed, he would have told me more before many days were out.

My dearest, when that man's strength is worn out, when enjoyment has brought satiety, when he begins to feel—I will not say degraded, but void of dignity, in your sight—the reproach of his own conscience will cause him a sort of remorse, which will wound you, inasmuch as you will feel that you yourself are guilty. And you will end by despising the husband whom you have not given yourself the habit of respecting. Remember this, scorn is the first shape a woman's hatred takes. Because you are a noble-hearted woman, you will never forget the sacrifices Felipe has made for you. But there will be none left for him to make, once he has offered himself up, as it were, at this first banquet, and the man, like the woman, from whom nothing more is to be hoped, is doomed to misery. Now I have said my say. Whether it be our glory or our shame, I know not, that is too delicate a point for me to settle, but the fact remains—it is only with regard to the man who loves her that a woman is exacting.

Oh, Louise, change all this—there is still time! If you will treat Macumer as I treat l'Estorade, you will yet rouse the sleeping lion in a truly noble-hearted man. It seems to me as if you desired, at present, to avenge yourself for his superior excellence. But would you not be proud to use your power otherwise than for your own profit—to turn a great man into a man of genius, just as I am making a superior man out of an ordinary individual?

Even if you had stayed with me here in the country, I should still have written you this letter. I should have been afraid of your petulance and your wit, if we had talked the thing out together, whereas I know that when you read what I have written, you will consider your own future. Dear soul, you have every element of happiness; don't spoil it all. And pray get back to Paris early in November. The whirl and absorbing interest of society, of which I once complained, are necessary diversions in your existence, the intimacy of which is perhaps almost too close. A married woman should have a coquetry of her own. The mother of a family who does not make

The Memoirs of Two Young Brides

her presence longed for by occasional disappearances from the bosom of her household, runs great risk of engendering satiety within it. If, as I devoutly hope for my own happiness, I have several children, I solemnly assure you that as soon as they have reached a certain age, I shall keep fixed hours entirely to myself. For we must see to it that our company is sought by every one, even by our own children. Farewell, dear jealous creature! Do you know that a vulgar-minded woman would have been flattered at the thought that she had stirred that jealous feeling in you. But it is nothing but a grief to me, for I have no feelings in my heart, save those of a mother, and of the truest friend. A thousand loves I send you. Say whatever you choose to account for your departure. If you are not certain of Felipe, I am quite certain of Louis.

XXXVII

**FROM THE BARONNE DE MACUMER TO THE VICOMTESSE
DE L'ESTORADE**

GENOA.

MY DEAR LOVE: The fancy took me to see something of Italy, and I am delighted at having carried off Macumer, whose plans about Sardinia are put aside for a time.

This country enchants and delights me. The churches, and above all the chapels, have an amorous and enticing look, which must make a Protestant long to turn Catholic. Attentions have been lavished on Macumer, and the King is delighted at having acquired such a subject. If he wishes it, Felipe might have the Sardinian embassy to Paris, for I am in high favour at Court. If you write to me, address your letter to Florence. I really have not time to write to you fully; I will tell you all about my journey the next time you come to Paris. We shall only stay here a week, then we go on to Florence by Leghorn, we shall spend a month in Tuscany, and another at Naples, so as to be at Rome in November. We shall return by Venice, where we shall be for the first fortnight in December, and then we shall get back to Paris by Milan and Turin, for the month of January.

The Memoirs of Two Young Brides

This is a real lovers' journey; the new scenes through which we pass renew all our dear delights. Macumer had never seen Italy, and we began by that magnificent Corniche Road, which seems as if it had been built by fairies. Farewell, my darling! don't be angry with me for not writing. I cannot snatch a moment to myself while I am travelling—all my time is taken up in seeing and feeling, and enjoying my impressions. But I will wait till memory has coloured them before describing them to you.

XXXVIII

FROM THE VICOMTESSE DE L'ESTORADE TO THE BARONNE DE MACUMER

September.

My Dear: A somewhat lengthy answer to the letter you wrote me from Marseilles is now lying at Chantepleurs. This lovers' journey of yours is so far from removing the fears therein expressed, that I beg you'll write and have my letter sent after you.

We hear the Ministry has decided on a dissolution. This is a misfortune for the Crown, which was to have employed the last session of this loyal legislature in passing laws which were indispensable to the consolidation of its power. But it is one for us as well, for Louis will not be forty until the end of 1827. Luckily, my father, who has agreed to accept election, will resign at a convenient moment.

Your godson has taken his first steps without his godmother's help. He is really magnificent, and he is beginning to make me little graceful gestures, which assure me he is no longer a mere thirsty being, and an animal existence, but a living soul. There is meaning even in his smiles. I have been so successful as a

The Memoirs of Two Young Brides

nurse that I shall wean our Armand in December. One year of nursing is enough—" Children who are nursed too long turn into fools." I have great faith in these popular proverbs. You must be desperately admired in Italy, my fair-haired beauty! A thousand loves to you!

XXXIX

**FROM THE BARONNE DE MACUMER TO THE VICOMTESSE
DE L'ESTORADE**

ROME, *December*.

I HAVE your wicked letter, which I desired my steward to send me from Chantepleurs. Oh, Renée! . . . but I spare you all the reproaches my indignation might suggest. I will only recount the effect your letter has produced. When we came back from the beautiful party the Ambassador had given for us, at which I had shone in all my glory, and whence Macumer had returned in an intoxication of adoration which I cannot describe to you, I read that horrible answer of yours to him—read it to him, weeping—though I risked seeming ugly in his eyes. My dear Abencerrage fell at my feet, and vowed you were talking twaddle; he drew me on to the balcony of the palace in which we are living, and which looks out over part of Rome, and his language was worthy of the scene spread out before our eyes—for it was a magnificent moonlight night. We have learnt Italian already, and his love, expressed in that soft language, so appropriate to the passion, seemed to me utterly sublime. He told me that, even if you were a true prophet, he preferred a single night of happiness, or one of our exquisite mornings, to the whole of an ordinary life. Reckoning thus, he had lived a thousand years already. He desired I should remain his mistress, and sought no other title than that of my lover. So proud and happy is he, to see himself daily preferred above all others, that if God were to appear before him and to give him his choice between living another thirty years under your rules, and having five children, or only living five, with a continuance of all our dear and beautiful delights, he would make his choice—he would rather be loved as I love him, and then die. These ardent vows, which he whispered in my ear, my head resting on his shoulder, his arm about my waist, were suddenly disturbed by the scream of a bat overtaken by some owl. This death-cry affected me so painfully, that Felipe carried me half fainting to my bed. But calm your fears! Although the portent re-echoed through my soul, I am quite well this morning. When I left my bed, I knelt down before Felipe, and with his eyes on mine, and my hands clasping his, I said:

"My dearest, I am a foolish child, and Renée may be right. Perhaps the only thing I love in you is love. But be sure, at all events, that there is no other feeling in my heart, and that I love you after my own fashion. And if in my ways, in the smallest matters of my life and being, there is anything at all contrary to what you have desired or hoped of me, tell me, make it known to me. It will be my happiness to listen to

The Memoirs of Two Young Brides

you, and to be guided solely by the light of your eyes. Renée loves me so much that she terrifies me."

Macumer could find no voice to answer me; he was in tears. And now, my Renée, I thank you. I did not know how much my beautiful, my kingly Macumer does love me. Rome is the city of love. Those who have a passion should come here to enjoy it—the arts and Heaven will be their accomplices. We are to meet the Duque and Duquesa de Soria at Venice. If you write to me again, direct to Paris, for we leave Rome within three days. The Ambassador's party was to bid us farewell.

P. S.—Silly darling, your letter is a clear proof that your sole acquaintance with love is theoretical. Let me tell you that love is a principle so various and dissimilar in its effects, that no theory can possibly embrace or govern them. This for my little doctor in petticoats.

XL

FROM THE COMTESSE DE L'ESTORADE TO THE BARONNE DE MACUMER

January, 1827.

My father returned to Parliament. My father-in-law is dead, and I am on the brink of my second confinement. These are the chief events of the close of this year. I mention them at once, so that the black seal upon my letter may not alarm you long.

My darling, your letter from Rome made me shudder. You are a pair of children. Either Felipe is a diplomat, who has deceived you, or a man who loves you as he would love a courtesan, to whom he would make over his whole fortune even though he knew her to be playing him false. But enough of all this. You think what I say is twaddle; I will hold my peace. But let me tell you that when I consider your fate and my own, the moral I draw is a cruel one. "If you desire to be loved, you must not fall in love yourself."

Louis received the Cross of the Legion of Honour when he was appointed to the Conseil Général. Now he has been on the Conseil for three years, and as my father, whom you will no doubt see in Paris, in the

The Memoirs of Two Young Brides

course of the session, has applied to have his son-in-law promoted to the rank of Officer, I will ask you to be so kind as to turn your attention to the functionary on whom the promotion depends, and see after this little business for me. And above all things, don't mix yourself up in the affairs of my much-revered father, the Comte de Maucombe, who wants a Marquisate for himself. Keep all your interest for me. When Louis is a Deputy—that will be next winter—we shall go to Paris, and we shall move heaven and earth to get him appointed to some permanent board, so that we may put away all our own income and live on his salary. My father sits between the Centre and the Right. He doesn't ask for anything except a title. Our family was famous in the days of King Renée—King Charles X will never refuse the request of a Maucombe. But I'm afraid my father may take it into his head to solicit some favour for my second brother, and if he has a little trouble in getting his Marquisate, he will not be able to think about anything but himself.

January 15th.

Ah, Louise, I've been in hell! The only reason I dare to speak of what I have suffered to you is that you are my second self. And even so, I do not know whether I can ever let my thoughts go back to those five hideous days. Even the word "convulsions" sends a shudder to my very soul. Not five days, but five centuries, of torture have I endured! Until a mother has gone through that martyrdom, she will

The Memoirs of Two Young Brides

never know what suffering really means. You'll judge of my distraction when I tell you I have called you happy, because you have no child!

The evening before the dreadful day, the weather, which had been heavy and almost hot, seemed to me to be disagreeing with my little Armand. He was peevish, quite unlike his usual sweet and coaxing self. He screamed about everything. He tried to play, and broke his toys. Perhaps this disturbance of the temper is always the precursor of illness in young children. My attention having been attracted by his unusual naughtiness, I noticed he had alternate fits of flushing and pallor, which I ascribed to the fact that he was cutting four large teeth at once. So I had him to sleep close by me, and kept waking up to look at him. He was a little feverish in the night, but this did not alarm me in the least. I still thought it all came from his teeth. Towards morning he called "Mamma," and made me a sign that he was thirsty. But there was a shrillness in his voice, and something convulsive about his gesture, that froze my blood. I jumped out of bed to get him some water. Conceive my terror when I brought him the cup and found he didn't move. Only he kept saying "Mamma" in that voice that wasn't his voice—that wasn't even a voice at all. I took his hand, but it didn't answer to mine, it stiffened. I put the glass to his lips. The poor little fellow drank, but in the most alarming manner, taking three or four convulsive gulps, and the water made a queer noise in his throat. Suddenly he clutched desperately at me. I saw his eye-balls turn, drawn up by some internal pressure, and his limbs lost all their flexibility. I screamed wildly. Louis came.

"A doctor! A doctor!" I shrieked, "he's dying."

Louis was off like a flash, and my poor Armand clung to me again, crying "Mamma! Mamma!" In another moment he was quite unconscious that he even had a mother. The veins on his pretty forehead swelled out, and the convulsions came on. For an hour before the doctors came, that lively child, so pink and white, that blossom which had lately been my pride and joy, lay in my arms as stiff and stark as a log of wood. And oh, his eyes! the very thought of them makes me shudder. Black and shrivelled, drawn and dumb, my pretty boy was like nothing but a mummy. First one doctor, and then two, fetched by Louis from Marseilles, stood over him, like birds of evil omen. The very sight of them made me shiver. One said it was a brain fever. The other said it was a case of infantile convulsions. Our village man seemed to me the most sensible, for he didn't prescribe anything. "His teeth," said the second; "fever," said the first. At last they agreed to put leeches on his neck, and ice upon his head. I thought I should have died. To sit there and gaze at a bluish-blackish corpse, that never moved or spoke, in place of that gay, lively little creature! At one moment I quite lost my head, and a sort of nervous laughter seized me when I saw the leeches fasten on the pretty neck I

The Memoirs of Two Young Brides

had so often kissed, and the darling head under an ice-cap. My dear, we had to cut off the pretty hair we used to admire so much, and that you had fondled, so as to apply the ice. The convulsions returned every ten minutes, just like the pains with which I bore him, and the poor little fellow struggled afresh, sometimes deadly pale, and then again purple in the face. Whenever his limbs, generally so flexible, touched each other, they gave out a sort of wooden sound. And that senseless creature had once smiled to me, and kissed me, and called me " Mother." A flood of agony surged over my soul at the thought, tossing it even as tempests toss the sea, and I felt a wrench at every cord that binds the child to the mother's heart. My own mother, who might have helped, advised, or consoled me, is in Paris. Mothers understand more about convulsions, I think, than any doctor. After four days and nights of ups and downs, and terrors, which almost killed me, the doctors all decided it would be better to apply some horrible ointment to blister the skin. Oh, sores on my Armand, who had been playing about only five days before, and laughing, and trying to say " Godmother! " I objected, and said I would trust to Nature. Louis scolded me, he believed the doctors—men are all alike. But at certain moments dreadful maladies like these take the form of death itself, and at one of these moments the remedy, the very thought of which had been an abomination in my sight, seemed to promise me Armand's salvation. My dearest Louise, his skin was so dry, so hard, so burnt up, that the ointment took no effect. Then I began to cry, and I wept so long over his bed that the pillow was all soaked. As for the doctors, they were at their dinner. Seeing I was alone I stripped all the medical appliances off my boy. Half wild as I was, I took him up into my arms, I strained him to my breast, I pressed my forehead to his, and I prayed to God to give him my own life which I strove to breathe into him. I had been holding him thus for several minutes, longing to die with him, so that neither death nor life might part us. My dear, I felt his limbs relax, the convulsions passed off, the child moved, the dreadful, hideous colour changed, I screamed, as I had screamed when he first fell ill. The doctors ran upstairs. I showed them my boy.

"He's saved!" cried the elder of the two.

Oh, those words! what music there was in them! Heaven opened to my sight. And indeed, two hours later, Armand was a new creature. But as for me, I was broken down, and nothing but the elixir of happiness saved me from being very ill. O my God! by what anguish dost thou bind the mother to her child! What nails thou drivest into her heart to hold him safely there! Was not maternal love passionate enough already in me, who wept with joy over my boy's first lispings and his baby-step, who watch him for hours together, so that I may do my duty well, and learn all the sweet business of a mother's life? Were all these terrors and these frightful sights needful for a woman who has made her child her idol?

The Memoirs of Two Young Brides

As I sit writing to you, Armand is playing about, shouting and laughing. Then I ponder the causes of this horrible complaint, remembering that I am about to bear another child. Is it the result of teething? Is it caused by some particular condition of the brain? Is there something faulty in the nervous system of children who suffer from convulsions? All these ideas alarm me, as much for the present as for the future. Our country doctor declares it is a nervous excitement caused by teething. I would give all my teeth to know those of our little Armand safely through. Every time I see one of those little white pearls peeping through the middle of his hot red gum, I feel a cold perspiration break out all over me. The heroic manner in which the poor little angel bears his sufferings shows me his nature will be just like mine; he cast the most heart-rending glances at me. Medical science knows very little of the causes of this species of *tetanus*, which disappears as swiftly as it comes, and can neither be foreseen nor cured. I tell you again, one thing alone is certain—that to see her child in convulsions is hell to any mother. How furiously I kiss him now! How long and closely I hold him when I carry him about! To have to endure such anguish when I am to be confined again within six weeks was a hideous aggravation of my martyrdom. I was terrified for the other child. Farewell, my dear and much loved Louise! Don't wish for children!— that is my last word to you!

XLI

FROM THE BARONNE DE MACUMER TO THE COMTESSE DE L'ESTORADE

PARIS.

POOR DARLING: We forgave your horridness, Macumer and I, when we heard how dreadfully you had been tried. I shuddered, and it was anguish to me to read the details of that double torture. I am less unhappy now at having no child. I lose no time in telling you that Louis is appointed Officer of the Legion of Honour, and may forthwith sport his rosette. You wish for a little girl, and you will probably have one, lucky Renée! My brother's marriage with Mlle. de Mortsauf took place on our return. Our dear King, who really is most exquisitely kind, has granted my brother the succession to the post of First Lord of the Bedchamber, which his father-in-law now holds.

"The office must go with the title," said he to the Duc de Lenoncourt-Givry. The only thing he has insisted on is that the Mortsauf escutcheon should be impaled with that of the Lenoncourt.

My father was right, a hundred times over. But for my fortune, none of these things could have taken place. My father and mother came from Madrid for the wedding, and are going back there after the party, which I am giving for the young couple to-morrow. The carnival will be very gay. The Duque and Duquesa de Soria are in Paris. Their presence here disturbs me a little. Maria Heredia is certainly one of the most beautiful women in Europe, and I don't like the way in which Felipe looks at her. So I have redoubled my love and tenderness. "*She* would never have loved you as I do," is a sentence I take good care not to utter, but it is written on all my looks and in everything I do. Never was coquette more elegant than I. Yesterday Mme. de Maufrigneuse said to me, "Dear child, we must all lay down our arms to you!"

And then I amuse Felipe so much that he must think his sister-in-law as stupid as a Spanish cow. I am all the more consoled at not being the mother of a little Abencerrage, because the Duchesse will most probably be confined in Paris, and so she'll grow ugly. If she has a son it is to be called Felipe, in honour of the exile—and spiteful Chance will make me a godmother once more. Farewell, my dearest! I shall go to Chantepleurs early this year, for our journey has cost something outrageous. I shall depart towards the end of March, so as to economize by living in the Nivernais. And besides, Paris bores me, and Felipe sighs as much as I do for the delightful solitude of our park, for our cool meadows, and our Loire, with its shimmering sands, so different from any other river in the

The Memoirs of Two Young Brides

world. Chantepleurs seems delightful, after all the pomps and vanities of Italy; for, after all, magnificence is wearisome, and one lover's glance is better than any *Capo d'Opera* or *bel quadro*. We shall expect you there. I won't be jealous of you any more. You can sound my Macumer's heart, just as you please. You can fish out interjections, and wake up scruples—I make him over to you with the most superb confidence. Since that scene at Rome, Felipe loves me more passionately than ever. He told me yesterday (he is looking over my shoulder) that his sister-in-law, the Maria of his youth, his former *fiancée*, the Princess Heredia, his first dream, *was dull*. Ah, dear, I'm worse than any opera-dancer—the slander delighted me. I've pointed out to Felipe that she doesn't speak good French—she says "esemple" for "exemple," "sain" for "cinq," "cheu" for "jeu." She is handsome, indeed, but she has no grace, nor the smallest liveliness of intellect. If any one pays her a compliment, she stares like a woman who has never been in the habit of hearing such things. With Felipe's nature, he would have left her before he had been two months married to her. She suits the Duque de Soria, Don Fernando, very well. He is a generous-minded man, but an evident spoilt child. I might be spiteful and set you laughing, but I confine myself to the truth. A thousand loves, my dearest one!

XLII

FROM RENÉE TO LOUISE

My little daughter is two months old. My mother stood godmother to the little creature, and an old great-uncle of Louis's was her godfather. Her names are Jeanne Athénais.

As soon as I can get away, I will start to join you at Chantepleurs, since you don't object to having a nursing mother. Your godson can say your name now, he pronounces it *Matoumer*, for he can't say his c's properly. You'll dote upon him. He has cut all his teeth, he eats like a big boy; he runs and trots about like a weasel. But I still keep an anxious eye on him, and I am in despair at not being able to have him with me during my recovery, which necessitates my keeping my room for more than two months, owing to certain precautions on which the doctors insist. Alas! my love, custom doesn't make child-bearing any easier. The same anguish and the same terrors have to be faced each time. Notwithstanding that (don't show this letter to Felipe) this little daughter has something of my looks. She may eclipse your Armand yet.

The Memoirs of Two Young Brides

My father thought Felipe had grown thin, and my darling looking a little thinner too. Yet the Sorias have left Paris, so there cannot be the smallest occasion for jealousy now. Are you hiding some sorrow from me? Your last letter was neither so long nor so affectionate in thought as your former one. Is that only one of my whimsical darling's whims?

I have written too much. My nurse is scolding me for having written at all, and Mlle. Athénais de l'Estorade is screaming for her dinner. Farewell, then. Write me good long letters.

XLIII

MME. DE MACUMER TO THE COMTESSE DE L'ESTORADE

For the first time in my life, my dearest Renée, I have sat crying alone on a wooden bench under a willow tree, beside my lake at Chantepleurs—a lovely spot to which you'll soon add fresh beauties, for the only thing lacking to it is merry children's voices.

Thinking of your fruitful motherhood, a sudden revulsion of feeling has swept over me, who am childless still, after nearly three years of married life. "Oh," I mused, "even though I suffer a hundred times more cruelly than Renée suffered when my godson was born, even though I should end by seeing my child in convulsions, grant, O my God, that I may bear an angel baby like that little Athénais, who, I can feel it, is as lovely as the day." For you didn't say a word about that, it was just like you, my Renée! You seem to have guessed I am unhappy. Every time my hopes are disappointed, I spend several days in the blackest melancholy. So there I sat composing gloomy elegies. When shall I embroider little caps and choose fine lawn for babies' gowns? When shall I sew dainty laces to cover a tiny head? Am I never to hear one of those darling creatures call me "Mother," and feel it pull at my skirt and lord it over me? Shall I never see the marks of a little carriage upon the gravel path? Shall I never pick up broken toys in my court-yard? Shall I never go to the toy-shop like the many mothers I have seen, to buy swords and dolls, and baby-houses? Shall I never watch the growth of a life and being that will be another and a dearer Felipe? I want a son, so that I may find out how a woman may love her lover better than ever in his other self. My house and park seem cold and deserted. Oh, my doctor in petticoats that you are, your view of life is true. And besides, sterility in any form is a horrible thing. My life is rather too like that in Gessner's and Florian's pastorals, of which Rivarol used to say that "one was driven to sigh for wolves." I, as well as you, want to devote myself to others. I feel I have powers in me which Felipe overlooks, and if I am not to have a child, I shall have to treat myself to a misfortune of some kind. This is what I have just been saying to my remnant of the Moors, and my words brought tears into his eyes. He got off with being told he was a noble-hearted silly. It doesn't do to jest with him about his love.

Now and then I long to go and say Novenas, to appeal to special Madonnas, or try special waters. I shall certainly consult physicians next winter. I am too furious with myself to say more about it to you. Farewell!

XLIV

FROM THE SAME TO THE SAME

PARIS, *1829.*

How's this, my dear? A whole year without a letter from you. ... I am rather hurt. Do you fancy that your Louis, who comes to see me almost every second day, can fill your place? It isn't enough for me to know that you are not ill, and that your business matters are doing well. I want to know your thoughts and feelings, just as I send you mine, and risk being scolded or blamed, or misunderstood, just because I love you. This silence of yours, and your retirement in the country, when you might be here, enjoying the Comte de l'Estorade's parliamentary triumphs—his constant speeches and his devotion to his duties have gained him considerable influence, and he'll no doubt rise to a very high position when the session closes—cause me serious alarm. Do you spend your whole life writing him instructions? Numa was not so widely parted from his Egeria. Why haven't you seized this opportunity of seeing Paris? I should have had your company for four whole months. Yesterday your husband informed me you were coming up to fetch him, and that your third

The Memoirs of Two Young Brides

confinement (indefatigable parent) was to take place here. After endless questions, sighs, and groans, Louis, diplomatic though he is, ended by telling me that his great-uncle, Athénais's godfather, is in a very bad way. And I conclude you capable, like the good mother you are, of turning the Deputy's speeches and his fame to account, to coax some handsome legacy out of your husband's sole surviving relative on his mother's side. Make your mind easy, my Renée. The Lenoncourts, the Chaulieus, all Mme. de Macumer's circle, are working for Louis. There is no doubt Martignac will send him to the Audit Office. But if you don't tell me why you are staying on in the country, I shall lose my temper. Is it so that nobody may suspect you of guiding the whole policy of the House of l'Estorade? Is it because of the old uncle's will? Are you afraid you may be a less devoted mother in Paris? Oh, how I should like to know whether it is that you don't choose to make your first appearance here in your present condition. Is it that, you vain creature? Good-bye.

XLV

FROM RENÉE TO LOUISE

You complain of my silence? Why, you forget the two little dark heads I have to rule and which rule over me. And, indeed, you have hit on some of the reasons that keep me at home. Apart from the state of the old great-uncle's health, I did not care, in my present condition, to drag a boy of four and a little girl of nearly three up to Paris; I wouldn't complicate your existence and burden your house with such a party. I don't care to appear at a disadvantage in the brilliant society over which you hold sway; and I have a horror both of furnished lodgings and of hotel life. When Louis's great-uncle heard the news of his great-nephew's appointment, he made me a present of two hundred thousand francs, half his savings, with which to buy a house in Paris, and I have commissioned Louis to find one, in your neighbourhood. My mother has given me thirty thousand francs to pay for the furniture. When I settle in Paris for the session, I shall go to my own house, and I shall try to be worthy of my dear "sister by election"— I say it without any intention of making a pun. I am

The Memoirs of Two Young Brides

grateful to you for having obtained so much favour for Louis. But in spite of the esteem in which he is held by MM. de Bourmont and de Polignac, who wish him to take office under them, I do not care to see him in such a prominent position. That is far too compromising. I prefer the Audit Office on account of its being a permanency. Our business here will be in very good hands, and once our steward has thoroughly mastered his work, I shall come and support Louis—you may be quite easy about that.

As for writing you long letters at present, how am I to do it? This one, in which I should like to give you a description of the ordinary tenor of one of my days, will have to lie on my writing-table for a week. It may be turned into tents for Armand's toy soldiers, set out in rows upon my floor, or into ships for the navy he sails upon his bath. One single day's work will be enough for you; and, indeed, my days are all alike, and only two facts affect them—whether the children are out of sorts, or well. Literally, in this quiet country-house, the hours are minutes, or the minutes hours, according to the children's state of health. My few exquisite respites are when they are asleep, when I am not rocking one, or telling stories to the other, to make them drowsy. Once I feel I have them both sound asleep close to me, I say to myself, "Now I have nothing more to fear." For really, my darling, as long as daylight lasts, a mother is always inventing some danger the moment her children are out of her sight. I think Armand is trying to play

The Memoirs of Two Young Brides

with stolen razors, I fancy his jacket has caught fire, that he has been bitten by a blind-worm, that he has tumbled down and cut his head, or drowned himself in one of the ponds. Motherhood, as you see, gives birth to a succession of poetic fancies, some sweet, some hideous. Not an hour but brings its terrors or its joys. But alone in my room, at night, comes the hour of my waking dreams, when I plan out all their future life, and see it lighted by the smiles of the angels I behold hovering above their pillows. Sometimes Armand will call me in his sleep. Then I kiss his unconscious forehead, and his little sister's feet, and gaze at their childish beauty. Those instants are my festivals. I'm certain it was our guardian angel who inspired me, in the middle of last night, to run in a fright to Athénais's cradle, where I found her lying with her head much too low, while Armand had kicked all his coverings off, so that his feet were blue with cold.

"Oh, mother darling!" he said, as he woke and kissed me.

There's a night scene for you, my dear!

How necessary it is for a mother to keep her children near her! Can any nurse, however good she may be, take them up and comfort them, and hush them to rest again, when they have been startled out of their sleep by some hideous nightmare? For children have their dreams, and it is all the more difficult to explain one of these dreadful dreams to them, because the child that listens to his mother at such a moment, is drowsy, scared, shrewd and simple, all at once—an organ pause, as it were, between his two slumbers. And I have learnt to sleep so lightly that I see my two little ones and hear them through my closed eye-lids. A sigh, even a turn in bed, awakes me. I see convulsions perpetually crouching like a cruel monster at the foot of their couch.

When daylight comes, my children begin to chirp with the earliest birds. I can hear them through my morning sleep. Their chatter is like the twitter of fighting swallows, merry or plaintive little chirpings, that reach me more through my heart than through my ears. While Nais does her best to get to me by crawling on her hands and knees, or toddling from her cot to my bed, Armand climbs up to kiss me, as nimble as a monkey. Then the two little creatures make my bed into their playground, on which their mother is at their mercy. The little maid pulls my hair, she still tries to find my breast, and Armand defends it as if it were his private property. I can never resist certain attitudes, and the peals of laughter that go off like rockets, and always end by chasing sleep away. Then we play at ogres, and the mother ogress devours the soft white baby skins, and kisses the merry roguish eyes and tender pink shoulders, till there is almost nothing left of them—and this, every now and then, results in the most fascinating fits of childish jealousy. Some days I take up my stocking at eight o'clock, and when nine o'clock strikes I have only contrived to put one on.

The Memoirs of Two Young Brides

But up I get at last, and dressing begins. I put on my wrapper, turn up my sleeves, tie on my waterproof apron, and with Mary's help I give my two little darlings their bath. I am sole judge of the heat or coolness of the water—for that matter of the temperature of the bath is the cause of half the screaming and crying among children. Then out come the paper boats and the china ducks. The children must be kept amused if they are to be properly washed. If you only knew what games have to be invented to please these absolute monarchs, if one is to get one's soft sponge over every corner of their small persons! You would be quite startled by the amount of cleverness and cunning a mother must employ if she is to carry her work to a glorious conclusion. Supplication, scoldings, promises, she needs them all, and her knavery grows all the more skilful because it must be so cunningly concealed. I don't know what would happen if God had not given the mother shrewdness to outwit the child's. A child is a wily politician, and he must be mastered, just like your great politician—through his passions. Fortunately, everything makes the little angels laugh. Whenever a brush tumbles down, or a cake of soap slips away, there are shrieks of delight. Well if all these triumphs are dearly bought, at all events they do exist. But God alone —for the father himself knows nothing of it—God alone, or the angels, or you yourself, can understand the glances I exchange with Mary when the two little creatures are dressed, and we see them all neat and clean amid the soap, and sponges, and combs, and basins, and flannels, and all the thousand impedimenta of an English nursery. I have grown quite English on this point. I acknowledge that English women have a genius for bringing up children. Although they only consider the child's material and physical comfort, there is sense in all the improvements they have introduced. Therefore my children shall always have warm feet and bare legs, they shall never be tightened or compressed—but then again they shall never be left alone. The French child's bondage in his swaddling-clothes means the freedom of his nurse, and that explains it all. No good mother can be free, and that is why I don't write to you—for I have to manage this place, and to bring up two children. The science of motherhood involves much silent well-doing, unseen and unpretending, much virtue applied to small things, a fund of never-failing devotion. Even the broths that are being made at the fire must be watched —why, you don't think I would shuffle out of any of these little cares? The least of them brings in its own harvest of affection. Oh, how good it is to see a child smile when he likes his dinner! Armand has a way of wagging his little head, which is better than a whole passion of love to me. How I can allow another woman the right, the care, the pleasure, of blowing on a spoonful of soup which is too hot for Naïs, whom I only weaned seven months ago, and who still remembers her mother's breast? When a *nurse* has burnt a child's tongue and lips, by giving

The Memoirs of Two Young Brides

it something too hot, she just tells the mother it is crying because it is hungry. But how can any mother sleep in peace when she thinks that an impure breath may have passed over the food her child swallows, and remembers that Nature does not permit of any interposition between her own breast and her nursling's lips? It is a work of patience to cut up a cutlet for Nais, whose last teeth are just coming through, and to mix up the carefully cooked meat with potatoes, and really, in certain cases, no one but a mother knows how to make an impatient child eat up the whole of its food. Therefore no mother, even though she have a numerous household and an English nurse, can be excused from taking her personal share of duty on this battlefield, where gentleness must wage war against the little griefs and sufferings of childhood. Why, Louise, one's whole heart must be in one's care of the dear innocents! No evidence must be trusted save that of one's own eye and hand as to their dress, their food, and their sleeping arrangements. As a general principle a child's cry, unless caused by some suffering imposed by Nature, argues a shortcoming on the part of the mother or the nurse. Now that I have two children to look after, and shall soon have three, there is no room in my soul for anything else, and even you, dearly as I love you, are only a memory. I am not always dressed by two o'clock in the day! And I have no faith in mothers whose rooms are always tidy, and whose collars and gowns and fallals are always neat. Yesterday, one of our first

The Memoirs of Two Young Brides

April days, the weather was lovely, and I wanted to take the children out before my confinement, which is close upon me. Well, to a mother, the taking of the children out is a perfect poem, and she looks forward to it from one day to the next. Armand was to wear a new black velvet coat, a new collar which I had embroidered for him, a Scotch cap with the Stuart colours, and a black cock's feather. Nais was to be dressed in white and pink, and a delightful *baby* bonnet. She is still the baby—she'll lose that pretty title when the little fellow whom I call " my pauper," for he'll be the second son, makes his appearance. I have seen my child already in a dream, and I know I shall have a boy. Caps, collars, coats, little stockings, tiny shoes, pink ribbons, silk-embroidered muslin frock, were all laid out upon my bed. When these two gay little birds who are so happy together, had had their dark hair, curled, for the boy, and brushed gently forward so as to peep out under the pink and white bonnet, for the girl; when their shoes had been fastened, when the little bare calves and neatly shod feet had trotted about the nursery, when those two " faces *cleanes* " (as Mary calls it in her limpid French!) and those sparkling eyes said to me, " Let us be off! " my heart throbbed. Oh, to see one's children dressed up by one's own hands, the beauty of their fresh skins, on which the blue veins shine out after one has washed and sponged and dried them, heightened by the brilliant colours of the velvet or the silk!—that's better than any poetry. With what hungry passion one calls them back to press fresh kisses upon their necks that look fairer in their simple collars than the loveliest woman's! Every day do I paint pictures such as these, which every mother pauses to admire, even in the commonest coloured lithograph.

When we were out of doors, while I was enjoying the fruit of my labours and admiring my little Armand, who looked like a prince of the blood royal as he led the baby along the narrow road you know so well, a wagon came in sight. I tried to pull them out of the way, the two children tumbled into a puddle, and so ensued the ruin of my master-pieces. We had to take them home, and dress them over again. I picked my little girl up in my arms, never noticing that I had spoilt my dress by doing it; Mary laid hands on Armand, and so we got back home. When a baby cries, and a boy gets wet, there's an end of everything—a mother never gives herself another thought, they are absorbed elsewhere.

As a rule, when dinner-time comes, I have got nothing done at all. And how am I to manage to help them both, to pin on their napkins and turn up their cuffs, and feed them? This problem I solve twice in every day. Amid these never-ending cares, these joys and these disasters, the only person forgotten in the house is me. Often, if the children are naughty, I haven't time to take out my curl-papers. My appearance depends upon their temper. To get a moment to myself so as to write you these six pages,

The Memoirs of Two Young Brides

I have to let them cut out the pictures on my ballads and build castles with books or chess-men or mother-o'-pearl counters; or else Nais must wind my silks and wools after her own method—a method so complicated, I can assure you, that she turns all her little mind to it, and never says a word.

After all, I have nothing to complain of. My two children are healthy and fearless, and amuse themselves with less trouble to others than you would think. Everything is a delight to them. They really need a well-ordered freedom more than toys. A handful of pebbles, pink and yellow, purple or black, a few little shells, and all the wonders of the sand, make them quite happy. To them wealth consists in the possession of a large number of small things. I watch Armand, and I find him talking to the birds, and the flies, and the cocks and hens, and imitating them all. He is on excellent terms with the insect world, for which he has the greatest admiration. Everything that is tiny interests him. He begins to ask me the why of everything. He has just been to see what I was saying to his godmother. Indeed he looks on you as a fairy—and see how right children always are!

Alas! my dearest, I had not intended to sadden you, by telling you of all these joys. This story will give you an idea of your godson. The other day, a beggar followed us—for the poor know that no mother who has a child with her will ever refuse them alms. Armand has no idea as yet of what it means to go hungry; he doesn't know what money is, but as he

The Memoirs of Two Young Brides

had just asked for a trumpet, and I had bought it for him, he held it out to the old man, with a regal air, saying, " Here, take it! "

" Have I your leave to keep it? " said the beggar to me.

Can anything on earth be compared with the joy of such a moment?

" For you see, madame, I have had children of my own," added the old fellow, as he took what I gave him without even looking at the coin.

When I think that such a child as Armand must be sent to school, when I think that I shall only be able to keep him for another three years and a half—I feel a shiver creep over me. State education will mow down the flowers of his blessed childhood, will pervert all his charm and his exquisite frankness. They will cut off his curly hair, that I have washed and brushed and kissed so often. What will they do with my Armand's heart?

And what are you doing all this time? You've told me nothing at all about your life. Do you still love Felipe?—for I have no anxiety about the Saracen. Farewell! Nais has just tumbled down, and besides, if I were to go on, this letter would grow into a volume.

XLVI

FROM MME. DE MACUMER TO THE COMTESSE DE L'ESTORADE

1829.

MY DEAR LOVING-HEARTED RENÉE: The news of the horrible misfortune that has fallen on me will have reached you through the newspapers. I have never been able to write a single word to you. For twenty days and nights I watched by his bed, I received his last breath, I closed his eyes, I knelt piously beside his corpse, with the priest, and I recited the prayers for the dead. All this dreadful suffering I imposed on myself as a chastisement. And yet, when I saw the smile he gave me just before he died still lying on his calm lips, I could not believe that it was my love that had killed him. Well, *he is no more*, and *I live on*. What more can I say to you, who have known us both so well? Everything is contained in these two sentences. Oh, if any one could tell me he might be recalled to life, I would give my hopes of heaven to hear the promise, for it would be heaven to see him again. To lay my hand on him even for two seconds, would be to breathe without a dagger in my heart. Won't you come to me soon and tell

The Memoirs of Two Young Brides

me that? Don't you love me enough to tell me a lie? . . . But no, long ago you warned me I was inflicting cruel wounds upon him . . . is it true? . . . No, I never deserved his love—you are quite right—I cheated him, I strangled happiness in my wild embrace. Oh, I am not wild now, as I write to you. But I feel that I am all alone. God! is there anything in hell more awful than that one word?

When they took him away from me, I laid myself down in his bed and I hoped I might have died. There was nothing but a door between us. I thought I was strong enough still to break it down. But I was too young, alas! and now after two months, during which a hateful skill has used every artifice known to dreary science to nurse me back to life, I find myself in the country, sitting at my window, among the flowers he had grown for me, enjoying the splendid view over which his eyes have often wandered, and which he was so proud of having discovered, because I loved it. Ah, dearest, it is extraordinary how it hurts one to move from place to place when one's heart is dead. The damp soil of my garden gives me a shudder. The earth is like one great grave, and I fancy I am treading on him. The first time I went out, I stopped in a fright, and stood quite still. It is very dreary to look at *his* flowers without *him*.

My parents are in Spain; you know what my brothers are; and you are obliged to be in the country. But let not that distress you. Two angels flew

The Memoirs of Two Young Brides

at once to my relief. Those kind creatures, the Duque and Duquesa de Soria, hastened to their brother's sick-bed. The last few nights saw us all three, gathered in calm and silent sorrow, round the bed on which one of those truly great and noble men, so rare and so far above us in all things, lay dying. My Felipe's patience was angelic. The sight of his brother and Maria cheered his heart for a moment and softened his sufferings.

"Dear," he said to me, in the simple way which was so peculiarly his own, "I was very nearly dying without leaving my Barony of Macumer to Fernando. I must alter my will. My brother will forgive me—he knows what it is to be in love."

I owe my life to the care of my brother and sister-in-law. They want to take me away to Spain with them.

Ah, Renée, I can't express the extent of my misfortune to anybody but you. I am overwhelmed by the sense of my own wrong-doing, and it is a bitter comfort to me to acknowledge it to you, my poor despised Cassandra. I have killed him with my unreasonableness, my ill-founded jealousy, my perpetual tormenting. My love was all the more fatal because we were both of us equally and exquisitely sensitive, we spoke the same language, his comprehension was perfect, and very often, without my suspecting it, my jests cut him to the very heart. You would never conceive the point to which that dear slave carried his obedience. Sometimes I would tell him to go away

The Memoirs of Two Young Brides

and leave me alone. He would go at once, without ever discussing a whim which quite possibly pained him. Till his very last breath he blessed me, saying over and over again that one forenoon spent alone with me was worth more to him than a long life spent with any other woman he might have loved, even were it Maria Heredia. My tears are falling while I write these words to you.

Now I get up at noon, I go to bed at seven; I dawdle absurdly over my meals, I walk slowly, I stop for an hour in front of one plant, I stare at the foliage, I busy myself solemnly and regularly over trifles. I love the shade and the silence and the night. I wage war with every hour, in short, and take a gloomy pleasure in adding it to my past. The peace of my own grounds is the only company I can endure. In everything around me, I can read some noble image of my dead happiness, invisible to other eyes, but clear and eloquent to mine.

My sister-in-law clasped her arms round me, when I said to her one day:

"I can't endure you. There is something nobler in your Spanish hearts than in ours."

Ah, Renée, if I'm not dead, it must be because God apportions the sense of misery to the strength of those who have to bear it. It is only women such as we who are able to realize the extent of our loss, when we are bereft of a love that knows no hypocrisy —the best of loves, a lasting passion, that satisfied nature and heart at once. How often does one meet a

The Memoirs of Two Young Brides

man whose qualities are so great that a woman can love him without degrading herself? Such an experience is the greatest happiness that any woman can know, and no woman is likely to come upon it twice. Men who are really great and strong—men who can cast a halo of poetry over virtue—men whose souls exert a mighty charm, men who are born to be adored—should never love, for they will bring calamity on the women they love, and on themselves. This is my cry as I wander along my woodland paths. And I have no child of his! That inexhaustible love which always had a smile for me, which poured out nothing but blossoms and delights for me, was barren. There is some curse upon me. Can it be that love, when it is pure and fierce, as it must be when it is complete, is as unfruitful as aversion—just as the excessive heat of the desert sands, and the excessive cold of the polar ice, both preclude the existence of life? Must a woman marry a Louis de l'Estorade, if she is to be the mother of children? Is God jealous of Love? I am beginning to rave.

I think you are the only person I can bear to have with me. So come to me; you alone must be with a mourning Louise. What an awful day that was when I first put on a widow's cap! When I saw myself in my black dress, I dropped down on a chair, and cried till dark. I am crying again now, as I tell you of that dreadful moment.

Farewell! writing to you tires me. I am sick of my thoughts; I won't go on putting them into words.

The Memoirs of Two Young Brides

Bring your children. You can nurse the youngest here. I shall not be jealous any more. *He* is gone, and I shall be very glad to see my godson—for Felipe longed to have a child like little Armand. Come then, and share my sorrows with me! . . .

XLVII

FROM RENÉE TO LOUISE
1829.

MY DARLING: When this letter reaches your hands I shall not be far away, for I start a few moments after sending it to you. We shall be alone. Louis is obliged to remain in Provence on account of the elections which are just coming on—he wants to be re-elected and the Liberals are intriguing against him already.

I am not coming to console you. I am only bringing my heart to keep yours company, and to help you to live on. I am coming to force you into tears; that is the only fashion in which you may buy the happiness of meeting him some day—for he is only journeying towards God, and every step you take will lead you nearer to him. Every duty you fulfil will break some link of the chain that parts you. Courage, my Louise. When my arms are about you, you will rise up again, and you will go to him, pure, noble, with all your unintentional faults forgiven, and followed by the good works you will dedicate to his name here on earth.

These lines are written hastily, in the midst of my preparations and of my children—with Armand shouting, "Godmother, godmother; let's go and see her!" till I am half jealous. He is almost your own son.

PART SECOND

XLVIII

FROM THE BARONNE DE MACUMER TO THE COMTESSE DE L'ESTORADE

October 15th, 1833.

WELL, yes, Renée, the story you heard is true. I have got rid of my town-house; I have sold Chantepleurs and my farms in Seine-et-Marne; but to say I am mad and ruined is a little too much. Let us reckon up. After all I have spent, I still possess some twelve hundred thousand francs out of my poor Macumer's fortune. I'll give you a faithful account of everything, like a dutiful sister. I invested a million francs in the three-per-cents when they stood at fifty francs; that gives me sixty thousand francs a year instead of the thirty thousand I got out of my landed property. What a burden and worry for a widow of seven-and-twenty, what disappointment and loss she must face, if she has to spend six months of every year in the country granting leases, listening to grumbling farmers who only pay when they choose, boring herself like a sportsman in rainy weather, struggling to sell her produce and getting rid of it at a loss—then living in a Paris house, costing her ten thousand francs a year, investing her funds

The Memoirs of Two Young Brides

through lawyers' offices, waiting for her interest, obliged to prosecute people in order to get it, studying the law of mortgage, and with business matters on her shoulders in the Nivernais, in Seine-et-Marne, and in Paris! As it stands, my fortune is a mortgage on the Budget. Instead of my paying taxes to the State, the State pays me. And every six months, without any expense at all, I draw thirty thousand francs at the Treasury, from a neat little clerk who hands me over thirty notes of a thousand francs each, and smiles at the very sight of me. "Supposing France should go bankrupt?" you'll say. In the first place, "*Je ne sais pas prevoir les malheurs de si loin.*" But even so, the country would not cut down my income by more than half, at most, and I should still be as rich as I was before I made my investment. And further, from now until that catastrophe takes place, I shall have been receiving twice as much as I received in the preceding years. Such financial crashes occur only once in a century, so if I economize I shall be able to lay up fresh capital. And besides, is not the Comte de l'Estorade a peer of the semi-Republican France of the July Revolution? Is he not one of the props of the crown offered by the people to the King of the French? Can I feel the least anxiety, when I remember that I number one of the presidents of the Audit Office, and a great financier to boot, among my friends? Now dare to say I'm mad. I reckon nearly as closely as your Citizen King. And do you know what it is that makes a woman so algebraically wise?

The Memoirs of Two Young Brides

Love! Alas! the time has come for me to explain my mysterious behaviour, the cause of which has escaped your clear-sightedness, your loving curiosity, and your shrewd wit. I am on the point of marrying privately, in a village close to Paris. I love, and I am loved. I love as deeply as a woman who well knows what love is can possibly love. I am loved as fully as a man should love the woman who adores him. Forgive me, Renée, for having hidden this from you, and from all the world. If your Louise has deceived every eye and baffled every curiosity, you must admit that my passion for my poor Macumer rendered this deception indispensable. You and l'Estorade would have plagued me with doubts, and deafened me with remonstrances; and circumstances might possibly have stood you in good stead. You alone know the extent of my constitutional jealousy, and you would have tormented me to no purpose. I was determined to commit what you, my Renée, will call my folly, on my own account, after my own will, my own heart, like some young girl eluding her parents' watchful eyes. My lover's only fortune consists of thirty thousand francs' worth of debts, which I have paid. What an opportunity for expostulation! You would have striven to convince me that Gaston was a schemer, and your husband would have spied upon the poor dear boy. I preferred making my observations on my own account. For the last two-and-twenty months he has been paying his court to me. I am twenty-seven; he is twenty-three. Between a woman and a man such a difference in age is something enormous. Yet another cause of misery! And finally, he is a poet, and lives by his pen—which is the same thing as telling you he has lived on very little indeed. The dear idler spent much more time basking in the sun and building castles in the air, than sitting in the shadow of his garret and working at his poems. Now matter-of-fact people very generally tax authors, artists, and all those who live by their brains, with inconstancy. They espouse and conceive so many fancies, that their heads are not unnaturally supposed to react upon their hearts. In spite of the debts I have paid, in spite of the difference in age, in spite of the poetry—after nine months of noble resistance, during which I had never even given him leave to kiss my hand—after the purest and most delicious of courtships, I am about—not to surrender myself, as I did eight years ago, in all my inexperience, ignorance and curiosity, but to bestow myself deliberately—and with such submission is the gift awaited, that if I chose I might put off my marriage for another year. But there is not a touch of servility in this—it is service, not subjection. Never was there a nobler heart, never was there more wit in tenderness, more soul in love, than in my affianced husband's case. Alas! my dearest, that is but natural. You shall hear his story in a few words.

My friend has no name save those of Marie Gaston. He is the son, not natural, but adulterous, of that beautiful Lady Brandon of whom you must have heard, and on whom Lady Dudley avenged herself by

The Memoirs of Two Young Brides

making her die of sorrow—a horrible story of which this dear boy knows nothing at all. Marie Gaston was placed by his brother, Louis Gaston, at the College of Tours, which he left in 1827. A few days after Louis Gaston had left him there, he himself left the country to seek his fortune—so Marie was told by an old woman who has acted the part of Providence to him. From time to time, this brother, now become a sailor, has written him truly fatherly letters, evidently dictated by a noble heart. But he is still struggling, far away. In his last letter, he told Marie Gaston he had been appointed a flag captain in the navy of some American Republic and that better times would shortly come. But for three years my poor poet has had no letter at all, and so devoted is he to his brother, that he wanted to sail away in search of him. The great writer, Daniel d'Arthez, prevented him from committing this mad act, and has taken the most noble interest in Marie Gaston, to whom he has often given, as the poet says, in his picturesque way, "*la patée et la niche.*" And, indeed, you may conceive the difficulties in which the poor boy has been. He fancied genius would provide him with the most rapid means of making a fortune. Is not that enough to set one laughing for four-and-twenty hours on end? So, from 1828 to 1833, he has been labouring to make himself a name in literature, and has naturally led the most frightful life of hopes and fears, toil and privation, that can be conceived. Led away by his excessive ambition, and in spite of d'Arthez's wise counsels, his debts have been constantly rolling up, like a snow-ball. Nevertheless, his name was beginning to attract attention when I first met him at the house of the Marquise d'Espard. There, at the first sight of him, though without his suspecting it, I felt a sympathetic thrill. How comes it that no one has fallen in love with him yet? How is it that he has been left for me? Oh, he has genius and wit, he has feeling and pride—and perfect nobility of heart always frightens women away.

Had not Napoleon won a hundred fields, before Josephine could recognise him in the little Bonaparte who was her husband? This innocent boy fancies he knows the extent of my love for him. Poor Gaston, he doesn't dream of it. But I'm going to tell it to you—you must know it. For this letter, Renée, is something of a last will and testament. Ponder my words deeply.

At this moment I possess the certainty that I am loved as much as any woman can be loved on earth, and I put all my faith in the adorable conjugal existence to which I bring a love hitherto unknown to me. . . . Yes, at last I know the joys of a mutual passion. That which all women, nowadays, are asking of love, marriage will bring to me. I feel in my soul that adoration for Gaston which my poor Felipe felt for me. I am not mistress of myself, I tremble in that boy's presence just as the Abencerrage once trembled in mine. In short, I love him more than he loves me. I am frightened of everything. I have the

The Memoirs of Two Young Brides

most ridiculous terrors. I fear I may be forsaken; I tremble at the thought that I may grow old and ugly while Gaston is still young and handsome. I tremble lest I may not seem lovable enough to him. Yet I think I possess the powers, the devotion, the intelligence necessary not only to sustain but to increase his love, far from the world, and in the deepest solitude. If I were to fail—if the glorious poem of this secret love were to end—end, did I say?—if Gaston should some day love me less than on the day before, and I were to find it out—remember, Renée, it is not him, it is myself that I should blame. It would be no fault of his, it would be mine. I know my own nature—there is more of the mistress than of the mother in me, and I tell you beforehand I should die, even if I had children. Therefore, before I make this bond with myself, I beseech you, my Renée, if misfortune should overtake me, to be a mother to my children. They will be my legacy to you. Your passionate devotion to duty, your precious qualities, your love of children, your tender affection for me, all that I know of you, will make death seem, I will not say sweet, but less bitter to me. This engagement with myself adds a touch of terror to the solemnity of my marriage. Therefore no one who knows me shall be present at it. Therefore it will be performed in secret. So shall I be free to tremble as I choose—I shall read no anxiety in your eyes, and none but myself will know that when I sign this new marriage bond, I may be signing my own death-warrant.

The Memoirs of Two Young Brides

I will not again refer to this compact between myself and that which I am about to become. I have confided it to you, only that you might know the full extent of your responsibilities. I am marrying with the full control of my own fortune, and though Gaston is aware that I am rich enough to enable us to live in comfort, he knows nothing about the amount of my income. In twenty-four hours I shall distribute my fortune according to my own will. As I don't choose my husband to find himself in a humiliating position, I have transferred an income of twelve thousand francs to his name. The night before our marriage he will find the bond in his writing-table, and if he were to object, I should postpone everything. I had to threaten I would not marry him, before I could get leave to pay his debts. I am tired with writing all these confessions to you, the day after to-morrow I will tell you more—but to-morrow I am obliged to spend the whole day in the country.

20th October.

Here are the measures I have adopted to screen my bliss from prying eyes—for I am bent on removing every possible cause likely to excite my native jealousy. I am like the lovely Italian princess who, having sprung like a lioness upon her prey, carried her love off, like a lioness, to devour it in some Swiss village. And I only mention my arrangements, that I may ask you to do me another kindness—never to come and see us unless I have asked you to come myself, and to respect my desire to live in solitude.

The Memoirs of Two Young Brides

Two years ago, I bought some twenty acres of meadow-land, a strip of wood, and a fine fruit garden, all standing above the lakes at Ville d'Avray, on the way to Versailles. In the midst of these meadows, I have had the ground excavated, so as to make a lake of about three acres, in the centre of which I have left an island with prettily indented shores. From the two beautiful wooded hills that shut in the little valley, several charming brooks run through my grounds, and my architect has taken cunning advantage of them. These streams all fall into the lakes on the Crown property, of which we catch occasional glimpses. The park, which has been laid out most beautifully by my architect, is surrounded, according to the nature of the ground, by hedges, walls, and sunk fences, so that the most is made of every view. In a most delightful situation, half-way up the slope, and flanked by the woods, with a meadow in front, sloping down towards the lake, I have built a chalet exactly the same in external appearance as that which all travellers admire on the road from Sion to Brieg, and which so took my fancy on my way back from Italy. Within doors, the elegance of the chalet defies the competition of its most illustrious compeers. A hundred paces from this rustic dwelling is a charming little house, communicating with the chalet by an underground passage. This contains the kitchen, offices, stables and coach-house. The façade of these brick-built edifices, most graceful and simple in design, and surrounded with shrubberies, is the only portion of them that is visible. The gardeners live in another building, which masks the entrance to the orchards and kitchen gardens.

The gate into the demesne, sunk in the wall that bounds it on the wooded side, is almost undiscoverable. In two or three years the plantations, which are already very tall, will have so grown up that the buildings will be quite concealed. The passer-by will never suspect the existence of our dwelling, except by the smoke he will see curling upward as he looks down from the hills, or else in winter time when the leaves are all fallen.

My chalet has been built in the middle of a landscape copied from what is known as the King's Garden, at Versailles, only that it looks out over my lake and my island. On every side are the hills, with their verdant masses, and the fine trees which are so admirably cared for under your new Civil List. My gardeners have orders to grow nothing but sweet-scented flowers and thousands of them, so that this corner of the earth may always be like a perfumed emerald. The chalet, the roof of which is hung with masses of Virginia creeper, is literally hidden under climbing plants—hops, clematis, jessamine, azaleas, and cobæa. The man who contrives to make out our windows may fairly boast of his good sight.

The said chalet, my dear, is a pretty and comfortable house, with its heating apparatus and all the conveniences known to our modern architects, who can design palaces to fit into a square of a hundred

The Memoirs of Two Young Brides

feet. There is a set of rooms in it for Gaston, and a set of rooms for me. The ground-floor consists of an ante-room, a parlour, and a dining-room. Above our own rooms are three more, intended for the nursery. I have five fine horses, a light brougham and a "milord," each to be drawn by a pair. We are only forty minutes' drive from Paris. When we have a fancy to listen to an opera or see a new play, we can after dinner, and come home to our nest at night. The road is a good one, and it runs under the shadow of our boundary hedge. My servants—the *chef*, the coachman, the groom, the gardeners, my own maid—are all very respectable people, for whom I have been looking about for the last six months, and they will be under my old Philippe's orders. Though I am sure of their attachment and discretion, I have bound them to me by their interest as well. Their wages are not very high, but they will be raised every successive year, by our New Year's gifts to them. They all know that the slightest failure in discretion, or even a doubt on that score, would cost them immense benefits. People who are in love with each other never worry their servants. They are naturally indulgent. So I can reckon on my people.

All the precious, pretty, and dainty things that were in my house in the Rue du Bac are now in my chalet. The Rembrandt (as if it were a mere daub) is on the stair-case. The Hobbima hangs in *his* dressing-room, opposite the Rubens. The Titian my sister-in-law Maria sent me from Madrid adorns the boudoir.

The Memoirs of Two Young Brides

All the beautiful bits of furniture Felipe picked up have found appropriate places in the parlour, which my architect has decorated in the most delightful manner. Everything about my chalet is exquisitely simple—with that simplicity that costs a hundred thousand francs. The ground-floor, built over cellars constructed of flint stones set in concrete, and almost hidden by flowers and climbing shrubs, is most deliciously cool, without being in the slightest degree damp, and a bevy of white swans floats on the lake.

Oh, Renée, there is a stillness in my valley that would rejoice the dead! In the morning I am roused by the songs of the birds or by the whisper of the breeze among the poplars. When my architect was digging the foundation of the wall that skirts the woods, he came upon a little spring that runs down into the lake, over a bed of silvery sand, and between two banks of water-cress. I don't think any money value could be set upon that rill. Won't Gaston take a horror of this overperfect bliss? It is all so lovely that I shudder with fear. Worms burrow into the choicest fruits, insects attack the loveliest flowers. Doesn't that hideous brown grub, whose greediness is like the greed of death itself, always choose the pride of the whole forest for its prey? Already I have learnt that an invisible and jealous power can lay an angry hand on absolute felicity. Long ago, you wrote it to me—and, indeed, you were a true prophet.

When I went down the day before yesterday, to see if my last whims had been duly comprehended, I felt the tears spring into my eyes, and, to the architect's great surprise, I wrote "Payment approved" across the memorandum of his charges.

"Your lawyer will refuse payment, madame," he said. "It's a matter of three hundred thousand francs."

Like a true daughter of my seventeenth-century ancestresses, I added the words, "without discussion."

"But, sir," I added, "I burden my acknowledgment with one condition. Never mention these buildings, nor the grounds in which they stand, to any living soul. Never tell any one the name of their proprietor. Promise me, on your honour, that you will observe this clause in our agreement."

Now do you understand the meaning of all my sudden journeys, all my secret goings and comings? Now do you see whither all the beautiful things I am supposed to have sold have gone? Do you understand the deep reason at the bottom of the alteration in my financial arrangements? My dear, love is a tremendous business, and the woman who wants to do that well must have no other. I shall never have any worry about money again. I have simplified my life, and I've played the notable housekeeper well and thoroughly, so that I may never have to do it again, except for my ten minutes' talk every morning with my old steward Philippe. I have watched life and its dangerous eddies closely. There was a day on which death taught me cruel things. I mean to profit by those teachings. To love him, to be his delight, to impart variety to that which seems so monotonous to ordinary folk—these shall be my sole and only occupations.

Gaston knows nothing at all as yet. At my request, he has registered his domicile, as I have mine, at Ville d'Avray. We shall start to-morrow for the chalet. Our life there will not cost a great deal of money. But if I were to tell you the sum I reckon for the expenses of my dress, you would say, and truly, "She is mad!" I mean to deck myself out for him, every day, just as other women deck themselves for society. Living in the country all the year round, my dress will cost me twenty-four thousand francs a year, and the garments I wear in the daytime will not be by any means the most expensive. He may wear blouses if he likes. Don't think I want to turn my life into a duel, and wear myself out in inventions for feeding passion. All I desire is to avoid ever having to reproach myself. There are thirteen years before me during which I may still be a pretty woman—I want to be loved more fondly on the last day of the thirteenth year than I shall be loved on the morrow of my secret marriage. I will always be humble, always grateful, this time; I will never say a sharp word. Since it was command that wrought my ruin in the first instance, I will be a servant now. Oh, Renée, if Gaston has realized the preciousness of love as I have, I am certain to be happy all my days! Nature is beautiful all around my chalet, the woods are quite entrancing. At every turn the most verdant landscapes

The Memoirs of Two Young Brides

lie before me, and the woodland views delight the soul and inspire the most exquisite fancies. These woods are alive with love. Heaven grant I may have prepared myself something better than a gorgeous funeral pyre! The day after to-morrow I shall be Madame Gaston. Good God! sometimes I ask myself whether any Christian ought to love a man so much!

"Well, it's legal, at all events," quoth my man of business, who is to witness my marriage, and who, when at last he perceived my object in realizing my fortune, cried, "This will cost me my client."

You, my beautiful—I dare no longer say my beloved—darling, you may say, "This costs me a sister."

My dearest, address your letters in future to Madame Gaston, Poste Restante, Versailles. We all send over there for our letters every day. I do not want our name to be known in this neighbourhood. We shall send up to Paris for all our provisions. By this means I hope to be able to live in mystery. My retreat has been ready for me for a whole year, and not a soul has seen it. The purchase was made during the disturbances which followed on the Revolution of July. My architect is the only being who has been seen in the country-side, nobody there knows any one but him, and he will never come again. Farewell! As I write the word, my heart is as full of sorrow as of joy. Does not that mean that I regret you as deeply as I worship Gaston?

XLIX

FROM MARIE GASTON TO DANIEL D'ARTHEZ

October, 1833.

MY DEAR DANIEL: I want two friends to act as witnesses at my marriage. I beg you'll come to me to-morrow evening and bring our good and noble-hearted friend, Joseph Bridau, with you. The lady who is to be my wife intends to live far from the world, and utterly unknown—she thus anticipates my dearest wish. You, who have softened the sufferings of my life of poverty, have known nothing of my love, but you will have guessed that this absolute secrecy was a necessity. This is why we have seen so little of each other for the last year. The morrow of our marriage will mark the beginning of a longer separation. Daniel, your heart was fashioned to understand mine—friendship will endure although the friend be absent. Perhaps I shall sometimes need you, but I shall not see you—in my own home, at all events. In this, too, she has forestalled our wishes. She has sacrificed her affection for the friend of her childhood, to whom she has been as a sister, for my sake, and I must give up my friend for hers. What I tell you here will doubtless show you that this is not a mere passion, but

The Memoirs of Two Young Brides

love—full, complete, divine, founded on intimate acquaintance between the two beings who thus bind themselves. My happiness is pure and infinite, but—since a hidden law forbids any man the possession of unalloyed felicity—at the bottom of my heart, and hidden in its inmost depth, I hide a thought which touches me alone, and whereof she knows nothing. You have helped me so often, in my incessant poverty, that you are well aware how dreadful my condition has been. Whence did I draw courage to live on, even when hope died, as it so often did? From your past, my friend, and from you—who gave me such liberal consolation and such delicate help. Well, my dear fellow, she has paid all those pressing debts of mine. She has wealth, and I have nothing. How often, in one of my fits of idleness, have I exclaimed, "Oh, if some rich woman would but take a fancy to me!" Well, in presence of the actual fact, the jest of careless youth, the settled determination of poverty that knows no scruple, have all faded away. In spite of my absolute certainty of her nobility of heart, I feel humiliated, even while I know that my humiliation proves my love. Well, she has seen I have not flinched from this abasement! There is a matter in which, far from my protecting her, she has protected me—and this suffering I confide to you. Apart from this, dear Daniel, my dreams are realized to the very uttermost. I have found spotless beauty and perfect goodness. In fact, as the saying is, the bride is too beautiful. There is wit in her tenderness; she has that charm and grace which impart variety to love; she is well taught, and understands everything; she is pretty, fair, slight, and yet plump—so that one would fancy Raphael and Rubens each had a hand in her composition. I don't know that I should ever have been able to love a dark woman as much as a fair one. A dark woman has always struck me as being rather like a boy who has been spoilt in the making. She is a widow, she has never had a child, she is twenty-seven. Though she is lively, active, and untiring, she knows how to find pleasure in melancholy meditation. In spite of these marvellous gifts, she is both dignified and noble looking; she has an imposing air. Though she comes of one of the proudest of our aristocratic families, she cares for me enough to overlook the misfortune of my birth. Our hidden loves had lasted for a considerable time: we have put each other to the test; we are both of us jealous; our thoughts are twin flashes from the same thunderbolt. With each of us, this is our first love, and the joys of this exquisite spring-tide have filled our hearts with all the most exquisite, the sweetest and the deepest feelings that imagination can conceive. Sentiment has showered down flowers upon us. Every one of our days has been complete, and when we were apart we wrote each other poems. It has never occurred to me to tarnish this glorious season with an expression of desire, although my heart was always full of it. She, a widow, and a free woman, has perfectly appreciated the tribute rendered her by this perpetual restraint—

The Memoirs of Two Young Brides

it has often touched her even to tears. Thus, my dear Daniel, you will catch a glimpse of a really superior being. We have never even exchanged our first kiss, we have each been afraid of the other.

"Both of us have a trifle to reproach ourselves with," said she to me.

"I don't know what yours may be."

"My marriage," was her answer.

You, who are a great man, and who love one of the most remarkable women of that aristocracy in which I have found my Armande, will divine her nature from those words, and gauge the future happiness of your friend, MARIE GASTON.

L

FROM MME. DE L'ESTORADE TO MME. DE MACUMER

WHAT'S this, Louise? After all the griefs a mutual passion, and that a married passion has brought upon you, you propose to live a life of solitude with another husband? After having killed one man, even when you lived with him in the world, you must needs go apart to devour another! What sorrows you are preparing for yourself! But I can see by the way you have set about it, that the whole thing is irrevocable. Any man who can overcome your horror of a second marriage must have the mind of an angel and the heart of a god. So I must leave you to your illusions. But have you forgotten all you used to say about the youth of men—that they have all been through vile experiences, and dropped their innocence on the filthiest crossings of the road of life? Which has altered —they or you? You are very lucky to be able to believe in happiness. I have not the heart to blame you, although my instinctive affection impels me to dissuade you from this marriage. Yes, a hundred times, yes! Nature and Society do agree together to destroy the existence of any complete felicity, because such

The Memoirs of Two Young Brides

felicity is hostile to Nature and Society—because, it may be, Heaven is jealous of its rights. My love for you, in short, dreads some misfortune, the nature of which no amount of foresight can reveal to me. I know not whence it is to come, nor from which of you it will spring. But, my dearest, immense and boundless happiness is certain to break you down. Excessive joy is more difficult to endure than the most crushing sorrow. I do not say one word against him. You love him, and I, no doubt, have never laid my eyes upon him; but one of these days, I hope, when you feel idle, you will send me some written portrait of this beautiful and curious animal.

You see I am making my mind up to the whole business cheerfully. For I am certain that once your honeymoon is over, you'll both reappear, like everybody else, and of your own free-will. One of these days, some two years hence, when you and I are out together, we shall drive down that road, and you'll say to me, "Why, there's the chalet I was never to have left again!" . . . and you'll laugh your merry laugh that shows all your pretty teeth. I've said nothing to Louis as yet. He would laugh at us too much. I shall simply tell him you are married, and that you wish your marriage to be kept secret. You need neither mother nor sister, alas! to attend you to your bridal-chamber. This is October. You are beginning your life in the winter, like a brave woman. If I were not talking about a marriage, I should say you were taking the bull by the horns. Well, you will al-

The Memoirs of Two Young Brides

ways find me the most discreet and understanding of friends. The mysteries of Central Africa have swallowed up many a traveller. And as far as your heart is concerned, you seem to me to be starting on a journey very like those in which so many explorers have perished, by the hand of negroes, or on those burning sands. But your desert is only two leagues from Paris, so I can waft you a cheerful " pleasant journey." We shall soon see you back!

LI

FROM THE COMTESSE DE L'ESTORADE TO MME. MARIE GASTON

1835.

WHAT has become of you, my dear? After two years of silence, Renée may really be excused for growing anxious about Louise. So this is love! It outweighs and utterly wipes out even such a friendship as ours. You'll admit, though my adoration for my children is greater than even your love for Gaston, there is a certain grandeur about the maternal feeling, which obviates any diminution of the other affections, and permits a woman to continue a sincere and devoted friend. I miss your letters and your sweet charming face. I am reduced to conjecturing about you, O Louise!

As for our own story, I'll tell it as concisely as I can. Reading over your last letter, I notice a somewhat tart remark as to our political position. You reproach us with not having resigned the office of Departmental Chief at the Audit Office, which we owed, like the title of Count, to the favour of Charles X. But how else—with an income of forty thousand francs, thirty thousand of which are settled on my eldest boy—was I to provide a suitable maintenance for Athénais, and for my poor little René? Does not our only chance lie in living on our official income, and carefully putting by whatever our landed property brings us in? In twenty years we shall have laid by some six hundred thousand francs, which will provide fortunes for my daughter and for René, whom I mean to send into the navy. My poor little man will have ten thousand francs a year, and perhaps we may be able to leave him as much, besides, as will make his share equal to his sister's. Once he is a Post-Captain, my penniless boy will make a rich marriage, and hold as good a position in the world as his elder brother.

These considerations of prudence decided us to accept the new order of things. The new dynasty has, very naturally, made Louis a Peer of France, and appointed him a Grand Officer of the Legion of Honour. Once l'Estorade had taken the oath, he could not well do things by halves, and since his adhesion, he has rendered valuable service to the throne in the Chamber of Deputies. He has now attained a position which he will peacefully enjoy for the remainder of his days. He is more of a pleasant speaker than an orator, but that suffices for all we want to get out of politics. His shrewdness, his experience in matters of government and administration, are much appreciated, and he is considered indispensable by men of every party. I may tell you that he has lately been offered an embassy and refused it, at my instigation.

The Memoirs of Two Young Brides

The education of my children—Armand is now thirteen, and Athénais is nearly eleven—keeps me in Paris, and I intend to live there until my little René's, which is now just beginning, is completed.

A married couple that proposes to maintain its allegiance to the elder branch and retire to the country on that account, must not have three children to educate and put out into the world. A mother, my dear love, must not be a Decius, more especially at a period when a Decius is a very uncommon bird. In another fifteen years l'Estorade will be able to retire to La Crampade on a handsome pension, and to leave Armand here behind him with the post of Referendary. As for René, I have no doubt the navy will turn him into a diplomat. At the age of seven, the little rogue is as cunning as an old cardinal.

Ah, Louise, I am a very happy mother. My children are an endless joy to me. (*Senza brama sicura richezza!*) Armand is at the Collège Henri IV. I settled he must be educated in a public establishment, and yet I could not make up my mind to part with him. So I have done as the Duc d'Orléans did before he was Louis Philippe, and, it may have been, with an eye to the attainment of that dignity. Every morning, our old man-servant Lucas, with whom you are acquainted, takes Armand to the college in time for the first class, and he fetches him home again at half past four. An excellent elderly tutor, who lives in the house, works with him at night, and wakes him every morning at the hour when the college pupils

The Memoirs of Two Young Brides

leave their beds. Lucas brings his luncheon to him at twelve, when there is a break for play. Thus, I see him at dinner, and before he goes to bed at night, and I am there every morning when he starts. Armand is still the delightful, affectionate, unselfish boy of whom you were so fond. His tutor is very well satisfied with him. I have my Nais and my little fellow with me constantly. Their buzzing never ceases. But I am as great a baby as they. I have never been able to make up my mind to being deprived of the sweetness of my dear children's caressing ways. It is a necessity of my existence to be able to fly to Armand's bedside whenever I choose, to look at him as he lies asleep, to take, or ask, or receive a kiss from my darling's lips.

Nevertheless, there are drawbacks to the system of bringing up children under the paternal roof, and I fully recognise their existence. Society, like Nature, is jealous, and brooks no interference with its laws. Nor will it permit any disturbance of its eternal economy. Thus, children who are kept at home are exposed to the action of the outer world at much too early an age. Incapable as they are of divining the distinctions that affect the behaviour of grown-up folk, they subordinate everything to their own feelings and passions, instead of subordinating their desires and requests to those of other people. They develop a sort of false lustre, more showy than solid virtue—for the world is apt to put forward appearances, and dress them up in deceptive forms. When a child of fifteen has the assurance of a man who knows the world, he becomes a monster. He is an old man by the time he is five-and-twenty, and that precocious knowledge unfits him for the genuine study on which real and serious talent must rely. Society is a great comedian. Like a comedian, it receives and reproduces everything, but it keeps nothing. Therefore, the mother who keeps her children at home, must make an unflinching resolution to prevent them from appearing in society; she must have the courage to stand out against their wishes and her own, and never to allow them to be seen. Cornelia must have kept her jewels in a place of safety, and I will do the same; for all my life is bound up in my children.

I am thirty now, the sultriest moment of the day is past, the most difficult part of my journey lies behind me. Before many years are out, I shall be an old woman, and I find immense strength in the thought of the duties I have performed. One would fancy these three little creatures realize my thought and share it. There is a sort of mysterious understanding between me and the children, who have never been parted from me. Indeed, they fill my existence with delight, as though they were conscious of all the compensations they owe me.

Armand, who for the first three years of his school life was slow and dreamy, and rather an anxiety to me, has suddenly taken a fresh turn. No doubt he has realized the object of these preparatory studies—an object children do not always perceive, that of giving them the habit of work, sharpening their intelligence, and inuring them to that obedience which is the cardinal principle of social existence. A few days since, my dear, I enjoyed the intoxicating delight of seeing Armand a prize-winner at the general examination at the Sorbonne, at which your godson was first in translation. At the Collège Henri Quatre he won two first-prizes—one for verses, and the other for composition. I felt myself turn white when his name was called, and I longed to scream out, " I am his mother!" Nais was squeezing my hand so tight that she would have hurt me if I could have felt anything at such a moment. Ah, Louise, such bliss as that is worth many hidden loves!

His elder brother's success has stirred my little René's ambition, and he longs to go to college too. Sometimes the three children make such a noise, shouting and running about the house, that I don't know how I bear it; for I am always with them. I never trust any one, not even Mary, to look after them. But there is so much happiness to be found in the noble work of motherhood. To see a child leave its game to kiss me, as if it felt a sudden need of me— what joy that is! And then, here again is one great opportunity for watching them. One of a mother's duties is to discern, from their earliest age, the aptitudes, character, and vocation of each child. This is what no schoolmaster can do. Children who are brought up by their mothers all possess good manners and the habits of society—two acquisitions which

The Memoirs of Two Young Brides

may take the place of natural understanding. Whereas natural understanding unaided can never replace what men learn from their mothers only. I can recognise all these various shades among the men I meet in society, and can always detect the woman's influence in a young man's manners. How can any mother deprive her child of such advantages? As you see, the duties I have accomplished yield me a rich and precious harvest of delight.

Armand, I am perfectly sure, will make the most excellent magistrate, the most upright administrator, the most conscientious Deputy that ever was seen. And my little René will be the boldest, the most adventurous, and at the same time the shrewdest sailor that ever lived. The little rogue has a will of iron. He gets everything he wants; he will find his way round a thousand corners to reach his goal, and if the thousandth trick avail him nothing, he will find another. When dear Armand submits quietly, and considers the reason of everything, my René will storm, and set his wits to work, and try one thing or another, chattering all the while, till he ends by discovering some tiny crack, and then if he can contrive to get so much as a knife-blade into it, he'll end by driving his little carriage through.

As for Naïs, she is so absolutely part of me that I can hardly distinguish her being from my own. Ah, my darling, my little precious daughter! whom I love to dress up, whose hair I braid so fondly, twisting a loving thought into every curl. I am resolved she

The Memoirs of Two Young Brides

shall be happy. But, good heavens! when I let her deck herself out, when I wind green ribbons in her hair, and put on her dainty little shoes—a thought springs to my heart and brain that turns me almost sick. Can a mother control her daughter's fate? She may fall in love with a man who is not worthy of her. It may be that the man she loves will not love her. Often, as I sit looking at her, the tears come into my eyes. Think what it will be to part with that darling creature, that flower, that rose that has blossomed in my arms like a bud upon a rose-bush, and to give her to a man who will carry her quite away from me! You, who in the last two years have never once written me those three words, "I am happy."—you, I say, it is, who have reminded me of the dramatic side of marriage, so terrible to a mother whose maternal feeling is as intense as mine. Farewell! for I don't know why I write to you—you don't deserve that I should love you. Ah, do let me have an answer, my Louise!

LII

MME. GASTON TO MME. DE L'ESTORADE

THE CHALET.

MY two years' silence has roused your curiosity, and you wonder why I have not written to you. Well, my dearest Renée, words, phrases, language itself, fail to express my happiness. Our souls are strong enough to bear it—there, in two words, you have the whole of my story. Not the slightest effort on our part is necessary to insure our happiness—we are agreed on every subject. Never in these two years has there been the slightest discord in the concert; the smallest disagreement in the expression of our feelings; the tiniest difference in our most trifling desires. In short, my dear, there has not been one of these thousand days but has borne its own special fruit, not a moment that fancy has not rendered exquisite. Not only are we certain now that our life will never be monotonous, but we feel it will most likely never be wide enough to hold all the poetry of our love—as fruitful as Nature herself, and just as varied. No, not one disappointment have we had! We love each other far more dearly than on the first day, and every moment we discover fresh reasons for mutual adoration. Night after night, we say to each other, when we take our walk after dinner, that we must go and look at Paris out of curiosity: just as one would say, "I must go and see Switzerland."

"Why," Gaston will cry, "there's such and such a boulevard to see, and the Madeleine is finished. We really must go and look at it."

Pshaw! when the next morning comes, we stay in bed; we breakfast in our room. By the time twelve o'clock comes, it has grown hot, we allow ourselves a little siesta. Then he'll ask me to let him look at me, and he'll gaze at me just as if I were a picture. He quite loses himself in this contemplation, which, as you will imagine, is reciprocal. Then the tears come into our eyes, we both think how happy we are, and we tremble. I am still his mistress—in other words, I seem to love him less than he loves me. This illusion is delightful to me. There is something so charming to us women in seeing sentiment override desire, and watching our master stop short timidly, just where we choose him to remain. You have asked me to describe him to you—but no woman, my Renée, can draw a truthful picture of the man she loves. And then between you and me, and prudery apart, we may acknowledge one strange and melancholy consequence of our social habits. Nothing can be farther apart than the man who succeeds in society, and the man who makes a good lover. So great is this difference, that the first may bear no resemblance whatever to the second. The man who will assume the most charming attitude known to the most graceful of

The Memoirs of Two Young Brides

dances, when he drops a word of love into a lady's ear as they stand beside the fire-place, may not possess a single one of those hidden charms for which every woman longs. On the other hand, a man who strikes one as ugly, without charm of manner, clumsily huddled into a black evening-suit, may possess the very genius of the lover's passion, and never look ridiculous at any of those moments in which we ourselves, with all our external charm, may show to disadvantage. To discover a man who does possess that mysterious agreement between what he is and what he seems to be, who, in the secrecy of marriage, displays that innate grace which can not be given or acquired, the grace expressed by the ancient sculptor in the chaste and voluptuous embraces of his figures—that innocent simplicity we find in the antique poems, and which even in its nakedness seems to drape the soul with modesty—that great ideal which depends upon ourselves alone and is bound up with the law of harmony, the guiding spirit, doubtless, of all things—that mighty problem, in short, after which feminine fancy hankers ever and always, finding its living solution in my Gaston.

Ah, dearest, I never knew before what love and youth and wit and beauty, all together, meant. My Gaston is never affected, he is instinctively graceful, and makes no effort to appear so. When we wander alone about our woods, his arm clasping my waist, mine resting on his shoulder, our bodies close together, and our heads touching, our step is so equal, our movement so uniform, so gentle, so absolutely alike, that any one seeing us pass by would take us for a single being gliding along the gravel path like Homer's Immortals. This harmony runs through all our desires and thoughts and words. Sometimes, when the leaves are still wet by a passing shower, and the green of the grass still sparkles with rain, we have taken long walks without ever uttering a word, just listening to the falling drops and admiring the ruddy sunset colours that lay smooth on the tree-tops or broken on their trunks. At such moments, truly, our thoughts have been a dim and hidden prayer, that lifted itself up to heaven, as though to excuse our happiness.

Sometimes, again, a cry will break from us both, at the same moment, at the sight of some sharp turn in the woodland path, opening on an exquisite distant view. If you only knew what sweetness and intensity there is in a kiss exchanged, almost shyly, in the presence of holy Nature! . . . it is enough to make one think God had created us on purpose to pray after this special fashion, and we always go home more in love with each other than ever. In Paris, such passionate love between two married people would appear an insult to society. We must live for it, like two lovers, hidden in the woods.

Gaston, my dear, is of middle height; like almost all vigorous men, he is neither fat nor thin, and very well built; there is a fulness in all his proportions; he is alert in all his movements, and will bound over a ditch as lightly as any wild creature. Whatever may be the position in which he finds himself, he has a sort of instinct which always makes him find his balance—and this is rare in the case of men who habitually spend much time in meditation. Although he is dark, his skin is exceedingly white. His hair is as black as jet, and contrasts strongly with the fairness of his neck and forehead. He is very like the sad-looking portraits of Louis XIII. He has let his moustache grow, and his *royale* too, but I have made him shave his whiskers and beard—everybody wears them now. His blessed poverty has kept him pure from all the contamination which has ruined so many young men. He has magnificent teeth; his health is splendid. His piercing blue eyes, full of the sweetest fascination when they fall on me, light up and blaze like a lightning flash, when his soul is stirred. Like all strong men of powerful intellect, he has an equability of temper that would surprise you, as it has surprised me. I have listened to many women's descriptions of their home sorrows—but all that changeableness and restlessness of the man who is dissatisfied with himself, who either does not choose, or does not know, how to grow old, whose life is full of the eternal reproach of his youthful follies, who carries poison in his veins, whose eyes always have a touch of sadness in them, who scolds to hide his lack of self-reliance, who makes us pay for one hour's peace with whole forenoons of misery, who avenges his own incapacity for being lovable upon his wife, and nurses a secret spite against her charms—all these discomforts are unknown to youth. They are the proper attributes of ill-proportioned unions. Oh, my dear soul, mind you marry Athénais to a young man. If you only know how I feed on that constant smile that varies never-endingly with every turn of a keen and delicate intelligence—a speaking smile, with thoughts of love and silent gratitude, hovering at the corners of the lips—a smile that is a perpetual bond between our past and present joys. Never is anything forgotten between us. We have taken the smallest of Nature's works into the secret of our happiness. Everything in these delicious woods lives and speaks to us of ourselves. An old moss-covered oak, close to the keeper's house on the road, reminds us that once, when we were tired, we sat down under its shade, that Gaston told me about the mosses growing at our feet, explained their history to me, and that from those mosses we worked upward, from one science to another, till we reached the ends of the world. There is something so fraternal in our two minds, that I think we must be two editions of the same work. You'll notice I have grown literary. We both of us have the habit or the gift of grasping the whole of a matter, and seeing all its meaning, and the proof we constantly afford ourselves of this clearness of our mental vision is an ever-new delight to us. We have reached the point of regarding this mental agreement as an evidence of our love, and if ever it were to fail us, that failure would affect us as an act of unfaithfulness another couple would affect.

The Memoirs of Two Young Brides

My life, full of joys as it is, would strike you, no doubt, as very laborious. In the first place, my dear, let me tell you that Louise Armande Marie de Chaulieu keeps her own room in order. I could never allow any paid servant, any strange woman or girl, to learn the secrets (literary woman again) of my private and personal arrangements. My scruples extend to the most trifling of the matters indispensable to the practice of my religion. This is not jealousy, but simple self-respect. And everything about my room is kept with all the care that a young girl in love lavishes upon her own adornment. I am as particular as any old maid. Instead of being a chaos, my dressing-room is a delightful boudoir. My care has provided for every possibility. My sovereign lord can enter whenever he chooses. Never is anything to be seen that might distress, astound, or disenchant him. Everything in the room—flowers, perfume, dainty refinement of all kinds—delights the senses. At daybreak every morning, while he is still sound asleep, and without his ever having found it out, so far, I get up. I slip into my dressing-room, and there, with a skill I owe to my mother's experience, I remove every trace of slumber by a liberal application of cold water. While we sleep the skin is less active, and its work less thoroughly performed. It gets heated, there is a fog upon it, a sort of atmosphere that the eye of the tiniest insect might detect. Under her streaming sponges the woman is transformed into a girl once more. My bath indues me with all the fascinating graces of the dawn. I comb out and perfume my hair, and after this careful toilet, I slip back like a mouse, so that when my master wakes he may find me as fresh as a spring morning. This way I have of blooming in the morning, like a newly opened flower, delights him, though he has never been able to discover its cause. My dressing for the day, which is done later, is my maid's concern, and takes place in a room set apart for the purpose. I make another toilet, as you may suppose, before I go to bed. Thus every day I make three for my lord and husband, and sometimes four—but this, my dear, is connected with quite different myths of antiquity.

We have our occupations as well. We take a deep interest in our flowers, in the beautiful treasures of our greenhouses, and in our trees. We are serious botanists, passionately devoted to our flowers—and the chalet is full of them. Our lawns are always green, our flower-beds are as carefully kept as those in the gardens of the richest banker in the world, and really nothing can be more beautiful than our grounds. We are excessively devoted to our fruit, and we watch our Montreuil peaches, our forcing pits, our espaliers, and our standards. But fearing these country interests might not satisfy the intellectual requirements of the man I adore, I have advised him to take advantage of the silence of our solitude to finish some of the plays—really fine compositions—he began to write in the days of his poverty.

This is the only kind of literary work which bears

taking up, and laying aside, for it needs prolonged reflection, and does not require the polish indispensable to style. Dialogue is not a thing that can be written always; it must be spontaneous, it demands conciseness, and flashes of wit, which the mind puts forth just as plants put forth their flowers, and which must be waited on rather than sought. This pursuit of ideas just suits me, I am Gaston's collaborator, and thus I never leave him, even in his wanderings athwart the wide field of fancy. Now you guess how I get through our winter evenings. Our service is so light, that since our marriage we have never had to say one word of reproach, or fault-finding to any of our servants. When they have been asked questions about us, they have been sharp enough to impose upon their questioners, and have passed us off as the companion and secretary of their employers, who, they have declared, are away on a journey. Knowing full well that permission will never be refused, they never go out without asking leave, and besides, they are comfortable, and quite aware that nothing but their own misdoing will alter their position. The gardeners have leave to sell the fruit and vegetables we do not want; the dairy-woman does the same with the milk and cream and fresh butter, only the best of everything is kept for us. The servants are all delighted with their profits, and we are enchanted with the abundance we enjoy and which no wealth can possibly procure in that dreadful Paris, where every fine peach costs you the interest on a hundred francs. There is a meaning, my dear, in all this! I must be the whole world to Gaston. Now the world is amusing, and therefore my husband must not be bored in his solitude. I fancied I was jealous in the days when I was loved and allowed myself to be loved. But now I know the jealousy of the woman who loves—real jealousy, in fact, and any glance of his that strikes me as careless sets me trembling. Every now and then I say to myself, "Supposing he didn't love me any more!" and I shudder. Oh, indeed, I adore him, even as a Christian soul adores the Deity.

Alas, my Renée, I am still childless. The moment will come some day, no doubt, when this retreat will need the cheering influence of parental love, when we shall both of us long to see little frocks and coats and little heads, dark-haired or golden, dancing and trotting among our garden-beds and along our flowery paths. Oh, there is something monstrous about flowers that bear no fruit! The thought of your beautiful children is painful to me. My life has narrowed, while yours has grown and spread itself abroad. Love is profoundly selfish, but maternity tends to widen all our feelings. I felt this difference deeply, as I read your dear and loving letter. I envied your happiness, when I saw how you lived again in three other hearts. Yes, you are happy; you have faithfully fulfilled the laws of social existence, whereas I stand outside all that. Nothing but loved and loving children can console a woman for the loss of her beauty. Soon I

The Memoirs of Two Young Brides

shall be thirty, and at that age a woman begins a course of terrible internal lamentation. Beautiful as I still am, the limits of feminine existence are within my sight—what will become of me after I have reached them? When I am forty, *he* will not be forty. He will still be young; I shall be old. When that thought strikes my heart, I spend a whole hour at his feet, making him swear to me that the moment he feels the slightest diminution of his love for me, he will tell me instantly. But he's a child! He swears it to me as though his love were never to grow less, and he's so beautiful that . . . you understand, I believe him. Farewell, my dearest love! Will it be years again before we write to each other? Happiness is very monotonous in its expression. Perhaps it is because of this difficulty that Dante strikes loving souls as being greater in his Paradiso than in his Inferno. I am not Dante, I am only your friend, and I do not want to bore you. But you, you can write to me. For in your children you possess a varied and constantly increasing happiness, whereas mine. . . . We'll say no more about it. I send you a thousand loves.

LIII

FROM MME. DE L'ESTORADE TO MME. GASTON

My dear Louise: I've read and reread your letter, and the more I ponder it the more I feel that there is less of the woman than of the child in you. You have not altered, you have forgotten what I have told you over and over again—Love is a theft practised on the natural by the social state. It is so essentially short-lived that the resources of society cannot alter its primitive conditions. Every noble soul essays to turn the child into a man, but then love becomes what you yourself have called it—a monstrosity. Society, my dear, desired fecundity, and when it substituted enduring feeling for the evanescent passion of Nature, it created the greatest of all human institutions, the Family—which is the eternal basis of social existence. Both man and woman are sacrificed to this object—for, let us not deceive ourselves, the father of the family bestows his activity, his strength, and all his fortune, on his wife. Is it not the wife who enjoys the benefit of almost every sacrifice? Are not luxury and wealth almost wholly spent on her who is the glory and the elegance, the sweetness and

The Memoirs of Two Young Brides

the beauty of the household? Oh, my dearest, you are making another great mistake about your life. The idea of being adored is very well for two or three spring-times in the life of a young girl, but it is quite inappropriate to the woman who is a wife and mother. A woman's vanity may be satisfied when she knows she can make herself adored. If you would be mother as well as wife, come back to Paris. Let me tell you again, that you will ruin yourself by happiness, just as many others are ruined by misfortune. Those things which do not weary us, such as silence, and bread, and air, are void of reproach because they are void of taste. Whereas strong-tasting things, which excite desire, all end by jading it. Hear me, dear child! Even if it were possible for me now to be loved by a man for whom I felt the love you bear Gaston, I would still be faithful to my beloved duty and my sweet children. To a woman's heart, my dearest, motherhood is a simple, natural, fruitful thing, as inexhaustible as those which constitute the elements of existence. I remember that one day, nearly fourteen years ago, I embraced a life of sacrifice in sheer despair, just as a drowning man clings to the mast of his ship. But now, when my memory calls up all my life before me, I would still choose that idea to be the guiding principle of my life, for it is the safest and most fruitful of all. The thought of your life, founded on the most utter selfishness, in spite of its being hidden under poetic sentiment, has strengthened my resolution. I shall never say these things to you again,

The Memoirs of Two Young Brides

but I felt obliged to speak of them this last time, when I learnt that your happiness is still holding out against the most terrible of tests.

I have thought over your life in the country, and this further remark, which I think it right to put before you, has suggested itself to me. Our life, both as regards the body and the heart, consists of certain regular movements. Any overstraining of the mechanism brings either pleasure or pain. Now both pleasure and suffering are a fever of the soul, essentially transitory, because it would not be possible to bear it long. Surely, to live in nothing but excess is to live a life of sickness. Your life is a sick life, because you force to a perpetual height of passion a feeling which marriage should turn into a pure and steady principle. Yes, my dearest, I see it clearly now, the glory of the household lies in that very calm, that deep mutual understanding, that exchange of good and evil, at which the vulgar scoff. Oh, how fine is that saying of the Duchesse de Sully, the wife of the great Sully, when she was told her husband, grave as he looked, had not scrupled to take a mistress!

"That's very simple," she replied. "I am the honour of this house, and should be very sorry to play the part of a courtesan within it."

You are more voluptuous than fond; you would fain be wife and mistress at once. You have the soul of Héloïse and the senses of St. Theresa; you indulge in excesses which are sanctioned by law, and, in a word, you deprave the institution of marriage. Yes, you who judged me so severely for my apparent immorality in accepting, on the very eve of my marriage, the means of happiness presented to me, you who have bent everything to your own purposes, now deserve the reproaches you then cast on me. What! you claim to subject both Nature and Society to your whim? You remain yourself, you never transform yourself into what a woman should do, you keep your young girl's wilfulness and unreasonableness, and you apply the most careful and mercantile calculation to your passion. Don't you charge a very heavy price for all those trappings of yours? These numerous precautions strike me as symptomatic of a very deep distrust. Oh, dear Louise, if you could only know the sweetness a mother finds in her endeavour to be good and tender to every member of her family! All my natural pride and independence have melted into a gentle melancholy which the joys of motherhood have first rewarded and then dispelled. If the morning of my day has been troubled, the evening will be clear and tranquil. I fear me, it may be quite the contrary with your life.

When I had come to the end of your letter I prayed to God that he might send you to spend one day among us, so that you may be converted to family life and all its joys, unspeakable, incessant, neverending, because they are true, simple, and eminently natural. But alas! how can my reasoning avail against a mistake in which you find happiness? The tears stand in my eyes as I write these last lines. I had honestly believed that after a few months devoted to your conjugal passion, satiety would bring you back to reason. But now I see you are insatiable, and that after having killed one lover, you will end by killing love itself. Farewell, dear wanderer! I have lost all hope, since the letter which I hoped would have lured you back to social life, by its description of my happiness, has only served to glorify your selfishness. For your love is nothing but your own self, and you love Gaston much more for your own sake than for his.

LIV

FROM MME. GASTON TO THE COMTESSE DE L'ESTORADE

May 20th.

RENÉE: It has come! disaster has fallen like a thunderbolt on your poor Louise, and—you'll understand the feeling—doubt to me dispels disaster, certainty will bring me death. The day before yesterday, after my early toilet, I hunted everywhere for Gaston to take a little walk with me before breakfast. He was nowhere to be found. I went into the stable-yard and saw his mare covered with sweat—the groom was scraping the flecks of foam with a knife, before rubbing her down.

"Who on earth has brought home Fedelta in such a state?" said I.

"My master," replied the boy. Looking at the mare's hocks, I saw they were covered with Paris mud —it is not in the least like country mud.

"He's been to Paris," thought I.

The idea sent a thousand others surging through my brain, and drove all my blood back to my heart. To go to Paris without telling me, to choose the hour when I leave him alone; to rush there and back so quickly as almost to knock up his horse—the terrible suspicion tightened round me till I almost choked. I moved away to a seat a few steps off, and tried to recover my self-possession. There Gaston came upon me looking pallid and appalling, as it seems, for he cried out "What's the matter?" so suddenly, and his voice was so full of alarm, that I rose to my feet and took his arm. But the strength had gone out of my joints, and I was obliged to sit down again. Then he took me up in his arms and carried me to the parlour close by, whither all our frightened servants followed us; but Gaston dismissed them with a wave of his hand. After we were left alone, I was able to get to our room—I would not say a word—and there I shut myself up to weep in peace. For a good two hours Gaston waited outside the door, listening to my sobs, and with the patience of an angel, putting one question after another to his creature, who gave him no reply. At last I said, "I will see you again when my eyes are not red, and when my voice is steady."

The second person plural which I had used, sent him rushing out of the house. I fetched cold water and bathed my eyes, I cooled my face, the door of our room opened, and there I found him. He had come back, without my having heard his footsteps.

"What is the matter with you?" he asked.

"Nothing," I said. "I recognised the Paris mud on Fedelta's tired hocks; I could not understand your going there without telling me, but you are free."

"Your punishment for your wicked doubts," he

The Memoirs of Two Young Brides

answered, " shall be not to know what my reason was until to-morrow."

" Look at me," I said.

I fastened my eyes on his, the infinite passed into the infinite. No, there was no sign of that cloud which unfaithfulness must cast over the soul, which must dim the clearness of a man's eyes. I pretended to be satisfied, though I was still anxious—for men can deceive and lie as well as women. We remained together. Oh, dearest, as I looked at him now and again I thought how indissolubly bound I was to him. What an internal tremor shook me, when he returned after leaving me alone for one short moment. My life is all in him, not in myself. I have given the lie in cruel fashion to your cruel letter. Did I ever feel this sense of dependence on that noble-hearted Spaniard to whom I was just what this terrible boy is to me? How I hate that mare! What an idiot I was to keep horses! But then I should have to cut off Gaston's feet, and keep him tied up in the cottage. You will conceive my demented condition when I tell you that such silly thoughts as these were in my mind. If love has not caged him, no power will ever restrain a man who is bored.

" Do I bore you? " said I to him suddenly.

" How you do torment yourself for no reason at all! " he answered, and his eyes were full of gentle pity. " You never have been so dear to me."

" If that's true, my dearest angel," I answered, " let me sell Fedelta."

The Memoirs of Two Young Brides

"Sell her!" he replied.

The answer crushed me. It was as if Gaston had said to me, "All the money here is yours—I am nothing, my will has no weight." If he did not think it, I fancied he thought it, and once more I left him to go to bed. Night had fallen.

Oh, Renée, in silence and solitude, one's thoughts play havoc, and lead one on to suicide. The exquisite gardens, the starry night, the cool breeze laden with the perfume of all our flowers, the valleys, the hills, were all gloomy and black and dreary to me. I felt as if I were lying at the foot of a precipice, with venomous snakes crawling over me, and poisonous plants about me. I could see no God in the heaven above me. Such a night ages a woman by years and years.

The next morning I said to him: "Take Fedelta and ride away to Paris. Don't let us sell her, I am fond of her: she carried you." Yet he did not misunderstand the tone of my voice, which betrayed the hidden fury I was striving to conceal.

"Trust me," he answered, and he held out his hand with such a noble gesture and cast such a noble glance at me, that I felt myself humbled to the dust.

"We women are all poor creatures," I exclaimed.

"No, you love me—that's all," he said, as he pressed me to his breast.

"Go to Paris without me," I said, and I made him understand that I had put all my suspicions away.

He went; I thought he would have stayed. I won't attempt to describe my misery. I found there was a being within me, the possibility of whose existence I had never realized. To begin with, my dear, these sort of scenes possess an indescribably tragic solemnity for a woman who loves; the whole of life appears to her in that silent moment, and no horizon bounds the view. A trifle becomes everything, there are volumes in a look, icebergs swirl down the stream of speech, and in one movement of the lips she may read her death-warrant. I had expected some return, for surely I had proved myself noble and great-hearted.

I went up on to the roof of the chalet; I watched him pass along the road. Ah, my dear Renée, I saw him disappear with a swiftness that agonized me.

"What a hurry he is in!" was my involuntary thought.

Then, when I was left alone, I fell back into a hell of hypothesis and a whirlpool of suspicion. There were moments when the certainty of his treachery seemed to me a blessing, compared with the horrors of doubt. Doubt is a duel fought within the soul, which causes horrid self-inflicted wounds. I went out, I walked about the paths, and back to the chalet, and out of it again, like a mad-woman. Gaston, who had started about seven o'clock, did not come back until eleven, and as it only takes half an hour to go to Paris through the Park of St. Cloud and the Bois de Boulogne, he must have spent three hours in the city. He arrived in triumph, bringing me an India-rubber riding-whip with a gold head. I have had no riding-whip for the last fortnight, having broken mine, which was old and worn out.

"Is it for this that you have been torturing me?" I inquired, as I admired the workmanship of the trinket, the handle of which contains a scent-box.

Then I realized that this gift concealed a fresh piece of duplicity. But I threw my arms quickly about his neck, and reproached him tenderly for having caused me so much misery about a trifle. He thought himself very clever, and then in his demeanour and his looks I recognised that sort of hidden joy which every one feels over a successful piece of trickery—a kind of flash of satisfaction and gleam of conscious cleverness, which is reflected on the features and revealed in every movement of the body. Still looking at the pretty bauble, I inquired, at a moment when his eyes could not escape mine, "From whom did you get this work of art?"

"From one of my friends, an artist."

"Indeed! I see Verdier mounted it," and I read the name of the shop which was stamped upon the whip.

Gaston is still very young. He coloured; I heaped endearments on him, to reward him for having been ashamed of deceiving me. I played the simpleton, and he fancied the whole thing had blown over.

May 25th.

The next day, toward six o'clock, I put on my riding-habit, and at seven o'clock I dropped in at

The Memoirs of Two Young Brides

Verdier's, where I saw several whips of the same pattern. One of the shopmen recognised mine, which I showed him. "We sold that yesterday to a young gentleman," he said, and when I described that impostor Gaston to him, there was no further doubt about the matter.

I'll spare you any description of the palpitations that half choked me as I rode to Paris, and during this little scene, on which the fate of my life hung. By half past seven o'clock I was back again and Gaston found me walking about in a fresh morning-gown armed with a most deceitful appearance of indifference, and certain that the secret of my absence, of which no one but my old Philippe was aware, would never be betrayed.

"Gaston," I said, as we strolled round the lake, "I am quite well aware of the difference between a work of art which love has procured as an offering for a particular person, and a thing which is merely one of many cast in a mould."

Gaston turned pale and looked at me, as I held out the terrible proof that convicted him. "My friend," I said, "this is no riding-whip, this is a screen behind which you are hiding some secret."

Thereupon, my dear, I allowed myself the pleasure of seeing him lose his way hopelessly, in masses of lies and labyrinths of falsehood, making extraordinary efforts to discover some wall that he might scale, but forced to stand his ground and face an adversary who ended by deliberately allowing herself to be deceived.

The Memoirs of Two Young Brides

As in all such scenes, this complaisance came too late, and besides, I had fallen into the mistake against which my mother had endeavoured to warn me. When my jealousy showed itself openly, war, with all its stratagems, was declared between Gaston and me. My dear, jealousy is an essentially stupid and brutish passion. I made up my mind I would suffer in silence, spy out everything, make quite certain, and then either have done with Gaston forever, or consent to my own misery; no other line of conduct is possible for a well-bred woman. What is it he is hiding from me? for he is hiding some secret from me. It is some secret about a woman. Is it some youthful *liaison* of which he is ashamed? What can it be? That *what*, my dear, is written in four letters of fire on everything I see. I read the fatal word on the glassy surface of my lake, upon my shrubberies, upon my flower-beds, in the clouds above me, on the ceiling, on the dining-table, on the pattern of my carpet. In the midst of my slumbers, I hear a voice that crys out, "What?" Ever since that morning a cruel interest has been added to my life, and I have known the bitterest thoughts that can corrode a woman's heart—the thought that I belong to a man whom I believe to be unfaithful. Oh, my dear, this life of mine touches both heaven and hell. Never before have I set my foot within this furnace—I, who have always been held in such holy adoration.

"Ah," said I to myself just now, "there was a day when you wished you might find your way into the cruel and gloomy halls of suffering. Well, the fiends have heard your fatal wish. Forward then, wretched woman!"

May 30th.

Ever since that day, Gaston, instead of working easily and deliberately like a rich man who can afford to play with his work, sets himself tasks, like the author who lives by his pen. He devotes four hours a day to finishing off two plays.

He is in need of money!

An inner voice breathed this thought into my ear. He spends hardly anything. There is no concealment between us. There is not a corner of his study which is not open to my eyes and fingers. His yearly expenses do not amount to two thousand francs. I know he has thirty thousand, not so much laid by as thrown into a drawer. You will have guessed my thoughts. In the middle of the night when he was fast asleep, I got up and went to see whether the money was still there. A cold shiver shook me when I saw the drawer was empty. That same week I discovered that he goes and fetches letters at Sèvres, and he must tear them up the moment he has read them, for in spite of all my cunning I have never been able to find even a vestige of one. Alas! my dearest, in spite of my promises, in spite of all the fine vows I had made to myself about the whip, an impulse which can only have been a sort of madness seized me, and I followed him on one of his hasty expeditions to the post-office. To Gaston's horror I caught him, on horseback, paying the postage of a letter which he held in his hand. He looked at me steadily. Then he turned his horse about, and galloped off so swiftly that even then, when I should have thought my mental anguish would have prevented my feeling any bodily fatigue, I was quite exhausted by the time we reached the gate leading into our wood. Gaston never opened his lips, he rang the bell and waited, without speaking to me. I was more dead than alive. I might be mistaken in my suspicions, or I might not —but in either case I had spied upon him in a manner unworthy of Armande Louise Marie de Chaulieu. I had fallen down to social depths, lower than the grisette, and the low-born girl. I had descended to the level of courtesans, actresses, and common creatures —what anguish in the thought! The gate was opened at last, he gave his horse to his groom and I slipped off mine, but into his arms, which he held out to me. I threw my riding-skirt over my left arm, I passed my right through his, and we walked away, still in dead silence. Those hundred paces should surely cut off a hundred years of purgatory for me. At every step, thoughts crowded on me, almost visible, darting tongues of fire under my very eyes, clutching at my heart—and every one with a sting and a venom of its own. When the groom and the horses were out of sight, I stopped Gaston, I looked at him, and with a gesture which you will imagine for yourself, I said, pointing to the fatal letter, which he still held in his right hand:

The Memoirs of Two Young Brides

"Let me read it."

He gave it to me; I broke the seal and read a letter in which Nathan, the dramatic author, told him that one of our plays, which had been accepted and rehearsed, was to be performed on the following Saturday. The letter inclosed a ticket for a box. Although this turned my martyrdom to heavenly bliss, the demon within me still disturbed my joy by whispering, "Where are those thirty thousand francs?" And dignity and honour, and all my former self, rose up to prevent me from putting the question. It was on my lips, I knew that if I put my thoughts into words I should have to throw myself into the lake, and yet I could hardly restrain myself from speaking. Dear, was not that agony more than any woman could bear?

"You are bored here, my poor Gaston," I said, as I gave him back the letter. "If you like, we will go back to Paris."

"To Paris! why should we go back there?" said he. "I only wanted to know what my powers were, and to taste the goblet of success."

It would be easy, while he was sitting at work, for me to feign surprise on opening the drawer and not finding the thirty thousand francs inside it. But would not that only serve to elicit the answer that such a clever man as Gaston would not fail to give me. "I have been helping So-and-so—a friend of mine."

My dear, the moral of all this is that the play which all Paris is now running to see, owes its success to us, though Nathan reaps all the glory of it. I

am one of the anonymous collaborateurs known as
"Messrs. ———." I watched the first performance
from the back of a stage-box on the pit tier.

July 1st.

Gaston is still working hard and running perpetually to Paris. He is toiling at fresh plays, so as to have a pretext for going there, and in order to earn money. Three of our pieces have been accepted, and two more are ordered. Oh, my dearest, I am lost! I am walking along in the dark. I will burn down my house, so that I may see clearly. What does his conduct mean? Is he ashamed of being rich through me? He is too noble-hearted a man to give a thought to such littleness, and besides, when such scruples as these begin to assail a man, they are inspired by something which affects his heart. A man will accept anything from his wife, but he does not choose to owe anything to a woman whom he intends to forsake, or whom he has ceased to love. If he wants so much money, no doubt it is because he has to spend it on some woman. If it were for his own purposes, would he not use my purse without the smallest ceremony? We have laid by over a hundred thousand francs. To sum it up, my dearest love, I have wandered through the whole world of supposition, and after weighing everything well, I am convinced I have a rival. I am forsaken—and for whom? I must see *her*.

July 10th.

I have seen; I am lost. Yes, Renée, at thirty—in all the glory of my beauty and all the wealth of my

The Memoirs of Two Young Brides

intelligence, armed as I am with all the charms of dress, and freshness, and elegance, I am betrayed—and for whom? for an Englishwoman with big feet, big bones, and a big chest, a sort of British cow. There can be no more doubt about it. This is what has happened to me within the last few days.

Sick of doubt, thinking that if he had helped one of his friends, Gaston might have told me, taking his silence for an accusation, and noting that a continuous thirst for money drove him to his work, jealous of that work, and alarmed by his perpetual excursions to Paris, I ended by taking my measures—measures that forced me to stoop so low that I can tell you nothing of them. Three days ago, I learnt that Gaston, when he goes to Paris, betakes himself to a house in the Rue de la Ville l'Evêque, where his loves are concealed with discretion such as was never seen before in Paris. The porter, a very silent man, said little, but enough to drive me to despair. Then I made up my mind that I must die, and I determined that I would know all first. I went to Paris, I took a room in a house opposite that to which Gaston is in the habit of going, and with my own eyes I saw him ride into the court-yard. Then, all too soon, I learnt a horrible and frightful thing—this Englishwoman, who seems to me to be about thirty-six, calls herself Mme. Gaston. That discovery was my death-blow. Well, I saw her go into the Tuileries with two children . . . two children, oh, my dearest, who are the living image of Gaston. No one could fail to be

The Memoirs of Two Young Brides

struck by the scandalous resemblance. And such pretty children, too, sumptuously dressed, as Englishwomen know how to dress their children. She has borne him children, that explains it all! This Englishwoman is a sort of Greek statue taken down off some monument; she is as white and cold as marble, and walks along solemnly like a proud mother. She's handsome, I must admit it—but she's as heavy as a man-of-war. There is nothing dainty or distinguished about her. I am certain she is no lady. She must be the daughter of some village farmer in a far-away county, or the eleventh child of some starving clergyman. I was half dead when I got home from Paris. On the road, a thousand thoughts assailed me, like as many demons. Is she a married woman? Did he know her before he married me? Was she the mistress of some rich man who has forsaken her, and has she not fallen back suddenly on Gaston's hands? I made endless conjectures, as if there were any use in hypothesis in the face of those two children. The next morning I went back to Paris and gave so much money to the porter of that house, that in answer to this question, " Is Madame Gaston legally married? " he answered:

" Yes, *mademoiselle!* "

July 15th.

Dear, since that morning I have been twice as tender to Gaston, and I have found him more in love with me than ever—he is so young. A score of times before we get up in the morning I have it on the tip

The Memoirs of Two Young Brides

of my tongue to say to him, " So you really love me more than the woman in the Rue de la Ville l'Evêque? " But I dare not explain the mystery of my self-denial, even to myself.

" Are you very fond of children? " I said to him.

" Oh, yes," he answered, " but we shall have children of our own."

" And how? " said I.

" I've consulted the best doctors, and they all advise me to go away for a couple of months."

" Gaston," I said, " if I had been able to love an absent person, I should have stayed in my convent to the end of my days."

Then he began to laugh, but that word " go away " gave me my death. Ah, indeed, I would far rather throw myself out of the window than let myself roll down the staircase and cling to every step. . . .

Farewell, my dearest! I have taken steps to insure that my death shall be quiet, refined, but quite inevitable. I made my will yesterday. You can come and see me now, the doors are opened wide. Come quickly then, that I may bid you farewell! My death, like my life, shall be full of distinction and of charm—I will die true to myself.

Farewell, my dear sister-heart! You, whose affection has never changed or wavered, who, like a gentle moonbeam, have always cheered my heart with your calm light. You have not known the ardour of love, but neither have you tasted its poisonous bitterness. You have looked wisely at life. Farewell!

LV

FROM THE COMTESSE DE L'ESTORADE TO MME. GASTON

July 15th.

My dear Louise: I send this letter on by a messenger, and am hurrying after it myself. Calm yourself, I beg. Your last words struck me as so demented that I thought I might venture, considering the circumstances, on confiding the whole story to Louis. For I felt you must be saved from yourself. Though we, like you, have employed odious means, the result is so satisfactory that I am certain you will approve. I even went so far as to call in the police, but that is a secret between the Prefect, ourselves and you. Gaston is an angel—here are the facts. His brother died at Calcutta, where he was employed by some mercantile company, just when he was about to return to France a rich, married, and happy man. The widow of an English merchant had bestowed her immense wealth upon him. After toiling for ten years to provide a subsistence for his brother, whom he worshipped, and to whom he never mentioned his disappointments, lest they should distress him, he was overwhelmed in the famous Halmer failure. The widow was ruined. The shock was so terrible that Louis

The Memoirs of Two Young Brides

Gaston's brain became affected. As his mind weakened, sickness took hold of his body, and he died in Bengal, whither he had gone to realize the remnant of his poor wife's fortune. The good captain had already forwarded a sum of three hundred thousand francs to a banker for transmission to his brother. But the banker was swept away in the Halmer bankruptcy, and thus this last hope disappeared. Louis Gaston's widow, that handsome woman whom you have taken for your rival, arrived in Paris with two children, who are your nephews, and without a centime. The mother's jewels had barely sufficed to provide for her own and her children's passage money. By means of the directions Louis Gaston had given the banker who was to have sent the money to his brother, the widow found her way to your husband's former place of residence. As your Gaston had disappeared without leaving a hint of whither he was going, the people of the house sent Mme. Louis Gaston to d'Arthez, the only person likely to know Marie Gaston's whereabouts. D'Arthez was all the more ready to help the poor young woman generously, because some four years ago, when Louis Gaston married, he had written to d'Arthez, whom he knew to be his brother's friend, to inquire about him, and find out how the three hundred thousand francs might be most safely transmitted to their destination. D'Arthez had replied that Marie Gaston was now rich, thanks to this marriage with the Baronne de Macumer. Alike in India and in Paris, the glorious gift of beauty bestowed on both brothers by their mother, saved them from misfortune.

Isn't it a touching story? D'Arthez ended naturally by writing to your husband to tell him of the situation of his sister-in-law and nephews, and of the generous purpose which chance had frustrated, but which the Indian Gaston had nursed with regard to the Gaston left in Paris. Your dear Gaston at once rushed up to Paris, as you will imagine. That accounts for his first excursion. In the last five years he has saved fifty thousand francs on the income you have made him accept, and with this money he has bought scrip to the amount of twelve thousand francs a year for each of his nephews, and besides, he has furnished the rooms in which his sister-in-law lives, and has promised to allow her three thousand francs a quarter. This explains his writing for the stage and his delight over the success of his first play. So Mme. Gaston is not your rival, and she has a perfect right to bear your name. A noble-hearted and delicate-minded man, such as Gaston, would, no doubt, conceal the story from you, out of fear of your generosity. Your husband doesn't consider what you have bestowed upon him as his own property. D'Arthez read me the letter he wrote him when he asked him to act as one of the witnesses at your marriage. In it Marie Gaston says his happiness would have been complete if he had possessed money of his own, and if he had not had any debts for you to pay. A pure heart cannot stifle this feeling. If it is there, it makes itself felt, and where

The Memoirs of Two Young Brides

it does exist its scruples and its sensitiveness may be easily conceived. It is very natural that Gaston should desire to provide secretly and suitably for his brother's widow, seeing the lady had originally sent him a hundred thousand crowns out of her own pocket. She is handsome and good-hearted, her manners are refined, but she is not clever. She is a mother, and you will understand that my heart went out to her the moment I saw her with one child in her arms, and the other dressed like a little lord and clinging to her skirts. "The children are all in all," that is her motto, even in the merest trifle. Thus, far from being angry with your darling Gaston, you ought to love him all the more. I have had a glimpse of him. He is the best-looking young fellow in Paris. Yes, dearest child, that one sight of him made me realize that a woman might well go crazy over him. His face is the index to his soul. If I were you, I would bring the widow and her two children down to the chalet. I'd build them a delightful cottage there, and they should be like my own children to me. So now calm your heart, and surprise your Gaston by playing this trick upon him.

LVI

FROM MME. GASTON TO THE COMTESSE DE L'ESTORADE

Ah, my dearest, hear the terrible, fatal, insolent words of the fool La Fayette to his master and his King, " It is too late! " Oh, my life! my beautiful life! what doctor can bring it back to me? I have dealt my own death-blow. Alas! what was I but a will-o'-the-wisp, doomed to flash gaily and then die out into the dark! The tears pour from my eyes, and . . . I must not weep when he is near me. . . . I flee from him and he follows after me! My despair is all hidden in my soul. Dante forgot my torture when he wrote his *Inferno*. Come and see me die!

LVII

**FROM THE COMTESSE DE L'ESTORADE TO THE COMTE
DE L'ESTORADE**

THE CHALET, *August 7th.*

MY DEAR: Take the children with you and go back to Provence without me. I must stay with Louise, she has only a few more days to live. I must be with her and her husband, who will go mad, I think.

Since the arrival of that note which made me fly to Ville d'Avray, taking the doctors with me, I have never left this exquisite creature, and I have not been able to write, for this is the fifteenth night I have spent out of bed.

When I got here, I found her sitting with Gaston, looking beautiful, exquisitely dressed, with a merry, happy face. It was all a splendid fiction. There had been an explanation between the two young people. For a moment I was duped, as Gaston had been, by her bold front. But Louise squeezed my hand, and whispered:

" We must deceive him, I am dying."

An icy chill fell on me when I felt her hands were burning hot, and noticed the rouge upon her cheeks. I congratulated myself upon my forethought. To avoid alarming anybody, it had occurred to me to tell the doctors to go and walk in the wood till they were sent for.

"You must go away," she said to Gaston. "Two women who haven't seen each other for five years have a great many secrets to tell each other, and I am sure Renée has something she wants to confide to me."

As soon as we were alone, she threw herself into my arms, and could not keep back her tears.

"What is it?" I cried. "In any case I've brought down the chief surgeon of the Hôtel-Dieu, and Bianchon. There are four of them altogether."

"Oh, if they can save me! If only they are in time! Let them come in," she cried. "The very feeling that made me long for death now makes me pine to live."

"But what have you done?"

"I've done my lungs the most frightful mischief, all in a few days."

"And how did you do it?"

"I used to put myself into violent perspirations at night and then run out and stand beside the lake in the dew. Gaston thinks I have a cold . . . and I'm dying."

"Send him off to Paris," said I, "I'm going to fetch the doctors." And off I ran like a mad-woman to the spot where I had left them.

Alas, dear friend, when the consultation was over, not one of the great men gave me the slightest hope.

The Memoirs of Two Young Brides

They all think Louise will die when the leaves begin to fall. The darling creature's constitution has served her purpose in the most singular way. She was already predisposed to the complaint she has set up. She might have lived for years, but now, in a few days, she has done herself irreparable harm. I will not tell you what I felt when I heard this perfectly well-founded verdict. You know my life has been as much in Louise as in myself. I sat there crushed, and could not even say good-bye to the merciless doctors. I know not how long I had been sitting with streaming eyes, wrapped in my agonizing thoughts, when I was roused from my stupor by a hand laid on my shoulder, and a sweet voice that said, " Well, so there's no hope for me." It was Louise; she made me rise and come with her to her sitting-room.

" Don't leave me," she begged, with a supplicating look. " I don't want to see despair all about me. Above all, I want to deceive *him*. I shall have strength to do that. I am full of youth and vigour, and I will die on my feet. For myself, I don't complain; I shall die just as I have often wished to die, when I'm thirty, with my youth and beauty still untouched. As for him, I should have made him miserable—I can see that clearly. I have entangled myself in the meshes of my own loves, like a doe that strangles herself in her rage at being caught. Of us two, I am the doe, and a very wild one. My fits of unreasoning jealousy were already so heavy on his heart that they made him wretched. And on the day when my suspicions met with indifference, the inevitable punishment of jealousy, I should have died. I have had my full share of life. There are some people who are supposed to have lived sixty years, and have really not had two years of life. On the other hand, I seem to be only thirty, but in reality I have had sixty years of love. So, for both him and me, this end is the best. But for us two, the case is different. You will lose a loving sister, and that is an irreparable loss. And you alone will have reason to mourn my death. . . . My death," she added, after a long pause, during which I could hardly see her through my tears, "carries a cruel lesson with it. My dear doctor in petticoats was right. Not passion, not even love, can be the true basis of marriage. Your life is a beautiful and noble life; you have clung steadily to your path, and grown closer and closer to your Louis; whereas, if conjugal life begins with an excessive ardour of passion, that cannot fail to cool as time goes on. I have fallen into a mistake twice over, and twice over Death's wasted fingers have snuffed out my happiness. They bereft me of the noblest and the most devoted of men, and now I am torn from the arms of the handsomest, the most attractive, the most poetic husband woman ever had. But I shall have made acquaintance, turn about, with the most perfect soul, and the most exquisite form, that ever existed. In Felipe's case the mind subdued the body and transformed it. In Gaston's, heart and intellect and physical beauty are all equal. I shall have been worshipped till I die;

what more can I desire? I will make my peace with God, whom I have forgotten somewhat, perhaps. I will turn to Him with my heart full of love, and pray that some day He will give me back my two angels in Heaven. For without them Paradise would be a desert to me. My example would be grievous, but I am an exception. As such beings as Felipe or Gaston can never be met with, the social law agrees, in this matter, with the natural law. Woman is really a weak being, who, when she marries, should utterly sacrifice her will to her husband, and he, in return, should sacrifice his selfishness to her. The noisy outcry our sex has raised, and the tears it has shed, of late, are follies which rightfully earn us the title of children bestowed upon us by so many philosophers."

She went on talking, in that sweet voice you know so well, saying the most sensible things in the most refined fashion, until Gaston arrived with his sister-in-law, the two children, and the English nurse, whom Louise had begged him to fetch from Paris.

"Here are my pretty executioners," she said, when she saw her two nephews. "Can you wonder I was mistaken? How like their uncle they are!"

She gave the kindest welcome to Madame Gaston, whom she begged to consider the chalet as her home. She did the honours of her house with the high-bred charm she possesses to such a marked degree. I instantly wrote to the Duc and Duchesse de Chaulieu, the Duc de Rhétoré, to the Duc de Lenoncourt-Chaulieu, and to Madeleine. It is well I did so. The very next day, Louise, worn out by her exertions, was unable to go out, and did not get up, indeed, till dinner-time. Her mother, and her two brothers, and Madame de Lenoncourt, came in the evening. The coldness between Louise and her family, arising from her marriage, has quite passed away. Since that evening her father and her brothers have ridden over every morning, and the two Duchesses spend all their evenings at the chalet. Death does almost as much to bring people together as to part them. It puts all paltry passions to silence. There is something sublime in Louise's good sense, and grace, and charm, and tender feeling. Even now, in her last moments, she reveals the taste for which she has been so celebrated, and pours out the treasures of an intellect which has made her one of the Queens of Paris.

"I mean to be pretty even in my coffin," she said to me, with that peculiar smile of hers, when she laid down in her bed, to linger out the last fortnight. There is not a sign of sickness in her room; all the drinks and lozenges and medical paraphernalia are hidden away.

"Am I not dying bravely?" she said yesterday, to the parish priest of Sèvres, to whom she has given her confidence.

We all treasure every moment of her, like misers. Gaston, whose mind has been prepared by all his anxiety and this cruel certainty, is full of courage, but it is a terrible blow to him. I should not be surprised if he were soon to follow his wife. Yesterday, as we were walking round the lake, he said to me:

"I must be a father to those two children," and he pointed to his sister-in-law who was walking with his nephews. "But though I do not intend to do anything to shorten my own life, promise me you will be a second mother to them, and that your husband will consent to accept the guardianship which I shall leave to him and to my sister-in-law."

He said all this without the slightest emphasis, like a man who feels he is condemned. He smiles back to Louise whenever she smiles to him, and I am the only person who is not deceived. His courage is as great as hers. Louise would have liked to see her godson, but I am not sorry he should be in Provence: she would very likely have done things for him which would have made me feel very uncomfortable.

Farewell, dear friend.

August 25th, HER BIRTHDAY.

Yesterday evening Louise wandered for a few minutes, but there was a real refinement even in her delirium, which proves that people of intellect do not lose their heads like common folk or fools. In a faint voice she sang a few Italian airs out of the Puritani, La Sonnambula, and Mosé. We all stood round her bed in silence, and there were tears in the eyes of every one of us, even of her brother Rhétoré, for we all saw her soul was slipping away. She was quite unconscious of our presence, but all her old charm lingered in the tones of her weak voice, with its exquisite

The Memoirs of Two Young Brides

sweetness. In the night the death agony began. At seven o'clock in the morning I helped her out of her bed myself—her strength came back to her a little, she wanted to sit by her window; she asked Gaston for his hand . . . and then, dear friend, the most charming creature that we shall ever see upon this earth left us nothing but her corpse! She had received the sacraments the night before, unknown to Gaston, who had been sleeping during the sad ceremony, and she had begged me to read her the *De Profundis* in French, while she looked her last on the beautiful natural surroundings she had created. She followed the words in her heart, and clasped her husband's hands as he knelt on the other side of her arm-chair.

August 26th.

My heart is broken! I have just been looking at her in her shroud—her face has grown white, and there are purple shadows on it. Oh, my children! I want my children! Bring my children to meet me!

PARIS, *1841.*

CURIOUS UNPUBLISHED OR UNKNOWN PORTRAITS OF HONORÉ DE BALZAC

CURIOUS UNPUBLISHED OR UNKNOWN PORTRAITS OF HONORÉ DE BALZAC

SKETCH OF BALZAC
As a young man.
From the drawing by Louis Boulanger, 1836, in the museum at Tours.

THE portraits of Balzac—should a list of them ever be attempted—would not provide the industrious personage who might undertake their methodical enumeration with matter for any very long or very curious pamphlet.

Balzac did not, like his contemporaries, much less celebrated than himself, furnish the subject for innumerable productions by caricaturists painters, engravers, and lithographers.

His portraits and caricatures are comparatively rare: the Print Room of the Bibliothèque Nationale hardly possesses more than fifteen presentments of Balzac, and it should be added that most of these are mere variations of the one monkish-looking type, of which Louis Boulanger's painting (1838), and the lithograph produced in 1840 by the *Galerie de la Presse*, are the types most frequently followed.

The Portraits of Honoré de Balzac

Private collectors are no better provided, and we have no means of tracing the evolution of this remarkable physiognomy from the days when the dweller in the garret of the Rue Lesdiguières signed his work "Horace de St. Aubin" or "Lord Rh'oone,"

PORTRAIT OF BALZAC.
Scarce lithograph by Emile Lassalle, published in 1841 in the *Galerie des Contemporains Illustres.*

up to the finest period of his talent, when he wrote *Les Parents pauvres* and *La Théorie de la Démarche.* This lack of portraits of Balzac, in any number, at that period of the century when lithography lent itself so willingly to the production of portraits of the men of the moment—when every newspaper, every periodical, every illustrated album, was striving to present the greatest possible variety of contemporary faces—can only be explained by the claus-

The Portraits of Honoré de Balzac

tral life of toil in which the great writer spent his days. It was only very occasionally that the fancy took him to be the fashionable society man, or the journalist of many acquaintances. More entirely than any other man did he escape the indiscretions of a commonplace publicity, and he succeeded in saving himself from the little gossiping paragraphs and scraps of detail of a journalism which has always proved its eagerness to scrutinize the private existence, all too readily revealed, of the artist and the novelist.

Thanks to his life of toil and to the triple bulwark of mystery which he ever carefully raised about him, the loves of the author of the *Comédie Humaine* were never discovered, and opportunities for snatching a furtive glimpse of his mobile features were few and far between.

It cannot be urged that Balzac, conscious of his own heavy appearance, and of a countenance which, at the first blush, conveyed an impression of vulgarity, shrank from all publication of his own lineaments. There is no truth in this idea. Balzac, like all other men, was very indulgent where his own person was concerned.

Though he was no coxcomb, he cannot be said

MEDALLION OF BALZAC.
After a lithograph, 1842.

The Portraits of Honoré de Balzac

to have been dissatisfied with his looks, or conscious of his lack of æsthetic grace; he was fond of his terrestrial envelope, he noted it with satisfaction, and the following remark, made when he was sitting to David of Angers for his medallion portrait, has in particular been preserved. "Above all things, dear sculptor, mind you study my nose; *there's a whole world*, look you, in my nose!"

One of the earliest known portraits of Balzac is that in the Tours museum, which represents him at the age of five-and-twenty; it presents the ordinary, rather commonplace face of a provincial employee. Julien's lithograph, published about 1832 or 1833, in the supplement of a newspaper, *Le Voleur*, comes next in order. This Balzac of over thirty summers appears as a stout fellow, beaming like some successful tenor singer. This is evidently quite a fancy portrait, got up to illustrate some novel, and the flattered face is designed to stir the fancy of sentimental little work-girls.

More typical is the curious caricature-portrait

UNSIGNED CARICATURE OF BALZAC.
Published in 1835 in the *Mercure de France*.

The Portraits of Honoré de Balzac

which is reproduced in this book, and which was buried in the position of tailpiece in the *Mercure de France*, of 1835, a most interesting collection, which was the supplement of the *Musée des Familles*, and the *Magasin Pittoresque*. Here

H. DE BALZAC.
After the portrait by L. Boulanger, 1840.

we really have the frank Balzac, the big comic dandy, the man with the walking-cane, as we love to fancy him. This picture recalls a statuette with a touch of caricature, modelled from his figure by Dantan, which, according to his contemporaries, reproduced with the most priceless fidelity his gait, his attitude, his face, his garb, his monumental cane, his very outline, in fact.

H. DE BALZAC.
Drawn from life, 1842.

The portrait published by Aubert in

The Portraits of Honoré de Balzac

the *Galerie de la Presse* (1839), is a charming lithograph, which would seem to be a study from the life. But it is so well known to Balzac worshippers that we will not dally over it now. The same cannot be asserted of the delightful lithograph-drawing by Emile Lassalle which appeared in 1841, in the *Galerie des Contemporains Illustres*, and has never been reproduced. This is a young and smiling face, pleasant to look upon, which would form an admirable frontispiece to the *Contes Drolatiques*. We give a fac-simile of this charming *Balzac in his armchair*, a pleasing change from the type of Balzac in a Rabelaisian frockcoat, which Hédouin, the etcher, has

SKETCH OF BALZAC.
Made by David d'Angers in 1845 (unpublished).

H. DE BALZAC
In 1844.

The Portraits of Honoré de Balzac

made only too well known in engravings after Boulanger's original.

In 1845, we find in that same *Galerie des Contemporains Illustres*, no lithograph this time, but a very curious etching, drawn and engraved by Adolphe

H. DE BALZAC.
After a daguerrotype taken in 1848. Only authentic portrait.

Forlet, and representing a very elegant Balzac indeed, wrapped in a dressing-gown, tall, slight, his face beaming with mirth and satiric humour, the very picture that should figure at the beginning of the *Physiologie du Mariage*, or of that subtle *Monographie de la Presse Parisienne*, which first saw the light in that same year 1843. The difficulties attending a reproduction of this etching very delicately

The Portraits of Honoré de Balzac

touched in a dry point, have prevented our displaying it here, although it is a hitherto unknown portrait belonging to this period. We also find a sketch of Balzac by David d'Angers, which was photographed at a later date, and the profile of which is exceedingly exact, very carefully worked up, and well deserving of study. Below the sketch the artist has written "À Madame de Surville, croquis fait de son illustre frère, par David, 1843." We could not do otherwise than instantly cause this curiosity to be engraved, and our readers will here find the profile, that of a warrior-monk and philosopher, whose close-pressed lips seem to have forgotten how to smile.

BALZAC.
After an anonymous engraving, 1836.

Another portrait, lithographed for the State, and long since vanished, is that which appears in heliogravure at the beginning of this book, and which gives us a respectable, substantial Balzac, comfortable-looking, quite the money-making author. This portrait is not in general circulation, and it exactly reproduces, to our mind, the great novelist's personal appearance.

As we are only considering in this notice those **portraits** of Balzac either little known or unknown

The Portraits of Honoré de Balzac

to collectors, or altogether unpublished, we will refer to the curious fact that Balzac gave a sitting one day to Gavarni, who, without troubling himself to make a pencil sketch, boldly laid hold of a big copper plate, and began to draw the great novelist on it, in dashing outline. We may take it that this sitting was not repeated, and that Gavarni threw his copper plate aside. But by a strange chance the plate fell one fine day into the hands of Bracquemont, who used it for the first state of a landscape. What was his astonishment, when he drew his first proof, at discovering the bold lines of Gavarni's Balzac portrait below the various foregrounds of his own picture? We need hardly say that Bracquemont did not finish his engraving, and that the great etcher still treasures the profile he has so unconsciously embowered in landscape scenery. No reproduction of this picture is possible. It is a landscape puzzle.

BALZAC.
After a sketch made by Eugene Giraud immediately after death.

Nevertheless Gavarni had made other rough

The Portraits of Honoré de Balzac

sketches of Balzac in dressing-gown and slippers, sketches no doubt made in the novelist's home, "aux Jardies," near Sèvres. One of these pencil sketches, reproduced by permission of the owner, M. Gavarni fils, forms the tail-piece to this Note.

One of the most authentic, most life-like, and most unconventional portraits of the great inventor of the *Comédie Humaine*, is that once owned by the photographer Nadar. This is a most remarkable daguerrotype, which shows us Balzac in his shirt-sleeves, his brace ill-fastened on the left side, his neck and chest exposed by his right hand, in the attitude of a condemned criminal just waking out of his last earthly slumber.

SKETCH OF THE REJECTED STATUE
By Auguste Rodin.

But we have been able to give a reproduction here of the most astonishing, the noblest, the finest portrait of Balzac, that taken just as he had passed out of human ken.

The Portraits of Honoré de Balzac

No public reference, indeed, has ever been made to the admirable tinted drawing made within an hour of the death of the Titan of literature, by Eugene Giraud. This fine portrait, which Madame de Balzac considered the best ever done of her husband, was left by her to her niece, Mlle. de Saint-Yves (Comtesse Keller by her first marriage). By the kindness of Mlle. de Saint-Yves, Lord Lytton, who was a great admirer of Balzac's genius, was enabled to obtain a photograph of Giraud's drawing. It was at the British Embassy in Paris, and in the Poet-Diplomat's own private study, that we had the good fortune some ten years ago of beholding this portrait, so solemn and so touching in the sight of every true Balzac worshipper. Lord Lytton was kind enough to send us the precious relic, and thus it comes about that we are able to give a fac-simile of this priceless memorial.

Balzac, lying dead, emaciated with suffering, looks a demigod already with the aureole of glory round his head, transfigured by the sight of the infinite eternity opening to his view. Never was there a face more noble, more superbly youthful, more mighty in its repose, than this, the image of which is Eugene Giraud's legacy to us. And of all the pictures of Balzac, this, which gives us the great repayer of his pitiful debts, when he had climbed the last step of his calvary, pallid, sublime, majestic, like a Christ in the Tomb, will ever be the most touching in the eyes of those who really comprehend and worship his genius.

The Portraits of Honoré de Balzac

Neither the deliberately caricatured portraits of Balzac, nor Rodin's recent statue of him, possesses much interest for us. The author of the *Deux Mariées* was not a fit subject for such disfigurements. Our respect for his memory is too great to permit us to remember his caricatures, and if this series of portraits closes with an outline of Rodin's marble, it is given rather with the object of comparing the sculptor's attempt at idealization with the expressive figures which reality has bequeathed to us.

OCTAVE UZANNE.

SKETCH OF BALZAC.
By Gavarni.